Dear Reader,

This year has b ... ! Our, particular brand ... readers in North America ... and we are also reaching audiences as far a... as Russia and New Zealand.

So, what delights are there in store for you this month? Characters from Angela Drake's book *The Mistress* are featured in *The Love Child*. Naughty-but-nice Ace Delaney from *Game, Set and Match*, returns in Kathryn Bellamy's new novel, *Mixed Doubles*. (But don't worry if you didn't read the authors' earlier titles – both of these books stand alone.) We are also absolutely delighted to announce the return to writing of much-loved romance author Margaret Pargeter, with a brand new book, *Misconception*, written especially for ***Scarlet*** readers. And finally, we are proud to bring you another author new to ***Scarlet***: Tammy McCallum has produced an intriguingly different novel in *Dared to Dream*.

I believe this time there is something to appeal to all reading tastes. But if there is a type of romance (say, time travel, ranch stories, women-in-jeopardy novels) we are not featuring regularly enough to please *you*, do let me know, won't you?

Till next month,

*Sally Cooper*

SALLY COOPER,
Editor-in-Chief – ***Scarlet***

## *About the Author*

**Kathryn Bellamy** was born in 1953 and educated at Queen Elizabeth's Grammar School in Horncastle, Lincolnshire. After gaining excellent examination results, she worked in a bank until ill-health forced her to resign. Since then, Kathryn has worked for her husband John, a chartered accountant, on a part-time basis, and has been able to spend more time writing fiction, which has always been a much loved hobby.

Kathryn still lives in Lincoln, and her hobbies include reading, tennis and yoga.

We are delighted to offer you Kathryn's second ***Scarlet*** novel which, as we promised you a short time ago, stars the gorgeous Ace Delaney from *Game, Set and Match* by the same author.

KATHRYN BELLAMY

# *MIXED DOUBLES*

*Enquiries to:*
Robinson Publishing Ltd
7 Kensington Church Court
London W8 4SP

First published in the UK by Scarlet, 1997


Cover photography by J. Cat



A copy of the British Library Cataloguing in Publication data is available from the British Library

ISBN 1-85487-988-X

Printed and bound in the EC

10 9 8 7 6 5 4 3 2 1

# CHAPTER 1

'How dare you interfere?' Alexa glared at her father across the polished mahogany of his desk. 'You've ruined my life – again!'

'Nonsense, girl!' Philip Kane roared back. 'On the contrary; I've saved you from making a fool of yourself – again!' He picked up some of the photographs that littered the desktop, and pushed them towards her. 'Here's the proof – see for yourself. Your precious Dimitri already has a wife and two children back in Cyprus. And, as for his claim to be "in shipping" . . .' his mouth curled derisively '. . . the nearest he's been to that is when he helps out on his uncle's fishing boat! Face facts, girl – you've picked another fortune-hunter.'

'No! He loves me,' she quavered. Her lip trembled and her large green eyes were luminous with unshed tears. She pushed back her long mane of auburn hair and squared up to her father. 'Dimitri loves me,' she repeated. 'And I love him. You've made a mistake – I'm going to see him. Now.'

'He's already left the country,' Philip said flatly. 'I

sent him packing this afternoon, and had one of my staff escort him to Heathrow.'

'I don't believe you; he wouldn't leave without seeing me.'

'He's gone. He cut his losses and ran – with some of my money, of course. Tell me, Alexa, who's been paying his hotel bill since he arrived here – you?'

'No,' she denied, but couldn't meet his gaze. 'Well, I lent him some money,' she mumbled. 'He lost his credit cards . . .'

'Oh, Alexa,' Philip sighed. His heart bled for her, and he hated having to dash her hopes. He moved around the desk to try and offer some comfort, but halted when a third person entered the room. Neither he nor Alexa had heard the front doorbell, nor been aware of their housekeeper, Mary, admitting a visitor, but now Philip's expression lightened and he stepped forward with a broad smile for the woman who had been his fiancée for less than twenty-four hours.

'Rose! You're early, I'm happy to say,' he greeted her with a kiss on the cheek. She looked lovely, he thought fondly; her cheeks flushed from the cold night air, her dark hair and eyes enhanced by the beige cashmere coat and matching hat.

'Is something wrong?' Rose Farrell looked uncertainly from Philip to Alexa, noting the girl's tears and clenched fists. Her heart sank. 'You've told her?' she faltered.

'What?' Alexa's head snapped up. 'She knows?' she demanded of her father.

'No, no,' Philip said quickly. 'Rose wasn't referring to Dimitri.'

'Then what?' Alexa demanded. Philip hesitated; this was hardly the time to tell her of his own engagement, when he had just put an end to hers. But Rose had already peeled off her gloves to reveal the magnificent half-hoop of diamonds on her left hand. Alexa's green eyes narrowed to cat-like slits.

'Cubic zirconia looks quite real, doesn't it?' she enquired snidely, before turning back to her father. 'I see it's okay for you to marry a fortune-hunter, but not me!'

'Alexa!' Philip thundered. 'Apologize to Rose. At once!'

'No!' She glared at them both before storming out of the room, slamming the door behind her.

'Oh, dear,' Rose sighed; she so hated any unpleasantness. 'Whatever's wrong with her? I thought she liked me.'

'She does,' Philip assured her quickly. 'That tantrum had nothing to do with you. I've had to break up her latest romance, that's all. She'll get over it; she always does. Let me get you a drink, darling. I know I need one – gin and tonic?'

'That would be lovely, thank you.' Rose took off her coat and hat and sank down on to the leather chesterfield.

Philip poured drinks for them both and settled down beside her, admiring her curves in the cherry-red dress, and her long, still-slender legs encased in sheer dark stockings. At forty-eight, Rose Farrell was still a very striking woman and, although Philip was almost sixty, he prided himself on keeping fit and trim with regular workouts at the gym.

He still had a full head of dark hair, greying slightly at the temples, and had retained the craggy good looks of his youth. But he had known for years that the blonde twenty-somethings who had until recently graced his arm and his bed wouldn't be with him if not for his wealth and success. Furthermore, he had nothing to say to them outside the bedroom; he disliked their friends, their taste in music and, most of all, their desire for marriage and children. He hadn't the energy or the patience to start another family – hell, he could barely cope with the one daughter he already had!

'Don't let Alexa upset you,' he said. 'I've been in this situation before. The trouble is, she inherited her mother's fortune when she turned eighteen, and there's been a seemingly endless procession of ski-instructors, Spanish waiters and God knows who else ever since!' He sighed heavily, then reached over to hold her hand. 'That's enough of my problems – what sort of day have you had?'

'Oh, wonderful,' Rose beamed, for her son and daughter-in-law had just produced her first grandchild. 'Jack and I took Lisa and the baby home this afternoon . . . oh, thank you for sending Lisa flowers,' she suddenly remembered his kind gesture. 'It's lovely to have a baby at Bellwood again. You don't mind marrying a grandmother, do you?' she asked anxiously.

'Not at all. You'd win *any* Glamorous Granny contests,' he said gallantly. 'When am I going to meet your children? Have you told them our news?'

'I told Jack today; he's very pleased for us.' She had also told Daniel, her ex-husband, and he had seemed to be happy for her. 'Melissa doesn't know yet – she and Nick, her husband, are flying back from their house in California in time for Christmas, and to see their niece, of course. Melissa sounded thrilled about the baby when I telephoned,' she said, but with a slight note of concern in her voice which Philip picked up on.

'Why wouldn't she be pleased for her brother?' he frowned.

'Oh, she is; she adores Jack, but it could be rather painful for her. You probably read about this in the Press – she had an abortion when she was nineteen,' Rose said regretfully. 'She and Nick broke up because of it; they were apart for more than two years, and I don't think she has ever really forgiven herself. I'm sure that was why she decided to give up tennis after winning Wimbledon – to try and make amends to Nick by giving him a child. So far, they haven't had any luck,' she sighed.

'I'm certain they will soon,' Philip comforted her. 'That daughter of yours seems to achieve all her goals – I just wish mine had one-tenth of Melissa's drive and ambition,' he added ruefully.

Alexa, who had decided to apologize to Rose after all, overheard the remark and promptly changed her mind. Damn Farrells! She snatched up her bag and jacket and ran out of the house, determined to see Dimitri and discover the truth for herself.

'Taxi!' She scrambled in and told him to hurry, desperate now to find Dimitri. Twenty minutes later, she stumbled out of the hotel where he'd been staying, numb with misery. He had gone, checked out, and not even left a message . . .

She stood on the pavement, shivering in the cold night air, oblivious to the impatient stares from passers-by as they pushed past her. It was almost Christmas and the streets were crowded with late-night shoppers and groups of girls tarted up for the annual office party, laughing and chattering loudly as they tottered along in high heels, leaving a cloud of mix'n'match perfume in their wake.

Utterly miserable and alone, Alexa wondered what she should do. Go home, back to Eaton Square? No fear! Visit a friend? She couldn't think of even one girlfriend who wasn't one half of a couple, and she shied away from having to explain another failed romance. I'm prettier than any of them, she thought resentfully, so why am I the one left on my own? Of course, her friends didn't have fathers who interfered in their lives as much as hers did, she decided, placing the blame firmly on Philip's shoulders.

She began walking aimlessly, heading for the bright lights of the shops. Cash, I need cash, she suddenly remembered; she'd had to ransack her bag to find enough to pay her cab fare. She queued at a cashpoint machine and slotted in her card. Her fingers began stabbing out the familiar number, the one she had used on an almost daily basis while Dimitri had been in London.

Suddenly, she paused in what she was doing; hadn't she known all along that Dimitri was everything her father said he was? Oh, not when she had first met him in Greece, of course, but since his arrival? When she had met him at the airport and he had told his tale of losing most of his luggage, including his credit cards? Who put their traveller's cheques and credit cards in their suitcase instead of keeping them during the flight? She must have been insane to have believed him, she thought sourly.

'Hurry up, love,' said an impatient voice behind her. 'We haven't got all night!'

'Oh!' Alexa looked at the display screen in front of her, then thumped the wall in frustration. She had dithered for so long that the damned machine had gobbled up her card and refused to give it back!

She turned and walked away, holding her head high as several of those in the queue either sniggered or looked at her pityingly, wrongly guessing that she had no funds in her account. Not looking at her feet, she failed to see a patch of frost on the pavement; her foot slipped and she fell to the ground. Oh, great! A perfect end to a perfect blasted day!

'Just what I like to see – a woman on her knees,' drawled a male, American voice. He sounded vastly amused and made no attempt to help her to her feet. Alexa pushed her hair back from her face to glare at the figure in whose path she had fallen.

He was tall and broad, his saturnine face certainly handsome and somehow vaguely familiar, although she was sure she had never met him before. His hair was over-long and jet-black; his features sharp and set in cold, harsh lines, with hooded, obsidian eyes and a cruel set to the well-shaped mouth.

'Leave her alone, Ace, she's crying,' his companion said, and Alexa noticed him for the first time. He, too, was tall and dark, but younger than the first man, and he wore a beard and one gold earring. He looked like a pirate, but a friendly one, Alexa thought, as she gratefully accepted his hand to help her scramble to her feet.

'You have been crying, haven't you?' the pirate persisted. 'What's the matter?' he asked, his voice warm and concerned, unlike that of his friend. Alexa was tempted to pour out her woes, but a glance at the older man made her change her mind about mentioning Dimitri. She was sure the pig would only laugh.

'I . . . came out without any cash, and the machine retained my card,' she explained instead.

'That's original,' sneered the older man. 'You're wasting your time, honey. I don't pay for it, and I'm sure Johnny doesn't, either.'

'You . . .!' Alexa turned on him in fury, her fingers curved into talons to claw at his hateful face. The expression – or lack of it – in his jet-black eyes deterred her and she backed off, her mouth dry, sensing that she had almost made a deadly mistake. Any blow inflicted on this man would be returned, with interest. She turned to the younger man in relief when he spoke again.

'I'm Johnny Dancer,' he said proudly. Alexa smiled slightly and nodded politely. The older man laughed.

'Hard luck, Johnny. The show isn't aired on British TV – she's never heard of you.'

'Oh.' He shrugged carelessly and grinned at Alexa. 'I'm an actor,' he told her. 'And this old reprobate you probably do recognize – he's Ace Delaney, the ex-professional tennis player who now pretends he's an actor! Ignore his rudeness – he's sulking because his best buddy has got a wife and new baby and can't come out to play!'

'I am not sulking, and Jack's still my best buddy,' Ace insisted.

'Not to mention his mother and his sister!' Johnny smirked. They had got drunk on the flight from LA and Ace had told him of his affairs with both Rose and Melissa Farrell.

'Shut up, Johnny!' Ace snapped, regretting the confidence. Jack would be furious if it became common knowledge. There had always been a lot of speculative gossip about him and Melissa before her marriage, but never a hint of a scandal about Rose.

'Let's go and eat; I'm starving. Bring her along, if you like,' he added, as if Alexa were a stray puppy. She smiled absently at Johnny and followed Ace Delaney, while pieces of an intriguing jigsaw slotted together. Of course. The Jack they spoke about must be Jack Farrell – he and Ace had been Doubles partners for years – she had seen them win Wimbledon on TV. Had Johnny really meant what his words had suggested – that Ace had been 'close' to both Jack's mother and his sister? Her father's frumpy fiancée? Things were looking up! How wonderful if she could dig up some dirt on her father's lover for a change!

Despite claiming to be hungry, Ace ate almost nothing, but his alcohol consumption was prodigious. There was no outward sign of drunkenness, but those who knew him well would have recognized the danger signs in the glitter of his eyes, the tension around his mouth and the restless tapping of his fingers on the bar-top.

Johnny had been correct in saying Ace was in a filthy mood, but wrong about the reason, although

Ace did want to talk to Jack about something other than his new daughter. The object of Ace's anger was out of his reach, fortunately for her, so he turned his attention to the silly bitch now pouring out her sob story to Johnny.

'My father ruins everything for me,' Alexa was telling him. 'I'm twenty, but he still treats me as if I'm a little kid. My mother died when I was ten and I'm an only child, you see.' She shot him a soulful glance from beneath her lashes and Johnny nodded sympathetically. 'So Daddy's very protective, and possessive,' she continued. 'He doesn't want me to get married, so he threatens and bullies my boyfriends into leaving.'

'Buys them off, you mean,' Ace put in caustically. He knew she was lying; knew Johnny did, too. His concerned act was just that, an act; behind the sympathy, he was wondering how soon to make a move on her.

Alexa glared at Ace, pushing her long, tawny hair away from her face. She couldn't understand why so many women apparently found him to be irresistible; he was so cold and arrogant, even cruel. It was easy to believe, now she had met him, in his claim to be of Apache descent. She'd bet he was a savage, especially in bed . . . She shivered and hunched her shoulder against him, and concentrated on Johnny, turning on the charm.

'You're an actor? Tell me about the films you've been in,' she smiled, surreptitiously checking in the mirror over the bar that her tears hadn't smudged her mascara.

'Only bit parts until *Country Club*,' Johnny told her. 'I play Ace's kid brother.'

‘Oh, well, I expect something better will come along soon,’ Alexa said snidely, loud enough for Ace to hear. He did, but pretended not to.

‘No, it’s a great part,’ Johnny said earnestly, misunderstanding her reply. ‘Big bucks. It’s a weekly serial, syndicated all over the States, and it might be shown over here soon. It was written especially with Ace in mind – he plays an ex-professional tennis player, who gets a new girl every week and generally causes havoc . . .’

‘No acting skill required, then?’ Alexa remarked. Ace did react to that, but not in the way she had expected. He smiled slightly and raised his glass in a mocking salute: he had never claimed to be an actor, it was something his agent had come up with and he had gone along with the idea. As Johnny had said – big bucks. Disconcerted, Alexa turned back to Johnny.

‘Why are you in London?’ she asked.

‘His girlfriend lives here,’ Ace replied for him. ‘Hadn’t you better phone her, Johnny? We’ll make up a foursome.’ He paused, ‘That is, if she has a decent-looking friend for me.’ He smiled evilly at Alexa and she flushed. Johnny shifted uncomfortably – why the hell was Ace being so rude? And he was deliberately ruining Johnny’s chances with this stunning redhead.

‘Er, yeah, I guess I ought to call her,’ he mumbled. ‘Do you need the cab fare home?’ he asked Alexa.

‘Just a loan, thank you,’ Alexa said quickly. Ace snorted derisively and she glared at him as she got to her feet. ‘Thanks for the drink, Johnny, it was so nice to meet *you,*' she stressed. He walked outside the hotel with her, but she placed her hand on his arm to stop him hailing a cab immediately.

'Is it true what you hinted at earlier – that Ace slept with Jack Farrell's mother and sister?'

'Well, not at the same time – much to his disappointment, I suspect.' Johnny laughed.

'But he did sleep with them both?' Alexa persisted. 'Surely the mother must be past it?'

'I've never seen her.' Johnny shrugged. 'It happened some years ago, I think, and Ace is over thirty,' he said, with all the arrogant disdain of one not much past twenty. 'Why are you so interested?' he asked suspiciously.

'No particular reason,' Alexa said airily. 'It just seemed so outrageous,' she said, and quickly hailed a passing taxi herself. 'I'll leave the money I owe you at Reception tomorrow,' she promised, as she clambered inside.

She sat back, well pleased with the way the evening had turned out. Rose Farrell and Ace Delaney! Daddy will have a fit, she thought happily. But she decided to hug the knowledge to herself for a while, perhaps until after he had officially announced his engagement . . .

Later, just before she drifted off to sleep, she realized, with a sense of shock, that she hadn't even thought about Dimitri for at least two hours . . .

Nick Lennox and his wife, Melissa Farrell, arrived at Gatwick Airport from Rose Arbor, their home in the wine-growing area of California, at two in the morning.

They were a striking couple, rating second glances even at that hour. Nick, now thirty-three years old, was an ex-Army officer from an aristocratic background, a tall, well-built ruggedly handsome man with short blond hair, strong features and shrewd grey eyes. A man of few pretensions, he had dropped his inherited title of Lord Lennox, preferring to use the title he had earned, that of the rank of Major.

Now a civilian, he co-owned a security company with another ex-Army friend, Dale 'Coop' Coupland. The firm supplied bodyguard-chauffeurs to rich and frightened people, and retaining their rank was good for business, especially with visiting Americans and Arabs.

Melissa, dubbed 'the English Rose' by the media, was as famous for her beauty as for her achievements in tennis. Her slender body, dark good looks and spectacular navy-blue eyes had earned her far more money in lucrative sponsorship deals than had her undoubted talent with a racket.

The pinnacle of her career had been claiming the Wimbledon Singles title six months earlier and, although still only twenty-three, she had decided to retire from competition to begin a family and lead a less nomadic existence. She hoped she was already pregnant, but had not yet mentioned the possibility to Nick, lest she had to disappoint him later.

'There's the limo,' Nick said, as they made their way out of the terminal building. Melissa pulled her jacket closer around her, shivering in the cold night air, which was in sharp contrast to the balmy nights she had become accustomed to in California.

'We'd better ask him to take us to London,' Nick continued; they had a flat there, and, although they were invited to spend Christmas at Bellwood, he felt it was unfair to descend on his brother-in-law at such an hour. But Melissa shook her head.

'No, Bellwood's nearer. And you left your Jag there,' she reminded him, stifling a yawn. 'I have a key – we can sneak in without disturbing them.' She was too eager to see her new niece to want to delay any longer than was strictly necessary. 'We'll ask the driver to drop us off on the road,' she added. However, when they approached the Tudor mansion that had been 'home' for most of her life, it became obvious that there was no need for caution, for lights blazed from both up and downstairs.

Melissa paused to gaze at the beauty of the ancient manor house, now bathed in moonlight, its whitewashed, timbered walls and diamond-paned windows beneath a gabled roof.

She had grown up here, as had countless generations of Farrells – the Bellwood estate had been in the family for over three hundred years, although history would show a brief interlude in ownership, when Melissa's father, Daniel, had faced bankruptcy and reluctantly put his heritage up for auction.

Jack, at that time a full-time professional player, had declined to buy, but Ace Delaney had surprised them all by becoming the new owner. However, the novelty, and expense, of playing the role of an English squire had quickly palled and he had been glad to re-sell the property to Jack after a car smash had ended his career prematurely.

The house nestled in a valley, surrounded and protected by wooded hillsides; there was a profusion of lawns, flower-beds, topiary hedges and even a maze. And, of course, a fenced-off tennis court. Jack had taught Melissa the rudiments of the game on that court; now he has a new generation to teach, she thought, and placed a hand lightly on her stomach. Perhaps even two members of the next generation . . .

She used her own key to unlock and push open the heavy, carved oak front door which led directly into the large reception hall. It was two storeys high, the walls and sloping ceiling washed a pale pink and heavily timbered. It retained many of its original features, including a large, open brick fireplace, yet was made comfortable by discreet modern central heating and lighting. A large Persian rug covered the oak floor, and plush sofas and chairs were scattered around the room.

From the hall, a narrow, low-ceilinged passageway led to the rear of the house, its walls adorned with photographs of Jack and Melissa winning junior trophies. Melissa walked past these to the kitchen, a huge room which was again a pleasing mixture of old and new, successfully maintaining its character while being comfortable and functional.

'Jack!' Melissa ran the last few yards and flung herself at her brother. Jack was five years older than Melissa, and was generally described by tennis fans as 'cute', with his shock of dark blond hair, twinkling hazel eyes and a ready grin. He smiled broadly now, not having heard their arrival, and hugged Melissa affectionately before nodding amiably at Nick.

'Sorry to burst in on you like this,' Nick apologized.

'It's my fault – I couldn't wait to see the baby,' Melissa interrupted. 'Have you decided on a name yet? And where's Lisa? Is she okay?'

'She's tired,' Jack answered the last question first. 'She's upstairs – she's feeding the baby while I feed the two of us,' he grinned, pointing to what was either a late supper or an early breakfast. 'And we're going to call her Kristin, Kit for short.'

'Kristin . . . Kit . . . Kit Farrell,' Melissa said slowly, trying the names for size. 'Yes, I like that,' she approved. 'Can we go up and see them?'

'Sure,' Jack agreed easily.

'I'll stay here,' Nick decided hastily, and Jack grinned as he guessed the reason.

'It's okay – she's being bottle-fed,' he assured him. 'You can come too.'

They trooped up the servants' stairs – the narrow flight that led from the kitchen – to the bedrooms. Jack put a finger to his lips before they entered the master bedroom and they tiptoed inside. Lisa, sitting in an armchair by the fire, glanced up and smiled tiredly; there were dark circles beneath her eyes, and her blonde hair was in disarray and in need of a shampoo, but she looked more beautiful than Melissa could remember seeing her as she cradled her baby.

Melissa walked slowly towards them and sank down on to her knees beside the chair.

'Hi,' she whispered to Lisa, but her eyes were feasting on the by-now sleeping baby. 'You clever thing – she's gorgeous.' Indeed she was; at a week old, her skin was creamy, a tuft of dark hair covered her tiny head and long lashes fanned her cheeks.

'Look at her little fingers.' Melissa gently reached out and touched the baby's hand. It was at that moment that the pain her mother had dreaded washed over her. More than four years had passed since the unmarried nineteen-year-old Melissa had allowed herself to be pushed into having an abortion, but suddenly it was as if it had happened yesterday. How could I have destroyed something as precious as this? she thought, in anguish. Not even her near-certainty that she was again pregnant with Nick's child eased her pain, and she struggled for control.

'Come on, sweetheart.' Nick had guessed her emotional turmoil, and drew her gently to her feet. 'You need some sleep – and I'm sure Jack and Lisa do, too,' he added, with a warm smile for his sister-in-law.

'You might need ear-plugs,' Jack told them cheerfully. 'You won't believe the lungs on this child!' he added proudly.

Gradually, the house and its occupants settled down. Kit, replete, slept peacefully, and her parents fell into an exhausted and probably short-lived slumber. Melissa, too, fell asleep quickly, tired from her journey. Only Nick remained wakeful, his body still on California time, but he was content to lie next to his wife's warm body as she relaxed against him. He finally dozed off, only to awake abruptly at six when Kit decided to inform them all she was hungry.

'Oh, God!' Melissa turned over and buried her head beneath a pillow. 'I feel as if I've only been asleep for five minutes,' she yawned.

'Stay where you are for a couple of hours,' Nick suggested. 'I'll bring you some coffee.'

'No, I'd better make myself useful now I'm here,' Melissa decided, reluctantly clambering out of bed and searching for a warm dressing-gown. Fortunately she still kept a wardrobe of clothes at Bellwood, as she did at all of her homes to cut down on the amount of packing she need do as she moved from one to the other. 'I'll make breakfast for us all.'

She padded down to the kitchen and raided the fridge. When Nick arrived, she raised an eyebrow in surprise at his smart suit and tie.

'I'm going to London,' he explained. 'I ought to see if I still have a business, and I'll check on the flat while I'm there.' Melissa nodded as she began whisking eggs. Nick watched for a while, marvelling at the change in his wife. For the first eighteen months of their marriage they had lived mostly in hotels as they travelled the tennis circuit, often eating in their suite to avoid Press and fans. Then, even during her breaks from competition, Melissa had rarely ventured into a kitchen.

Nick sat down and helped himself to coffee and toast, and they chatted idly while Melissa prepared a tray for Jack and Lisa.

'Come and see Kit again before you go,' she urged.

'Okay.' Nick carried the tray upstairs while Melissa dashed to unpack the baby clothes and cuddly toys she had purchased before leaving San Francisco, too impatient and excited to wait until she arrived in England to indulge in a shopping spree.

They knocked and entered the master bedroom, and gazed down at the baby, now quietly feeding.

'She really is a pretty little girl,' Nick said truthfully.

'You would think that – Mum and Dad reckon she looks just like Melissa,' Jack told him.

'Lucky baby,' Nick said lightly, and all three missed the look of resentment Lisa threw in their direction.

'Your car should be okay,' Jack said, when Nick told them of his plans for the day. 'I started it up and took it for a spin yesterday.'

'Thanks.' Nick nodded his appreciation and took his leave. 'I'll be back this afternoon,' he told Melissa, as he kissed her goodbye.

After she'd showered and breakfasted, Melissa spent some time with Lisa and Kit, but left Lisa to rest when Daniel Farrell, Melissa and Jack's father, arrived from neighbouring Brook Farm towing a huge Christmas tree on a trailer behind his Land Rover.

Daniel and Jack hauled the tree into the hall while Melissa hurried to fetch the boxes of decorations from the attics, feeling about ten years old as she sorted through the familiar objects. When Rose arrived, the family picture was complete; fortunately, Daniel and Rose had remained friends after their divorce and the four of them laughed and joked and caught up on each other's news as the tree was gradually transformed into a magical display of colour and lights. None of them noticed Lisa standing rather forlornly at the top of the stairs.

Jack had already told Melissa about Rose's engagement to Philip Kane, a multi-millionaire merchant banker. She was eager to hear all about him, but, with her father present, she contented herself with a quick hug and a whispered word of congratulations.

Finally, the last baubles had been tied on to the branches, the final strands of tinsel draped in shimmering cascades, and they stepped back to admire their handiwork.

'Oh, Lisa, good morning. How are you feeling today?' Daniel asked pleasantly, the first to spot her as she carefully negotiated the stairs, cradling Kit in her arms.

'These stairs are a death-trap,' she said crossly. 'They're dreadfully uneven!' They were actually very safe, broad and shallow, although hundreds of years of use had worn hollows in the middle of the treads.

'You'll soon feel more confident,' Rose told her, after exchanging a quick glance with Daniel. 'I remember I was terrified I would drop Jack when I first brought him home from the hospital.'

'That would explain a lot!' Melissa grinned at her brother.

'May I hold Kit?' Rose asked eagerly. It seemed to Melissa that Lisa hesitated before handing the baby over, and she looked at Jack searchingly – what was wrong? Lisa had been offhand with Melissa earlier, but she'd assumed that was due to exhaustion. Now she wasn't so sure. Jack shrugged slightly and looked away.

'What do you think of the tree?' Daniel asked Lisa.

'It's okay,' she said coolly. 'But then, you've had centuries of practice, haven't you?'

'Not me personally – I'm not that old!' Daniel forced a laugh.

'Lisa – would you like me to make you some tea?' Melissa asked.

'I don't like tea! I'm an American, I prefer coffee!' Lisa snapped.

'Okay, I'll make coffee,' Melissa said amiably.

'I can do it myself, thank you!' Lisa stalked off in the direction of the kitchen and, after an uncomfortable pause, Jack followed her.

# CHAPTER 2

Jack watched his wife for a moment as she struggled to hide her tears, then he pushed her gently into a chair and sat down beside her.

'What's wrong, love?' he asked quietly. 'Are you in pain? Or upset about something? Is it because you can't breast-feed? That's not your fault, you know.' He waited patiently for a response, but none was forthcoming. 'I can't put it right if you don't tell me what's troubling you,' he went on. Lisa plucked at the sleeve of her dressing-gown, struggling to find the words to convey what she was feeling.

'I'm fine, really,' she began, obviously untruthfully. 'It's just . . . oh, this is going to sound awful,' she bit her lip. 'Your parents are great, and Melissa was my friend before you and I got together, but . . .' She paused and sighed heavily. 'I feel as if they still live here and I'm just a guest!' she burst out. 'They all have keys to the house and just walk in as and when they please . . .'

'I couldn't run Bellwood without Dad's help, especially with my TV work,' Jack said. 'And Melissa gave me – gave, not lent,' he stressed, 'half a million quid when I bought the estate back from Ace.

Do you really expect her to knock on the door before she can come inside? And it was you who suggested she and Nick come for Christmas,' he reminded her.

'I know! I love you all, and I know your mother's just trying to help, but . . . I wish my mom could be here,' she finished wistfully.

'Your parents are welcome here any time, you know that,' Jack said. Both Joshua and Hannah Renwick were successful lawyers in San Francisco and wouldn't be coming to England to see their new granddaughter until Christmas Eve. Which Jack felt wasn't his fault, nor that of his family. But he didn't say so. 'They'll be here in a few days,' he said comfortingly instead.

'I know, but my brother won't,' Lisa went on resentfully. 'Hal's still in love with Melissa.'

'You can't blame her for that,' Jack sighed.

'Yes, I can. She slept with him, after she broke up with Nick. She just used Hal.'

'I don't recall hearing him complain at the time,' Jack said, rather unwisely, he realized, and he rushed on. 'Look, we'll go to California for an extended stay just as soon as you feel up to it. You can spend as much time as you want with your family – okay?'

'Okay, I'd love that.' She nodded, and smiled.

'Sorry to interrupt,' Melissa said from the doorway. 'You have a visitor, Jack – Ace has just arrived.'

'Oh, great, that's all I need!' Lisa muttered crossly, her momentarily regained happiness disintegrating almost immediately.

'Tell him I'll be there in a minute,' Jack said to Melissa, and she sauntered back out into the hall to pass on the message.

'What have you brought Kit?' she asked.

'Who?' Ace enquired blankly.

'The baby,' Melissa sighed.

'Oh.' Ace pulled two bottles of scotch from the pockets of his overcoat and grinned. 'Will these do?'

'Perfectly,' Jack said, as he joined them. 'Good to see you, mate. Come into the study.'

'Sure,' Ace said, but paused to give Melissa's face and figure a speculative once-over. 'You're looking good, honey – not bored with marriage yet?' he asked hopefully.

'No. And you look terrible,' she told him. 'Were you up all night?'

'Yes,' he said, leering suggestively. 'Up was definitely the word to describe the state I was in! Great girl; her name was . . . Stacey, I think,' he added vaguely.

'You are awful,' Melissa scolded.

'You should know,' he retorted. 'We had some fun, didn't we, honey?' he drawled.

'I don't remember,' she lied, trying not to blush. Ace laughed derisively but dropped the subject. Teasing Melissa was so much more enjoyable when her husband was around. 'Where's His Lordship?' he asked next, referring to Nick in his usual scornful tone. He'd submit to torture rather than admit he envied Nick his aristocratic background and title.

'Don't call him that. It's not even correct any more – he dropped the title,' she told him.

'Careless of him,' Ace remarked, and she giggled.

'Leave her alone and come and get this drink,' Jack called from the study. Ace winked at Melissa and went to join his friend. 'Melissa's right – you do look rough,' Jack commented, handing him a large glass of scotch.

'Yeah, Johnny Dancer certainly knows some wild girls – he's worse than I am.'

'He is? Keep him away from my womenfolk, then,' Jack said, in some alarm. 'How are things working out in Hollywood?' he asked, and Ace grimaced.

'Easy money. Easy women. Too easy,' he said moodily. 'I've signed up for another series of *Country Club*, then I think I'll pack it in.'

'To do what?' Jack asked. Ace shrugged.

'Something in tennis, I guess, to keep me involved in the sport until I'm eligible to join the over-35s tour. I gather that's a lot of fun and a much less gruelling schedule. I really miss competing; I even miss the discipline, believe it or not.'

'Not,' Jack said promptly.

'Really,' Ace insisted. 'Going on a bender isn't as much fun when I can do it all the time – those end-of-tournament parties were really something, weren't they?' He grinned. 'And I do miss the rivalry: beating the hell out of the opposition, especially in New York. We had some great Doubles matches on Stadium Court at Flushing Meadow – twenty thousand fans yelling their support . . .' he mused. Jack nodded; for a moment he was transported from the English country house in midwinter to a hot and humid New York in September – he could almost hear the noise, smell the hot-dogs . . .

'It wasn't so great when the twenty thousand were yelling for the other side,' he said ruefully.

'Oh, I don't know,' Ace said thoughtfully. 'I played Jimmy Connors out there early in my career. He was the crowd favourite, of course – it was just me and my talent against a legend and twenty thousand people. I lost the match but I took a set off him – it was better than sex . . . Oh, God, pour me another drink,' he said, a little embarrassed to be giving so much of himself away, even to Jack.

'Sure,' Jack refilled both glasses and sat back, surveying his old friend with a slight frown. He felt it was more than booze and late nights that were making him look tired, and something more than the artificiality of life in Hollywood that was getting him down. There were deep furrows of discontent grooved either side of his mouth, and a bleakness to his eyes that boded ill for someone.

'What else is on your mind?' Jack asked. Ace smiled slightly.

'There is something,' he admitted slowly, gazing down into his glass of scotch as if that held an answer. 'There's trouble on the way, big trouble,' he went on glumly. Jack raised an eyebrow and waited for him to continue. 'Do you remember a freelance reporter named Flanagan? A ferret-faced bastard who's always had it in for me?'

'You did thump him once,' Jack reminded him.

'Occupational hazard.' Ace shrugged. Jack grinned, then his expression hardened.

'Of course I remember him – he was the little sod who broke the story of Melissa's abortion. What about him?'

'He phoned me just before I left LA. He's persuaded my bitch of a mother to collaborate with him on a biography of me,' Ace said bitterly.

'I thought you paid her to keep quiet?' Jack asked.

'I do. Or I did. She won't get another cent from me. He must have made her a better offer – she was never one to turn down money from strange men,' he added savagely.

'Can't you persuade her not to go ahead with it? Even if it means topping his offer?' Jack suggested.

'I'd silence her permanently if I knew where to find her,' Ace said wrathfully. 'But I don't. Flanagan's installed her in an apartment somewhere so I can't get to her.'

'I realize you must be angry at her betrayal, but she can't do you much harm, can she? It's not as if you've ever tried to portray yourself as the middle class all-American hero,' he pointed out. 'Everyone already knows you pulled yourself out of the gutter, and she can't reveal too much about your early life without admitting she was a hooker who forced her child to fend for himself on the streets. She's hardly likely to do that.'

'If Flanagan gets her drunk, or high on drugs, she'll say anything he wants her to,' Ace said morosely. 'And he must have a file on me a foot thick. On us,' he amended, shooting Jack a sideways glance. 'I doubt he'll leave you out of it, buddy. Our Doubles partnership lasted longer than most marriages – just think how many groupies we bedded who'll tell him their story for a few bucks.'

'I'd rather not,' Jack said drily, then he shrugged. 'Oh, to hell with him – we were both single back then, and Lisa knows I was no saint before we got together.'

'Mmm. He also mentioned Rose and Melissa,' Ace said reluctantly, loath to bring up the thorny subject.

His affair with Rose had caused a rift between the two men and Jack hadn't been exactly overjoyed when he'd learned of the fling with Melissa, either. Jack frowned and stared at him rather accusingly.

'There were always rumours about you and Melissa,' he acknowledged, 'but never a word about Mum,' he said flatly. 'How did Flanagan get wind of that?'

'I don't know; I thought it was better not to pursue it. I pretended I'd misheard, and that I thought he was referring to Melissa as the English Rose, but he's bound to dig around.'

'Damn!' Jack sighed. 'Mum's just got engaged; this could really screw things up for her. Is there anything else I should know about?'

'I'm not sure,' Ace said thoughtfully. 'Flanagan was almost gloating, as if he knows something I don't.'

'He was probably just fishing, hoping you'd give something away. What could he know?'

'The name of my father?' Ace said slowly.

'Don't get me wrong, but isn't that something even your mother doesn't know?' Jack asked, rather awkwardly, but Ace didn't take offence.

'So I always believed. But, as I said, she'll say anything if the price is right. And, so far as Flanagan's concerned, the more sensational the story, the better.'

'Sure, but he's not stupid enough to risk a libel suit,' Jack pointed out. 'DNA testing is too accurate for him to name names without solid proof.'

'Yeah, I guess you're right. I suppose I'll just have to wait and read about it – unless I get to my mother first. I've hired a private detective to try and find her.'

'Good. Let's hope . . .' Jack broke off and motioned to Ace to keep quiet as the door opened and Rose appeared.

'We're about to have some lunch – chicken casserole – do you want to join us or shall I leave some in the oven?' she asked.

'We'll eat later, thanks.' Jack smiled at her, aware that she was always a little uncomfortable in Ace's company.

'Right.' She disappeared as quickly as she had arrived. 'Melissa! Lunch! she called.

'Should I warn her about Flanagan?' Ace asked. Jack considered for a moment, then shook his head.

'Not yet. There's no point in upsetting her while there's a chance you can stop it. I'll probably tell Melissa, though. Flanagan's more likely to approach her first since she's a celebrity, and she's more capable of handling it than Mum.'

'More capable of handling what?' Melissa had overheard on her way to the dining room and popped her head around the door.

'It's not important – I'll tell you later,' Jack said quickly.

'Okay.' She shrugged, and went on her way. Daniel had returned to Brook Farm, so only Rose, Lisa and Melissa sat down to lunch.

'Have Jack and Ace already eaten?' Melissa asked, as she helped herself to a large jacket potato and a spoonful of casserole.

'No, they're drinking their lunch,' Lisa said sourly.

'I suggested they eat later,' Rose put in quickly, but Lisa wasn't mollified.

'Jack's so irresponsible when Ace is around – I hope they don't go near Kit when they're drunk!' she snapped. Melissa thought the possibility of Ace going anywhere near a baby, drunk or sober, was too remote to even consider, but said nothing. Rose opened her mouth to defend her son, but a burst of raucous laughter from the men in the study caused her to change her mind.

'I thought I'd go into Brighton shopping this afternoon,' she said instead. 'Unless you'd like me to stay, Lisa?'

'No, I'm fine,' Lisa said shortly.

'Melissa? How about you? Would you like to come with me?'

'Yes, I still have some Christmas shopping to do,' she said.

Mother and daughter enjoyed their time alone, shopping and gossiping, and Rose told Melissa all about Philip Kane and their rather whirlwind romance.

'You'll meet him on Boxing Day – he and his daughter are coming to the party at Bellwood,' she said happily, then she frowned. 'That is, if we still hold the party – do you think it will be too much for Lisa?'

'Ask her – we can always hold it at Brook Farm instead. Dad won't mind,' Melissa said.

'I daren't ask Lisa anything,' Rose grimaced, then sighed. 'I always hoped I'd love the girl Jack married, but I suppose all mothers think the girl who marries their son isn't good enough . . . I used to be fond of her,' she went on, but rather doubtfully, 'but, well, she's just so hard to please. Jack bends over backwards to make her happy – she has him, a beautiful home, plenty of money and now Kit. I thought she'd be better once the baby was born but she seems worse, if anything.'

'Have they been arguing a lot?' Melissa asked, surprised by what she was hearing. They had seemed fine when she and Nick had last been in England, and she had assumed the birth had taken its toll on Lisa's usual good nature. 'The pregnancy was planned, wasn't it?'

'Oh, yes. They were both thrilled about it. Oh, I expect they'll settle down,' Rose said brightly. 'Ignore me, I'm probably just being one of those dreadful, interfering mothers-in-law . . . feel free to contradict me any time you want to!' she added tartly, and Melissa grinned.

'I'm just glad I had the sense to marry an orphan!' she said brightly.

'Oh, that reminds me – should we invite Nick's sister to the party?' Rose asked.

'No, they've all gone to Scotland for the holidays,' Melissa was happy to report. Nick's sister, Caroline Stanton, was much older than Nick and Melissa had never felt comfortable with her, knowing Caroline had hoped Nick would marry their cousin's widow, Sheena Lennox. And, although Melissa had once been friendly with Nick's older niece, Jessica, she loathed the younger, Juliet, a fellow professional player who had vowed to take over Melissa's spot as the highest-ranked British player.

That was fair enough – Melissa had more than her own share of ambition – but it was Juliet who had leaked the story of Melissa's abortion to the Press, and that was what she, and Nick, found unforgivable. Nick had been helping Juliet financially, but promptly withdrew his support when he discovered her perfidy.

He had expected her to run home to her parents with her tail between her legs, but instead Juliet had surprised them all by buckling down and working hard to earn prize money and the even more valuable computer points. Experts doubted she would ever be as successful as Melissa, but she was steadily climbing the rankings and, owing to Melissa's retirement, looked set to replace her as the British number one. By default, Melissa insisted firmly.

Nick had already returned from London when Rose dropped Melissa off at Bellwood, and had gone upstairs to shower and change. After hearing of Ace's visit, thankfully a short one, he wished he had stayed at Bellwood; although he trusted Melissa completely, he didn't trust Ace Delaney as far as he could kick him, and the violent jealousy he had once suffered over Melissa's affair with the American resurfaced whenever the other man was around. He didn't blame Melissa for seeking solace elsewhere during the two years of their separation, but regretted that the two men she had chosen were still part of their lives – Ace, Jack's best friend, and Hal Renwick, Jack's brother-in-law!

He had already begun stripping off when Melissa entered the bedroom, laden with shopping. She let the bags drop to the floor and cast a smouldering glance at her half-naked husband. Instantly, his mood lightened and he forgot all about Ace – and his intention to take a shower. Just one look from his wife's incredible navy blue eyes was all it ever took for him to forget everything but his need to have her.

Melissa smiled slightly as he visibly hardened; she loved his desire for her, but it was a two-way street. Always, the touch of his hands and mouth on her body instantly aroused her, and now she pulled impatiently at her clothes, needing to feel her bare skin against Nick's.

She sighed blissfully as they fell on to the bed, their bodies fitting so well together in the wonderfully familiar way. She pushed her hips against him, wanting him inside her, now, but Nick resisted, pulling back slightly to tease and torment her into even greater need. He bent his head to nuzzle her breasts, hearing with delight the soft moans of pleasure deep in her throat.

'Now!' Melissa said insistently, and he smiled, more than ready and willing to comply. He closed his eyes at the ecstasy of his entry into her hot, moist body and groaned his delight as she wrapped her slender thighs around him, urging him deeper inside.

He raised his head and opened his eyes – watching her pleasure always increased his own. He loved seeing the flush of desire suffusing her skin, loved hearing the sound of her ragged breathing, the soft endearments and urgent demands – all served to push him to the brink of climax. He understood her needs as well as he knew his own, and held back until she was at the point of orgasm, then carried them both inexorably over the edge.

He eased his weight from her and rested on his elbows, gazed down at her and dropped a kiss on her softly curved mouth.

'I have always adored making love to you,' he murmured, 'but it's even better now we're trying to make a baby.' Melissa smiled, but said nothing; it was too soon.

Nick waited in vain for a response – why does she think I can't count? he wondered fondly, but he understood the reason for her secrecy. To him, a baby would be the icing on an already wonderful cake, but it would mean so much more to Melissa.

They rarely spoke about the abortion which had all but ended their relationship, but he knew she was haunted by what she had done. He hoped a child would finally grant her peace of mind and allow her to forgive herself.

He realized that she wasn't going to confide in him yet, and began telling her about his day in London. His business venture with Dale Coupland continued to flourish and Coop had hired six more men, all ex-Army, during Nick's absence in California.

'How many of us are there for dinner?' he asked, as they finished dressing.

'Just four, I think,' Melissa replied, but, when they ventured downstairs they discovered the four had become three.

'Lisa's in bed – she's nursing the baby and I'm nursing a hangover,' Jack said ruefully. 'I'd forgotten what it was like to try and out-drink Ace!'

'Shall we send out for pizza?' Melissa suggested. Despite her retirement from full-time tennis, she wasn't one to spend too much time in the kitchen unless it was strictly necessary.

'I'll go and fetch it; it'll be quicker,' Nick decided. 'And I've worked up quite an appetite!' He winked at Melissa as he picked up his car keys, and she laughed. Jack looked at her quizzically.

'Fun and games, huh? Lucky you.'

'Mmm, there's something deliciously illicit about having sex in the bedroom I had as a child,' she confided. 'I feel like a naughty schoolgirl!'

'So do I,' Jack sighed wistfully, deliberately misunderstanding. 'Oh, so do I. God, don't tell Lisa I said that – I'm already in the dog-house for boozing with Ace earlier. I haven't dared tell her he'll be coming to the party on Boxing Day.'

Lisa declined to join them for the meal and, when Melissa took her some food on a tray, spurned her offer to keep her company upstairs, pleading tiredness. As Melissa returned to the dining-room she heard Jack telling Nick his plans to take Lisa and Kit to California in the New Year.

'. . . not until after the Australian Open – I'll be too busy,' Jack said, referring to his job with satellite TV, which would be offering extensive coverage of the tournament.

'You're not going to Melbourne, are you?' Melissa asked him.

'No, of course not. But I'll be presenting the coverage from the studio in London,' Jack explained. 'Lisa might want to stay in California for a while – if we're underfoot at the Renwicks', can we use Rose Arbor?' he asked casually, for the whole family used Melissa's house in the Napa valley as a holiday home.

'Sure,' Melissa said easily.

'Thanks. God, I've just remembered something!' he exclaimed; the booze had made him temporarily forget Ace's problem with the Press, a problem which might involve them all, but now he repeated as much as he knew about Flanagan and his plan to write Ace's life story.

Both Nick and Melissa were shocked; Flanagan had broken the scandal of Melissa's abortion, two years after the event, by which time she had confidently expected it would remain a secret. Nick's lip curled with distaste as he recalled the little creep offering him money in return for the story of his affair with the English Rose.

'For once, I'm with Ace,' he said tightly. 'I damn near put my fist through Flanagan's face!'

'Yeah, well, he might dredge all that up again,' Jack told them. 'Flanagan asked Ace to comment on his affairs with . . . sorry, Nick . . . you and Mum,' he told Melissa.

'Oh, no,' she sighed heavily. 'Can't Ace stop him? Or pre-empt him by telling his own story? A sanitized version?' she suggested hopefully.

'It's a book we're talking about, not a pamphlet,' Jack said drily.

'But I thought Ace's mother was dead?' Melissa frowned. 'He's always denied having any family.'

'There is only the mother, Loretta, and he hasn't seen her since he was about sixteen,' Jack told her. 'I don't know the whole story, but he's let slip a few things over the years. He grew up in a bad neighbourhood, as you know, and she more or less left him to fend for himself from the age of eight. She became a drug-user and turned to prostitution to feed her habit. That was around the time she stopped feeding her child,' he added grimly.

'Poor Ace,' Melissa said, appalled. Even Nick felt some sympathy for the young Ace, but he had no patience with those who used a bad childhood as an excuse for adult misdeeds. Nick's own parents had been killed in a car crash when he was eight and, although he had been offered a loving home with relatives in Scotland, he had been deeply unhappy for quite some time. The tales of Ace's debauchery and dirty tricks were legendary – any pain he had suffered in his early years had since been inflicted tenfold on his hapless victims.

'Sorry, I probably shouldn't have mentioned it,' Jack said quickly, catching the grim expression on Nick's face. He had forgotten quite how much trouble Ace had caused for Melissa and Nick in the past, and how he had so nearly succeeded in keeping them apart forever. 'I just thought you ought to be warned in case Flanagan approaches you,' he added to Melissa, who nodded resignedly. One of the bonuses of retiring from competition was the lessening of Press interest in her and her private life. At least, it had been, she amended silently.

Jack poured out more wine for them all and raised his glass.

'Let's forget Ace and drink to us, our family, and its newest member.'

'To Kit,' Nick said, his gaze softening as he smiled at Melissa. She had barely sipped at her wine, another sign that she believed, as did he, that Kit would not be the youngest member of the family for very long. Ace Delaney can't hurt us, Nick thought confidently; he's already done his worst and failed. However, he still dreaded the renewed gossip Flanagan's exposé would generate – he had hoped never again to see Melissa's name linked with Ace in the Press.

The forthcoming book was on Melissa's mind, too. She was rather quiet all evening and wakeful after they went to bed. Suddenly, she turned and snuggled up to Nick, needing comfort and his approval for what she felt she had to do.

'Please don't mind too much about Ace,' she whispered.

'Why should I mind the whole world reading about his affair with my wife?' he asked, but he wrapped his arms around her and held her close.

'I wasn't your wife at the time . . . sorry, that's not much consolation, is it?' she sighed. 'But I've been thinking: if Flanagan contacts me, it will be better if I don't try to deny it. If I do, he'll dig around and maybe find out about Mum. She was always terrified of people knowing and it could cause trouble between her and Philip Kane.'

'So, you're going to offer yourself up as the sacrificial lamb to save your mother's blushes, are you?' Nick asked, after a pause.

'I don't think I have much choice,' she said sadly. Nick hugged her tightly.

'I love you, Mrs Lennox,' he said fiercely.

'I love you, too. So much,' she whispered, and began rubbing her thigh against his, wanting to make amends in the best way she knew.

She sat up to straddle him, and Nick lay back, content to let her soothe him with her clever hands and mouth until they both forgot Ace and nothing existed but their love of and pleasure in each other.

Lisa's spirits rose when her parents, Joshua and Hannah Renwick, arrived on Christmas Eve, and she became much more relaxed and confident with Kit once she had her own mother to help and advise her.

Rose tried not to feel insulted by Lisa's obvious, and perfectly natural, desire for Mrs Renwick's assistance instead of her own. Christmas Day was generally enjoyed by everyone, although Hannah Renwick complained of the cold, and of not sleeping well.

'These old houses are so noisy; I expect it's the ancient timbers creaking,' she opined.

'They're not in the room next to ours, are they?' Nick muttered to Melissa, and she suppressed a giggle.

'I hope not. Why can't she just have jet-lag like everyone else?' she responded. She had stayed at the Renwicks' house in San Francisco on several occasions in the past, and they had always made her welcome. But that was before her marriage to Nick, which had caused a great deal of pain to their only son, Hal, who had been Melissa's friend, one-time coach and, for a short time, her lover.

'Hal sends his love to you and the baby,' Hannah told Lisa loudly. 'He's longing to see you both, but he had already arranged to spend the holidays with his girlfriend, Debbie.' Her gaze rested briefly on Melissa before she continued. 'She's such a lovely girl, and she's lasted longer than any of the others, so we might be hearing wedding bells soon.'

'I do hope so,' Melissa said sincerely, which earned her a sideways glance and the merest sniff from the older woman.

Caterers, supervised by Melissa, had done all the work for the Boxing Day party, and Lisa cheered up even more when she discovered she could fit into one of her pre-pregnancy party frocks. Guests began arriving at seven; the women trooped upstairs to admire Kit, while the men headed for the booze. Melissa began watching out, with some trepidation, for Philip Kane and his daughter, who were picking up Rose on the way.

'I do hope he's nice – and the daughter. What's it like having a little sister?' she asked Jack.

'Purgatory,' he sighed gloomily, but the accompanying hug belied the sentiment. 'It's not as if she's a kid – she's twenty, so I expect she leads her own life. She's not likely to bother us much, or Mum for that matter,' he added airily.

If Melissa was nervous at meeting her prospective stepfather and sister, Alexa was positively panic-stricken, but prepared to die rather than admit it. After all, as her father continually pointed out, both of Rose's children had accomplished much in their lives and were millionaires by their own efforts, and not through inherited wealth as was Alexa herself.

She had still to drop her bombshell regarding Rose's fling with Ace Delaney. Many times, over a boring Christmas spent in the company of deadly dull aged aunts, she had been tempted to say something, so sick was she of hearing her father boast about his lovely and classy fiancée. But she had resisted the urge – so far.

She changed her outfit several times, making them late leaving the house, so her father was in a foul temper when she finally emerged wearing a slinky mini-dress in shimmering green satin. On the journey he proceeded to give her a long list of dos and don'ts, which ensured her mood matched his by the time they arrived at Rose's flat.

'Let Rose sit in the front,' Philip ordered. Alexa seethed silently, but obeyed. Not that sitting in the back seat of a Rolls-Royce entailed any hardship, of course, but it was the principle that irked her, condemning her to child status. She vented her spleen on Rose.

'Hello, Granny,' she greeted her, with a sneer.

'Alexa!' Philip said warningly.

'I don't mind,' Rose said quickly. 'I love being a grandmother,' she added, so patently sincere that Alexa ground her teeth in annoyance.

'Who will be at the party?' she asked next, seemingly casual.

'Oh, my family, of course. And my daughter-in-law's parents, plus some friends and neighbours. It won't be too much of a crowd this year because of Kit.'

'Will any of Melissa or Jack's famous friends be there?' Alexa persisted. 'You know, tennis players?'

'Possibly,' Rose said vaguely.

'There was a piece in the gossip column about Jack's Doubles partner, Ace Delaney. He's here in London – did you know?'

'Er, yes, I did. Can you turn the heating down, Philip? It's rather hot in here,' she said, flushing.

'Is it true he slept with your daughter?' Alexa continued.

'Alexa, really!' Philip protested.

'What?' she asked guilelessly. 'There was often gossip about Melissa and the male players.'

'Exactly. Locker room gossip,' Rose said firmly. 'That's all it was.'

'I thought so,' Alexa agreed. 'I'm sure Melissa would have more sense than to become involved with someone as promiscuous as Ace Delaney. No woman with any self-respect would become part of his harem,' she said scornfully. 'He probably has some awful disease!'

'I'm sure he's not that irresponsible,' Rose said faintly.

'Alexa!' Philip thundered. 'That's quite enough! You're embarrassing Rose.'

Not half as much as I'm going to embarrass the pair of you soon, she thought silently, but sat back with a meek, 'Sorry, Daddy.'

# CHAPTER 3

Rose heaved a huge sigh of relief when Bellwood came into view, and quickly pointed it out to Philip. He slowed the car as they approached and nodded his appreciation.

'It's a beautiful house,' he approved. 'It's one of the oldest of its type still privately owned, isn't it?'

'Yes, it's mentioned in guide books,' Rose said, as proudly as if she still lived there. 'Often, in summer, tourists stop and ask if it's open to the public. Melissa used to say it was and charge them a small fortune for a guided tour and a cup of tea,' she told him. 'Once, during a heatwave, I was resting stark naked on my bed and opened my eyes to find four Japanese tourists in my room!' She laughed at the memory but had been furious at the time. 'At least she stopped them taking any photographs.'

'I'm looking forward to meeting your daughter – she sounds delightful,' Philip said, with a smile. He didn't notice his own daughter screw up her face and poke out her tongue at him.

Rose led the way inside and introduced Philip and

Alexa to her family. Alexa nodded unsmilingly and glanced around the room rather haughtily.

'Let me take your coat,' Melissa offered. 'Would you like a drink? Or do you want to come and see the baby?'

'No,' Alexa said coldly.

'No to which? The drink or the baby?' Melissa asked pleasantly, maintaining a smile for her mother's sake. Alexa flushed.

'I'll have a vodka and tonic,' she mumbled.

'I'll fetch it,' Jack said hastily, exchanging a rueful glance with Melissa as he hurried away. Melissa tried gamely to engage Alexa in conversation, but it was a thankless task. Alexa continued her perusal of the room, but there was no sign of Ace Delaney. It was mostly a collection of wrinklies, she thought scornfully. Suddenly, her restless gaze lit on a ruggedly handsome blond man and she brightened.

'Who's that?' she pointed him out. 'You can introduce me to him, if you like.'

'That's my husband, Nick Lennox,' Melissa said drily, but she effected the introductions. Nick talked to Alexa at length, trying to make her feel welcome, and she cheered up perceptibly.

Ace arrived later than anyone else and with two stunning girls in tow, both blonde and buxom. He had been partying non-stop over Christmas and hadn't been completely sober for days. He was gaunt from lack of sleep and needed a shave; in fact, he looked even more dangerous and disreputable than usual, but was still drop-dead gorgeous and immediately had the attention of every woman in the room – even Melissa, briefly, although she was now immune to his charms. Alexa looked at him and shivered; how would he react when she exposed his affair with Rose Farrell? She stepped closer to Nick, as if seeking protection.

'Hi,' Ace greeted Jack. 'This is Stacey . . .'

'No, I'm Stacey,' said the second girl resignedly.

'Oh, right. So this is . . .'

'Sophie,' she supplied, giggling.

'Yeah – a present for you.' Ace grinned at Jack. 'I figured Lisa would be out of action for a while . . .'

'Shut up!' Jack hissed; his mother-in-law was within earshot and rigid with disapproval. 'I'm not interested.'

'No? You won't get anywhere with that one,' Ace squinted at the shy fifteen-year-old daughter of a neighbour with whom Jack had been trying to converse. 'A virgin,' Ace proclaimed loudly. 'They're too much like hard work. The last one I had didn't even know what I meant by oral sex. And, when I told her, she looked so horrified I immediately went as limp as a fag's handshake!' He looked around for applause, while Jack groaned. The men guffawed uncomfortably while the women pretended not to have heard. Mrs Renwick glared at both Ace and her son-in-law before stalking off.

'What exactly *is* oral sex?' enquired the suddenly not-so-shy fifteen-year-old, gazing at Ace with adoration. Jack ignored her and pulled Ace aside.

'Mum's here with her fiancé, so behave yourself,' he ordered quietly.

'Sure, Jack,' Ace agreed amiably. 'Where's that gorgeous sister of yours?'

'Out of bounds,' Jack said firmly. 'You don't want to upset her husband again, do you?'

'No way, he fights dirty,' Ace said indignantly, as if he didn't. After years of mutual dislike, he and Nick had finally had a showdown which had left both men in agony and needing hospital treatment. 'Oh, there's His Lordship,' Ace spotted Nick talking to a girl who had her back to him. All he could see of Alexa was a mane of tawny hair which almost reached to her slender waist. The mini dress showed a cute rear and long, shapely legs. 'If that girl gets any nearer to Nick, she'll be wearing his trousers!' he said, grinning. 'I'm surprised Melissa hasn't sent her packing.'

'Oh, that's Alexa Kane, our soon-to-be stepsister,' Jack told him after turning around to check. 'She's a bit of a madam, but we're all trying to be nice to her for Mum's benefit,' he explained.

'Alexa?' Ace frowned, trying to clear his drink-sodden brain. 'I think I know her.'

'Oh, hell!' Jack groaned.

'No, listen. She was all over Johnny Dancer a few nights ago, telling him some sob story about a broken love affair. She got over it pretty quickly; within minutes she was making bedroom eyes at Johnny. I soon broke that up,' he said, with some satisfaction, remembering how Alexa had slunk off home alone.

'Why did you break it up?' Jack asked curiously. 'Were you annoyed that she preferred Johnny to you? If so, tonight's your chance to get her for yourself.'

'You must be joking,' Ace said flatly. 'She's trouble, more dangerous than a limpet-mine. She's the sort of girl you bed once and then can't get rid of, the type who breaks into your house and creates a scene . . . you know what I mean.'

'Not really, no,' said Jack drily. 'That's never happened to me.'

'Well, it has to me,' Ace said, with a shudder. Jack shook his head in despair.

Ace decided to sit down before he fell, and sprawled the length of a sofa with Stacey draped all over him, feeding him titbits of food in an effort to soak up the alcohol. She fed him pieces of smoked salmon from her mouth to his in an incredibly erotic display.

Alexa watched them covertly for a few moments, then curled her lip in disdain when Ace began gnawing at a piece of chicken. What a savage he is, she thought, and again felt that the rumour concerning his Apache heritage might well be true.

She was peeved that he had not yet noticed her, and purposely tried to catch his eye. When she did, his gaze passed over her seemingly without recognition. Damn! He'd probably been drinking so much that he had completely forgotten Johnny Dancer letting slip the choice item about him and Rose.

She sauntered over to her future stepmother and asked a question about the baby – something designed to keep Rose busily occupied for eternity. Linking arms with Rose, Alexa turned and faced Ace squarely – surely now he would make the connection?

Ace had actually been watching her performance, and recognized it for what it was. He was an excellent poker player and few people ever saw anything in his expression that he didn't want them to read. He remained where he was, seemingly ensconced for the evening with Stacey, and forced Alexa to make her move. Eventually, she did, her courage bolstered by the certainty that she held the upper hand.

'Hello,' she said, standing directly in front of him.

'Hi, honey,' Ace said vaguely.

'Don't you remember me?' Alexa asked tightly.

'Er, no.' He squinted at her. 'Sorry, honey, did I forget to call? I've been tied up,' he added, with a suggestive wink at Stacey, still draped all over him. Alexa almost stamped her foot in vexation.

'We met last week,' she reminded him. 'I had a long chat with Johnny Dancer – he was telling me all about your love-life . . .'

'That *must* have been a long chat,' Ace drawled. Stacey giggled.

'As I was saying,' Alexa bit out, 'he told me all about your conquests, especially my future step-mother and sister!'

'Yeah?' Ace raised one eyebrow. 'Yeah, I remember you now. You still owe Johnny the twenty quid he lent you for your cab fare,' he told her, sounding bored. Alexa flushed and dug in her purse, luckily finding a twenty pound note which she held out to Ace.

'I've been too busy to drop it off,' she snapped. 'Will you give this to him?'

'Sure.' Ace plucked the note from her fingers and casually tucked it into Stacey's cleavage. 'Look after that for me, honey.'

'That's hardly a safe place!' Alexa sniffed, and had to look away when Ace's long fingers began stroking the other girl's plump breast. Stacey almost purred with pleasure and nestled closer to Ace. He bent his head and kissed her hungrily, completely ignoring Alexa. Feeling dismissed – no, feeling as if she didn't even exist, she stomped off, pausing to speak to Rose.

'Ace Delaney's having fun – is there anyone here who hasn't slept with him? Or is that like searching for a virgin in a brothel?' She didn't wait for a reply, but went and helped herself to another drink, tossing it back in one gulp.

She calmed down a little and scanned the room for someone, anyone, interesting to talk to. Nick Lennox was dishy, but he seemed to have disappeared; besides, he was obviously too straight and too much in love with Melissa to want to play around. Where was Jack Farrell? Might as well keep it in the family . . .

Ace was well aware of her actions; he had seen her aside to Rose, although he hadn't been able to hear it. However, judging by the look of distress on Rose's face, it had been nothing pleasant. He tipped Stacey unceremoniously off his lap and went after Rose, catching her hand and pulling her to a halt.

'Jack tells me you're getting married. Congratulations,' he said sincerely, for Rose Farrell was one of the few women he genuinely liked. 'Have you told what's-his-name about me?'

'Philip? No, I haven't,' she said, looking around nervously.

'Do it,' Ace advised. 'Before someone else beats you to it,' he added. Rose paled.

'No one knows,' she whispered. 'Only Jack and Melissa, and they won't say anything.'

'Hasn't Jack mentioned the book Flanagan's writing about me?' Ace asked, and, when she shook her head, quickly told her about it. 'And that's not all.' He shifted a little uncomfortably, for he had been at fault in hinting of the relationship to Johnny Dancer. 'I have a hazy recollection of a friend of mine telling Alexa about it, so I suggest you get to Philip with your version first. I'm really sorry, honey, I hope it won't louse things up for you.'

'So do I.' She bit her lip and forced a wan smile. 'Thanks for the warning.'

'Why is Alexa so hostile to you? You're hardly the wicked stepmother,' Ace went on.

'She was fine until a few days ago. Then she had some bad news of her own, and I'm afraid she's not inclined to share anyone else's happiness at the moment,' Rose sighed. 'The main trouble is that she has too much time on her hands and too much money she's not had to work for.'

'Mmm, she doesn't strike me as the sort who's ever grafted for anything,' Ace said disparagingly. 'Those long nails are a giveaway – they're usually a sign of a useless woman. And they're hell on a man's back,' he added, with a sideways glance at Rose. But she was no longer shocked by anything Ace said or did.

'You've already considered that, have you?' she queried.

'No, of course not. She's not my type,' Ace said crossly. Jack had insinuated much the same earlier, and it annoyed him that two people who ought to know him well could be so wrong – since when had he gone after neurotic, poor little rich girls? Alexa Kane would need about a thousand years of psychotherapy before I'd be interested in her, he thought.

'Have you seen Melissa recently?' Rose asked, scanning the room for a glimpse of her daughter – Philip wanted to ask her about life on the tennis circuit.

'No.' Ace shook his head, glancing around. 'His Lordship is missing, too – perhaps they've gone to bed?' he said, with a suggestive grin and a slight pang of regret. Melissa was a great kid; beautiful, sexy and independent. She didn't cling, or demand too much of a man's time or attention. He'd once briefly considered marriage to her, but had known he was incapable of being faithful to her, and that would have brought Jack's wrath down on his head. Besides, Melissa had laughed at the very idea, he remembered, with a scowl.

Melissa had, in fact, gone upstairs to the nursery, where the Farrells' cleaning lady was sitting with Kit. It was reasonably quiet in this far corner of the house and Kit was sleeping peacefully, undisturbed by the party taking place below.

'I'll stay with her for a while – why don't you go and get some supper?' Melissa suggested to Mrs Charles.

Alone with the baby, she sat next to the cot and resisted the urge to pick her up, contenting herself with gently stroking her tiny arms and hands, which were curled into loose fists either side of her head.

'Do you want to know a secret?' she whispered. 'You might have a cousin to play with soon. Wouldn't that be wonderful?'

'I thought I might find you up here,' Nick said from the doorway. Melissa jumped slightly, not sure if he had heard. She glanced at him and smiled a welcome.

'I'm surprised you even noticed I'd left the party,' she said drily. 'But I'm glad you managed to tear yourself away from Alexa!'

'Don't pretend to be jealous,' Nick said. 'You know it took me too long to win you for me ever to risk losing you. Besides, that one would eat a man alive,' he grimaced. 'She's slinking around downstairs like a Black Widow spider, searching for prey!'

'I can well believe that!' Melissa said tartly. 'I don't think I'm going to like that girl. In fact, I think Mum should consider postponing the wedding until Alexa has grown up and left home, which will probably be in about thirty years' time!'

'Don't worry about it,' Nick said dismissively; he didn't want to talk about Alexa, or even Rose for that matter. He hunkered down beside Melissa and took her hand, dropping a kiss on her palm. 'Let's be very rude and forget the party and go to bed,' he suggested huskily, reaching over to kiss her and slipping his tongue inside her mouth.

'Mmm.' Melissa leaned against him, then glanced at Kit. 'I can't; I told Mrs Charles I'd stay with Kit while she went for something to eat,' she said regretfully. Nick watched Kit for a moment, then sighed.

'I hope Mrs Charles is on a diet,' he said, and Melissa smiled.

'Me too.'

'I'll go and collect some food for us and take it to our room,' Nick decided. 'Join me there as soon as you can?'

'You bet.' Melissa nodded, and, after another deep

kiss, full of promise of what was to come, he left her to continue her stint of babysitting.

When Mrs Charles returned, Melissa was pacing the floor, impatient for the pleasures awaiting her in her bedroom. She dashed along the corridor and into Nick's waiting arms. In addition to fetching refreshments, he had lit candles and placed them on tables and cabinets, bathing the room in a soft, cosy glow.

Nick had already stripped off and, despite his obvious arousal, took his time over undressing Melissa, revelling in her mounting impatience as he slowly bared her body to his gaze, kissing and caressing each newly exposed area of skin until she was quivering with desire.

His lovemaking was slow and sensual, gradually building to a peak of incredible sensations that left Melissa utterly sated and content. She snuggled into his embrace and glanced at him, dropping a kiss on his shoulder.

'You're being wonderfully gentle with me recently – you know, don't you?'

'Know what?' he prompted. 'I know that your period is late, and I know there's an unopened pregnancy testing kit in the bathroom. Why haven't you used it?'

'I'm scared to, in case it's negative,' she admitted. 'I don't want our hopes dashed.'

'I understand, but do it,' Nick urged. 'Do it now.' Melissa hesitated.

'I think it gives a more reliable result if I do it first thing in the morning,' she said.

'Okay.' Nick decided not to push; to let her take things at her own pace.

They remained in bed, cuddling and chatting idly, neither of them in the mood to rejoin the party downstairs. But then there were unmistakable sounds of a commotion outside, car engines revving and a lot of shouting.

'That sounds as if we have gatecrashers,' Nick decided, and was out of bed in a flash, pulling on his trousers. 'You stay here, sweetheart, while I check it out,' he said, pausing to draw aside the curtains to see what was going on. 'It's okay.' He relaxed and smiled at Melissa. 'Your brother and Ace are putting on a show.'

'Oh, dear. Is it decent?' she laughed, and scrambled out of bed to join him at the window, shrugging on his discarded shirt for warmth.

Jack and Ace were out on the tennis court, which was illuminated by the headlights from the guests' cars lined up alongside. They squared up to each other, both obviously the worse for drink, with Stacey and Sophie, giggling and even more drunk, preparing to act as ball-girls. Melissa winced at the sight of them tottering around the court in their high-heeled shoes.

'They'll ruin the court,' she fretted. 'Jack must be drunk not to notice the damage they're causing.' Then she fell silent and watched the two men.

Despite their inebriation and the poor light, it was an impressive display of power and dexterity. They weren't trying to score points; they played to each other's strengths, not weaknesses, their aim to entertain, not to win. They both hit some spectacular shots; the talent which had won them numerous Doubles titles around the world was very much in evidence.

Melissa watched rather pensively, her admiration tinged with sadness. A car smash had cut Jack's career short, and Ace had never really fulfilled his potential, certainly not as a Singles player. He could have been at the very top of the sport if he had cut out the booze and the late nights, and attempted to channel his talent properly. In Doubles, Jack had managed to keep him focused and out of trouble with officials, but in Singles he had so often lost matches he should have won through lack of concentration or poor fitness and preparation.

The party guests were enjoying the match; their cheers and whistles were clearly audible to Nick and Melissa inside, as were Stacey's and Sophie's shrieks as they stumbled around the court. The impromptu show finished abruptly when Ace twisted an ankle as he lunged for a shot, falling heavily on to the frost-hardened surface. Too drunk to register any pain, he lay back and burst out laughing as he realized his foot was entangled in the bottom of the net. Jack grinned and ambled over to extricate him, but Stacey beat him to it. Ace ignored the bystanders and grabbed her outstretched hand, not to lever himself up, but to pull her down on to his lap.

'Uh-oh, the cabaret's just become X-rated.' Nick smiled at Melissa and drew the curtain on the scene. She scurried back to bed and snuggled beneath the covers, shivering a little.

'Would you like some coffee?' Nick asked, noticing she was chilled.

'Mmm, yes please.' She nodded. She was still wearing Nick's shirt and he didn't bother replacing it, but went bare-chested on his errand, using the rear stairs to reach the kitchen unseen.

Ace was there, limping a little. He had appropriated the ice-bucket and was wrapping cubes in a towel to make an ice-pack for his injured ankle. Nick ignored him and busied himself preparing Melissa's drink. Ace eyed him speculatively; his half-undressed state spoke volumes and it still irked Ace that Melissa had chosen this upper-class Brit over him.

'Is that coffee for Melissa?' he asked casually.

'Yes.'

'Having trouble keeping her awake?' Ace smirked. Nick balled his hands into fists as he counted slowly to ten, refusing to rise to the bait. But Ace never knew when not to press his luck.

'Need some advice on how to handle her?' he continued his needling.

'From a man who could only hold on to her for a week?' Nick enquired mildly. 'I think not,' he added dismissively.

'Yeah, but what a week,' drawled Ace. Nick had heard enough; he walked over to where Ace was sitting, nursing his injured ankle, and calmly tipped the remaining contents of the ice-bucket over his head before turning and leaving the room.

When he re-entered the bedroom, Melissa was standing by the adjoining bathroom door with tears streaming down her face.

'Sweetheart, whatever's wrong?' Nick asked, in alarm, completely forgetting his irritation with Ace. Then he noticed the pregnancy indicator in her hand. 'You've done the test? Oh, don't upset yourself; it will happen soon,' he tried to reassure her, but she shook her head wildly.

'It already has!' she finally managed to say, and he realized they were tears of joy and relief, not of disappointment.

'That's wonderful!' Nick drew her close and rested his cheek on her hair. They remained like that, unspeaking, each content to hold the other while they absorbed the enormity of the knowledge that they had created a new life.

Meanwhile Ace, dripping wet and deprived of the pleasure of tormenting Nick, was seeking a diversion when Alexa wandered into the kitchen in search of more ice. She came to an abrupt halt when she saw him, and almost retreated but something in her refused to back down.

He had discarded his jacket before going out on the court and his white shirt was open at the throat, the sleeves rolled up to reveal the muscular strength of his arms. Despite the injured ankle, he looked tough, handsome and very, very masculine. She flushed when she realized she had been staring, and that he was regarding her with evident amusement.

'Er – are you okay?' she enquired, rather breathlessly.

'Fine. I didn't know you cared,' Ace mocked her concern, and she flushed.

'I don't, but I was brought up to be polite!' she retorted. 'Do you know where I can get more ice?' she asked. Ace obligingly pointed out the huge freezer stored in one of the pantries, and watched her as she fumbled to refill a container.

'Put some more on my ankle, will you, honey?' he asked, stretching out his long, muscular leg. He was aware that he was in danger of receiving yet another shower of cubes over his head, but wanted to see how she would react. He accompanied the request with a devastating smile and Alexa's protest died on her lips; he looked younger, almost boyish, with a lock of black hair flopping onto his forehead.

She balked at actually ministering to him, though – she was damned if she would let him think she was as docile and subservient as the two simpering blondes he had brought with him – and silently held out the ice for him to help himself.

'Thanks, honey,' Ace said casually. He stood up to tower over her and flexed his foot before putting it to the ground. 'It's okay now. Do you feel like going clubbing?' he asked, with another smile that ought to have signalled a warning. But Alexa didn't know him that well, and her heart skipped a beat.

'Cl . . . clubbing?' she stammered. 'When?'

'Tonight. This party will be over pretty soon.'

'Er, well, yes. I'd love to,' she beamed, forgiving him for his earlier boorishness, both at the party and when he had been with Johnny Dancer. After all, she hadn't exactly been in a wonderful mood herself that evening . . .

'Good. There's a guy in the drawing room – Gareth somebody – he's off the booze and has agreed to do the driving. Go and ask him if there's room in his car for you,' he suggested.

'Okay.' Alexa sped off and soon found herself crammed into the back seat of a Mercedes.

'Right. We're off,' Gareth declared, getting in behind the wheel, squeezing against the fifteen-year-old who had earlier asked about oral sex.

She was now tipsy and telling everyone she was eighteen so she'd be allowed into the nightclub. Only a last-minute intervention by her frantic mother saved her from probably learning what she wanted to know, and she was hauled bodily from the car, kicking and screaming, and insisting she was an adult.

'Hell, I didn't know she was only fifteen!' Gareth grumbled, red-faced from the assault on his ear-drums by the girl's irate parent. 'Let's get out of here!'

'Hang on a minute!' Alexa called out. 'Ace isn't here yet.'

'Ace Delaney? He's not coming with us – I did ask him, but he's staying here overnight with those two blondes, lucky devil!' Gareth told her cheerfully, gunning the engine into life and speeding down the driveway.

Alexa sat back and silently fumed, mentally going through her repertoire of swear words. The swine! He knew I thought he was inviting me out on a date, she realized, squirming in her seat. In fact, he deliberately set me up . . .

Her face grew hot with mortification, and she pressed her cheek against the cold glass of the car window to cool it. Never again will I let Ace Delaney score points over me, she vowed. Next time, *he'll* be on the receiving end!

Alexa hadn't bothered to inform her father that she was leaving the party, and consequently Philip was in a bad mood when he and Rose finally stopped searching for her and headed for home.

He drove in silence, his brows drawn together in a frown, and Rose decided to defer confessing her affair with Ace. But then, to her horror, he told her he intended announcing their engagement the next day to his board of directors. She mulled that over for a while, then sighed heavily, knowing she mustn't delay. When they reached her flat, she persuaded him to come inside for coffee, despite the lateness of the hour.

'Before you make the engagement official, there's something you ought to know,' she began falteringly, twisting her hands nervously. 'You might change your mind about marrying me.'

'Never,' he declared stoutly. 'What have you done that's so dreadful?' he asked, smiling indulgently. He was so proud of her, her elegance and poise, her impeccable background. He even approved of her children, which was a novel experience for him. Other women of Rose's age always seemed to have brattish teenagers who expected him to provide them with sports cars and pay for expensive holidays. He didn't anticipate either Jack or Melissa approaching him for a handout!

'Well, it's about Ace Delaney,' Rose mumbled, already beginning to blush. 'Years ago, after my divorce from Daniel . . . well, Ace and I had an affair . . .'

'You and that . . . that friend of your son's,' he amended.

'Yes.' Rose hung her head like a naughty schoolgirl. 'I never cheated on Daniel,' she said earnestly.

'But I was so lonely after the divorce, and Ace . . . well, it just happened.' Philip stared at her in shocked amazement. Ace Delaney? The man who could have any woman he wanted? The man who, during his years as a professional tennis player, had appeared in gossip columns more often than the sports pages, always linked with some young beauty? The stories were the stuff of legend; the groupies smuggled into locker rooms around the world, the three-in-a-bed sessions . . . This man had bedded Rose?!

Suddenly, unaccountably, he became aroused at the thought of Superstud making love to Rose. For some inexplicable reason, the knowledge made him want her even more. His chest swelled almost as much as his manhood and he moved swiftly, pushing Rose down onto the sofa.

'Philip!' Rose gasped, her eyes wide with fear. Briefly, she braced herself for violence, then realized what was on his mind. 'Philip,' she said again, half-laughing, half-relieved, when he began tearing at her dress.

It was the best sex they had ever shared, half on, half off the sofa, until they finally tumbled to the floor in a tangle of limbs and discarded clothing. Philip was harder than he could remember being in years, his climax stronger and more satisfying, and Rose's soft cries of approaching fulfilment echoed in his ears and spurred him to even greater effort.

'Oh, darling, that was wonderful!' Rose sighed happily. 'You're not at all angry about Ace, are you?'

'No.' He gazed down at her flushed cheeks and sparkling eyes. 'Was sex as good with him as it is with me?' he demanded roughly.

'Oh, no,' Rose had enough sense to lie. 'He's quite selfish in bed, actually,' she went on glibly, and quite untruthfully. No woman ever left Ace's bed without being utterly sated and exhausted, and barely able to walk!

'Hm!' Inordinately pleased with himself – and with his future bride – Philip got dressed and declined Rose's eager invitation to stay overnight. She might want a repeat performance and he was afraid he might not come up – literally – to expectations. Not twice in one night. He left her with a chaste goodnight kiss and drove back to London feeling ten years younger than when he had set out for the party eight hours earlier.

He slept deeply and awoke in fine humour, which persisted even when Alexa slunk in around noon, quite unapologetic about sloping off without a word, and still wearing the dress she'd donned for the party.

He was on the phone when she returned downstairs after a shower, and she listened with quiet satisfaction as he phoned his secretary and instructed her to place the official announcements in the Press. He then proceeded to call all the members of his board, plus senior members of his staff to acquaint them with the news of his forthcoming marriage. She decided to drop her bombshell at dinner.

'Isn't Rose joining us?' she enquired sweetly.

'No, she's at Bellwood again this evening. Melissa has some wonderful news, too. She's pregnant,' Philip announced, as proudly as if he were the prospective grandfather.

'Yuk!' Alexa feigned an attack of nausea. 'She must be mad, giving up all that fame and fortune to have a kid. At least Rose is too old to have another baby . . . or is she?' she asked slyly. Philip looked momentarily alarmed, then dismissed the notion.

'I don't think you need worry about your status as my only child,' he said benignly.

'Good,' Alexa muttered, then, 'So Rose is at Bellwood? Is Ace Delaney still there?'

'I shouldn't think so – why do you ask?'

'Oh, I was talking to a friend of his recently. Apparently Ace brags about his conquests,' she said airily. 'It's probably an idle boast, but he says he slept with Rose,' she added, watching for signs of apoplexy.

'Really? That's not very gentlemanly of him,' Philip responded mildly. 'Bad form to name names, but then, he is an American,' he added, with just a hint of disapproval. Alexa stared at him, unable to believe his reaction.

'Don't you believe it's true?' she persisted.

'Oh, yes, I know it's true. Rose told me herself.' He smiled in happy memory of what had followed her confession. Alexa ground her teeth in vexation. The words 'damp' and 'squib' sprang to mind!

# CHAPTER 4

Two weeks later, Alexa debated long and hard over whether to attend her friend Clarissa's hen-party. Still smarting over Dimitri, she hated the prospect of putting on a brave face to celebrate someone else's marriage. But if she failed to show, her friends might guess that Dimitri had dumped her and not she him, as she had told them, and their pity would be unendurable.

Finally, pride won and she decided to go. Besides, it was too boring to remain home in Eaton Square, with her father away on business and Rose in residence, forever shoving baby pictures of Kit under Alexa's nose and wittering on about Melissa's pregnancy. To listen to Rose banging on, anyone would think the Farrells had invented a whole new process of reproduction!

She chose a dress she considered to be 'lucky', one in which she had always enjoyed herself. It was in her favourite colour, green, made of taffeta with shoestring straps over a fitted bodice and a short, full skirt. She paid particular attention to her hair and make-up and was feeling almost light-hearted at the prospect of a night on the town when she left her room.

Her good mood vanished abruptly when she saw Rose, standing on the wide staircase, studying the collection of fine art which adorned the walls. The pictures were investments that Philip Kane had accumulated over the years, with an eye for profit, not colour or style, and Alexa shared his view. She assumed, wrongly, that they also represented mere money to Rose.

'Valuing the house contents?' Alexa enquired frostily. What was the blasted woman doing here, anyway? Babysitting? She knew her father didn't trust her not to go chasing after Dimitri – on impulse, she had looked for her passport and found it missing, no doubt locked in Philip's safe until he felt she had come to her senses!

'N . . . no, of course not,' Rose stammered. 'There are some beautiful pieces here . . .' She stopped speaking and silently assessed Alexa's dolled-up appearance. 'You're going out? When will you be back?'

'It's none of your business, but I'm meeting friends at the Gemini Club, and I might not be back until morning if I get lucky!' Alexa said as she pushed past her. 'Don't get too fond of those paintings, Rose,' she warned. 'My father's much older than you and when he dies, you'll be out of here so fast your feet won't touch the ground!' she spat. Rose stared after her in dismay, but Alexa hadn't finished yet. She reached the marble vestibule and looked up at Rose.

'There's a quote in the evening paper you might like to read – I left it in the drawing room.' She smiled coldly and left the house.

Rose walked slowly downstairs and into the drawing room. She picked up the paper as if it might bite, well aware she would read nothing to cheer her. Alexa had circled the article, which concerned mistresses – the quote to which she had referred was the old maxim that a man who marries his mistress automatically creates a job vacancy. Beside it, Alexa had scrawled: 'Noticed any job applicants yet?'

'Oh, dear.' Rose sighed heavily, and couldn't stem the tears that sprang to her eyes. She sympathized with Alexa over Dimitri, truly she did, but why did the girl so resent anyone else's happiness? Is it just me, or would she be like this with anyone Philip wanted to marry? she wondered unhappily.

For a few moments she contemplated packing her bag and returning home, but eventually decided not to give up; to run away. She loved Philip, not with the intensity with which she had adored Daniel Farrell in the early years of their marriage, but she did love him and had grown accustomed to the comforting thought that she no longer faced the prospect of reaching her fiftieth birthday alone. I won't let Alexa drive me away, she thought determinedly, but she was still rather tearful and red-eyed when the doorbell sounded, shortly before midnight. Mary, the live-in housekeeper, had already retired to bed, so Rose, rather warily, opened the door herself.

She was surprised and delighted to see Jack, not quite so pleased to discover Ace with him. Jack had been in London recording a TV programme previewing the forthcoming Australian Open and had invited Ace to guest on the show. They'd had a lot of fun, Jack told Rose, although many of Ace's comments concerning his former opponents on the tour would have to be edited out before transmission! He had called at Eaton Square to bring Rose the latest photographs of Kit.

'What's wrong, Mum?' he asked in concern, noting the signs of recent tears.

'Oh, Alexa. What else?' She tried to smile, but it was a poor effort. 'Philip asked me to keep an eye on her while he's away, but she's impossible. She went out earlier and said she might not come back until morning.'

'Good riddance,' Ace muttered.

'Oh, don't say that. I promised Philip I'd try to make friends with her. What on earth can I say if he phones and I've no idea where she is?' she asked, distressed.

'Tell him she's a bitch and not your responsibility,' Ace suggested, not very helpfully. Jack flapped his hand at him to be quiet.

'What else is wrong?' he asked shrewdly. 'She said something to upset you, didn't she?'

'Oh, she's just making sure I know I'm not welcome here. But I still wish she'd come home,' she said, her lip quivering.

'Where did she go?' Ace asked.

'The Gemini Club, I think she said.'

'I know it.' Ace nodded. 'Come on, Jack, let's go and drag her out of there. She needs a few lessons in manners,' he added grimly.

'Listen who's talking?' Jack muttered, but he followed Ace out of the door. 'Don't worry, Mum, we'll bring her back,' he promised.

Ace was driving a hired Mercedes; the third of his stay in London, the other two having been clamped and then towed away. Now, he parked on double yellow lines and marched into the nightclub with Jack at his heels.

Alexa had arrived three hours earlier, stepping warily in her high heels as she negotiated the stairs leading down to the bar and dance floor. She haughtily declined the offer of a drink from a man she had never seen before and paused while her eyes adjusted to the dim lighting, scanning the room for a glimpse of her friends. She spotted them almost immediately and threaded her way through the crowd towards them.

'Hi,' she greeted Clarissa, the bride, a friend from schooldays.

'Hi, glad you could make it,' Clarissa beamed at her, obviously already tipsy.

'What are you drinking?' Alexa asked her.

'We've each put twenty quid in the kitty and told the barman to keep 'em coming!' Clarissa explained, so Alexa added her contribution, wondering as she did so if Ace had passed on her twenty pound note to Johnny Dancer in repayment of her cab fare. One thing was for sure – he'd definitely have retrieved it from Stacey's bra! she thought crossly.

'I'm surprised you turned up tonight,' Bella, Clarissa's sister, said knowingly to Alexa. 'After all, you were hoping to hear wedding bells yourself soon.'

'Oh, Dimitri, you mean?' Alexa shrugged carelessly. 'No, that would have been a mistake. He seemed very charming and sophisticated when I met him in Greece, but let's just say he didn't travel well! His English is rotten and my Greek is non-existent, and one can't spend all one's time in bed!'

'Really?' Clarissa exclaimed, in mock horror. 'In that case, the wedding's off!' she announced dramatically, and they all laughed. Alexa relaxed and began to enjoy herself.

As the evening wore on, the group of girls dominated the scene more and more as, with each successive round of drinks, their voices became shriller and their laughter rang out louder. Several more of Clarissa's friends arrived to swell the number, gathering on this, her last night of 'freedom', to ply her with drinks and wish her luck for the future.

'Ooh, I say, who's that?' Clarissa peered drunkenly at two men approaching their table. 'He looks familiar . . . it's Ace Delaney!' she exclaimed, and Alexa's heart lurched. She carefully stared down at the table, and wished Clarissa would shut up and not draw attention to them. She didn't.

'And Jack Farrell!' Clarissa continued excitedly, for she was an avid tennis fan. 'I watched them win Wimbledon, and the US Open a few years ago when I was in New York. 'Cooee! Can I have your autographs? I'm getting married tomorrow,' she informed them, hiccuping loudly. Ace grinned down at her, admiring her blonde prettiness and taking absolutely no notice of Alexa.

'Of course you can, honey,' he drawled. He took out a pen and proceeded to scribble his name along her exposed collarbone. Clarissa squinted horribly in an effort to read it.

'That'll look great with your wedding dress!' Alexa said sourly, miffed at being ignored. She stood up, somewhat unsteadily, and wrapped herself around Jack, pressing close to his body.

'Jack's going to be my new brother – aren't I lucky?' she purred. Ace narrowed his eyes and grabbed her wrist to pull her away. Jack was too easygoing to spot trouble when it was staring him in the face – he'll probably be as soft with this bitch as he is with Melissa, he thought disgustedly.

'Come on, I'm taking you home,' he said abruptly.

'That's not fair,' Clarissa protested. 'Who's going to take *me* home?' she pouted.

'That's my job,' Bella interrupted, screwing up her eyes in an effort to focus on Ace. 'I'm the chief bridesmaid, so you can rely on me to see her home safely,' she told him, with the utmost dignity, but then spoiled the effect by sliding smoothly off her chair to land in an ungainly heap on the floor.

Alexa took one look at the expression of mingled disgust and disbelief on Ace's face as he surveyed the unconscious girl lying at his feet, and promptly dissolved into giggles. Once started, she found it impossible to stop, and her laughter proved infectious. That, plus the sight of Bella sprawled on the carpet sent all of the girls into renewed fits of merriment.

'I suppose this is your bad influence!' Ace growled at Alexa, most unfairly, she thought.

'No, it isn't. They were halfway drunk before I even got here!' she told him indignantly.

'Look at the state of them!' Jack muttered helplessly. 'We'll have to get them all home, not just

Alexa.' He sighed unhappily. It would be the middle of the night before he got back to Bellwood, and Lisa would be furious.

'I'll take Alexa home first. You get some coffee down the rest of them and we'll pour them into taxis,' Ace decided. 'If they can't remember where they live, that's their problem.'

'But I don't want to go home yet,' Alexa pouted, reaching for her glass. 'I'm getting drunk!'

'Getting?' Ace stressed the tense. 'You've already succeeded, so come along; you've upset Rose and you're going to apologize to her,' he ordered.

'No! This is a hen-party – you and Jack weren't even invited,' she informed him.

'We invited ourselves.' Ace took the glass from her hand and put his arm around her waist as she swayed.

'You smell nice.' She leaned against him happily, completely forgetting how much she hated him. 'But I want to stay here,' she added, with what she hoped was a winsome smile.

'Tough.' Ace ignored her protests and hustled her out of the club, pulling her ruthlessly after him up the stairs and out into the street, practically frog-marching her to where he had parked the car.

'Ace! Stop! I've lost a shoe!' Alexa wailed, and he jerked her to a standstill, glancing down at her feet and sighing heavily as he noticed she was hobbling along in just one high-heeled shoe. He looked back in the direction of the club but there was no sign of the second shoe on the pavement.

'You must have lost it on the stairs – it isn't important. Get in the car; I'm on double yellow lines.' He opened the door and pushed her, none too gently, inside.

'Ouch! You banged my head!' Alexa complained. 'And my shoe *is* important,' she insisted. 'These are my favourites, my very *best* favourites,' she emphasized, when he climbed in behind the wheel. 'Do you know how much they cost?'

'No, and I bet you don't either. Fasten your seat belt . . . oh, leave it; I'll do it!' He almost snatched the restraint from her fumbling hands and clipped it into place, then gunned the engine into life and eased out into the traffic.

Alexa had a vague idea that she had intended never speaking to him again, but couldn't remember why, so dismissed the thought as being irrelevant and settled comfortably back in the seat.

Ace reached Eaton Square easily enough, but then couldn't recall which house she lived in – they all looked the same!

'Which number?' he asked irritably. 'Hurry up, or I'll dump you on the pavement!'

'Well you're in a bad mood! It was your idea to bring me home, not mine,' she told him huffily. She tried to climb out of the car in a dignified manner, but had forgotten she was strapped in and almost strangled herself in the attempt. Ace swore under his breath and unbuckled the belt before dragging her out of the car.

Rose had been watching out for them, and hurried to open the front door.

'Where is her room?' Ace asked tersely.

'Up the stairs, the third one on the right, but I can manage her now,' Rose said.

'You can't manage what I have in mind,' Ace informed her ominously, and Rose looked alarmed. Alexa, if sober, would have been terrified; unfortunately she was as high as a kite.

'Ooh! Lucky me; it's my turn now!' she shrieked. 'You had your fun with him, Granny, so butt out and leave us alone.'

'You vicious little bitch! That's something else you'll apologize for when you sober up,' Ace said furiously, hauling her up the long flight of stairs.

'Else what?' Alexa goaded. She soon found out.

Ace pulled her into her room, ignored the lace-trimmed four-poster bed and headed for the adjoining bathroom. He reached inside the shower cubicle and switched it on, turning the setting to 'cold' before thrusting Alexa beneath the jet of water.

Alexa screamed and struggled violently to be free, but his grip was too strong. He moved only to shrug off his jacket, briefly using his left arm to hold her instead of his right.

She gasped for breath as icy-cold water streamed down her face and body, soaking her taffeta dress and leaving her hair a mess of rats' tails while her make-up smudged and ran, painting her cheeks a sludgy brown-green colour.

'You bastard! Stop it! I can't breathe!'

'You wouldn't be able to scream if you couldn't breathe,' Ace responded, obviously not too concerned if she could breathe or not. Rose appeared, rather nervously, in the doorway. She felt Philip would prefer to come home to discover his daughter was missing, rather than to find her corpse . . .

'Is she all right? I thought you were murdering her.' She tried to make light of it.

'Not yet,' Ace said grimly. 'Are you ready to apologize to Rose?' he asked Alexa, giving her shoulders a vigorous shake.

'No! Let me go! Look at my dress!' she wailed. 'It's ruined! My favourite dress!'

'As well as your favourite shoes? It's not your night, is it?' Ace enquired cheerfully, with an evil grin. He was beginning to enjoy himself enormously.

'Ace, let her go,' Rose was still hovering anxiously.

'In a minute. Had enough?' he asked Alexa, giving her another shake.

'Yes!' she spluttered.

'Right.' Ace turned off the shower. 'Apologize to Rose for upsetting her earlier, and for being rude to her when we came in,' he said sternly.

'I didn't say anything . . . oh, all right. I'm sorry,' she muttered.

'Go and make her some black coffee, will you, Rose?' Ace asked, simply to be rid of her. He hadn't finished with Alexa yet. When Rose had gone, he picked Alexa up as if she were a rag doll and tossed her on to the bed. Her soaked dress left nothing to the imagination and clung to the curves of what he had to admit was a wonderful body.

Alexa didn't even attempt to rise; she lay back, gazing up at him expectantly, recognizing the glitter of desire in the jet-black eyes and experiencing a delicious aching need between her legs. It would be different with him, she thought, with a surge of hope and excitement. His touch would surely give her pleasure, not turn her cold and dead as a statue . . .

Amazed by her daring, she reached out and grabbed the leather belt cinched at his lean waist and tugged, but to no avail. He didn't move an inch nearer.

'Ace,' she pleaded huskily; she knew he was aroused, yet, unbelievably, he took her hand from his belt and pushed it away.

'No,' he said coldly. 'I don't want you.' He realized, even as he spoke, that his desire must be obvious, so continued quickly, 'Oh, I admit you're well put-together, but I do have certain standards, despite what you may have read in the Press.'

'You . . .' His words were like a dash of water, far colder and more shocking than the enforced shower she had just taken. She sprang at him, her hands curled into claws, nails raking at his face and aiming for his eyes.

Fortunately for Ace, his reflexes were still as lightning-quick as they had been during his days as a tennis pro, and he dodged back out of reach, then grabbed her wrists to restrain her, tightening his hold until she stopped struggling and went limp, staring up at him helplessly.

'Don't play games with me, honey, or you'll really get hurt,' Ace warned. 'If you make Rose cry again – or upset any of the Farrells for that matter,' he added, remembering her blatant invitations to both Jack and Nick, 'you'll have more trouble from me than you can begin to imagine. In case you haven't noticed yet, I am not one of the restrained British gentlemen you're used to dealing with. If you don't behave, I'll destroy you. Count on it.' He stabbed his finger into her shoulder for emphasis. 'If you had any sense at all, you would realize how lucky you are to be welcomed into that family,' he added, and, after one long, final hard stare, full of menace, he turned and left the room.

As he ran down the stairs, Rose was climbing towards him, a tray of coffee in her hands. Ace grabbed a cup and quickly drained its contents.

'Leave her to stew for a while,' he advised. 'I'd better go and rescue Jack – he's been married for so long, he's probably forgotten what to do with half a dozen drunken girls!'

Alexa awoke early, with nothing worse than a dull headache, a raging thirst and partial amnesia. She sat up, rather gingerly, and tried to put her thoughts into some sort of order. She clearly remembered meeting Clarissa and the others, but the latter part of the evening was a complete blank.

She looked disdainfully at the damp, crumpled taffeta which had once been a dress and frowned. Why was she still wearing this? Surely she hadn't been so drunk she had passed out before getting undressed? And how did it get wet? she wondered.

She tottered unsteadily into the bathroom and drank several glasses of water. Then she reached to switch on the shower and gave a scream of outrage as her memory flooded back. He almost drowned me! she fumed. And hurt my wrists, and then threatened me, she recalled furiously. Her hair had dried overnight into a tangle which required an entire bottle of conditioner to restore it to its usual sheen.

Rose had wisely left the house early to go shopping and visit Melissa, now staying for the duration of her pregnancy at Nick's flat in Chelsea. Rose knew Clarissa's wedding was due to take place at noon, and she had decided to stay away until then. She dreaded to think what kind of mood Alexa might be in.

Alexa arrived at the church with only minutes to spare, dashing the last few yards along the pavement to ensure she'd be seated before the bride's entrance. A car, driven through a deep and muddy puddle, splashed her cream silk suit and handmade shoes with filthy, cold water.

'Ohh! You stupid idiot!' Alexa screamed, and added a choice swear word which obviously shocked the vicar, who was waiting outside the church to greet Clarissa and her father. 'Sorry,' she smiled weakly, and turned her back on him to glare at the driver of the car. 'You can't park there – you're on double yellow lines . . .' She stopped speaking and frowned slightly; that seemed familiar, as did the car and the face and lithe figure emerging from it. Ace Delaney!

'You!' she spat. 'How dare you show your face here? You nearly drowned me; I ought to call the police . . .'

'Quit moaning. You deserved it; you'd have had my eye out with those talons of yours if I hadn't ducked,' he said coldly, without a trace of contrition. 'And, as for what I'm doing here.' He gave a self-satisfied smirk. 'The bride invited me.'

'Clarissa did? When?' she gasped.

'Oh,' the smile broadened as he consulted his watch, 'about eight hours ago. I've finally discovered something I like about you, Alexa – you have some extremely pretty and obliging friends!'

'You . . . eight hours . . .' Alexa gaped at him as realization dawned. 'You and Clarissa?' she asked incredulously.

'That's right. I took her home last night, or rather, this morning,' he admitted smugly.

'She's getting married today,' Alexa said stupidly. 'You can't sleep with a girl eight hours before her wedding!' Ace hadn't, actually, but saw no reason to enlighten Alexa.

'Better eight hours before than eight hours after,' he pointed out logically. 'She'll be here any moment. Come along, Alexa, I'm sure it's bad manners to arrive after the bride,' he said reprovingly, and began marching along the path to the church door.

A large crucifix hung above the porch, and Alexa half-expected it to topple and crush him, rather than let him enter the sacred portal. But nothing happened, dammit, and she had no choice but to follow him meekly, all the while trying in vain to remove the stains on her mud-splashed skirt with a damp tissue.

'Bride or groom?' enquired the usher.

'Bride, definitely,' Ace grinned. Oh, strike him dead, please strike him dead, Alexa prayed. He had the gall to stride right to the front of the congregation and squeeze into a pew between two of Clarissa's aunts, who seemed delighted by his presence.

Alexa took a seat at the back, still fuming. His behaviour was absolutely appalling – first he'd half-drowned and threatened her, and then he'd returned to the nightclub to take his pick of her friends! She burned with shame to remember her own clumsy attempt at seduction, wishing she still had the amnesia with which she had awoken.

When Clarissa arrived she looked positively radiant, and very demure in her gown of white satin and frothy lace. Alexa couldn't bear to look at her and turned away, unwittingly noticing how Ace watched her approach and give her a broad, knowing wink as she took her place next to the waiting groom.

After the ceremony, Alexa ground her teeth in annoyance as Ace casually kissed the bride and informed the groom, Peter, that he was a lucky man.

'How did you meet?' Peter asked, his arm around his new wife.

'He's a friend of Alexa's,' Clarissa explained quickly. Ace raised an eyebrow at Alexa, daring her to contradict.

'Well, a friend of a friend,' she demurred.

Ace began signing autographs for practically every female guest, ranging in ages from seven to seventy, but then, to Alexa's relief, she heard him making his excuses for not attending the reception: he was returning to LA later that day, he explained to Clarissa's blushing mother, and had some business to attend to before he left.

He didn't bother to say goodbye to Alexa and she brooded bitterly throughout the reception, rudely rebuffing the attempts of Clarissa's brother, Derek, to flirt with her. Derek Fenton was a creep, a real dope, in every sense of the word. He had been in prison and rehab clinics because of his drug habit . . . Hold on, hadn't Ace a reputation for taking drugs? She was sure she recalled reading that he had been disqualified from a tennis tournament because he had tested positive. An idea grew in her mind and refused to go away; a plan to gain revenge for all the humiliation he had heaped on her in recent weeks . . .

'Derek.' She smiled sweetly, and took him to one side. 'I'm sorry I'm so grouchy today, but you know how it is when you . . . need something,' she hinted. He looked interested but wary, and she leaned close, brushing her body against his as if by accident. 'My father found my – er – stash, and destroyed it,' she whispered. 'I couldn't reach my regular supplier on the phone earlier. I'm getting desperate, Derek; I don't suppose you could help me out . . .?'

'Follow me outside in a couple of minutes,' he said, and she nodded. She checked her bag; fortunately she had plenty of cash with her and the transaction was quickly completed. Not knowing how much time she had, she didn't delay, but slipped away without a word to anyone, busily working out how to slip the small package into Ace's possessions.

'Taxi!' First, to Bond Street, for one of the quickest shopping expeditions of her entire life, where she bought two pairs of shoes, a suit and a party frock, and also a man's watch. Next, to Ace's hotel on Park Lane – at least, she hoped he was still staying at the same place as on the night she had first met him and Johnny Dancer. She went first to the powder room and locked herself into a cubicle.

She carefully eased off the watch's gift-wrapping and lifted the box lid, took the watch from its bed of satin and tucked the sachet of heroin in the bottom of the box. Then she replaced the contents and re-wrapped it, satisfied that it didn't appear to have been tampered with. She took a deep breath and emerged from the powder room, walking purposefully to the reception desk.

'Ace Delaney's suite number, please,' she demanded crisply.

'I'll phone him for you – what name shall I say?' she asked. Alexa hesitated.

'Melissa,' she said finally. The receptionist spoke briefly to Ace and the turned back to Alexa, who was desperately fighting a desire to run away.

'You can go up – Suite 212,' she said.

Alexa hurried to the elevator before she could lose what little courage she had left. Her legs were shaking and she had a horrid sick feeling in the pit of her stomach. But he deserves this, she thought, and bolstered her nerve by reminding herself of all the vile things he had said and done to her over the past few weeks.

She paused outside his door and had to take several more deep, steadying breaths before knocking.

'It's open,' Ace called. 'Come in, honey. There's nothing . . . oh, it's you.' His welcoming tone for Melissa changed to one of cold disdain when he saw Alexa in the doorway. 'What do you want? As you can see, I'm packing to leave.' He gestured to the open suitcase on the bed.

'I heard you say you were leaving today; that's why I'm here,' she said, rather breathlessly. 'I'd like you to give this to Johnny Dancer – as an apology for forgetting to repay the money he lent me.' She handed him the watch, her heart thudding with fear.

'And I also want you to settle this before you go,' she went on quickly, thrusting the receipt for the clothes she had just bought into his hand. As she had hoped, he lost interest in Johnny Dancer's gift and casually dropped it into his suitcase before turning his attention to the bill she'd handed him.

'What the hell's this?'

'You owe me for the dress and shoes I was wearing last night, plus this suit and these shoes.' She pointed to the dried-on mud splashes. 'They're all ruined because of you. I've just been shopping to replace them and that's the bill,' she added, amazed at how cool she sounded.

'You don't seriously expect me to pay for your clothes?' Ace asked incredulously. No, but I expect you to pay for all the snubs and slights you've subjected me to, she thought. She shrugged carelessly.

'I thought it was worth a try. The answer's no, is it?'

'You bet it is.' His eyes suddenly took on a speculative gleam and she forced herself to look at him and not stare at Johnny Dancer's watch. 'You knew I wouldn't pay,' Ace declared flatly. 'So why are you really here?' he persisted. Alexa couldn't think of a reply and merely shrugged again as she backed slowly towards the door.

'Do you want a sample of what Clarissa enjoyed last night?' he asked, with a smug grin. You arrogant pig! Alexa thought furiously, and some of her faltering courage returned.

'No. As I said, I hoped you'd honour your debts. My mistake. You're an American – you can't even spell the word properly, let alone understand what it means!' she snapped. She turned and ran from the room, with his hateful laughter ringing in her ears.

She spent the rest of the day in turmoil, one moment fearful, the next elated. One thing was for sure – she didn't want him detained before leaving England, so she waited until she was sure he would be airborne before phoning the authorities to inform them Ace Delaney was on a flight to LA and carrying drugs.

The call itself posed a problem; she dared not use her own phone, not even the mobile, as she was uncertain how easily a call could be traced. Instead, she had to use a public phone box, something she had never done in her life. She stared at the instructions in rising exasperation; the wretched thing didn't seem to take money, nor credit cards.

'What the hell's a phone card?' she muttered crossly, and finally swallowed her pride to ask for help from a passer-by. She made the call and went home feeling decidedly ill and apprehensive. He deserved it, but, what form would his revenge take?

# CHAPTER 5

The Customs officials at LA couldn't believe their luck, and they almost outnumbered the passengers as even those off-duty gathered to greet the arrivals from the London flight.

Ace couldn't believe it, either. He submitted, with his usual ill grace, to being searched, and the barely concealed triumph on the officer's face convinced him that a member of the airport staff had planted the package of heroin in his luggage. But then he discovered precisely where the heroin had been found, realized at once who had put it there, and exploded into fury. The resulting fracas hit news headlines around the world.

'ACE DELANEY IN DRUGS BUST!'

'EX TENNIS STAR IN JAIL ON ASSAULT CHARGES! – TWO OFFICERS IN HOSPITAL!'

It was even featured on TV news bulletins and Alexa watched in horror. What have I done? she wondered wretchedly. She hadn't expected Ace to be put in jail, nor anticipated that he would resist arrest and start thumping people! Admit it, Alexa, you didn't think it through at all, she admonished herself. She was uncomfortably aware that she had acted as she had, not primarily because of the way he had treated her, but because he had bedded Clarissa after spurning her, Alexa.

She couldn't eat or sleep, couldn't relax nor settle to doing anything. She knew she ought to own up, but didn't dare. After all, she had bought heroin and hidden it in someone else's luggage! At least he's not in Thailand or somewhere where he would be facing life imprisonment, she thought, but it afforded her scant consolation.

After another sleepless night, she plucked up the courage to phone Bellwood and speak to Jack. If she didn't discover what was happening, she'd go nuts! Lisa answered the phone and Alexa forced herself to make polite conversation, belatedly thanking her for the Boxing Day party and enquiring after Kit – as if Rose hadn't already provided her with every damned detail of the child's existence, ad nauseam.

'May I speak to Jack?' she finally asked casually.

'He's not here – he's gone to LA,' Lisa said tartly. 'Ace is in trouble – again.' It had been bad enough for Jack to come home at three in the morning, two nights before, reeking of perfume and booze and blaming Ace, but then he had gone dashing off to rescue him from his latest act of irresponsibility.

'Yes; I heard something about that,' Alexa said vaguely. 'What will happen to him, do you know? How long will they keep him in prison?'

'Oh, I expect he's already out on bail,' Lisa said, which was a great relief to Alexa until she realized he might come gunning for her as soon as he was free. She swallowed nervously as Lisa continued speaking.

'Apparently, he's due to start filming a new series of *Country Club*, so the studio's lawyers are doing all they can to get him off,' she said. 'Of course, he made it worse for himself by pretending the drugs weren't his and going berserk when they tried to arrest him. It would have been much better if he had accepted he'd been caught and owned up to it.'

'Quite,' Alexa said faintly.

In fact, Ace was persuaded, against his better judgement, to do just that – own up to something he hadn't done. The studio bosses wanted the case settled as quickly as possible and Ace's own lawyer, Larry Knight, agreed there was little to be gained by going to trial.

Ace's arrogant attitude didn't help one bit; his assertion that he would never bother smuggling drugs into LA, his home city, because he knew exactly where he could buy top quality merchandise the minute he hit the streets if he wanted to made Larry drop his head into his hands in despair.

Eventually, a deal was struck. Ace paid a hefty fine, and even heftier compensation to the two officers who'd arrested him – 'I hardly touched the bastards!' Ace said disgustedly. He also agreed to attend a rehab course and, worst of all, to undertake coaching underprivileged children in the city.

'Can you believe that?' he demanded irritably of Jack. 'If I'm such a bad character, why the hell do they want to let me loose on young kids!'

'Stop complaining,' Jack advised tersely. 'You were bound to be caught sooner or later.'

'Yeah, but I didn't do it!' Ace said, for the umpteenth time. 'I keep telling you – that heroin was planted in my suitcase before I left England!'

'Honestly? Who would do that? Stupid question; half the husbands in London, probably!' Jack grinned.

'Very funny,' Ace scowled. 'No, it was that bitch Alexa Kane. I warned you she was trouble.'

'It's a pity you didn't warn yourself,' Jack said drily. 'Are you sure it was her?'

'Positive,' Ace grunted.

'What did you do to make her so angry and vindictive?' Jack asked curiously.

'Mmm, well, I dunked her under a cold shower that evening she upset Rose,' Ace said. 'I guess I was a little rough on her,' he admitted quietly.

'Are you going to call it quits, then?' Jack asked, but without much hope.

'Yeah. For now,' Ace added ominously. 'I'm going to let her think she's got away with it. When you get back to England, I want you to casually mention that I'm convinced the Customs guys planted the stuff in my luggage.'

'Okay,' Jack agreed, then he began to laugh. 'She's got more guts than I gave her credit for!' Ace glared at him for a moment, then gave a reluctant grin. If he could have got his hands on Alexa while he was in jail, he'd have cheerfully throttled her in front of the prison warders and gone quite contentedly to Death Row. But, since his release, he had begun to cool down – it had been rather clever, especially distracting his attention from the watch by trying to make him pay for her clothes. And he guessed he had been pretty lousy to her; he was to most women, of course, but none had paid him back so swiftly or effectively.

'Let's go and get drunk,' he suggested now.

'Sure, but first I want to book my flight home. I really miss Kit,' Jack confessed.

'Kit? Not Lisa?' Ace queried.

'Of course,' Jack said quickly. 'It's just that Kit changes every day. By the way, what's happening with Flanagan's biography?' he asked, wanting to change the subject. 'Did the private detective you hired find your mother?'

'No, there's no trace of her after she left the city. I've told him to stop looking – I'm not spending another dime on that woman. Except her funeral expenses; I'll gladly pay those!' he added viciously.

'You don't mean that!' Jack said, shocked as much by the venom in his voice as by the actual words.

'I do mean it! Don't preach at me, Jack! You had great parents who looked after you – you never had to steal to eat.'

'No; sorry,' Jack said quietly. 'Let's go for that drink – somewhere quiet, though; I'm in enough trouble with Lisa already without the paparazzi photographing you and me at some Beverly Hills nightclub!' he added ruefully.

'Suits me,' Ace agreed: he rarely went to the trendy places in town, spurning the Hollywood smart set. He didn't consider himself to be a part of the acting world and still thought of himself as a professional tennis player. The sport which had brought him fame and fortune and provided the high spots of his life would always be his first love.

They spent the evening at the house Ace had rented next door to Johnny Dancer, on a quiet stretch of beach between Malibu and Topanga Beach. It was large and airy, but impersonal and uncluttered, as if it was only a temporary home – which it probably was, Jack thought. The furnishings had come with the house; all Ace had added were framed photographs of his tennis victories and replicas of the trophies he had won during his years on the circuit. The only non-tennis adornment was an enlarged photograph of Bellwood, and Jack wondered if Ace regretted selling it back to the family.

'Hell, no,' Ace denied quickly when asked. 'I was glad to get my two million quid back from you and Melissa. Besides, it's a family home; there'll be a whole new generation of Farrells there soon.'

'And Lennoxes,' Jack reminded him. 'Don't forget Melissa is Mrs Lennox now.' Ace grinned.

'I bet her husband wishes he could forget me!' He drained his glass and got up to pour them both a refill. Jack wasn't drunk, but he wasn't entirely sober, either. If he had been, he might have thought twice before speaking; particularly he would have considered what Lisa's reaction might be to what seemed, at the time, to be a perfectly natural offer to his friend and old Doubles partner. Ace's lack of a real family, his seeming inability to put down roots, made Jack want to strengthen their own bond, especially as they had moved in different directions since their retirement from tennis.

'How would you like to be Kit's godfather?' he asked suddenly. 'The christening will be after the

Australian Open, before Lisa and I go to stay with her parents.'

'Godfather?' Ace looked taken aback: no one had ever asked that of him before.

'Not as in Mafia!' Jack grinned. 'And I wouldn't expect you to look after her spiritual welfare, either,' he added drily.

'What would I have to do?' Ace asked suspiciously, unaware that most people would consider it an honour to be asked.

'Oh, forget it; we'll ask Nick,' Jack shrugged.

'Like hell you will! I want to do it,' Ace decided. 'Do I just have to buy her presents?' he asked, thinking that was a task he could easily delegate to a girlfriend.

'Yeah. And don't forget to mention her in your will,' Jack said, straight-faced.

'Oh? Okay; fine.' Ace accepted that readily. He had no one else to leave his money to; Jack's kid might as well have what was left – not that he intended leaving much, of course!

Jack returned home the following day, eager to see his daughter. He was sure she smiled in recognition and he scooped her up into his arms for a cuddle.

'Hello, darling,' he crooned. 'Has she missed me?' he asked Lisa.

'Oh, sure. She never stopped asking about you!' Lisa snapped sarcastically. Jack sighed heavily.

'Now what's wrong?' He had meant to sound concerned, but he was tired, jet-lagged and a little hungover and instead sounded irritable.

'Your damn family, that's what! Your mother was here yesterday – she wants us to ask Alexa Kane to be Kit's godmother – "to make her feel part of the family"!' she mimicked Rose. To her fury, Jack laughed. Alexa and Ace? In the same church?

'Is now a good time to tell you I've asked Ace to be her godfather?' he enquired, without much hope.

'Ace!' Lisa stared at him in disgust. 'Whatever possessed you to ask him? I suppose you were drunk at the time? This christening is going to be a complete farce!'

'Oh, lighten up,' Jack pleaded. 'It's not as if we're deeply religious or anything. You weren't bothered if we had a christening or not. You suggested we wait and let her make up her own mind when she was old enough to,' he reminded her.

'Oh, all right; I suppose it's too late to alter it now,' she gave in, but with bad grace.

Jack was extremely busy over the following two weeks, presenting extensive coverage of the first Grand Slam of the year, the Australian Open in Melbourne. It meant long hours in the television studio and he often stayed overnight in London, in the spare room of Nick and Melissa's flat in Chelsea, instead of driving back to Bellwood.

'Why don't you come into the studio with me?' he asked Melissa one day. 'You know more about the women's game than I do, and I'm sure the viewers would love to see you and hear what you have to say. You can't sit here getting fat and idle just because you're pregnant,' he teased.

Melissa wrinkled her nose at him; she wasn't fat, in fact, she still didn't feel pregnant, just pre-menstrual with sore boobs! As yet there was no other sign of her condition – except for the permanent proud grin on Nick's face!

'Okay,' she agreed to Jack's proposal. 'I'd like that.'

It had been a casual, spur-of-the-moment suggestion, and it occurred to neither of them that Lisa might be upset. In fact she was furious. She had been a professional player longer than Melissa, and okay, she'd never risen so high in the rankings or won a major title, she conceded, but that was beside the point. To her, it was yet another sign that Jack thought more of his family than he did of her and her feelings.

The atmosphere at Bellwood became decidedly frosty and Jack spent even more time in Chelsea, although he was unhappily aware that absenting himself from home was not the answer. He pinned his hopes on a prolonged stay in California after the Open to mend the alarming cracks in his marriage.

One day, he noticed a stack of house brochures in Melissa's drawing room, all featuring properties for sale in the same area of southern England as Bellwood.

'Are you and Nick moving?' he asked.

'Mmm, probably, although we'll keep this flat,' Melissa said. 'It will be useful for overnight stays in London, but it's not really big enough to live in, and we certainly don't want to bring a child up here.'

'If you're not in any hurry, wait a while. Bellwood might be vacant soon,' Jack said heavily.

'Bellwood? Why?' Melissa asked sharply. 'You're not thinking of selling?'

'No, but a semi-permanent move to California might be on the cards. Lisa simply isn't happy here. Isn't happy with me,' he added, with a rueful grin.

'In which case a move to California won't help much,' Melissa pointed out. 'What about your TV work?'

'Judging by the viewers' response to your appearances on the programme, I should think you could take over my job,' he said lightly, then he frowned. 'I don't want to move, but I have to do whatever it takes to save my marriage. I'm not prepared to lose Kit,' he said flatly.

'I'd no idea things were that bad,' said Melissa, deeply concerned for her brother. He had always been so happy-go-lucky, so sunny-tempered and cheerful. He didn't deserve the grief Lisa was threatening to cause him; was already causing him. 'When did it start to go wrong?'

'God knows; I sure as hell don't,' he sighed. 'Maybe we should never have married. We might not have done, if not for that car smash,' he said broodingly. Melissa nodded, and they both fell silent, thinking back to the dreadful time when Jack had almost lost his life. The injuries he had sustained to his back and legs had ended his career abruptly and taken almost two years to heal.

'Lisa felt guilty about what had happened to me,' Jack continued. 'I was driving, not her, but she had suggested we go out for the day. As you know, she pulled out of her scheduled tournaments to be with me while I recuperated and, once I was better, she had slipped so far down the rankings she didn't feel she could ever make up the lost time.'

'Is that why you proposed?' Melissa asked slowly. 'Because you felt she had given up her career for you?'

'I didn't rationalize it like that at the time, but yes, I suppose that was one of the reasons. I could hardly say, "Thanks for keeping me company while I was an invalid, now go and get on with your life," could I? And we both wanted children. It seemed like a good idea at the time.' He forced a smile.

'You both seemed happy with each other until fairly recently – maybe Lisa's suffering from post-natal depression?' Melissa suggested, and Jack grimaced.

'She bit my head off when I said that – she says I'm blaming her hormones for my shortcomings!'

'You don't have any shortcomings,' Melissa objected loyally. 'I bet she'll be happier when you go to California – remember how she cheered up when her parents arrived at Christmas,' she reminded him. 'My baby won't be born for another six months, but I already know I'm going to need Mum around. I'm sure Lisa feels the same about having her mother to help,' she said encouragingly.

'I hope you're right,' Jack said, but he wasn't optimistic. 'I'm sorry, love, I shouldn't be dumping my problems on you,' he said, and quickly turned the subject back to the tennis tournament, arranging for Melissa to come back into the studio to review the Ladies semi-finals.

She remained troubled, though, and needed a comforting hug from Nick when he returned home.

'I wish they could be as happy as we are,' she said wistfully. 'Do you think I should talk to Lisa?'

'No,' Nick said firmly. 'She'll know you're on Jack's side, and won't thank you for interfering.'

'I wouldn't be interfering . . .' she began indignantly.

'No, but she'll think you are. Leave it, sweetheart, and just hope the holiday in San Francisco does the trick,' he advised.

'Okay,' she agreed reluctantly.

Ace borrowed his gardener's beat-up old truck for his first trip in over fifteen years back to the slums where he had grown up, and where he had hoped never to return. It was another black mark against Alexa Kane and he cursed her with every mile that took him back to his roots.

He had also dressed scruffily, in old jeans and sweatshirt, and hoped to hide his identity behind cheap sunglasses and baseball cap. To have done anything else would have been akin to tattooing 'victim' across his forehead!

Those who could remember the young Ace Delaney would know he was too tough to tangle with; others might consider the wealthy man he had become to be an easy target. If so, they'd receive the shock of their miserable lives, he thought grimly. No one got the better of him – besides, he had a gun tucked into his waistband . . .

The community centre to which he had been assigned was only a few blocks from his old neighbourhood: the graffiti, the litter, the burned-out old cars and menacing groups of youths on street corners were all depressingly familiar.

He had worked hard to pull himself out of this

hell-hole and a rich, spoilt madam had put him back here, simply out of spite and because no one had ever thwarted her before. I ought to bring her here and just dump her, he thought grimly. She wouldn't survive five minutes.

Being back in his old territory also reminded him of his mother, Loretta, even now holed up somewhere with the creep journalist, Flanagan, spewing up her sordid life story and tainting her son with her venom. He hadn't a clue what she might say – after a lifetime of drugs and booze she probably didn't even remember the truth. However, one thing was for sure: Flanagan wouldn't be interested in anything other than gossip and scandal, the more scurrilous the better . . .

He sighed heavily as he parked the truck and locked it – a useless gesture, of course, since every kid over the age of five could hot-wire it if they wanted to.

'Mr Delaney? I'm Mike Elliott, the youth leader. Glad you could make it,' the man who came to greet him said heartily, holding out his hand in welcome and trying not to quail beneath the icy glare Ace bestowed upon him.

'I'm not here because I want to be!' Ace snarled, ignoring the outstretched hand. 'It was either this or jail, and I'm beginning to think I made the wrong choice!'

'They're good kids,' Mike protested.

'Don't try to kid me – I grew up around here,' Ace said.

'Then you know the problems they face: bad schooling, constant exposure to drugs and crime, parents who can't or won't cope . . .'

'Yeah, yeah,' Ace interrupted impatiently. 'Let's get on with it. How many kids do you coach?'

'Coach is too strong a word – I'm not much of a player, I'm afraid,' Mike confessed cheerfully. Ace rolled his eyes in despair. 'I'm just glad to get the kids off the streets and taking healthy exercise. They aren't taught tennis in school and we use the public courts, but they're in a bad state of repair.'

Five minutes later, Ace made no attempt to hide his dismay as he surveyed the courts, although that was too grand a name for the disused car lot, its surface pot-holed and covered with debris. The nets had holes a shark could swim through. Even more daunting was the large group of teenagers awaiting him, a motley crew of all colours, shapes and sizes, only a few of whom clutched a racket. The rest no doubt hoped for a handout, or had come merely to gawp.

'So,' Ace began heavily. 'You all want to be professional tennis players?' he asked. 'You've read how much money the top guys earn and you think it sounds good?' Most nodded eagerly; a few just looked at him with a mixture of awe and envy. For them, the only way out of the slums was through sport or Hollywood, and Ace Delaney had succeeded in both spheres.

'You think, with a bit of luck, you can become the next Sampras or Agassi?' Ace continued. He knew there was no point in telling them about the guy ranked around one thousand, who was lucky if he could scrape together the bus-fare to the next minor tournament. Even the players breaking into the top one hundred were struggling to make ends meet – the sheer cost of travel and basic accommodation was prohibitive.

'I don't! I want to be the next Melissa Farrell!' piped up one of the girls. Ace smiled slightly; it could be true, although a fellow American was a more likely role model. Probably it was a shrewd move from a girl who knew he was friendly with the Farrells. At least she'd done her homework.

'I doubt that, honey – she's pregnant,' Ace drawled, then wondered belatedly if Melissa had yet made an official announcement. Oops! 'What's your name, honey?' he went on quickly.

'Ella,' she replied, with a cheeky grin. She reminded Ace a little of Melissa when he had first met her at Bellwood, almost ten years before. Melissa had been tall and skinny, all eyes and pigtails and bursting with enthusiasm. This girl was very similar, but had olive skin and soulful brown eyes, more wary and knowing than those of the youthful Melissa, born into privilege and cushioned from the harsh realities of life.

'Daniella Cortez – she's very keen,' Mike Elliott told Ace.

'Have you had any formal coaching?' Ace asked her.

'Yes,' Ella said.

'No,' Mike contradicted sternly, and Ella giggled, not a whit perturbed at being caught lying.

'I practise a lot,' she said earnestly. 'And I have loads of tennis magazines and coaching manuals.' Oh, hell! Ace thought.

'At least you have a racket,' he sighed. He glanced at the crowd of teenagers, gazing at him as if hoping for a miracle, yet with a weary resignation that expected disappointment. He sighed again. He had come unwillingly, intending to make only a token gesture to appease the legal system, but reluctantly decided to give it his best shot.

'There are too many of them,' he said to Mike. 'I'll have to concentrate on just a few.' He thought for a moment; he was pretty sure one of his old sponsors would donate free equipment in return for publicity photographs. If not, what the hell? He had more money than he could spend. He turned to address the waiting group.

'Those of you without rackets – clear off,' he said baldly. 'Come back tomorrow and I'll give each of you a new racket, autographed by me. I know my signature is worth a few bucks so, if you want to sell your racket, that's fine by me – but then don't come back,' he warned. 'For those who keep theirs, I'll be here to teach you a thing or two.'

His first few words had pleased those with begged, borrowed or, more likely, stolen rackets, but they were looking glum by the end of his little speech, muttering amongst themselves and feeling cheated. Ace reconsidered.

'All right, cheer up. You'll *all* get new rackets,' he told them, and they brightened immediately.

'That's very generous,' Mike Elliott said, pleased. Ace shrugged.

'Let's get to work and see if there's a spark of talent among this lot,' he said heavily. If Jack could see me now, he'd laugh himself silly, he thought. As for Alexa Kane, well, we'll see who has the last laugh.

Over the following weeks, Ace continued to coach the few who remained interested in learning how to play tennis. Most had drifted gradually away, disillusioned by Ace's refusal to gossip about the famous players and his insistence on hard work.

The only one with any real talent was Ella Cortez. She was quick around the court, had excellent hand-eye co-ordination and an instinctive touch with a racket. A new stroke, an added spin or slice was quickly mastered, and she would spend hours practising her new skills. In fact, she was a natural.

'How old are you, honey?' Ace asked one day.

'Fifteen.' He grimaced; that was very late to begin serious training. She had an enormous amount of ground to make up even to bring her level with her peer group.

He began toying with the idea of sponsoring her; of sending her to one of the many excellent tennis academies which provided intensive coaching. It would cost a bomb, but, in return, he would ensure he had a contract entitling him to a percentage of all her future earnings. There was a strong possibility that he might make a loss, but his gut instinct told him he would eventually make a packet. And there were two things he was expert at – girls and tennis! How could he go wrong? Besides, he could probably offset the expense against his taxes . . .

He said nothing to Ella, hanging back to see if her enthusiasm would wane at the first twinge from a pulled muscle, or blistered feet, but she was always waiting impatiently for him to arrive from the studio.

However, he did mention his idea to Mike Elliott and noticed with wry amusement the man's obvious dilemma – he desperately wanted Ella to have a chance to succeed, but he was suspicious of Ace's motive in taking a pretty young girl away from her home.

Ace said nothing to reassure him or explain his reasons; he rarely felt it necessary to justify his actions. Besides, whatever he said, now or in the future, would make no difference to the malicious gossip and innuendo. It was something he – and Ella – would have to live with and learn to ignore.

'You'll have to have permission from her parents, of course,' Mike said, evidently relieved he didn't have to make the decision. 'I don't think the father's around much, though,' he added, frowning.

'In that case, I'll talk to her mother,' Ace said. 'But not for a couple of days – I'm going to England; I've a christening to attend!'

Jack and Lisa had decided to have Kit baptised before they flew off to California to spend some weeks with Lisa's parents and her brother, Hal, who had not yet seen his niece. Excited by the prospect of going home, Lisa had forgiven Jack and Rose for lumbering her – and Kit – with Ace and Alexa as godparents.

'I suppose I should have known he'd ask Ace,' she sighed to Melissa as they prepared for the ceremony. 'After all, he asked Ace to be his best man at our wedding. Huh, best man – that's a misnomer if ever I heard one.' She glanced slyly at Melissa. 'I've never understood what you saw in him. I know he's good-looking, but he just uses women. I think I'm the only one who's immune to his so-called charms!'

'Not quite – Katy could never stand him, either,' Melissa said idly. 'Oh, sorry,' she grimaced. Katy Oliver, her long-time coach, had been Jack's on-off girlfriend for a couple of years before Lisa came on to the scene.

'That's okay,' Lisa shrugged. 'What's Katy up to these days?'

'She's in New York, coaching some American juniors,' Melissa told her. 'Once she stopped yelling at me for quitting just after I won Wimbledon, she decided she'd had enough of the constant travelling and applied for a job near her home.'

'Mmm, I . . . oh, look, here's Alexa. I'm not so sure about having her for a godparent, either – is your mother still going to marry Philip Kane? She seems to be putting off naming a date. Is she finding Alexa too daunting a prospect as a stepdaughter?'

'I don't think so.' Melissa frowned a little; she had also noticed Rose's reluctance to actually make wedding plans. 'I wondered if Alexa was causing her trouble, but Mum says she's been quite subdued and pleasant recently. I think it's Philip who's the problem – he asked Mum to sign a pre-nuptial contract.'

'So?' queried the American, daughter of two lawyers. She had been surprised that Jack hadn't wanted her to sign one, and couldn't understand Rose's reluctance.

'It's demeaning,' Melissa protested. 'He's more or less insinuating that the marriage won't last and that Mum would try to take him for every penny if they *did* divorce.'

'Are the terms stingy?' Lisa asked.

'No, very generous, apparently,' Melissa replied. 'But that's not the point.' Lisa shrugged, disagreeing, but not sufficiently interested to pursue the matter.

However, Melissa was only partly correct – the financial settlement was not the point, nor was it the whole problem. Although dismayed at being presented with the contract, Rose's real concern was Philip's behaviour in bed.

Ever since she had confessed to having slept with Ace, he had become almost obsessed by it, insisting she tell him details of what Ace had said and done to her. It was as if he could only get an erection by imagining her in bed with Ace, and his constant dwelling on the affair meant Ace was in her thoughts more and more. He really had been a delightful lover; demanding and often moody, and never faithful, of course, but utterly sensational . . .

# CHAPTER 6

Ace arrived by helicopter with only minutes to spare. He wasn't in the best of tempers; first he'd had to get permission from the court to fly to England for the weekend – and Ace wasn't accustomed to asking anyone's permission to do anything – and then his flight had been delayed. He had also been stopped and searched at Customs – an indignity he had half-expected, but irritating all the same.

His latest girlfriend, Gail Adams, a small-time actress currently playing a bit-part in *Country Club*, had bought a gift for Kit on his behalf, a silver bangle which she had assured him was suitable for a christening gift. Luckily, Ace had thought to declare it at Customs before his luggage was searched.

He spotted Alexa immediately; she was inappropriately clad for a February afternoon in a short suit that appeared to be made up of golden cobwebs. She looked half-frozen; she also looked apprehensive and ready to bolt, he noticed with satisfaction. She was obviously wary of meeting him again, despite Jack's assurances that Ace blamed the LA Customs officers for placing the heroin in his luggage. He afforded her only a vague, 'Hi, do I know you?' half-smile of recognition, before turning to Melissa and giving her a friendly hug.

'Hi, honey, you're looking good,' he said admiringly: although still slender, pregnancy had filled out her curves and added inches to her bust – to her dismay, but to the delectation of most males. 'Where's that bastard husband of yours?'

'Right behind you, Delaney,' Nick said grimly. Ace glanced over his shoulder and grinned, quite unabashed. But he was careful never to push Nick Lennox too far – the one brawl they'd had had been more than enough! The contest between the unprincipled street-fighter from the slums of LA and the military-trained aristocratic Englishman had been a battle neither would forget.

'You have remembered to bring Kit a present, haven't you?' Melissa asked.

'Of course I have,' Ace replied indignantly, and showed her the bangle. 'Is that okay? I had it inscribed – and there's a cheque to go with it. I thought Jack could start a savings plan for her or something.'

'It's lovely,' Melissa said, then went on solemnly, 'You do know what you're committing yourself to this afternoon, don't you?' knowing 'commitment' was a dirty word to Ace.

'Er – Jack said not to bother about the religious bit,' Ace said, beginning to feel a little uneasy. 'I just have to buy her gifts on her birthday and at Christmas, don't I? And, as she was born just before Christmas, a joint present will suffice. Even I can remember that!'

'That's fine. But, if something happens to Jack and Lisa, you'll have to adopt her,' she told him, straight-faced. Just.

'Do what?' Ace asked, alarmed.

'Adopt her. Have her live with you. Take her to school . . .' She began listing parental duties on her fingers and Ace paled beneath his tan.

'Jack never said anything about that . . . oh, very funny,' he scowled when Melissa began to laugh.

'Sorry,' she said insincerely. 'Don't worry – Jack and Lisa have appointed Nick and me her guardians if the need arises.'

'Great,' Ace said, vastly relieved. Jack was probably the only person in the world he would have qualms about letting down, but looking after a baby was just too much!

'Have you given her a cuddle yet?' Melissa persisted.

'Er, no, I'll wait until she's human . . . oh, you know what I mean,' he said crossly, as Melissa glared at him. 'Walking and talking . . . human,' he repeated. She shook her head in despair, but let it go.

The ceremony passed off without a hitch; Kit gave a small yelp of outrage when she was baptised and screwed up her little face in annoyance before going back to sleep. Alexa was terrified of dropping her, too scared even to worry about standing next to Ace, and thankfully handed her back to Lisa as soon as she could.

'Ace sounded quite sincere when he said his lines – he's a better actor than I gave him credit for,' Nick muttered to Melissa.

Ace had ignored Alexa throughout – even he maintained a pretence of civility while inside a church! But, back at Bellwood for refreshments, he began to put his pre-laid plan into action. Like a cat toying with its prey, he gave her time to relax and imagine she was escaping scot-free before he sauntered towards her. She tensed slightly as he approached and offered a tentative smile.

'Have you forgiven me for dunking you under the shower?' he asked, smiling pleasantly. Alexa visibly relaxed again, but a flush of guilt stained her cheeks.

'Oh, yes! I expect I deserved it,' she allowed. 'I had been rude to Rose, – but I did apologize,' she assured him hastily, as if fearing he might repeat the punishment.

'That's good.' He nodded approvingly. 'Your glass is empty,' he noted, and took it from her. 'I'll get you another drink.'

'Th-thank you,' she stammered.

'Stay here; I'll be right back,' he said, and wandered off. Once out of her sight, he dumped the glass on a table, walked outside and beckoned to his helicopter pilot.

'Take the chopper up and fly off, will you? Be back here in half an hour,' he instructed.

'Fly where?'

'Anywhere,' Ace said impatiently. 'Just do it.'

'Okay.' The pilot shrugged and went off to what Ace requested.

Ace returned indoors and found Alexa obediently waiting in the same spot.

'Where's my champagne?' she asked, noting he was empty-handed.

'I haven't a clue,' Ace said cheerfully. 'But your glass is . . . up there.' He pointed out of the window as the helicopter rose from the ground.

'Excuse me?' Alexa looked at him and puzzlement gradually gave way to apprehension. Why was he looking so smug? 'Did you say my glass . . .?' She trailed off; the expression in his eyes was utterly chilling. She felt colder than she had in the icy church and deathly afraid. She licked her lips nervously.

'I did. The glass with your fingerprints on,' he said smoothly, and watched the colour drain from her face. 'I have no doubt they will match the fingerprints the LAPD lifted from the packet of heroin found in my luggage,' he went on softly. Alexa appeared to have trouble breathing, and he wondered briefly if she suffered from asthma. She was certainly too pole-axed to realize that the LAPD wouldn't be remotely interested; nor that the 'evidence' wouldn't hold up in a court of law. She hadn't even committed a crime in America, and the British police had never been involved in the case.

'Jack said the Customs officers planted it on you,' she finally managed to whisper.

'That's what I thought had happened at first,' Ace lied smoothly, to prevent her plotting future revenge against Jack for his part in the deception. 'But then I remembered you bringing that package for Johnny Dancer to my room, and guessed what you'd done. Very clever, Alexa, distracting me with a bill for your clothes. I hope this isn't what you bought?' he asked disaparagingly, flicking the cuff of her jacket with his finger and thumb. 'If so, you were robbed, if I recall the exorbitant sum correctly.'

'What?' Alexa felt as if she were in a nightmare, where nothing made any sense, but which was nevertheless wholly terrifying.

'You do remember coming to my hotel?' Ace persisted. 'Suite 212?'

'Well, yes, of course . . .'

'Good. Because I have the same suite booked for tonight,' he said, which was true. He had also booked a second suite for himself and Stacey, the girl with whom he'd spent much of Christmas, but he didn't feel inclined to tell Alexa that. 'Be there, in bed, naked, at eight o'clock this evening,' he instructed. 'I've told Reception to give you a pass key. If you're . . . entertaining enough, I'll forget about the heroin and we'll call it quits,' he said, as calmly as if he were making a perfectly reasonable suggestion.

'What?' Alexa gasped.

'Are you deaf?' Ace demanded irritably.

'N-no, but you can't mean . . .' She trailed off under his cold, unyielding gaze. 'You really are as bad as people say you are,' she ground out, but he merely raised one quizzical eyebrow at that. 'It will be rape,' she whispered, and gave a shudder of revulsion. Ace nearly hit her.

'Really?' he drawled. He was becoming angrier by the second, affronted by her repugnance at the idea of sleeping with him, and even more annoyed by her readiness to believe him. He had never forced a woman in his life, and this trouble-making, toffee-nosed madam thought he was so desperate to bed her that he would resort to blackmail! Didn't the little bitch realize that most women considered a night with him a reward, not a punishment? Evidently not, judging by the pallor of her face and stricken, tear-filled eyes. He hardened his heart; tears seldom worked with him.

'You don't *have* to be there, of course . . .' He paused to let her take the bait, which she did.

'I don't?' she asked eagerly.

'No.' He shook his head, and gave her a few moments to think she had won a reprieve. 'But I doubt you'd like the alternative, Alexa,' he continued. 'If you disliked the shower I gave you, just imagine how much you'll hate the communal showers in jail. They're dangerous places, I hear, especially for an upper-class young girl like you. The other prisoners would eat you up – literally. You'd be much more comfortable in my bed,' he went on. Alexa gazed up at him, her stomach churning with fear. She couldn't please him in bed! She couldn't please any man . . . And, even if his super-stud reputation was based on fact, she wasn't stupid enough to think he intended making the evening a pleasurable experience for her. It would be an act of revenge, designed to humiliate and degrade . . .

She glanced wildly around the room, searching for an ally. Her father was there, talking to Rose, but she couldn't approach him, not unless she was prepared to tell him the truth, which she wasn't. He hated drugs and drug-users and his anger and contempt would know no bounds. He'd probably hand her over to the police personally!

'Well?' Ace demanded impatiently. 'Jail, or me?'

'I don't suppose it would help if I said I'm sorry,' she ventured, without much hope.

'No,' he said bleakly, and she sighed, bowing her head to the inevitable.

'Very well,' she capitulated. 'I'll be there.'

'Good. One other thing – cut those claws of yours. I prefer my women unarmed,' he added, then he turned on his heel and left her alone with her dark thoughts.

She watched dully as he circled the room, chatting pleasantly to everyone, utterly charming now that he had got what he wanted. Some people spoke to her, but she didn't even hear them, much less respond, and they moved away, wondering aloud why Jack and Lisa had chosen her to be a godparent and why on earth Rose Farrell was prepared to take on such a sullen girl as her stepdaughter.

'Are you okay?' Melissa lightly touched her arm. 'You're awfully pale. Would you like a cup of tea?' she asked. She had seen Ace and Alexa deep in conversation, seemingly unaware of anything going on around them, but Alexa didn't have the happy, expectant look of a girl who had been chatted up by Ace Delaney!

Alexa just shook her head in despair. She felt an insane urge to ask Melissa what Ace was like as a lover, but the question was irrelevant as well as crass. This wasn't about sex; it was all about power.

'Come with me,' Melissa urged. 'I'm going to make some tea for myself; I'm not drinking alcohol for the next few months.' Alexa allowed herself to be led away. The hot tea stopped her shivers, but the numbness of her emotions remained. She wished she could feel angry, but she didn't, just resigned to her fate and very, very frightened. She had been an idiot to think she could remain unpunished for what she had done.

'Are you feeling better now?' Melissa asked. 'I'm not trying to interfere, but is there anything you want to talk about?'

'Well . . .' Alexa hesitated, not sure Melissa would even want to help if she knew the truth. A loud and obviously phoney cough from the doorway stopped any confidences and she looked up fearfully as Ace strolled into the kitchen.

'Shouldn't you be heading back to London?' he asked Alexa casually, adding to Melissa. 'She has a hot date tonight.'

'Really?' Melissa looked uncertainly from one to the other, a slight frown marring her brow. Something was definitely going on here, but nothing pleasant . . . I'll ask Jack; he'll know, she decided with relief. He would also know how to put a stop to whatever Ace had in mind, if necessary.

'Yes, I have to go.' Alexa hastily finished her tea and fled from the room. Ace's eyes narrowed to slits as he watched her go. She looks as if she's heading for the gallows, he thought bleakly.

'I don't suppose you'd like to tell me what you're up to?' Melissa asked him.

'Me? I'm not up to anything,' he said guilelessly. 'I've turned over a new leaf now I'm a godparent. I might even join a nunnery.'

'Don't you mean a monastery?'

'No.' He winked and grinned at her. Melissa shook her head in despair, but couldn't help returning the grin.

'Oh, get outta here!' she said, exasperated.

Jack proved to be just as annoying when she asked him later what, if anything, was occurring between Ace and Alexa. He pleaded ignorance, but she didn't believe him either, and was left to wonder. Alexa certainly wasn't behaving like one of Ace's usual conquests. Was Ace the 'hot date' to which he had referred? If so, she wouldn't mind being a fly on the wall!

Alexa wouldn't have minded being a fly on the wall, either, or a spider in the bath, or anything but what she actually was – a victim staked out for the marauding Apache! As time passed, she became more and more convinced that the rumour concerning his Native American heritage was based on truth . . .

She had arrived punctually at the hotel, quaking with fear, and had been given a key to his suite. It had taken all her courage simply to unlock and open the door, and then, when she did, she discovered the room was empty. Not only was Ace not there, nor was there any of his belongings; the wardrobe and cupboards were empty, the bathroom devoid of any toiletries save what the hotel provided. Maybe it was all a huge wind-up? His sick idea of a joke? She expelled a huge pent-up breath and gradually allowed herself to hope that he would be satisfied by merely forcing her to do be here against her will. Her relief was short-lived. Just as she was wondering if she dared leave, the phone rang. She approached it as warily as if it were a venomous snake about to strike – which it was.

'Hello?'

‘So glad you could make it,’ Ace’s voice mocked her, and she bit her lip in vexation and renewed fear. He was ensconced in the other suite with Stacey and had asked Reception to inform him of Alexa’s arrival. He was pleased by her promptness. ‘Are you naked yet?’ he demanded, hastily placing his hand over Stacey’s mouth to stifle her protests over a ‘rival’. It would ruin everything if Alexa realized he had someone with him.

‘N-no,’ she stammered.

‘Then do it. Now. And get into bed. I don’t intend wasting time. And cut your nails, if you haven’t already,’ he instructed before hanging up.

Alexa had already trimmed her long nails, cursing him with every cut of the scissors, for she was very proud of her elegant hands. But that command was as nothing compared to the other . . . Tears of fright and humiliation spilled over as she fumbled with her clothes and climbed, shivering uncontrollably, into the huge bed. I can’t please him, I know I can’t. He’ll laugh at me, hate me . . . He already hates you, jeered an inner voice and she sobbed out loud.

Time passed agonizingly slowly, and then too quickly as she became sure he would arrive any moment. He hadn’t said anything about being sober, she realized suddenly. Perhaps, if she was drunk, she could relax sufficiently, or at least be too numb to care overmuch . . .

At eleven o’clock, Ace decided Alexa had waited long enough and had learned her lesson. He had spent the evening in bed with the luscious and oh, so willing Stacey, so he was pleasantly exhausted and in a good humour when he dressed and walked the short distance to Suite 212. Alexa had sounded suitably cowed on the phone and his only intention was to send her home.

He opened the door and paused on the threshold.

'Okay, you can . . .' He ducked smartly as a bottle crashed into the door above his head; only his lightning reflexes saved him from concussion, or worse.

'You little bitch!' he snarled, and sprang at her before she could find another missile.

She was kneeling on the bed, gloriously naked, her tawny hair falling around her shoulders and framing her face. She fell back, laughing, and Ace stopped in his tracks. She's beautiful, he thought and, despite bedding Stacey four times in as many hours, he felt renewed desire as he gazed at Alexa's body stretched out before him.

She was slimmer than he usually preferred, small-boned and small-breasted, but exquisite. And those gold-green eyes were bright with laughter now, not flashing with hostility. But it was alcohol-induced amusement, he realized. The empty bottle which had almost brained him had once contained vodka.

'Plastered again? Didn't anyone ever tell you that drunkenness in a woman is deeply unattractive?' he said disapprovingly. Alexa just gaped at him for a moment, then resumed giggling.

'You sound like my father!' she said scornfully. 'Still, you do have a lot in common, don't you? Rose, for instance.' Ace took a step towards her, then forced himself to move back. He didn't trust himself to go near her; he was so furious he could throttle her. She needed to get plastered before she could bear my touch, he thought savagely. The snooty, haughty, worthless baggage . . .

'Get dressed and go home!' he snapped.

'W-what? Have we done it?' she hiccuped, and he balled his hands into fists.

'If we had done it, as you so delicately phrase it, you wouldn't need to ask!' he ground out. 'No, we have not. And never will. I didn't force you to come here to violate your skinny body – I don't want you,' he said forcefully, but knew it was a lie. 'In case you haven't worked it out yet, let me spell it out for you – I made you come to this hotel only to teach you a lesson. Cause trouble for me and you'll get it back tenfold – is that clear now?' he demanded.

'You don't want me?' Alexa only grasped those few, hurtful words and her face crumpled. 'No one does. I'm useless in bed . . .'

'You're useless, full stop,' Ace snapped, turning on his heel to leave. He caught his foot in the skirt she had dropped to the floor and stumbled to one knee. Alexa's mood veered back to laughter in an instant.

'I knew you'd fall for me eventually!' she shrieked, leaning forwards and pushing her hair back from her face. The action unwittingly pushed her breasts near to Ace's face and he mistakenly thought she had done it deliberately, to tease and tantalize now he had told her he didn't desire her.

'May I have my skirt back? I don't think it's quite your colour.' She smiled winningly and hiccuped gently.

'You want your skirt? And these?' Ace held up her jacket, shirt and underwear. 'Fine. Go and fetch them!' As he spoke, he pulled open the window and tossed the garments down into the street below. Alexa was too inebriated to care, and seemed to find his action genuinely amusing, which only added to his irritation.

He stalked to the door, wrenched it open so violently it almost parted from its hinges, and walked out, shaking with anger. He should have won that encounter; he'd held all the cards, but he felt like a loser, something he hadn't felt for years and had intended never to feel again. She claimed to be useless in bed? With that body, those eyes? He snorted in disgust; he was surprised she hadn't tried to convince him she was a lesbian – she was obviously desperate enough to do or say anything to avoid sleeping with him.

At least Stacey was pleased to see him return so quickly. She was as naked as Alexa, but far more willing. Only now her body seemed too lush, overripe, her breasts too large and soft, her buttocks too fleshy. Hardly aware of what he was doing, Ace began to use her roughly, venting his anger on her, ignoring her whimpers of protest that quickly changed to gasps of delight.

She matched his furious pace, accepting each hard, deep thrust with welcoming cries, biting his shoulders and clawing at his back, receiving and inflicting pain-pleasure and enjoying every threshing moment of the coupling.

'Phew!' Ace rolled off her, his sweat-slicked body glistening, his powerful chest heaving with exertion. 'Sorry, honey, did I hurt you?' he asked, when his breathing returned to normal.

'Yes, but I loved it,' Stacey purred, snuggling up to him. Ace pushed her away, but did it gently; he felt a bastard for using her so, even if she had enjoyed it.

'I need a shower,' he explained when she pouted, and shut himself in the bathroom.

He closed his eyes under the force of the spray; beneath his lids there was an image of Alexa, her face pale and tear-stained, her huge green-gold eyes fearful as they gazed imploringly at him.

'Aw, hell!' he muttered. He switched off the jet of water and grabbed up a towel. Back in the bedroom, he quickly dressed and began packing.

'You're not leaving?' Stacey frowned. 'I thought you were staying until tomorrow?'

'Change of plan,' Ace said briefly: he had to get out of this hotel as soon as possible. 'Sorry, honey, but you can stay here overnight if you want to.'

'No, I might as well go home,' she sighed, and sulkily began to put on her clothes. Ace phoned Reception, asking for his bill and a cab to the airport. He checked his wallet, kept back enough for his fare and handed Stacey the remainder of his sterling.

'Buy yourself something nice, honey,' he said absently.

'Thanks!' Her face brightened as she took the wad of fifty pound notes. 'You will call me when you're coming back to London?'

'Sure,' he agreed, although he doubted he would. 'Bye, honey; it's been great,' he said, hustling her out of the room.

When she had gone, he returned to Suite 212 but it was empty. Alexa had obviously swallowed her pride and asked a member of staff to retrieve her clothes, or phoned a friend to bring replacements. He wondered briefly what explanation she had given. The thought of her embarrassment should have made him feel good, but it didn't. And, when he went to pay his bill, he learned that Alexa had already settled the account for Suite 212. And that made him feel even worse.

# CHAPTER 7

From London, Ace flew straight to LA, and was back on the set of *Country Club* the following day, tired and jet-lagged, and in a thoroughly bad temper. Everyone, even Johnny Dancer, stepped warily around him. Especially Johnny, as he had slept with Gail Adams, Ace's current girlfriend, during his absence, and wasn't sure how he would react if he found out.

At three o'clock, one of the gofers approached Ace, cautiously, and flanked by two others for moral support.

'I know you don't want to talk to the Press . . .' she began nervously.

'I don't,' Ace scowled.

'But this guy's insisting you'll want to take his call. He says it's about your mother . . .'

'Name?' Ace snapped.

'Rita.' She flushed.

'Not yours! His!' Ace ground out.

'Oh. Thomas Flanagan.'

Ace snatched the phone from her hand. 'Clear off,' he said, to the three girls. 'Not you,' he added hastily to the caller. 'Not yet, anyhow. What do you want, Flanagan?'

'Loretta wants to see you,' Flanagan told him. It was the last thing Ace had expected to hear and he was stunned into momentary silence.

'Why?' he asked finally. 'Does she think I'll offer her money to pull out of her deal with you? If so, you can tell her I won't give her a dime!'

'No, it's not that. I think she's having second thoughts about the whole project,' Flanagan said. 'Delaney?' he said sharply, when there was no reply.

'Where is she?' Ace rapped out.

'Right here in LA. 1612 Mullaney Drive, apartment 2B. You'd better get over here quickly before she changes her mind. She's afraid of you; I had to promise her you wouldn't upset her. You won't, will you?'

'Upset her? I'm going to wring her scrawny neck!' Ace said wrathfully, as he broke the connection.

He walked off the set without a word to anyone and drove at breakneck speed, his stomach churning at the prospect of meeting his mother again. He didn't want to do it, but he had no choice if he wanted to stop Flanagan's book.

He soon realized that Mullaney Drive was only two blocks away from Loretta's own apartment, and resolved grimly to have words with the private detective who had failed to locate her. The man had been sure Flanagan had taken Loretta out of the city – maybe he had, but only as a bluff, and must have quietly sneaked her back into LA, where she had been living under their noses all these weeks.

Ace was so annoyed with the detective, and wound-up about seeing Loretta, that unfortunately it didn't occur to him to wonder why Flanagan was suddenly being so helpful . . .

No one answered his knock on the door of apartment 2B; too impatient and angry to think straight, Ace kicked savagely at the flimsy lock, smashing it with one blow from his heel.

'Flanagan? Loretta?' He stepped inside; it was dim and musty, stiflingly hot, curtains and windows closed. 'Loretta? Mother dearest,' he called mockingly, walking over to the window and pulling back a blind to let in some daylight.

He turned back and surveyed the room, staring in shock at the figure lying on the sofa. He didn't recognize her at first; Loretta Delaney had always taken care of her appearance and this wizened old crone bore little resemblance to the smart, if cheaply dressed and over-made-up woman he remembered. But, beneath the straggly grey hair and wrinkled skin, there remained the dark eyes and sculptured bone structure she had bequeathed to her son. God, that *is* her! was Ace's first thought. His second, with a skin-crawling sense of horror, was the realization that the eyes staring at him were sightless – she was dead.

He swallowed bile and forced himself to step closer, noting the empty liquor bottles, over-spilling ashtrays and a hypodermic needle. It took an immense effort of will for him to reach out and touch her, feeling for a pulse, but there was none. Track marks of recent injections scarred the skeletal arm and he dropped her hand, rubbing his palm against his jeans as if to wipe away contamination.

She is – was – my mother, he thought. I should care; should at least feel something! But he didn't. She gave birth to me, he reminded himself desperately, but that thought only provoked revulsion.

He took a deep breath and turned away, noticing for the first time a small voice-activated tape recorder on the coffee table near to Loretta's hand. He quickly pressed the eject button, but the machine was empty. Damn! He realized that Flanagan must have already taken the tape, and that Loretta had probably been dead or dying when Flanagan phoned him. He guessed the heating had been turned on full blast in an attempt to prevent rigor mortis setting in too soon and so cause confusion over the exact time of death. He's set me up to take the rap for this, he thought, and fought down an urge to flee. He knew it was too late for that.

Calmly, he used his mobile phone to call his lawyer, Larry Knight, and then used what time he had to search the apartment, hoping there was a slim chance Flanagan had hidden the tapes or a manuscript. He found nothing. All the while, he could hear police sirens getting louder, then the sound of car doors slamming and heavy feet pounding up the stairs.

He turned to face the two uniformed cops who rushed in, guns drawn, and held out his arms to show he was unarmed. They still approached him warily; one covered him with his weapon while the other checked Loretta for signs of life before cuffing Ace's hands behind his back. He gritted his teeth against the ignominy of it all and refused to say a word as they led him away. They had to force a path through a crowd which had quickly gathered to gawp and speculate. Ace stared stonily ahead, his face expressionless.

The news of Loretta Delaney's death and Ace's arrest spread like wildfire, first through LA, and then beyond, as Press and TV picked up the story and broadcast it throughout the States.

But, when Jack and Lisa flew into San Francisco a few hours later, they were still unaware of what had happened. Kit had disliked her first experience of air travel and had made her feelings known throughout the journey, so consequently all three were tired and irritable.

As usual, a small crowd of reporters and photographers were hanging around the Arrivals hall, hoping for impromptu interviews or pictures of celebrities passing through.

'Hey! There's Jack Farrell!' They surged forward, surrounding the trio, their camera flashes startling Kit and making her cry.

'Get out of the way!' Jack snarled, most uncharacteristically.

'Have you heard about Ace Delaney? Is that why you're in California?'

'We're here on a private visit,' he told them shortly.

'So, you haven't heard the news?'

'No,' Jack snapped.

'Ace Delaney has been arrested – his mother was found dead in her apartment this afternoon,' one told him, with evident relish.

'He doesn't even know where she lives,' Jack said, only to regret it a moment later.

'He was arrested at the scene,' the same reporter informed him, with a note of triumph in his voice. Jack swore under his breath.

'Do you have any comment?'

'Yes. Back off,' Jack growled unhelpfully. 'Shut up,' he added quietly to Lisa, when she opened her mouth to speak. She obeyed, temporarily.

'Do you think he killed her?' she asked him, when they were finally free of the reporters.

'Of course he didn't,' Jack said curtly, but wished he could be sure. Ace had been angry enough to kill, and he recalled the vehemence with which he had said he would gladly pay Loretta's funeral expenses. He sighed heavily. 'I suppose I'd better get a flight to LA,' he said reluctantly.

'Well, that decision took around ten seconds longer than I expected,' Lisa said huffily. 'What about Kit and me?'

'You'll be okay with your parents, won't you?' he asked, exasperated. Anyone would think he was dumping them in the middle of the Sahara, instead of the city which had been Lisa's home for most of her life. 'I have to go and see if I can help – surely you can understand that?'

'Sure.' She shrugged, but refused to talk to him during the short drive to her parents' house.

Joshua and Hannah Renwick were waiting to greet them, as was Lisa's brother Hal, eager for his first glimpse of his niece. Jack separated his luggage from Lisa's and Kit's, and explained why he couldn't stay. His in-laws' welcome cooled perceptibly, and became positively icy when Lisa burst into tears. Her distress prompted a piercing wail of sympathy from the baby, and Jack felt about as popular as King Herod in a maternity ward!

'Don't cry, poppet.' He chose to comfort Kit, not Lisa, and cuddled his daughter close. 'I'll be back soon,' he crooned to her.

'At least come inside for a while,' Hal urged him. He was keen, yet dreading, to hear news of Melissa. He had fallen in love with Jack's kid sister years before and had hoped to marry her. He had supported her in the aftermath of the abortion and consequent break-up with Nick Lennox, only to lose her to him again. Everyone but Hal had known Melissa had never stopped loving Nick; Hal guessed he had known too, deep down, but had chosen to ignore it.

'I'll drive you back to the airport when you're ready,' Hal continued, leading the way indoors.

'Thanks,' Jack nodded his appreciation. 'What have you heard about Ace's mother?' he asked.

'I was surprised to learn he ever had one!' Hal said caustically. He had never been friendly with Ace, despite being a fellow pro as well as a fellow American, and could not understand why Jack remained friendly with the arrogant bastard.

'Get serious!' Jack snapped, his customary easy-going manner rapidly vanishing beneath the weight of exhaustion and worry.

'No details have been released yet, but apparently Ace was arrested at her apartment. Someone saw him kicking the door in and dialled 911. When the cops arrived, she was already dead,' Hal said baldly. He hesitated, then continued, 'I think you should steer clear of this one, Jack,' he advised.

'Do you?' Jack countered grimly. 'How did she die?'

'Dunno,' Hal shrugged. 'They haven't said, but it doesn't make much difference, does it? God knows what his motive could have been, though. Have you any idea?'

'Not a clue,' Jack lied. 'He hadn't seen her since he was a kid. You seem awfully keen to find him guilty,' he added.

'Oh, come on, Jack! We've both witnessed his vicious temper – how many times did he have to be restrained from beating up some poor guy? And usually for no real reason. Anyone who has ever shared a locker room with Ace can be lined up as a prosecution witness.'

'You sound as if you'll be first in the queue,' Jack commented sourly.

'No, I'm just stating facts,' Hal shrugged. 'The cops will sort it out, I expect.' He realized he was alienating Jack and changed the subject, offering him a drink and food. 'Er – how's Melissa?' he asked, ultra-casual.

'Pregnant. Blissfully happy. Nick adores her.' Jack rapped out, far too annoyed with Hal to want to spare his feelings. Besides, it was high time he stopped mooning over what he could never have.

He made his peace with Lisa, more or less, and saw Kit settled into the new crib her grandparents had bought for her, then headed back to the airport to catch the shuttle to LA.

'Has Ace mentioned Daniella Cortez to you?' Hal asked, as he drove.

'Mm, don't think so. Who's she – a new girl-friend?'

'I hope not – she's only fifteen. He wants me to take her on at the academy. I haven't had an opportunity to see her play yet, so I don't know if it's her talent or her body he's interested in.'

'Her talent,' Jack decided. 'He did say he was thinking of sponsoring one of the underprivileged kids he was coaching,' he remembered. 'He didn't mention any names, but I guess it must be this girl.'

'Mm.' Hal was unconvinced. 'It's a bit out of character for Ace to go out of his way to help someone.'

'Oh, get off his back, will you?' Jack demanded. 'Oh, look, sorry; I'm just tired. Thanks for the lift – I'll phone Lisa as soon as I find out what's going on, and how long I'll have to stay,' he added, as he clambered out of the car.

He checked in and called Ace's house, leaving a message on the answerphone giving his time of arrival, and hoping Ace's current girlfriend, whoever that might be, would have more details of the arrest and know Ace's whereabouts.

In fact, it was Johnny Dancer who listened to the message and went to meet Jack. Johnny, now famous in LA courtesy of *Country Club* – and Ace Delaney – had to push his way through a crowd of autograph-hunters to greet Jack.

Johnny, despite his friendship with Ace, was more concerned about his own career than Ace's problems. If *Country Club* folded – and the studio bosses were less than pleased with the publicity Ace was currently generating – Johnny's lucrative role as Ace's brother would be history. And Johnny didn't relish the prospect of returning to the obscurity of bit parts and TV adverts that had been his lot until his superficial resemblance to Ace Delaney had handed him the plum part in *Country Club*.

'Jack?' Johnny recognized him from the photographs of the Doubles partners which littered Ace's house. 'I'm Johnny Dancer.'

'Thanks for meeting me.' Jack briefly shook his hand. 'What's the latest? All I've heard is that he was arrested at his mother's apartment,' he said, following Johnny outside.

'Right. Well, he hasn't been charged yet – the cops are waiting for the result of the autopsy. His lawyer's trying to get him out of jail, but without much luck. Apparently there was enough heroin in the apartment to kill an elephant.'

'Heroin!' Jack exclaimed.

'Yeah,' Johnny sighed. 'It's a pity that Ace got busted for possessing the stuff just a few weeks ago. It looks bad.'

'That was planted on him,' Jack said grimly. 'I have to call England,' he decided.

He didn't have Philip Kane's ex-directory phone number with him and called Melissa, forgetting that it was still the early hours of the morning in the UK. Nick answered the phone, somewhat grumpily, and was even less inclined to be helpful when he learned it was Ace who was in trouble. So far as Nick was concerned, jail was the best place for him.

'I'm not waking Melissa,' he snapped at Jack. 'She needs her rest . . . oh, too late,' he sighed, as Melissa stirred and rubbed her eyes.

'Who is it?' she yawned.

'Jack. Ace is in trouble with the police again,' Nick handed her the phone. 'I think Jack's lost his mind – he seems to think Alexa Kane can help.'

'Jack?' Melissa was wide awake now. 'What's happening?' She listened incredulously as he briefly filled her in on Alexa's earlier trickery and how that was affecting the current investigation into Loretta Delaney's death.

'Alexa has to get over here and tell the police what she did. Have you got her number?' Jack asked.

'Yes, just a sec.' She quickly found her phone book and reeled off the Kanes' number. 'Is there anything I can do?'

'No,' Nick said firmly.

'I was asking Jack,' she hissed.

'I know, but I'm telling you to stay out of it.' Nick settled the argument by taking the handset from her and breaking the connection. Jack grinned slightly as he imagined the scene that would follow, then he quickly punched out the number Melissa had given him. Luckily, Alexa had risen early and picked it up almost immediately. Once again, Jack rapped out the bare details.

'I don't give a damn about the games you and Ace are playing – this is serious. You're getting on the first available flight to LA, and telling the truth about the heroin you put in his luggage,' he told her curtly. Alexa paled at the very thought.

'I can't! Daddy will kill me,' she said, horrified. 'Ace bought himself out of trouble last time – can't he do that again?' she asked hopefully.

'Don't be stupid. This time he could be facing a murder charge,' Jack said brutally. 'They have the death penalty here in California,' he added, for good measure. Alexa bit her lip; that was a bit extreme, even for someone who ruined as many of her clothes as Ace had . . .

'Oh, all right,' she muttered ungraciously.

'Good girl,' Jack sighed with relief. 'Let me know which flight you'll be on and I'll meet you,' he promised, quickly rattling off Ace's phone number and then breaking the connection before she could change her mind.

He turned back to Johnny and Gail Adams, Ace's current flame-haired girlfriend, who had been listening.

'She's agreed to come?' Johnny asked.

'Yes. Her testimony will prove the first drugs bust was nothing to do with Ace, so it has to cast doubt on who supplied the heroin which killed Loretta Delaney.' Jack said. The other two nodded their agreement, but when Ace's lawyer, Larry Knight, arrived later, he was doubtful that Alexa's statement would help, although he understood Jack's need to be doing something.

'Don't forget, Ace told the cops he knew exactly where to buy drugs in this city,' he reminded them. 'Besides, they'll probably think Alexa is lying to help him. They'll figure she's just another of his broads . . . sorry, Gail,' he apologized hastily. Gail merely shrugged, unconcerned. She knew she didn't have exclusive rights to Ace, but then, neither did he to her . . . She cast a smouldering glance at Johnny, but he frowned slightly and jerked his head warningly towards Jack. Jack had missed the by-play; his thoughts were on Ace and Alexa.

'No way,' he answered Larry. 'Alexa loathes him, and the police will realize that as soon as they speak to her.'

'Perhaps,' Larry nodded. 'At least they're listening to Ace's story, and they're trying to locate Flanagan, which is a good sign as it means they're prepared to concede he could have been the last person to see Loretta Delaney alive. Ace searched the apartment for tapes or a manuscript, but couldn't find anything, which seems to indicate Flanagan was there when she died and did a bunk, taking everything with him. He must have phoned Ace to get him there to take the rap.'

'Who called the police?' Jack asked.

'There were two calls, both anonymous, ten minutes apart. All 911 calls are automatically recorded, so they'll be checked out,' Larry told him. 'Flanagan could have hung around and made the first call when he saw Ace arrive, and the second was probably genuine, from someone who actually saw Ace kick down the door but didn't want to get involved. That's not unusual in that sort of neighbourhood.'

'How long will they keep Ace in jail?' Jack asked next.

'They'll hold him until they get the result of the autopsy tomorrow, then they'll have to charge him or release him. But hopefully, they'll have found Flanagan by then and got his statement. And Alexa Kane's, of course,' he added quickly, for Jack's benefit. Jack nodded, rather grimly, no longer confident he was helping. If Ace's freedom depended upon a journalist who wanted to destroy him and a spoilt girl who hated him, God help him!

Alexa half-hoped all flights to the United States had been inexplicably cancelled, but, once her seat was booked, she resigned herself to the inevitable. Jack was right; this was no time for games. Her feelings for Ace were confused, to say the least. She had hated him so much for forcing her, as she thought, to sleep with him, but then he had told her, somewhat bluntly, that that had never been his intention – or his desire – and had told her to go home! That had been no easy task, either, not after he had thrown her clothes out of the window! Luckily she had been drunk enough to find the situation amusing and hadn't batted an eyelid when asking the hotel staff to retrieve her suit from the street below.

She booked a cab and packed quickly, hoping to be out of the house before her father and Rose awoke. She would just leave him a note, she decided cowardly.

'Oh, damn!' she exclaimed; her passport was locked in her father's safe, where he'd placed it to thwart her threat to follow Dimitri . . . Dimitri? She realized she couldn't even remember what he looked like.

'Daddy!' She rapped on his bedroom door, and walked inside, averting her gaze from Rose's nude body lying beside him in the huge bed. 'Daddy!' she hissed again, moving nearer.

'Huh?' Philip rolled over and squinted at her in the light cast from the hallway behind her. 'What is it? Are you ill?'

'No, I'm fine. I'm sorry to wake you, but I need my passport, and it's in your safe,' she told him.

'Passport?' He sat up, still groggy. Rose was awake now too, but pretended not to be. 'Why do you suddenly need your passport?' he demanded irritably.

'I have to go to the States. Please, Daddy, hurry! I've a plane to catch,' she said urgently. 'Get up, please. I'll explain while you unlock the safe.'

'Oh, very well,' Philip sighed and reached for his robe. Alexa had already left the room and was waiting impatiently in the study for him to open the safe.

Twenty minutes later, Alexa was on her way to Heathrow and Philip made his way slowly back upstairs. He didn't know which shocked him the most – Alexa's relationship with Ace Delaney, or her involvement with drugs.

'What's going on?' Rose asked excitedly, but her eager expression quickly changed to one of concern. Philip looked grey, tired and old, his craggy face set in lines of weariness.

'Ace Delaney's in prison – his mother's dead,' he told her baldly.

'Oh, my God! And they think Ace killed her?' Rose gasped.

'Apparently,' he nodded. 'According to Jack, she died from an overdose of heroin.'

'And Ace was caught smuggling heroin recently . . .' Rose said slowly.

'That's where Alexa comes into it,' Philip said reluctantly. 'She's just told me she placed that heroin in his luggage and then tipped off the authorities. She doesn't even seem to have a good reason for doing such a thing; just said they don't get along. I can't believe she could be so spiteful,' he shook his head sorrowfully.

'Ace often brings out the worst in people.' Rose sighed.

'But how did she become involved in drugs? When? Have I been blind not to notice? She swears she's never taken the filthy stuff herself, but refuses to tell me where she got hold of it.' He sat on the bed and buried his head in his hands. Rose knelt behind him, placing her hands on his shoulders, and he leaned back against the comforting cushion of her breasts.

'Where did I go wrong with that girl?' he asked sadly. Rose wisely didn't reply, and he reached up to pat her hand. He tilted his head slightly and gave her a small smile, touched by the concern evident in her expressive eyes.

'I know; I spoiled her rotten,' he confirmed Rose's unspoken words. 'But it was hard not to,' he excused himself. 'She was only ten when Elizabeth – her mother – died and, soon after, she lost her nanny, too. It was a dreadful time,' he sighed.

'Her nanny? Did she die as well?' Rose asked, frowning slightly. Surely she couldn't have been very old?

'No, she resigned,' Philip said shortly.

'When Alexa had just lost her mother? How heartless!' Rose exclaimed.

'No, Magda was a sweet girl,' Philip refuted quickly. He wished he'd never brought up the subject – he and Alexa never discussed it, but he supposed Rose ought to know. 'You see, after

Elizabeth died, one of the papers picked up on the fact that she'd left her fortune to Alexa and ran a piece on this "poor little rich girl", making Alexa out to be in the same league as an Onassis heiress. Maybe I should have foreseen trouble and taken steps to avoid it, but we're not celebrities, or well-known to the public, so a kidnapping never even occurred to me.'

'Kidnapping!' Rose repeated in horror.

'Yes,' he confirmed, and paused to take a deep breath. Even now, the memory of that day brought him out in a cold sweat. 'Magda was taking her to school, as she did every day. The two of them were bundled into a van and driven off. Luckily, an off-duty policeman witnessed it and put out the alert quickly and they were rescued later that same day. Magda, quite understandably, just wanted to go home to her family in Germany, so I let her go. What else could I have done, even though I knew it hurt Alexa to see her go?' he asked, shrugging helplessly.

'Nothing. Of course you had to let her go,' Rose said firmly, giving him a hug of reassurance. 'The poor girl! What an ordeal. And for Alexa, too . . . she must have been terrified.'

'Yes, although she never speaks of it, not then or now. I sometimes think she must have forgotten all about it, but then I wonder why she stays living here, with me, instead of striking out on her own. Lots of her friends have travelled the world, but not Alexa. Oh, she often holidays abroad with a crowd of people, but seems happier here.' He paused and glanced at Rose. 'I'm afraid she'll probably want to stay here, even after we're married, probably until she finds a husband of her own,' he said, rather apologetically. 'Will you mind too much?'

'No, I won't mind,' Rose assured him, not altogether truthfully, although Alexa had at least been more friendly recently, not nearly so prickly and sarcastic. 'I can see why she would want to cling to you and her home; obviously she feels safe here.' At least, she did, until Ace practically attacked her in her own bedroom, she thought guiltily. She had never mentioned the events of that evening to Philip and Alexa had refused to discuss it, save for a rather stiff apology to Rose for her rudeness – the apology Ace had insisted on. Was that why Alexa had planted heroin on Ace? Not because he had bruised her pride by half drowning her under an icy shower but because he had proved to her that her sanctuary wasn't invulnerable to attack?

'Will Alexa be in trouble with the police by confessing?' she asked.

'I doubt it; she hasn't committed a crime in the States, but I told her to be sure and have a lawyer with her when she goes to make her statement.' He paused, then, 'You know Ace Delaney as well as anyone,' he said, and Rose tensed, but for once there was no sexual undertone to his questioning. 'Tell me. Do you think he's capable of murder?'

# CHAPTER 8

Is Ace Delaney capable of murder? It was a question that was repeated a million times as the world awoke to the news of his arrest. Ace's legion of fans, mostly female, declared: no way! Others, like Hal Renwick, who had witnessed his temper first-hand thought it more than possible. And most tennis umpires who'd had the misfortune to referee his matches were surprised that such a charge hadn't been levelled against him long before! Larry Knight, while loudly protesting about the Press speculation, was secretly pleased it was making headlines; trial by media made a courtroom trial less likely, he told Ace when he saw him in prison the following morning.

'Just get me out of here!' Ace snapped. He hadn't enjoyed his night in jail; the smell of hopelessness, anger and despair permeated the very walls. At least he'd had a cell to himself, but he hadn't been able to sleep. He was gaunt, his stubbled cheeks hollow as he drew deeply on a cigarette.

'They'll have to charge you or let you go today,' Larry assured him. 'The DA won't relish the prospect of another celebrity trial. I guess you'll walk.'

'You guess?' Ace glowered. 'I don't pay you to guess!'

'No.' Larry shifted uncomfortably. 'Jack Farrell's here,' he told him.

'Yeah?' Ace brightened slightly. 'That was quick.'

'He was in San Francisco when he heard the news – do you want to see him?'

'I hope I'm not going to be here long enough to have visitors! Pull you finger out, Larry – I didn't touch the woman,' he said coldly.

'No.' Larry looked even more uncomfortable; talking about his mother in such a derogatory manner did nothing to help Ace's cause. 'But your fingerprints are all over the apartment, and your record for possession of heroin . . .' He shrugged. Ace almost laughed out loud. Fingerprints and heroin! Alexa Kane would enjoy the irony of that combination, he thought.

'Loretta's used heroin for years – if the cops do their job, they can find her own supplier. And it wasn't me,' Ace said flatly.

The police were rapidly coming to the same conclusion: the autopsy report revealed such long-term drug and alcohol abuse that it was surprising Loretta Delaney hadn't killed herself sooner. The private detective Ace had hired before Christmas to try and find Loretta confirmed he had been unable to locate her, and the staff at the TV studio verified Ace's presence on the set until the phone call from Flanagan. And the journalist was still missing; hadn't returned to his apartment at all overnight.

'I'm going to have to let the bastard go,' said the police captain in disgust. Larry was right – the last thing the DA wanted was another celebrity trial, especially one that would end in acquittal.

At noon, Thomas Flanagan walked into the precinct, accompanied by his lawyer. He admitted that Loretta had died shortly before he had phoned Ace, but insisted her death was an accident. She had become greedy, demanding more money for the juiciest details of Ace's young life, and he had given her vodka to loosen her tongue, but vehemently denied supplying her with heroin.

'She had her own regular supplier somewhere in the neighbourhood,' he told them. 'Look, I wanted us to get the hell out of LA while we collaborated on the book, well away from Ace Delaney's wrath, but she refused to leave. She was scared she'd be unable to buy the stuff elsewhere and I refused to try and find her any,' he added virtuously.

'Aw, Loretta Delaney was just another hooker who killed herself with drugs and alcohol – we've a dozen like her in the mortuary. If it weren't for her son we wouldn't be wasting time on her,' the captain decided. 'Let Delaney go. And Flanagan, too, when he's signed a statement.'

Ace left first, shielding his face from the photographers and ignoring the questions fired at him by the assembled Press. He was relieved to be free, but the matter wasn't finished, not so far as he was concerned.

'Can we stop the book?' he asked.

'We can try, but he might have already done a deal,' Larry pointed out.

'I doubt it. She was still holding out on him, wasn't she? Get him to come and see me, Larry.'

'What if he doesn't want to come?'

'Bribe him, blackmail him – what do I care?' Ace asked impatiently. 'He tried to set me up for a murder charge, and, if he didn't give Loretta the drugs that killed her, he certainly gave her the money to buy them. Threaten to tie him up in court for the next ten years, but also hint that I'm prepared to buy him off. Carrot and stick, Larry. Just get him to meet me.'

'Okay, I'll hang around here until they release him.' Larry sighed.

'Thanks. I don't suppose you know what happened to my car, do you?' Ace asked, resigned to hearing the worst. The odds on its still being in one piece in Mullaney Drive were about a million to one.

'Gail drove Johnny Dancer over to collect it – it's back at your house,' Larry told him.

'Great. I'm going home – I need a shower, a drink and a change of clothes. See you later, Larry.' He strode off and hailed a cab, breathing deeply of the smoggy, polluted but gloriously free air.

His house was empty, save for the couple who looked after the place, Maria and Raul, and Ace revelled in the solitude and comfort of his surroundings. Hell, that had been a close one! Only now could he let himself consider what might have happened.

After a long shower, he dressed in black jeans and a white silk shirt and wandered out on to the terrace, staring out at the ocean and swigging occasionally from a bottle of scotch. He waved Maria away when she offered food and remained outside, trying to unwind, but he was as tense as a virgin on her wedding night. If such a creature still existed, of course!

After a while he went to check if his Porsche had been damaged, but it was fine; even more amazingly, nothing was missing, not even the car phone or stereo. Presumably there had been too many cops milling around for anyone to risk going too near. He had Gail and Johnny to thank for that . . . His mouth twisted. He had guessed from their demeanour with him and their careful avoidance of each other that neither of them had been lonely during his trip to London. He had been with Stacey, of course, but he dismissed that as being irrelevant. He didn't appreciate it when someone who was supposed to be a friend tried to make a fool of him by sleeping with his girlfriend.

'Ace!' He spun around, a ready smile on his face at the sound of Jack's voice.

'Where have you . . .?' He stopped speaking, his expression hardening as he spotted Jack's companion. Alexa Kane. 'What the hell is she doing here?' he demanded harshly. It was the last straw for Alexa: she'd had a dreadful journey, alternately reliving the tense interview with her father, knowing he was both angry and disappointed with her, and dreading the ordeal of confessing her crime to the LAPD. Ace had still been in custody when Jack had collected her from the airport, so they had gone straight to the precinct, Alexa quaking with fear. Fortunately, Larry Knight had spotted them and assured them her confession was no longer necessary. Now she had come here, at Jack's insistence, and all Ace could do was shout and glower at her. She burst into tears.

'Oh, God!' Ace turned away in disgust.

'You lousy ungrateful bastard,' Jack ground out. 'She came here to help you!'

'To help? Oh, sure,' Ace swivelled around to face them again. 'To gloat, more likely,' he sneered. 'Sorry, honey, the cops had to let me go – save your prison visiting for some other guy.'

'You're wrong,' Jack told him quietly. 'I phoned her and asked her to come and clear up the drugs bust, and she got on the first flight she could. I thought you would want to thank her. My mistake.' He turned and took hold of Alexa's hand. 'I'm flying on to San Francisco – do you want to come with me, or shall I take you to a hotel?' he asked gently.

'Oh, a hotel,' she decided; she couldn't bear to board another plane so soon, not even for the short hop to San Francisco.

'Don't be ridiculous; she can stay here,' Ace snapped.

'She's already seen how welcome she is,' Jack shot back.

'She'll stay here,' Ace insisted. 'Maria!' he yelled, and the housekeeper came running.

'Yes?'

'Take Miss Kane up to the guest room, will you? She'll be staying for a few days,' Ace said casually. A few days? Jack thought incredulously. He glanced from Ace to Alexa and back again, and decided not to interfere. Whatever was going on between these two – and he was certain there was something – would be better sorted out by themselves. He raised one eyebrow questioningly at Alexa, waiting for her to decide.

'Perhaps I'll just rest for a while,' she said, drooping with exhaustion. 'Then I'll book into a hotel later.' Ace shrugged and then ignored her, and began talking to Jack.

Maria led the way upstairs, casting curious glances at the girl treading wearily behind her. It was the first time a pretty young lady had stayed in the guest room. Alexa was too tired to notice either Maria's curiosity, or take in much of her surroundings, noting only that the house was cool and uncluttered, but expensively fitted and furnished. As Jack had on his first visit, she vaguely sensed the impersonality, as if Ace didn't intend putting down roots; the only personal touches came from his tennis trophies and photographs.

The guest room was plainly decorated, in cool greens and cream, with dark furniture – more suited to a man than a woman, but Alexa only noticed the large, comfortable bed which seemed to beckon to her. She barely waited for Maria to leave the room before she pulled off her outer clothes and almost fell into the welcoming softness of the bed.

When Ace looked in two hours later she was fast asleep, lying on her tummy with her cute backside sticking invitingly into the air. He watched her for several moments, wondering why she had come to help him. If, indeed, she had. She was such a devious little madam, she could have had an entirely different idea in mind, he thought. But he wanted to figure her out, for some reason he didn't even try to fathom, and that could take a while!

Stepping cautiously nearer the bed, he picked up the shoulder bag she had let drop to the floor and rifled the contents. His fingers closed over her passport and he drew it out, then backed out of the room, closing the door softly behind him.

He moved into his own bedroom and tossed the passport into a drawer, a slight smile curving his mouth. That would slow her up for a time! At the least, it would give Rose a much-needed break from her trouble-making, he excused himself.

'What have you got there?' Gail asked, startling him as she emerged, nude, from his bathroom, rubbing water from her hair with a towel. Taken by surprise, he merely glowered by way of reply, and she bit her lip, wondering if he had guessed about her dalliance with Johnny Dancer.

'Ace, honey, you're so tense,' she purred, going over to him and rubbing her splendid body against his. For once, he didn't react and she quickly unbuttoned his shirt and then his jeans, moving down his body, kissing and licking until he became erect.

She tried to draw him to the bed, but his hands remained firmly on her shoulders and she sank to her knees, taking him in her mouth and bringing him to orgasm. It took forever; her knees hurt and her jaw ached by the time he finally climaxed. She sat back on her heels and gazed up at him with a small smile of triumph on her face.

'Now it's my turn,' she said huskily.

'Go and ask Johnny Dancer – I'm not in the mood,' Ace said curtly. 'Get dressed and get out, and take all your belongings with you. Don't leave anything here as an excuse to come back,' he added, from past experience.

'You can't be jealous of Johnny!' Gail exclaimed, then her eyes narrowed to cat-like slits. 'It's not Johnny you're bothered about, is it? You want me out of the way because of that pale-faced waif you've installed in the guest room!'

'That "waif" happens to be a millionaire,' Ace said drily. 'You don't know what you're talking about – this has nothing to do with her. I just don't like sharing, that's all.'

'Huh!' Gail wasn't convinced, but she realized the futility of arguing with him. She made enough noise to wake the dead as she left, but Alexa didn't even stir.

Ace dined alone on the terrace with just the noise of the ocean and his own dark thoughts for company. What the hell was taking Larry so long? he wondered irritably, reaching for one of the cigarettes he had vowed to give up. I will quit, just as soon as all this is over, he promised himself, drawing smoke deep into his lungs.

He exhaled slowly, gazing up at the night sky; it was a clear night, the stars seemingly close enough to reach out and touch. May you get to heaven an hour before the devil even knows you're dead . . . He smiled slightly; that was the only way Loretta would ever get to heaven, probably the only way he would, too . . .

He stood up and began to pace restlessly, glancing at his watch at regular intervals. He hoped Larry could get his hands on all the material Flanagan had gathered. The empty tape recorder in the apartment haunted him; just what information had Loretta, drunk and high on drugs, spilled into that damned machine? Nothing that would make pleasant reading, that much was certain, but he could live with that, just so long as it wasn't broadcast to the world. Why the hell is everyone so interested, anyhow? he glowered. Why couldn't people just accept that he had pulled himself out of the gutter and not try to drag him back down again?

At nine, Larry finally phoned.

'Where the hell are you?' Ace growled.

'In a bar. Flanagan's with me. He's really scared of meeting you and flatly refuses to come out to the house. I've hinted you might pay him to scrap the book, and he's interested in a deal. The publishers he approached have all dropped out now because of the bad publicity surrounding Loretta's death.'

'Good,' Ace grunted.

'Can you come and join us? We're at the Shamrock, on Penfold.'

'I know it. Okay, I'll be there in fifteen minutes,' Ace said. He snatched up his car keys and left at once.

The moment he entered the Shamrock, he spotted Flanagan and realized that he was, as Larry had said, terrified. The man looked even more ferret-like than usual, his eyes darting nervously from Ace to the open doorway, as if prepared to bolt. Which he was. He almost wished the police had charged him and locked him up; meeting Ace Delaney after trying to set him up for murder was not exactly a bright idea. Only greed kept him in his seat; that, and Larry Knight's presence.

'What can I get you to drink?' Larry asked Ace.

'Nothing; it's not a social call,' he said, glaring at Flanagan. Besides, he could do without the cops pulling him over for drink-driving. 'I want all the tapes, computer disks, typed manuscript . . . whatever material he has,' Ace said, speaking as if Flanagan weren't there, which suited the journalist just fine. 'I also want a signed guarantee that he's handed over everything, plus a pledge never to write so much as a paragraph about me in the future, or to pass on information to any of his colleagues. Tie him up in knots, Larry – if he steps out of line, he'll be in court for the rest of his life. Which won't necessarily be a long time,' he added, with a casualness that fooled no one.

'Leave it to me,' Larry nodded. He coughed, then, 'Money?' he ventured. Ace hesitated, his lips tightening to a thin, cruel line. Until this moment, he had been prepared to buy Flanagan's co-operation, but now he just couldn't do it. He would prefer to set fire to a stack of thousand-dollar bills than to hand over a cent to this creep, even though his refusal to pay increased the chances of a double-cross at some time in the future.

'He gets nothing. He's out of jail and healthy, which is more than he deserves,' he said flatly. 'If he wants to stay that way, he'll sign whatever you tell him to and he'll keep out of my way. He can count himself lucky I'm not hauling him into court for causing Loretta's death and setting me up to take the blame for it. I could sue him for every dime he has if I felt like it,' he finished, his jet-black eyes glittering with menace. Flanagan shot a reproachful glance at Larry, who had promised payment, but wisely remained silent. Loretta Delaney's death had shaken him badly; he knew he was lucky to be out of it with his skin intact.

Ace fixed Flanagan with another steely glare, then turned on his heel and walked out. Larry rushed after him.

'Ace, I think you're making a mistake . . .' he began.

'You do?' Ace enquired politely. Too politely.

'Well, yes. He's not going to stay scared forever,' Larry pointed out.

'He will for as long as it takes to hand over his material and for you to get that signed guarantee,' Ace said. 'Get on with it, Larry,' he added impatiently, turning once more to leave.

'Okay,' Larry sighed, and watched him go. He hadn't bothered asking what Ace wanted to do about his mother's funeral arrangements, or about her effects. 'Deal with it, Larry,' he muttered out loud. Not for the first time, nor for the last, he suspected, he wondered if the retainer Ace paid him was worth all the hassle. One thing was certain, though – life was never boring with Ace Delaney as a client!

Alexa slept soundly until morning, and woke to find a tray of freshly squeezed orange juice and warm croissants by her bed. There was also a scribbled note from Ace: 'Stick around and I'll take you sightseeing later.' Short and fairly sweet, she thought, swinging her legs off the bed.

Maria heard the sound of the shower and began preparing a more substantial breakfast. When Alexa emerged from the bedroom she followed the delicious aroma of fresh coffee down to the large, sunny kitchen.

'You look rested,' Maria noted approvingly; Alexa looked nothing like the wan, exhausted girl who had arrived the day before.

'Yes, I feel much better,' Alexa told her, sitting down and tucking hungrily into a fluffy omelette and home-baked bread rolls, washed down with gallons of strong black coffee.

'I unpacked and hung up your clothes to save them getting creased,' Maria continued. 'And the suit you were wearing yesterday is at the cleaners – I'll collect if for you tomorrow.'

'Oh. Thank you, that was kind of you, but I'm not staying here,' Alexa said quickly. 'I didn't even intend staying overnight. I have to find a hotel.'

'Mr Delaney said I was to make you comfortable here,' Maria said, beginning to look distressed, as if Ace's word was law around here, which it probably was, Alexa thought. 'Is there anything else I can do for you?' Maria asked anxiously.

'No, everything's fine,' Alexa assured her, wondering if Ace would sack the poor woman if he didn't have his own way.

She finished her late breakfast and, as she still felt a little tired after the flight, decided to do nothing more strenuous than stroll along the beach. She was a little wary of venturing into LA by herself – one read about so much crime here – but the beach looked safe and peaceful enough; joggers were out in force and there were couples taking a leisurely walk, hand in hand. But first she phoned England, and luckily spoke to Rose, not her father.

'We heard Ace was released from prison; it's a pity you had to make the journey for nothing,' Rose said.

'I expect he's very grateful, though,' she prattled on happily.

'Er, yes,' Alexa grimaced, remembering his less than polite greeting. 'I'm whacked after the flight, so I thought I'd stay on for a couple of days,' she said casually. 'Jack suggested I visit San Francisco while I'm here,' she added, even more casually, and wondered why she felt the need to imply she was still in Jack's company.

'Good idea,' Rose agreed. 'The weather's foul here, and I'm really missing Kit,' she went on gloomily. 'I hope Jack and Lisa won't be away for too long.' Alexa rolled her eyes and ended the call as soon as she could, and pretended not to hear Rose asking which hotel she was booked into.

She was strangely excited by the prospect of Ace's return, nervous too, lest this be another wind-up. Maria had told her he was filming an episode of *Country Club*, and she wondered if he intended taking her to the film studio. She dressed carefully in a cream linen suit and emerald-green silk shirt, which emphasized the red glints in her hair and accentuated her green-gold eyes, then sat on the terrace and tried to read while she awaited his arrival.

'Hi, honey, I'll be with you in a sec,' Ace appeared and disappeared so quickly she almost missed him. He was later than he had expected; Gail had been a bitch all day, acting up . . . no, definitely not acting, he amended silently. She had deliberately messed up their scenes together, piqued because he had thrown her out of the house the night before. Johnny Dancer had been tense and uptight, too, and they had needed retake after retake – and they were already behind schedule because of Ace's arrest.

He showered quickly and changed into scruffy jeans and T-shirt, and pushed his feet into worn trainers before bounding back downstairs and outside.

'C'mon, honey,' he instructed, leading the way to a battered old truck, not his gleaming black Porsche. Alexa came to an abrupt halt and eyed him suspiciously.

'We're going sightseeing in . . . that?' she queried.

'Yep. If you want to go shopping on Rodeo Drive or to gawp at the Hollywood homes of the stars, you'll have to go alone,' he told her. 'Today I want you to meet a few people.'

'Oh, yes?' she said, still wary. 'Am I suitably dressed?' she asked.

Ace eyed her thoughtfully, belatedly realizing she looked too well-groomed and wealthy for what he had in mind.

'Not really, no, but I don't have time to wait while you change. Don't you have any running shoes?'

'Not here, no. Why do I need running shoes?'

'To run, of course!' Ace grinned. 'You'll do,' he decided, and pushed her into the truck. There were several tennis rackets on the seat, and a box of new balls, which she had to move before being able to sit down. She wasn't at all sure she should be going along with this, but he seemed to be in such a good mood she was loath to risk spoiling it. She just wished she could be sure she wasn't about to become the butt of another of his jokes.

'I really did fly over here to confess I planted the drugs, not to gloat,' she told him earnestly, hoping to win some Brownie points. He nodded.

'I know; Jack put me straight on that. I appreciate it,' he said, casually, but with the devastating smile that could weaken knicker-elastic at a hundred paces.

Alexa swallowed painfully and turned her head away; the smile had relaxed her fears but caused alarm of a different nature. He's out of my league, she thought despairingly, cringing at the very thought of the contempt with which he would regard her if he ever attempted to treat her as a desirable woman. Unless she was drunk at the time, of course; that helped, a little, but never enough, and certainly not with a man like Ace Delaney.

She forced herself to stop brooding and looked around her with interest as he drove. She had been too tired, and too apprehensive about her interview with the police, to take much notice of her surroundings during the journey from the airport with Jack.

But soon her interest changed to dismay and then to downright horror as the wide freeways and modern skyscrapers gave way to crowded streets and dilapidated buildings, with smashed windows and covered in graffiti.

'Not exactly Knightsbridge, is it?' Ace asked, evidently amused by her shocked silence.

She shook her head and glanced at him worriedly. What on earth would she do if he threw her out of the truck and left her in this slum? Was this where he used to live? she suddenly wondered. At least he can't be taking me home to meet his mother, she thought, with black humour born of near hysteria. She was becoming more frightened with every passing mile, and the next horrific sight made her scream out loud.

'What the . . .?' Ace accelerated instead of braking. 'What the hell was that for?' he demanded, glancing in the rear-view mirror and seeing nothing untoward. He had expected a gun-toting crack addict at the very least from the noise she had made.

'Rats!' Alexa shuddered violently, feeling sick.

'Two-legged or four?' Ace enquired, matter-of-factly.

'Four, of course! Huge black things . . .' She almost retched.

'That's okay, then, It's the two-legged variety you have to watch out for around here,' he informed her cheerfully.

'You're a riot,' she told him dourly.

'Don't even think that word in this neighbourhood!' Ace exclaimed, in mock horror. He laughed at the expression on her face and she glared at him, still shaken, then gave a reluctant grin.

'How did you and Jack come to be partners?' she asked curiously. 'You're an unlikely pair. If you don't mind my saying so,' she added hastily, still not too sure he wouldn't leave her in this dreadful place to find her own way back to civilization.

'I don't mind; it's been said before,' Ace shrugged. 'I'd have agreed with you at one time. I'd been on the tour for about four years when Jack appeared on the scene, wet behind the ears. He had heard about my unsavoury reputation, of course.' He cast a sly glance at Alexa before continuing, 'And I thought he was just another stuffed-shirt Englishman – it's the snooty accent that does it,' he added, with another sideways glance.

'Jack doesn't have an accent,' Alexa demurred, in almost the same British upper class clipped tones as the Farrells. Ace grinned and shook his head slightly. 'Sorry, go on.'

'We were both at a tournament in Chicago – my regular Doubles partner injured his back in practice and I needed a replacement, quickly. Jack was available, so I asked him to join forces. We won the tournament, which was a pretty amazing feat for two guys who had never played together before, so we decided to continue the partnership. After that first victory, we went out to celebrate and I discovered he wasn't such a kid after all. He knew how to party, without any guidance from me.'

He lapsed into a thoughtful silence, remembering the mounting tally of titles they had accumulated; the good times, both on and off the court. Most commentators of the sport would say that he, Ace, had been the dominant partner, the player with the greater talent, but Ace disputed that – if only to himself! He knew that, without Jack's steadying influence and easygoing good humour, he would probably have let drugs, booze and women drag him down and cut short his career.

'We're here.' He pulled the truck over to the side and stopped the engine. Alexa looked around her and caught the interested gaze of a group of teenagers lounging on the street corner. Ace picked up the rackets and balls and clambered out of the truck, with Alexa hastily scrambling after him. She followed in his footsteps, sticking as close to him as possible, for he suddenly seemed safe and strong and her only protection in an alien world. God help her!

As they rounded the corner, she saw a crowd of kids messing around on what looked to her to be a patch of waste ground; some were playing tennis or basketball, most just sitting around in small groups.

'Ace! Ace! I knew you'd come back!' A pretty, dark-haired girl pelted across the ground and flung herself at Ace. He laughed and caught her up in his arms, secretly delighted by her welcome.

'Ella! Pleased to see me, huh?'

'Oh, yes! I knew you'd be back. I've been practising every day, and doing the exercises you taught me,' she told him earnestly. Belatedly, she noticed Alexa and peeked at her, her brown eyes alight with curiosity and a little hostility.

'Hi.' She smiled, wanting to please Ace and trying not to feel overawed by Alexa's obviously expensive clothes or jealous of her apparent closeness to Ella's hero.

'Hello.' Alexa smiled politely.

'This is Ella Cortez. She's my star pupil,' Ace said, and Ella beamed her delight. 'I've been coaching some of these kids as part of my punishment for smuggling heroin,' he explained, deadpan.

'Oh.' Alexa flushed and bit her lip. 'Sorry,' she mumbled.

'Don't be. If not for you, I'd never have met this little treasure.' He smiled down at Ella and she gazed adoringly back at him.

'Oh,' Alexa repeated uncertainly. Surely he wasn't involved with this child? She was certainly a beauty, but . . . 'How old are you, Ella?' she asked pleasantly.

'Fifteen,' Ella told her.

'She's a little too old, of course,' Ace said, and Alexa's jaw dropped. He could see what she was thinking and his lips tightened in annoyance. Not even his worst enemy could accuse him of seducing under-age girls!

'Go and fetch Mike, will you, honey?' he asked Ella. 'Ask him if he'll look after Alexa while I coach you guys. I want to see how much you've improved while I've been away.'

'Okay.' She scampered off, ponytail flying behind her.

'Mike Elliott looks after these kids, and tries to keep them off the streets. You'll like him,' Ace told Alexa, rather coolly, she thought, and she sought to make amends.

'You're obviously doing a wonderful job here,' she enthused. 'Ella's very keen, isn't she?'

'Yeah, she soaks it up like a sponge and is prepared to practise all day. I thought about her a lot while I was in jail – I'd already considered sponsoring her, and I've decided to go ahead with it. If she fails, I can afford the loss, and if she succeeds, I make a profit. Either way, she'll have a chance to get away from here,' he said casually, as if what he was proposing was no big deal. Alexa mulled it over for a moment.

'Are you . . . repaying some sort of debt?' she hazarded a guess. 'Did someone give you a similar chance to get out of this neighbourhood? I am right in thinking you grew up here?'

'Not far away,' he nodded. 'And I guess someone did give me a chance – not intentionally, though. One of my mother's boyfriends –' his mouth twisted into a sneer at the word '– was a tennis player. Not a pro, just a keen amateur, and he paid for me to have lessons, merely to get me out of the apartment.' He paused, remembering, and a small, bitter smile played around his mouth. 'The women at the sports club were rich, bored and willing to pay for what they wanted – which was me. When Loretta's boyfriend was history, those women continued to pay my coaching fees, in return for certain favours, of course!'

'Oh, Ace,' Alexa said wretchedly.

'Don't you dare feel sorry for me!' he snapped, instantly regretting the confidence. 'I learned a lot, and I don't just mean tennis strokes! Ah, Mike.' He turned to Mike Elliott in relief.

'Glad to see you.' Mike shook his hand. 'Sorry about that dreadful business with your mother,' he said awkwardly.

'Thanks,' Ace shrugged off the sympathy. 'Look after Alexa for me, will you? And, Mike, I'd like to meet Ella's parents; I've a proposition to put to them.'

'Oh?' Mike guessed what it was; he was eager but still cautious. Although he had come to think that Ace's none too savoury reputation was somewhat exaggerated by the Press, Ella was an extremely pretty girl . . . He was reassured by Alexa's presence, though. 'She lives with her stepmother,' he told Ace. 'I think the mother died when she was a baby, and the father's not around any more,' he said, matter-of-factly. Absent fathers were not exactly a rarity.

'Fine. I'll talk to the stepmother. Arrange it, will you?' Ace asked, thinking she would probably be glad to be relieved of the responsibility of raising someone else's kid. 'Come on, Ella, let's get to work!'

# CHAPTER 9

Linda Cortez had heard nothing but, 'Ace says . . .' 'Ace thinks . . .' 'Ace is wonderful . . .' from Ella for weeks, and was heartily sick of the sound of his name.

The recent Press coverage of Loretta's death had been extensive, and the tabloid papers had rehashed old stories of Ace's conquests amongst the female tennis players and the groupies who followed the circuit, all of which fuelled her suspicions that Ace Delaney wasn't particularly interested in Ella's career, just her pretty face and nubile body.

She was therefore alarmed, rather than pleased, when Mike Elliott told her Ace wanted to discuss Ella's future with her, and was very much on the defensive, even when Ace arrived with a very glamorous and beautiful tawny-haired girl in tow.

Linda bristled with indignation when Alexa gazed around the poor but clean, apartment with barely concealed distaste. Ace nudged Alexa none too gently in the ribs.

'Can I get you some coffee?' Linda offered, rather stiffly.

'No, thanks,' Ace declined, with a warm smile that he realized at once was wasted on Linda Cortez.

She wasn't at all what he had expected; of course, Cortez was merely her married name, and she wasn't Ella's birth mother, but her pale blonde looks and extreme youth surprised him. She looked barely thirty, was small and slight, and could be pretty, he thought idly, his experienced eye ridding her of the dreadful, ill-fitting, shapeless clothing, imagining her elfin face made up to highlight her soft, large grey eyes, her silver-blonde hair let loose instead of being scraped severely back into a tight knot.

Of course, the husband was absent, Ace remembered; Linda probably didn't want to draw attention to herself. In fact, keeping Ella safe must be almost a full-time job, a job he was prepared to take over. What he wasn't prepared for was her resistance to the idea, a very generous and costly idea at that!

'Don't you want to get her away from this neighbourhood?' he demanded irritably. Linda drew herself up to all of her five feet three inches of height.

'She's doing fine,' she said, with dignity. 'She gets good grades at school and steers clear of the street gangs. She's never been in trouble with the police, or involved with drugs,' she added proudly, with a look that plainly said: unlike you! Mike Elliott hastily turned a laugh into a cough when Ace glared at him.

'Perhaps I'd better talk to her father after all,' Ace muttered to Mike, rather helplessly. He had expected this to be a pushover, a mere formality; had been sure Ella's stepmother would jump at the opportunity of a better life for Ella and to be relieved of the responsibility of caring for a teenage girl who wasn't even her own flesh and blood.

'Marcelo isn't here; he's in the military,' she said, as if that explained why she and Ella hadn't seen him at all for more than five years. At least he still sent money occasionally, so Linda counted herself luckier than most. 'I've looked after Ella since she was three years old. I'm not handing her over to you now,' she declared.

'I want to sponsor her, not adopt her!' Ace said, exasperated.

'Aw, Linda, please!' Ella begged. 'Mom,' she wheedled. Linda sighed.

'This tennis camp – where is it?' she asked Ace, making the words 'tennis camp' sound like 'brothel', he thought irritably.

'It's near Santa Barbara,' he said, as patiently as he could. 'Her education wouldn't suffer, but she needs the extensive coaching they offer if she's to make up for lost time. Evenings and weekends just aren't enough to bring her up to the required standard.'

'And what happens if I agree and she still doesn't come up to this standard?' Linda asked.

'She'll be no worse off than if she stays here,' Ace shrugged.

'That's not true. Coming back here with broken dreams would be harder than never going away,' Linda pointed out shrewdly.

'All the more incentive for her to work hard!' Ace snapped; he was becoming thoroughly fed up with her attitude. 'There are plenty of other kids I can sponsor . . .'

'No!' Ella's wail was one of pure anguish. Linda looked at her and bit her lip.

'I'm not sure,' she wavered.

'Look, why don't you and Ella come out to my place this weekend?' Ace suggested. 'My lawyer will draw up a contract . . .'

'Your lawyer?' Linda said doubtfully.

'Oh, for heaven's sake. Bring your own damned lawyer!' Ace bit out.

'I can't afford a lawyer . . . but, okay, we'll come,' she agreed, as if granting him a huge favour.

'Fine. I'll send a car to pick you up,' Ace said, deciding to let Larry Knight persuade the silly woman his offer was both genuine and generous. 'I'll see you tomorrow, as usual,' he added to Ella, as he got up to leave.

'Actually, you've already put in the number of hours the court decreed,' Mike told him.

'Have I?' Ace was surprised; it had seemed like a life sentence at the time. 'In that case, Ella can come out to my house after school – the court's better. Alexa will be there,' he added quickly to reassure Linda. Oh? Alexa thought. I'm here to play the part of chaperone, am I?

She put the question to Ace once they were back in the truck and heading, she hoped, for civilization. Where did these people go for a restful holiday – Beirut? She had to repeat the question, for Ace had lapsed into a brooding silence and didn't hear her. He regretted bringing Alexa along; regretted telling her so much about himself, showing her his lowly origins. He had divulged more of himself to her – a girl he didn't even like – than he could ever remember doing before. Except maybe when he'd been drunk.

'I said, am I here just to act as a chaperone for Ella?' Alexa raised her voice slightly. Ace seized the opportunity she had just handed him to put her back in her place.

'Of course,' he said coolly. 'I figured Mike Elliott would kick up a fuss if he thought Ella would be alone at my place. You can pretend to be my girlfriend when Linda comes over at the weekend,' he added.

'I'm not that good an actress,' Alexa bridled.

'I noticed. Did you have to make it so obvious to those people back there that you consider them beneath contempt?' he asked savagely.

'I . . . I'm sorry,' she stammered. 'I certainly didn't mean to upset anyone,' she faltered.

'I suppose you can't help being a snooty bitch,' he responded, and not another word passed between them for the rest of the journey.

Larry Knight was waiting at the house, and Ace quickly made it clear to Alexa that the conversation was to be private.

'I'm staying in this evening,' he told her brusquely. 'If you want to go out, phone Johnny Dancer – he likes being seen in all the smart places.'

'I'd prefer to stay here,' Alexa demurred.

'Suit yourself. Maria will get you something to eat.' He nodded dismissively, and went to pour drinks for himself and Larry, excluding Alexa, and she went miserably to her room. Perhaps she should phone Johnny? Or go to a hotel? Anything other than stay where she wasn't welcome. But she did neither.

'So. How's it going?' Ace asked Larry, when they were seated.

'Great,' Larry said, with satisfaction. 'Thomas Flanagan came in to my office this afternoon, still subdued, I'm glad to say. Here,' he pulled a copy of a twenty-page contract from his pocket and handed it to Ace, 'If he so much as mentions your name in public we can haul his ass into court!'

'Good.' Ace glanced briefly at the contract, then put it aside. 'And the material for the book?' he asked casually, only the tight grip on his glass betraying his tension.

'It's all in the trunk of my car. There's a ton of the stuff,' Larry said ruefully. Ace's eyebrows shot up.

'He has been busy,' he remarked lightly.

'Most of it is just old Press clippings, I think. I didn't look closely,' he added hastily. 'And no one from my office has seen any of it.' Ace nodded his approval.

'The tapes?' he enquired next, topping up both Larry's glass and his own.

'There are five of them. Again, I haven't checked them, but Flanagan told me a couple are question-and-answer sessions with Loretta, and the others he left with her for her to use when she was alone.'

'Mmm,' was all Ace said to that. His flesh crawled just imagining what drunken revelations were on those tapes. He forced himself to relax; they belonged to him now. 'Before you go, Larry, there's another contract I want to discuss,' Ace continued, and briefly outlined his plans for Daniella Cortez.

'Is she pretty, this Ella?' Larry asked, with a grin. Ace shook his head slightly; talk about giving a dog a bad name!

'Of course; I wouldn't be interested otherwise,' he drawled, and Larry started to look a little uncomfortable.

'If she's only fifteen . . .' he began.

'Oh, don't be such an idiot!' Ace exclaimed. 'The pretty girls on the tour earn far more than their butch counterparts. They get around five times as much in endorsements as they do in prize money. Right now, there's plenty of room for another beauty – Melissa Farrell has already retired and Lucia Conti has said that this will be her last year on the tour.'

'Oh, I see,' Larry looked relieved. 'Right. I'll get on with it tomorrow,' he said, getting to his feet. 'Thanks for the drink.'

Ace accompanied him to his car and removed the box that contained the details of his life from the trunk.

'Goodnight, Larry,' he said, and carried the box back to the terrace. He poured himself another scotch and sat back to drink it slowly, for once uncertain as to what he should do. It would be sensible to burn the whole lot without even glancing at it, he thought. But, contract notwithstanding, Thomas Flanagan's memory hadn't been erased and it would be prudent for Ace to know the secrets – whether they be true or alcohol-induced fantasies – that his mother had confided.

Forewarned was forearmed; at least there would be no unpleasant shocks awaiting him in the future if Flanagan pushed his luck and printed part of Loretta's story. Ace would be surprised if the creep hadn't retained copies, just in case an opportunity arose for him to use them, at some later date.

Eventually, he tore open the sealed box; the five small tapes were in a separate container and he realized at once that he couldn't listen to them now even if he wanted to, as they were too small to be played on his own cassette deck. With a sense of having been reprieved, he locked them away in the safe in his bedroom, together with the computer disks. He put aside the stack of typescript and settled back to read through the mass of Press cuttings, already sorted methodically into chronological order, which spanned his career in the public eye.

He read with interest the earlier ones, most of which he was seeing for the first time, and grimaced at photographs of the seventeen-year-old new kid on the tennis block. His arrival on the tour had initially been greeted with enthusiasm; his looks and flamboyant style of play quickly earned him an army of fans, mostly female, and the Press had hailed him as a welcome breath of fresh air into a sport that some denounced as boring.

But the media loved to put someone on a pedestal for the sheer hell of then knocking him off it, and after a while the tenor of their articles became disapproving, citing his outbursts on court, his drunken orgies off it . . .

'Orgies?' Ace murmured, with a grin. Did three in a bed count as an orgy? He couldn't remember anything more outrageous than that.

Absently, he moved his chair nearer to the light and continued reading; of his triumphs and disasters, thankfully the former outnumbered the latter; of his Doubles partnership with Jack Farrell; of the seemingly endless procession of women in and out of his life, well, in and out of his bed . . . He felt exhausted just reading about it!

Perhaps, one day, he ought to have someone he trusted write all this down, he thought idly – it would be a best-seller! He put aside the clippings to pick up the partially completed manuscript. The early chapters were barely begun, but the later ones were almost complete, covering much of what Ace had just been reading, only Flanagan had portrayed him in the worst possible light, he noticed, his mouth tightening in annoyance. Each story had been slanted in favour of Ace's disgruntled beaten tennis opponents, or his dumped girlfriends.

At the very end, there was an index of Ace's lovers; he ran his finger down the long list, frowning in an effort to remember some, smiling in fond memory of others. Both Melissa and Rose Farrell were listed, although there was a question mark against Rose's name, Ace noticed, with a satisfied smile.

He turned his attention, finally and reluctantly, to the early part of his life, the years of poverty before he had become a success. Flanagan had talked to his neighbours, and even schoolteachers, but had learned little, it seemed. Loretta Delaney had arrived in the neighbourhood thirty years before with a small child and no husband. Big deal.

Flanagan had obviously asked Loretta repeatedly for the name of Ace's father and evidently received no satisfactory reply. Across one printed page, he had scored, so heavily he had ripped the paper, 'the bitch is holding out on me!!' Ace laughed out loud at that. No doubt Loretta either didn't know the answer, or was indeed holding out for more money, but Ace decided to give her the benefit of the doubt and assume that a belated sense of loyalty to her son had stilled her tongue.

'Way to go, Mom,' he said softly.

He burned the typescript, but kept the Press cuttings and, with the tapes securely locked away, decided to forget about it for a while and go out for a drink and some company. Briefly he considered inviting Alexa to join him, but decided against it, for a reason he couldn't quite explain. He just felt the need to put her firmly back in her place, an uninvited and not very welcome guest, here only to act as a chaperone to Ella, and that only until after Linda Cortez had signed the necessary paperwork to give him control of Ella's future.

He didn't return until the early hours of the morning; three forty-five to be precise. Alexa knew to the second, because she had been unable to sleep, wondering miserably what she had done wrong. Just for a while, Ace had seemed to like her company; he'd been open and friendly, but then she had obviously done or said something to ruin everything and he had reverted to the sarcasm and coldness she hated. Was it just because she had been unable to hide her distaste for the slums? Did he feel her reaction was a personal insult? It never occurred to her that he regretted confiding even a small part of his young life to her; that he rarely mentioned to anyone the bleakness of his childhood, let alone took them on a guided tour . . .

Ella arrived late the following afternoon. Initially she seemed a little overawed by her surroundings, and, as Ace hadn't yet returned from filming for the day, evidently felt free to display her hostility towards Alexa.

'Are you living with Ace?' she demanded, rather rudely. Alexa raised a disdainful eyebrow at her tone, but answered calmly, as it was obvious the poor girl had a huge crush on Ace.

'Only very temporarily, and not in the way you mean – I'm sleeping in the guest room,' she told her.

'Oh.' Ella lost her scowl and smiled sunnily instead. 'Isn't this a great place?' she enthused. 'And look – he's got a lobster machine!' she exclaimed ecstatically, and raced from the terrace at breakneck speed to the tennis court below.

'A what?' Alexa frowned, thinking of seafood for dinner. But the machine in question turned out to be a contraption that, when switched on, lobbed tennis balls in all directions and at varying speeds, enabling a player to practise alone.

Ella quickly figured out how to use it, and was soon blasting balls all over the court. Alexa remained in the comfort of the terrace and watched idly while sipping coffee. Alexa hadn't picked up a tennis racket in years, not since her schooldays, but she thought Ella seemed very proficient, and far stronger than she looked. Her long, skinny legs carried her swiftly around the court and her thin arms and delicate wrists belted the ball with a surprising amount of power.

Despite concentrating on her tennis, Ella spotted Ace before Alexa was even aware of his arrival, and she dashed to greet him, her large brown eyes bright with adoration.

'The machine's great, but will you come and practise with me?' she pleaded.

'Sure. Just give me a couple of minutes to get changed,' he said amiably. 'Alexa,' his tone changed imperceptibly; became harder, colder, 'make yourself useful and pick up all those loose balls, will you? In fact, you can be our ball-girl,' he added. She sensed he expected her to refuse, so she smiled sweetly instead and got to her feet.

'I'd be happy to,' she lied.

In fact, she quite enjoyed herself, and was soon relieved to have been assigned such a lowly task, thereby escaping Ace's bullying. He yelled at Ella constantly, finding fault and belittling her efforts. Alexa was surprised Ella didn't either burst into tears or break her racket over his head. Or both.

But the youngster gritted her teeth and took everything Ace threw at her, even when her body ran with perspiration and her face was scarlet from her exertions. Her breathing became so laboured that Alexa feared she might suffer a heart attack. Ace, of course, looked as cool as when they had started; he worked harder than this when merely warming up before a match.

'Okay, that's enough for today,' Ace finally decided, and Ella flopped to the ground in exhaustion. Alexa heaved a sigh of relief, too; she was worn out from simply picking up the discarded balls! After checking to make sure Ace wasn't watching her, she rubbed at her aching back and the backs of her thighs, which had been complaining ever more insistently at the constant bending and stretching.

'You're doing really well.' Ace at last bestowed some praise and encouragement on his pupil. 'You've improved immensely these past few weeks.'

'I have?' Ella immediately perked up, and bounced back to her feet. 'I can come tomorrow, can't I? All day? It's Saturday,' she reminded him.

'Sure you can. And don't forget to bring your stepmother – my lawyer has a contract for her to sign. She *is* your legal guardian, isn't she?'

'I guess so.' Ella shrugged, unconcerned. 'She signs stuff for school; anyway, there isn't anyone else – we haven't seen my dad for years,' she added cheerfully.

'That's fine,' said Ace, rather vaguely. 'I'm going to take a shower – Alexa, show Ella where she can freshen up, will you?' he asked. 'Then I'll take you both out for a meal – okay?'

'Oh, thank you!' Ella beamed, and sighed wistfully as Ace disappeared from her view. 'He's terrific, isn't he?' she asked Alexa.

'He has his moments,' Alexa agreed drily. 'Come with me – you can use my bathroom,' she said, and led the way upstairs. She noticed that Ella hadn't brought a change of clothes with her, and rummaged through her own garments, wishing she had the vast contents of her wardrobes at home at her disposal, but eventually finding a short black skirt and a fuchsia top which fitted well enough.

'This is all like a dream come true – I can't wait to go to the tennis academy and play every day,' Ella confided, completely won over by Alexa's non-girlfriend status and the loan of the lovely clothes.

'Won't you have any regrets about leaving your friends?' Alexa asked.

'No, not really,' Ella said honestly. 'I don't like leaving Linda, though. She'll be all alone,' she said sadly. Alexa nodded and repressed a shudder at the memory of the cheerless apartment the Cortez family called home.

'That top looks better on you than on me – you can keep it if you like,' she offered casually.

'*Thank* you! It's lovely!' Ella smiled broadly, and told Ace about her gift when they met up downstairs. Alexa hadn't made the gesture to earn herself Brownie points with Ace, but the look he bestowed upon her was warmer than any she could remember, and once again she found herself wishing she could magically transport all her clothes from Eaton Square to give to this young girl. I'm as pathetic as she is where Ace is concerned, she thought disgustedly; since when had she wanted or needed his approval?

Alexa saw a different side to Ace that evening, when he took her and Ella to an unpretentious pizza parlour to dine. He was in a rare good humour, and took time to scribble autographs and chat to the young girls – and often their mothers, too – who approached their table.

He and Ella did most of the talking, mainly about tennis, but Alexa wasn't in the least bored. She found herself listening as avidly as Ella to his stories of life on the tour, most of which were scandalous, some downright libellous, but all of them entertaining.

However, she was careful to school her features, afraid she might be wearing the same look of adoration on her face as the younger girl. I do hope she achieves her dreams, she thought, and said as much to Ace, when they had taken Ella home and were heading back to the ocean.

'She'd better; she's going to cost me a fortune over the next couple of years,' he said, matter-of-factly. 'After that, I hope to see a return on my investment.'

'Investment? You're not helping her to make money for yourself, are you?' Alexa asked, rather taken aback.

'Of course. Why else?' he asked carelessly.

'Oh.' She sat back, feeling strangely disillusioned, which was a strange emotion when she had never harboured any illusions about him to start with! 'You said you were repaying some sort of debt . . .' she began. Ace laughed derisively; he still deeply regretted those confidences.

'You really ought to stop being so gullible,' he said easily, and she bit her lip.

'But Ella thinks you're helping her out of the goodness of your heart,' she told him earnestly. 'And she has an enormous crush on you.'

'I know. She'll work all the harder because of it, just to please me,' he said, with a complacency that made her seethe.

'I think I'll book a flight home,' she broke the suddenly strained silence.

'Okay.' Ace shrugged indifferently, but shot her a sideways glance. Evidently she hadn't yet noticed her passport was missing. He still wasn't sure what had prompted him to steal it, but, for some reason he didn't try to explain, he didn't replace it . . .

* * *

On Saturday, Ella arrived early with Linda in tow. The latter was still wary about Ella's seemingly too-good-to-be-true fortune, but a comforting chat with Larry Knight won her over. The lawyer was homely, middle-aged and respectable – everything Ace wasn't. With a final stipulation that she should visit the academy personally, she and Ella signed the contract Larry had drawn up, which effectively gave Ace control over Ella's life.

'Hal Renwick will look after her – he's a real good guy,' Ace told Linda: it was true enough, but Ace didn't add that he considered the man a wimp, and that he was confident his own ideas for Ella's career would take precedence. So far as Ace was concerned, Hal was little more than a babysitter, admittedly one who could play and teach tennis, until Ace felt Ella was ready to join the circuit as a professional player.

'Hal Renwick will coach me?' Ella exclaimed joyously. 'He's Jack Farrell's brother-in-law, and he coached Melissa for a while,' Ella told Linda. 'Oh, I do hope I'll be as good as Melissa one day,' she sighed.

'Ella's a huge fan of Melissa's,' Ace explained, unnecessarily, to Alexa.

'Aren't we all?' she responded, rather tartly, and received a sharp look from Ace. Retaliation was swift.

'Have you booked your flight yet?' he rapped out.

'Er – no,' she flushed slightly. 'You wanted me to be here today for Linda's peace of mind,' she reminded him.

'So I did.' He stood up and stretched; the movement pulled his sleeveless T-shirt taut across his muscular chest. Alexa found herself, somewhat reluctantly, admiring his physique. Despite his hedonistic lifestyle, he kept in great shape; his body was still as lean and hard as in the heyday of his career as a top athlete.

'Come on, Ella, let's get back to work,' he called, and she jumped up and followed at his heels like an eager puppy.

Larry took his leave soon after, and Alexa found herself alone with Linda. The conversation was stilted, as the two women had absolutely nothing in common. Linda felt rather in awe of the younger, beautiful and obviously wealthy girl, and resented feeling that way. Alexa's cut-glass English accent made her seem haughty to the American, even when Alexa was trying to be pleasant.

Linda, rather stiffly, thanked Alexa for the silk top she had given Ella the evening before.

'It was nothing,' Alexa tried to shrug off the gesture, which was a mistake, as Linda had never before seen material so fine.

'I suppose you're a model, are you?' Linda asked.

'Good grief, no!' Alexa laughed.

'So what do you do?' Linda persisted.

'Er – nothing, really,' Alexa confessed. 'How about you?'

'I work as a waitress.'

'Oh.' How dreary, Alexa thought, but luckily didn't say so. She stared down at the court, debating whether to go and offer her services as ball-girl. Raul had been performing the task, but he seemed to have disappeared. She shaded her eyes with her hand, searching for him, and spotted another figure in the distance, strolling along the beach towards the house.

'Oh, look! There's Johnny Dancer!' she exclaimed. The arrival of another rich celebrity was too much for Linda and she fled into the house, mumbling something about preparing cold drinks for the players on court.

Johnny paused to speak to Ace, then bounded up the stone steps to the terrace. He grinned broadly at Alexa, recognizing her from his trip to London, and pulled up a chair after helping himself to a drink.

He was even more tanned than when she had met him at Christmas, and the tight black jeans and loose white shirt, open at the throat, enforced her impression that he resembled a pirate. He still wore a full black beard and his hair was longer, brushing against his collar.

'I'm having a party tonight – I've just invited Ace; I'm trying to make amends for Gail!' He flashed a sparkling white grin.

'Who's Gail?' Alexa frowned.

'Ace's girlfriend. Or, at least, she was. I'm afraid she and I became a little too friendly while Ace was in England!' He grinned again, obviously unrepentant. 'He chucked her out, the night he got out of jail.'

'Oh.' Alexa nodded slowly. His first choice of chaperone had cheated on him, hence her own invitation to stay. 'I see,' she said tightly.

'So. The party – do you wanna come?'

'I . . .' Her gaze slid past him to Ace.

'You don't need his permission, do you? He's just told me there's nothing going on between you two,' Johnny told her.

'That's right; there's nothing,' Alexa confirmed quickly.

'I'm glad to hear it, because I've already trodden on his turf once and I'd hate to do it again – I want to live!' he proclaimed dramatically, and Alexa smiled. 'Although, on second thoughts, I think you would be worth the risk,' he added softly, with a soulful glance from twinkling brown eyes. 'So. You'll come?'

'Yes, I'd love to,' Alexa decided. 'When and where?'

'Whenever you want. Just follow the sound of champagne corks popping and music from over there.' He pointed in the direction from which he had come. 'My house is the next one along – you can't miss it.'

She mentioned the party to Ace later, and was stung by his indifference.

'Fine. Enjoy yourself,' he said curtly.

'Won't you be coming too?'

'Doubt it,' he said, with no explanation as to where he might be instead.

'Did anyone ever tell you you're a lousy host?' she snapped.

'Only to uninvited guests!' he shot back. 'Have you booked your flight yet? Linda's signed the contract, so there's no need for you to stay any longer.'

'No, none at all,' she agreed. 'Perhaps Johnny will give me a bed for the night, and I'll return to England tomorrow,' she added, before storming off to shower and change.

She hadn't brought any clothes suitable for a showbiz party and had to settle for a simple, black slinky number and lots of gold jewellery, but felt quite satisfied with her appearance. She looked elegant, in an understated way; the severity of the black threw into contrast the shining tawny mane of hair, and her make-up was dramatic, emphasizing the cat-green of her eyes. The house was deserted when she returned downstairs. Raul and Maria had the night off, and she supposed Ace was driving Linda and Ella home before going on to do whatever he had planned for the evening. She was hurt by his refusal to accompany her to the party, and by his obvious desire to be rid of her now that Linda Cortez had signed the contract. But what had she expected? He had always made it perfectly plain he considered her a complete waste of space. She'd bet she was the only woman who had ever slept in his guest room instead of sharing his. She didn't want to sleep with him, of course; the very idea terrified her, but it would have been nice to be asked!

She was more than a little nervous of arriving at any party by herself, let alone one hosted by Johnny Dancer and attended by other celebrities, but set out determined to enjoy herself.

A string of coloured lights blazed brightly around Johnny's house and down to the beach, illuminating the path she had to follow. Soon, she could hear voices, laughter and music, then loud shrieking as a naked man chased an equally naked girl into the ocean. Alexa almost turned around to retrace her steps, but she hated to sit at home, docilely awaiting Ace's return, as if she had nothing better to do with her time.

'Hi, gorgeous!' She jumped when a strong arm snaked around her waist, then relaxed as she recognized Johnny. 'Ace not with you?' he asked casually.

'No, I don't know where he is,' she replied truthfully.

'Ah, well, who needs him?' Johnny grinned. 'Come on, honey, let me get you a drink and show you around.' He led her into the house, which was not at all like Ace's modern clean-cut structure, but built in a Spanish-hacienda style that she liked.

Johnny put a glass of champagne into her hand and kept refilling it as the evening wore on. He was intrigued by Alexa; so stunning and sexy, but somehow aloof. And he would dearly love to know the real story about her and Ace, and why she had planted drugs in his luggage.

'I was real sorry we didn't get together while I was in London,' he told her, as they swayed to the music. He dropped a light kiss on her shoulder and grabbed a bottle of champagne from a waiter to top up her glass once more. 'Why don't we leave this rabble and find somewhere private?' he suggested huskily. Alexa hesitated, then thought of Ace, no doubt 'somewhere private' with a woman, and she nodded.

## CHAPTER 10

Ace could hear the distant sounds of revelry as he sat on the terrace, listening to the soothing, peaceful swell of the ocean waves lapping at the shore. Or, at least, he was trying to, he thought irritably, as someone turned up the volume of Johnny's powerful music system, yet again.

'I must be getting old!' he muttered. 'I'll be calling the cops next to complain about the noise!' He lit and then stubbed out a cigarette – he was still smoking too many, but he certainly dared not risk keeping any illegal substances in the house. He felt the local cops would turn over his place for drugs any time they got bored. Damn Alexa! It was all her fault, he brooded. The little green-eyed witch was getting under his skin, and he didn't like it, not one bit.

He couldn't understand his own actions – why didn't he either bed her or send her packing back to London? He shied away from the former, sensing she was too emotionally insecure for the uncomplicated it's-been-great-but-now-it's-over type of relationship he preferred. So why was she still here? And why was her passport still hidden in his bedroom?

Linda Cortez's suspicions had been allayed, the contract had been signed, but all that had been an excuse, he was well aware of that; he just didn't understand *why*?

After a while, he decided to go along to Johnny's party, after all, but had only walked a few yards along the beach when a slight figure, dressed in black and sobbing uncontrollably, cannoned into him. Alexa!

'Hey, steady on!' Ace grabbed hold of her arms and she screamed, then began flailing at him with her fists.

'Let me go!'

'Fine.' He dropped his hands and she lost her balance, toppling backwards to land in an ungainly heap on the sand. She made no attempt to rise and Ace stared at her, for once feeling helpless in a situation with a woman.

'What's the matter?' he asked, quite kindly, and hunkered down beside her.

'I hate men!' she said vehemently.

'Is that why you dress like a high-class hooker and apply make-up with a trowel?' he asked interestedly. Alexa glared at him murderously.

'I hate all men, but I especially hate you!' she hissed.

'I'm not too fond of you, either,' he told her. 'But you already knew that, so why the tears? Did someone make the mistake of assuming you're an adult and make a pass at you?'

'More than a pass!' she spat. 'The men at that party – they're all pigs! Especially Johnny Dancer – your friend,' she emphasized, as if he were responsible for

Johnny's actions. Ace sighed and wondered briefly if he could phone Jack and ask him to come and take care of his soon-to-be stepsister. Perhaps not, he decided reluctantly; Jack had enough women problems of his own.

'Go indoors and have a glass of brandy,' he suggested. 'It will calm you down.' I hope.

'All right,' she agreed dully. She seemed to have lost all her spirit in an instant; the virago disappeared, leaving behind a trembling, tearful child. Ace stifled a sigh.

'Go on,' he urged. 'I'll be back in a minute.' He watched her trudge wearily towards the terrace – minus her shoes, he noticed. She seemed to make a habit of losing her shoes, he thought, or perhaps she had kicked them off in order to run away . . . His expression hardening, he swiftly covered the distance to Johnny's house. He had to step round couples lying on the beach in varying stages of undress, and reluctantly avoided the clutches of a stark naked voluptuous blonde who tried to latch on to him as soon as he walked into the house.

'Maybe later, honey,' he said, absently patting her backside, glancing around for a glimpse of Johnny. 'Hi, Jen,' he said, recognizing Jennifer Patterson, one of the PAs on *Country Club*. 'Have you seen Johnny recently?'

'He was in a clinch with someone – they were dancing, and then they went upstairs, I think,' she said.

'A slim girl, English, long reddish-gold hair and wearing a black dress?'

'Yeah, that sounds like her,' Jen nodded.

'Thanks.' Ace pushed his way towards the stairs. The bedrooms were all occupied, but not by Johnny. He declined several invitations to join in the fun and continued his search, and eventually found Johnny outside by the pool.

'Johnny! A word!' He jerked his head towards a quieter spot and stalked off.

'Sure.' Johnny took one look at his face and inwardly quailed. 'If it's about Alexa . . .' he began.

'It is. What did you do to her?' Ace demanded. 'She's hysterical, for God's sake!'

'Don't blame me. She's psychotic!' Johnny said disgustedly. 'She was coming on to me as if she'd not had a man in years! We went upstairs – she was still hot for it, and then suddenly she went nuts! Scratching and kicking like a wild animal! Look what she did to me!' He pointed to a deep scratch on his neck.

'More to the point – what did you do to her?' Ace asked grimly, not in the least concerned with Johnny's injury.

'I let her go, of course, and she ran out of the house.'

'That's it? You didn't force her?' Ace frowned, watching him closely for his reaction.

'I'm not that desperate! No, of course I didn't force her. But, if she carries on like that, one day she'll get more than she bargains for!'

'Maybe she already has,' Ace said thoughtfully, speaking half to himself. But that didn't make sense. If her looks and provocative behaviour had gotten her into trouble before, why would she persist? Was she one of those weirdos who led men on and then went running to the cops, crying rape? Oh, God, she's staying in my house! he thought, with a shudder. Twice already this year he had been hauled off to jail for crimes he hadn't committed – was Alexa after a hat-trick?

'Honestly, Ace, I didn't hurt her – I let go of her as soon as I realized she'd changed her mind,' Johnny said earnestly.

'Yeah, I believe you,' Ace nodded.

'Stay and have a drink?' Johnny suggested, relieved not to be on the receiving end of the notorious Delaney temper.

'No, thanks. I just want a quick word with Jennifer Patterson and then I'll be on my way.' Ace had remembered that, prior to *Country Club*, Jen had worked on a talk show, in which the great unwashed spilled out their secrets to the nation. He went in search of her and drew her aside.

'Jen – that talk show you worked on – you must have covered stories of people with sexual problems,' he said.

She choked on her drink. 'Not you?' She grinned. 'Now that would make an interesting programme!'

'No, of course it's not me!' he said impatiently. 'I'm talking about women with hang-ups about sex.'

'Yeah, we did loads of those. Why?' she asked curiously.

'Could you get me some tapes?' Ace ignored her question.

'Sure; I keep copies of all the shows I help produce,' she said proudly. 'But what specifically are we talking about here? Date rape? Child abuse? Did she see her parents screwing when she was three years old and still has nightmares about it? What?'

'I haven't a clue,' Ace admitted. 'Probably date rape. Maybe frigidity; I just don't know.'

'Frigidity!' Jen snorted disgustedly. 'That's extremely rare. It's a word sexually inept men use to describe a woman who's sick of being treated as nothing more than a receptacle for sperm! Some men haven't the slightest idea how to give pleasure – they don't even know they're supposed to give . . .'

'Okay, okay,' Ace interrupted, 'you don't have to give me lectures on sexual technique.' She grinned.

'I'm sure I don't – not if the gossip around the set is only halfway true,' she said. Ace arched one eyebrow.

'Yeah? Anyhow, these tapes – can you let me have a look at some of them?'

'Sure. I have them at home – I'll bring them to the studio on Monday,' she said. 'Or I can drop them off at your place tomorrow,' she suggested eagerly.

'Thanks, I'd appreciate that.' He paused. 'And Jen – I'd also appreciate it if you didn't mention this to anyone.'

'Okay.' She nodded, and watched him as he shouldered his way out of the room. Ace Delaney and a frigid girlfriend? The one who'd been hitting on Johnny Dancer? The tabloids would love that story! she thought. Not that she would ever speak to those creeps; they were always nosing around the studios, panting for gossip about the stars.

Ace strolled back to his own house, deep in thought and in no hurry to see Alexa. Delving into a woman's mind instead of her underwear was a new experience for him, and he wasn't sure it was one for which he was ready. He'd sooner dive into shark-infested waters than try to untangle the mess inside Alexa Kane's head! So why had he asked Jen for the tapes? Why didn't he send Alexa to a shrink? Or, better still, send her back to England with a note for her father suggesting she shouldn't be allowed out?

When he entered the sitting room, Alexa was huddled on the sofa, still barefoot, a pitiful sight with traces of tears on her face; her make-up smudged so that she resembled nothing more than a small girl experimenting disastrously with her mother's cosmetics.

He noticed what small and delicate feet she had; she looked very young and vulnerable, her gold-green eyes huge in a pale face as she glanced warily at him, then quickly away, seemingly unable or unwilling to meet his gaze. Was that a sign of guilt? Or merely embarrassment? Ace wondered, frowning a little as he pondered how best to proceed.

'Johnny says he didn't touch you,' he said finally.

'Huh!'

'Okay, he might have touched you,' Ace acknowledged, 'but he let you go when you objected. Is that the truth?'

'I suppose so,' she said listlessly, as if it was of no importance.

'So, why all the fuss? You went to his bedroom willingly, didn't you?' he snapped, suddenly angry with both her and Johnny.

'A woman has the right to say no at any time,' she replied, very much on her dignity. That was too politically correct for Ace.

'Sure, but she also has to take responsibility for her actions. *You* have to take responsibility,' he stressed. 'You can't expect to lead a man on and then be surprised when he gets an erection and wants to screw you,' he said bluntly.

'Do you have to be so crude?' Alexa snapped, her cheeks burning with mortification. 'Look, it's no big deal,' she lied. 'I fancied Johnny, then I changed my mind. That's it. End of story.'

'How often has this happened?' Ace asked shrewdly. She looked up quickly, startled by his perception, then lowered her gaze and began twisting strands of hair in her fingers, pulling the shining tresses forward to cover her face.

'Quite often,' she mumbled finally.

'Always?' he guessed again. She bit her lip, then nodded reluctantly.

'Yes,' she whispered.

'So, what's the problem? A bad first experience put you off? Frightened you? Hurt you?'

'A bad first experience, yes, then a bad second experience, then a third . . .'

'God, how many have there been?' Ace pretended to be shocked. 'You're only a baby!'

'I'm nearly twenty-one – I should have worked it out by now, shouldn't I?' she asked bitterly.

'What about the guy you were engaged to at Christmas? The Greek waiter?'

'Dimitri? He was a fisherman, not a waiter. He was just another holiday romance; someone I need never see again once I returned home, if it turned into another fiasco – which it did. But he was more persistent than most, or, I should say, more greedy

– I finally realized he was more interested in my money than my body. I think I knew it all the time, really; I just kidded myself he was sincere when he said he preferred passive women.'

'Passive!' Ace muttered, with a grimace.

'Only "passive" is the wrong word; "dead" would be more accurate,' she continued, then Ace's exclamation of disgust registered, and she blushed furiously, cringing inwardly. 'Why am I even talking to you about this?' she asked, horrified.

'Because I'm here, I guess,' he said calmly. 'And because I'm asking questions, ones to which you obviously want to find answers for your own happiness.' He paused, frowning a little, as one possible answer presented itself to him, and it was one he didn't like one bit, he realized uncomfortably.

'Alexa, you said you fancied Johnny – was that true? Or are you secretly attracted to other woman? If you are gay, you might as well admit it, even if only to yourself.'

'I'm not gay,' she denied quickly. 'I like men. I even like being touched . . . to start with, then . . . I just don't like it any more,' she finished miserably.

Ace regarded her silently for a moment; she's like a little girl, pretending to be a grown-up, he thought. Then she suddenly stretched and uncoiled her lithe body from the corner of the sofa. The clinging Lycra dress moulded to her curves – and quite delectable curves they are, too, he noted approvingly. All she needs is careful handling; hours, maybe whole nights of non-penetrative sex, just sensual massage and kisses to both arouse and relax her . . .

'Come to bed with me,' he said softly. Alexa's stomach lurched, and she had to fight back hysterical laughter, or tears, she wasn't sure which. Go to bed with him? Mr Sex-on-legs? And then endure his contempt and sarcasm forever? She could just picture the scene in twenty years' time, when, as godparents, they would both have to attend Kit's wedding. 'Still frigid, honey?' he'd drawl, with a knowing smirk. She shuddered at the very thought; she must have been insane to confide in him as much as she had already.

'You must be joking! You're the very last person on earth I'd go to bed with,' she said vehemently. Ace's lips tightened in annoyance. If this was the result of trying to be a New Man, well, to hell with it, he'd revert to being a male chauvinist pig! It was a lot more fun.

'Your loss, honey!' he snapped. 'Sort out your own hang-ups! What do I care?' he added, as he stalked from the room.

He went for a long walk along the beach to cool off, but ignored Johnny's party, which was still in full swing. He thought briefly of the full-breasted naked blonde who had propositioned him earlier, but found, to his disgust, that he wasn't interested. His mind was full of the tawny-haired child-woman he'd left at his house. Somebody, or something, had damaged her, but it wasn't his problem, he told himself firmly. I'm definitely sending her back to her father, he decided, as he eventually turned to retrace his steps.

He didn't manage to sleep much that night; he could hear Alexa sobbing quietly in the guest room, but was damned if he was going to try and comfort her. She'd probably accuse him of attempted rape, or something. Her sex-life, or lack of it, was her problem and she would have to sort it out by herself, or with the help of a shrink, or a gynaecologist, perhaps both.

'I've just booked my flight home,' Alexa said, when she emerged, red-eyed from weeping, next morning. Ace didn't look up from the newspaper he was perusing. 'I'm leaving this afternoon.'

'Fine. I'll run you to the airport,' he said casually.

'No, that's okay, I'll call a cab,' Alexa said quickly. 'You'll be busy – Ella's coming over again today, isn't she?'

'So she is,' Ace slowly unwound his muscular form from the chair and handed her the paper as he passed. Neither looked the other in the eye: Alexa was too embarrassed by what she had told him the night before; she would prefer to have him still think her an immoral slut than feel sorry for her. Or laugh at her. She didn't know which would be worse. Ace didn't look at Alexa because he didn't want to see the ravages the night's weeping would have wrought.

Raul went to collect Ella, and Ace found working with her took his mind off Alexa. Ella had been given much less in life than Alexa Kane, yet she was full of enthusiasm and joy. He was really pleased with his decision to help the kid – especially as he had been putting out some feelers amongst the companies who had sponsored him during his years as a pro, and found several would be interested in having a protégée of his endorse their products – *if* she was talented enough. No one would pay her to use their equipment or wear their clothes if she persistently lost in the first or second round of tournaments, of course.

But Ace felt sure she had the talent and will to succeed, although there was helluva lot of hard work to be done first. That was where Hal Renwick came into the picture; Ace had neither the time, inclination or patience to put in the thousands of hours' coaching needed to bring out Ella's potential.

He had almost forgotten talking to Jennifer Patterson at Johnny's party and frowned in annoyance at being interrupted when she arrived, shortly before noon.

'I've brought those tapes you were asking about,' she explained hurriedly, seeing his frown. 'It seemed kinda urgent, so I thought I'd get them to you today instead of taking them to the studio tomorrow.'

'Great. Thanks,' he said. 'Have a drink now you're here?' he suggested, but without much enthusiasm, and her face fell.

'No, it's okay, I can see you're busy,' she mumbled, eyeing Ella with interest. She'd assumed Ace's problem lay with the snooty English girl, but now wondered about the dark-haired pretty girl on the tennis court, who was ostensibly practising her serve, but was all the while constantly looking impatiently over at Ace, as if resenting every moment apart.

Ace glanced at the stack of tapes rather helplessly; it had seemed a good idea at the time, but what was he going to do now? Force Alexa to sit down and watch them all until she freaked out?

'Ace? Can I have a word?' It was Alexa, and he turned quickly, hiding the boxed – and labelled – videos on the table behind him.

'What's up?' he asked casually.

'I don't know what to do – I can't find my passport,' she said worriedly. Ace sighed heavily. He would 'find' her passport before her flight, but he couldn't resist the opportunity to wind her up.

'Alexa, honey, if you've changed your mind about leaving me, just say so,' he drawled kindly.

'Oh!' Alexa stamped her foot in annoyance; her eyes sparkling with anger. Ace was secretly pleased by this display of temper; she still had plenty of spirit, he thought approvingly, it just needed channelling in a more pleasurable direction!

'You arrogant pig! I do not want to stay here!' she yelled. 'I am telling you the truth – I've lost my passport. How am I going to get back to England?' She was truly desperate to leave, to return to her life of pretence, flirting with everything in trousers, gossiping and giggling with her girlfriends about her supposed army of conquests. It was strange how her closest friends believed her wild stories, accepted that she was promiscuous, yet Ace Delaney had seen through her act in an instant; hence the reason for his instinctive disdain – he would have no time at all for a frigid woman.

'It will be around here somewhere,' Ace shrugged. 'Have you checked with Maria?' he asked, knowing his housekeeper would be at church. 'She unpacked for you when you arrived, didn't she?'

'Well, yes, but my passport was in my shoulder bag . . .'

'Don't start panicking just yet. It wouldn't be the end of the world if you had to stay here until you could get a replacement, would it?' he asked, quite sharply. He wanted to be rid of her, but it irked him that she was just as eager to leave. He didn't wait for her to reply, but turned his back on her and shouted for Ella to come indoors.

'Take a short break, honey,' he told her. A glance over his shoulder showed him that Alexa had returned to the sitting room and was flicking through the newspapers. He beckoned Ella to come closer and lowered his voice. 'Do me a favour?' he asked.

'Of course!' Her dark eyes shone with adoration for this God-like creature, whom she had always admired as a role model and who had miraculously returned to the slums to help her follow in his footsteps to fame and fortune. She would have done anything for him, and Ace knew it. She's too trusting, he thought. If I were as debauched as everyone thinks I am, I could have seduced her long before now.

'Don't ask me to explain this, but I want you to go and watch these tapes while Alexa is in the room. If she asks, tell her it's a school project you're working on. Try this one first,' he said, handing her the tape labelled 'date rape'.

'Okay,' Ella said amiably. She picked up a bottle of water and then went to do his bidding.

Ace decided to remain on the terrace for a while to judge Alexa's reaction for himself, and stretched out on a sun-lounger as if half-asleep, his eyes covered by dark glasses.

Alexa looked up in surprise when Ella switched on the TV, but said nothing and continued reading. An image of a tearful girl filled the screen, sobbing out her story of trusting her boss and inviting him into her apartment for coffee when he had given her a lift home after working late. She went on to describe his attack on her, and how she'd kept silent because he had threatened she would lose her job if she spoke out or reported him to the police.

Ace listened with mounting impatience – if that was all true, why had the silly bitch spilled her guts out to millions of strangers on TV? he wondered cynically. He watched Alexa closely; she glanced up, cast a disdainful all-men-are-pigs look at the screen, then turned her attention back to the article she was reading. Ace grimaced slightly; apparently that hadn't hit a chord . . . He mimed to Ella to slot in another tape, but that one received even less attention from Alexa.

Ah, well, it had been worth a shot, Ace thought, as he got to his feet and wandered back to the tennis court to begin picking up the balls scattered around from the morning's work. Ella watched him wistfully; she was already bored and itching to be back outside, but Ace had asked her to do this apparently pointless favour, so she pretended to concentrate and even occasionally scribbled some notes.

'How many of those are you going to watch?' Alexa asked, exasperated by the constant changeover of tapes. 'What are you doing, anyway?'

'It's for school,' Ella replied vaguely.

'My teachers would have had a fit if we'd watched that kind of programme,' Alexa commented. The remark wasn't intended as a criticism but, to Ella, Alexa's clipped, cut-glass tone always sounded aloof and arrogant. The gift of the silk top had gone a long way towards softening Ella's original hostility to the girl she had feared was Ace's lover, but now she threw down her pen in annoyance. She wanted to be outside with Ace, not stuck indoors watching boring TV.

'Yeah, I'm sure they would. But I don't go to a posh school, where the teachers have nothing worse to worry about than the kids having midnight feasts in the dorm!' she snapped, recalling hazy details of a novel she'd once read set in an English boarding school, and assuming Alexa had had much the same kind of education. 'I bet you never had the cops raiding your school to arrest drug-pushers or search for guns, did you?'

'Well, no,' Alexa said faintly, rather taken aback.

'And I bet you didn't have to make sure you were always with a crowd of other girls to avoid being raped, did you?' Ella yelled. Alexa just shook her head dumbly: where had all this come from? And why?

'Er – it was an all-girls school,' she finally managed to say, rather stupidly, she felt.

'How nice,' Ella jeered. 'You rich people! All you have to worry about is how to avoid paying taxes. And making sure you're protected so you're not kidnapped and held to ransom, of course!' The last was a sarcastic afterthought, and she turned away to remove the cassette and switch off the TV set. It was only when she turned back that she realized Alexa had stood up and backed into a corner, staring wildly at . . . nothing. Ella followed her terrified gaze and frowned.

'What's wrong?' Ella asked apprehensively. 'There's nobody there.'

Alexa didn't hear Ella. She heard a male voice; a voice from ten years before, but it was as vivid and loud as if the man were in the room with her. 'The paper says the kid is worth ten million quid! I say we should ask for more . . . shut that bitch up!' She backed away even further, until she was pressed against the wall, whimpering, her face as white as the ghost Ella feared she had seen. Ella crossed herself and ran to fetch Ace, afraid he would blame her for whatever was happening to Alexa.

'Ace! Come quickly!' she gasped. 'It's Alexa – she's gone nuts! Seeing ghosts, or something. She's not on drugs, is she?' Bingo! Ace thought, with mingled satisfaction and trepidation. What can of worms had he opened?

'Ella, you stay out here and practise your serve; I'll be back as soon as I've calmed Alexa down,' he said. 'Which video were you watching when she flipped?'

'The one about fathers abusing their daughters,' she told him. Oh, God! Ace thought, in horror. Philip Kane? Ultra-respectable, wealthy, upper class . . . but so what? Child abuse wasn't confined to the slums, he reminded himself as he raced back to the house. Unbidden came a memory from the night he first met Alexa, when she had confided to Johnny Dancer about her broken love affair; she had told him how protective and possessive her father was, how he always scared away her boyfriends . . .

# CHAPTER 11

'Alexa?' Ace said gently. She was sitting on the floor, pressed tightly into the corner, her knees drawn up against her chest as if she were trying to make herself as small and insignificant as possible, he thought.

'Alexa, honey?' He hunkered down to her level, but was careful to keep his distance. 'Can you talk to me? Can you tell me what's wrong? Whatever, whoever it is, can't hurt you here. There's just me and Ella,' he said soothingly, although a tiny part of him registered the fact that she might not consider his presence to be a plus!

He moved to fetch her a glass of brandy, and forced it into her hands, and then, when she ignored it, placed it to her lips. Automatically, she sipped the fiery liquid, then pushed his hand away.

'Can you talk to me?' he said again. After what seemed an eternity, she drew a deep, shuddering breath and gazed at him steadily.

'I forgot, until just now,' she whispered. 'How could I forget?' she asked wonderingly. She didn't really expect, or even want, an answer, but Ace supplied one anyway.

'Because you didn't want to remember it, whatever it is,' he said calmly.

'So much happened, so many horrible things, in such a short space of time . . . I forgot,' she repeated.

'You forgot because you weren't strong enough to cope with it,' he told her. 'But now you are,' he prompted, knowing he was taking a huge risk in encouraging her to talk. 'Tell me what happened,' he said, quietly, but firmly. Alexa drew another deep breath.

'I was ten years old . . . Mummy died . . . I didn't really understand what that meant; I kept expecting to still see her.' She frowned slightly. 'I think she had been ill for a long time; she was often in bed. Then, soon after, Magda . . .' Her lip trembled and she bit down hard on it to stop herself screaming. Magda had been with her the day they were snatched off the street. Poor, poor Magda. Alexa heard, as if for the first time, Magda's cries of pain and rage as one of the kidnappers forced himself on her.

'Magda? Who's Magda?' Ace queried softly.

'My nanny,' Alexa whispered. 'He raped her. I didn't understand that, either . . . oh, God! Poor Magda – she was only there to look after me.' She struggled to control her emotions but huge tears welled in her eyes and rolled slowly down her ashen cheeks. Ace balled his hands into fists at his sides; what a bastard Philip Kane must have been, forcing himself on the hired help the minute his wife had died. Hadn't he heard of hookers?

'Then what happened?' he prompted.

'Magda left. I think she loved me,' she said, in a high, childish voice. 'But, after what he did to her, she wouldn't stay. At least now I understand why – it wasn't because she no longer cared about me,' she said, and tried to smile, but it was a poor, watery effort, and Ace struggled to hide his own anger and disgust.

Alexa breathed deeply and fell silent as she tried to put the jumble of memories into some sort of order; to finally make sense of it all. Why did I think Magda had deserted me? she wondered; why did I forget? The answer came suddenly, shockingly; she heard Magda's guttural voice as loudly as if she were in the room, seemingly as real as that of the kidnapper had a few moments, or was it hours, ago? 'Alexa, you tell no one, do you hear me? No one! If your father asks, you tell him they didn't hurt me. No one must know what he did! Promise me?' Alexa had promised; indeed, she had not realized the enormity of what had happened, only sensed and been terrified by the ugly brutality of it all. She might eventually have told her father, she thought now, but he had panicked after the kidnapping, fearing other members of the gang might still pose a threat, and had sent her to stay with her grandparents . . .

'Oh, my God!' Alexa wailed and buried her head in her hands.

'You're doing great,' Ace told her; he had been watching the conflicting emotions on her face, none of them pleasant, and hoped to hell he wasn't making things worse for her. 'What happened after Magda left?'

'He . . .' She faltered and briefly closed her eyes. She was remembering her grandfather, but Ace assumed, as before, that she was talking about

Philip Kane. 'He said he missed Mummy so much,' she whispered. 'I look like her, you see, and he . . . he said we should . . . hug each other, since we couldn't hug her any longer.' She fell silent and Ace forced himself to speak calmly, despite being consumed by a murderous rage against her father.

'He came to your bed?'

'Yes.' It was the faintest whisper, almost a sigh.

'He raped you?'

'I . . .' She frowned, as if part of her wanted still to defend her father, Ace thought. 'I suppose so,' she said dully. 'He was . . . gentle, though, it wasn't like it had been for Magda.'

'How often did it happen?' Ace asked gruffly.

'Just once,' she said, and frowned again. 'I think Granny must have found out. There was a lot of shouting, and I remember she slept in my room after that. Just once,' she repeated. Once too often, Ace thought grimly. He was uncertain how to proceed; this was far worse than the date rape he had assumed she had suffered. She needed professional help.

'Honey, do you think you could repeat all this to a shri . . . doctor,' he amended hastily.

'Not now,' she said wearily, rubbing her hands over her face like a tired child.

'No, not right now,' he agreed. 'But soon. You must talk to someone who can help you sort it all out.'

'I don't know.' She shied away from that. She hadn't really been talking to Ace, just remembering out loud. 'I'm so tired.' She sighed; she felt utterly drained.

'I know you are, honey. Go and get some rest,' he suggested. She nodded but made no attempt to move, so he reached for her hand and gently tugged her to her feet. She followed dutifully as he led her upstairs and into her room.

'Get undressed and into bed,' he ordered, and she again obeyed, as if she were a ten-year-old child again. Ace watched her, frowning, and wondered if he should call a doctor, but decided against it. She'd had enough, for now.

He went and rifled through his bathroom cabinet, searching for the sleeping pills he occasionally used when travelling on long-haul flights. He found them and tipped one, then, after a pause, a second tablet into his hand. A double dose should knock her out for around twelve hours, he figured, and the healing process could begin while she slept. Hopefully, she would be refreshed and mentally strong enough to cope with it when she finally awoke.

'Come on, swallow these,' he instructed, and again she obeyed without question. He noticed she was shivering; her hands were like ice as he passed her the pills.

'I want to go home,' she whispered. Unfortunately, Ace had gone to fetch a spare quilt, and didn't hear her.

The pills took effect almost immediately, and he quietly left the room. Temporarily, he put Philip Kane to the back of his mind and remembered how he had blackmailed Alexa into meeting him at his hotel in London after Kit's christening, letting her believe he intended forcing her to have sex.

He cringed, now, at the memory of that night, struggling to come to terms with an unfamiliar emotion – guilt. It took a while for him to even recognize it for what it was. But, damnit, she didn't give the impression that she was scared of men, he thought, seeking an excuse for his behaviour. Quite the opposite, in fact. She had flirted outrageously with Johnny Dancer that first evening, and then appeared to be doing her damnedest to seduce both Nick Lennox and Jack at the Bellwood party.

Ace had sensed she was playing games, but had never come close to guessing what she was really doing, but now he knew. All that showy packaging and sensuous posturing was a desperate attempt at proving she was 'normal'.

But . . . Philip Kane? He was a powerful, wealthy man; he could buy all the women he needed! What made him prey on those supposedly under his protection, his employee and his daughter? And now he was engaged to marry Rose Farrell! Ace frowned darkly at that thought. This was no longer exclusively Alexa's problem. Rose would never marry Philip if she knew the truth. And she mustn't marry him – she would, in all innocence, have Kit to stay at the house, and Melissa's child when it was born . . . His blood ran cold at the very thought. Jack and Melissa would warn their children about talking to strangers, and then unknowingly hand them over to a pervert!

'Not likely!' he muttered, his decision made. He wouldn't bother Jack, trying to repair his marriage; he would go to England himself.

'Maria!' He yelled for his housekeeper, and gave her a list of instructions regarding Alexa's care, depending upon her state of mind when she awoke. He booked a flight and packed an overnight bag, forgetting all about Ella until she reappeared, anxious to know what was going on, and afraid that Ace might be angry with her for upsetting Alexa.

'Sorry, honey; I have to go to England,' he apologized, with a rather absent-minded smile that at least reassured her she wasn't in trouble. Still her face fell at the news of his departure.

'Can I stay here? I'll work on my serve, and set up the lobster machine to work on my ground strokes by myself,' she said earnestly.

'Okay, but be sure and let your mom know what's happening. In fact,' he paused, 'do you think she'd come over here? Alexa isn't feeling too well,' he explained vaguely.

'She's at work – I can call her there,' she nodded. 'I'm sure she'd come and look after Alexa.'

'Great. Tell her I'll send Raul over to pick her up after he's dropped me at the airport.'

'Will you be back in time to take me to the academy on Wednesday?' she asked anxiously. Damn, Ace thought; he'd forgotten about that.

'Yeah, I hope so,' he said.

'It's just that I don't want them to think I'm not serious,' she said earnestly, hopping from one foot to the other in her agitation.

'Don't worry about that. I'll call Hal Renwick and explain – he knows what an unreliable sod I am. He won't think badly of you if you're a couple of days late,' he assured her.

'Okay.' She relaxed slightly. 'Will Alexa be okay? What's wrong with her?' she asked tentatively, wondering if the English girl had complained about her angry outburst.

'She's just a bit upset,' Ace said vaguely. 'Look after her while I'm away, will you?' he asked, and she nodded eagerly, keen to make amends. It didn't seem at all incongruous to either of them that he should ask the fifteen-year-old to care for the twenty-year-old. In many ways, Ella was much older and wiser.

Ace checked on Alexa before leaving the house: she was sound asleep and looked peaceful in repose. No nightmares, then . . .

Ace was unable to get a direct flight, and travelled to London via New York. From Heathrow he took a cab to Eaton Square and arrived early on Monday evening, only minutes after Philip Kane had returned from his office. He and Rose were in his study, enjoying a quiet drink before dinner, when the housekeeper showed Ace into the room.

'Ace!' Rose saw him first, but her smile of welcome slowly faded as she registered the grim expression on his face. 'What's wrong? Isn't Alexa with you?'

'No, she's at my house,' he said tersely, his jet-black eyes glittering with fury as they fixed on Philip Kane.

'Your house!' Philip exclaimed. 'I thought you said she was with Jack and Lisa,' he said accusingly to Rose, who shrugged slightly and looked away. 'Why didn't she come back with you?' he demanded of Ace. 'I expected her home days ago, after we heard you were released from prison. And what's this about heroin?' he continued, without pausing for breath.

'Did you introduce her to the filthy stuff?' He had been mulling over Alexa's story ever since her hasty departure, and could still make no sense of it. Ace ignored him and spoke to Rose.

'Pack whatever belongings you have here – you're leaving. And you're not marrying him either,' he said brusquely.

'Not marrying . . . how dare you!' Philip spluttered, puce with anger. 'Get out of my house!'

'It will be a pleasure. But Rose is coming with me,' Ace said coldly, and turned to Rose. 'You see, I've discovered why Alexa is so screwed up. It's because of him.' He jerked his head towards Philip. 'He raped her when she was a kid.'

'What?' Rose gasped. 'No.' She shook her head in denial.

'Yes!' Ace insisted.

'You filthy lying bastard!' Philip roared. 'I'll sue!'

'Go ahead,' Ace shrugged. 'If you weren't an old man I'd rip your head off,' he said contemptuously. 'In fact, I think I will, anyway,' he decided. 'After all, *you* don't care about the age of your victims, do you?' He took a purposeful step towards Philip and Rose sprang forward and grabbed at his arm.

'No, don't! Let's talk about this, please, Ace,' she begged. He glanced down at her troubled face and, with a sigh, stepped back. 'Alexa couldn't really have told you that . . . that . . .' She couldn't even say the words.

'He raped her, yes, that's what she told me,' Ace confirmed.

'She must have been lying,' she faltered, for to accuse Alexa of that was almost as bad as the charges she had levelled at her own father. 'Maybe she was desperate for your attention . . .'

'If she was pretending, then Hollywood is the right place for her. She could win more Oscars than Tom Hanks. She wasn't lying,' he said flatly.

'No – *he* is the liar!' Philip glared at Ace. 'Alexa would never say such a dreadful thing. Never! Because it never happened,' he added for good measure. 'Answer me this – if it had happened, why would she have continued living with me? She has her own money, she could have left on her eighteenth birthday.'

'That's right,' Rose nodded. 'You must have been mistaken,' she told Ace, rather lamely. He looked at her incredulously.

'Don't be stupid,' he said coldly. 'She lives here, or lived, I should say, since I doubt she'll ever come back, because she had blanked it out. She only remembered it when she was watching a TV programme about fathers abusing their children,' he explained to Rose, with another contemptuous glance towards Philip Kane, who was almost apoplectic and incoherent with rage and disbelief.

It was dawning on him that Ace Delaney sincerely believed the obscenity he was saying to be true. Alexa, his lovely, if rather spoilt and wayward daughter, had accused him of . . . He struggled to breathe; there was a loud buzzing in his ears and he moved awkwardly to pour out a glass of brandy which he downed in one gulp. Rose watched him, with a look of mingled horror and confusion in her expressive eyes.

'She was only ten,' Ace told Rose. 'After her mother died, he turned his attention to the nanny, who walked out, and then to Alexa, who couldn't leave. His pathetic excuse was that he missed her mother!'

'Elizabeth?' Philip mouthed the word. His marriage hadn't been happy, certainly not in the latter years, and her death had been, shameful though it was to admit, something of a relief, for he could never have brought himself to divorce an invalid. The nanny? Magda? But I never touched her; she left because of the kidnapping . . . oh, dear God!

He suddenly realized what must have happened to the poor girl during their captivity. Alexa too? Had she somehow muddled it all up in her young mind and attributed the dark deeds to him? But why invoke Elizabeth's name? His brow furrowed as he struggled to make sense of the incomprehensible. Had Alexa felt abandoned because he had sent her to stay with her grandparents after Magda's return to Germany?

'Oh, God,' he groaned, as the likeliest answer hit him with the force of a thunderbolt. His father-in-law! Peter Beauchamp's love for Elizabeth had always grated on Philip, considering it to be overly protective and possessive. He had always assumed it sprang from concern over Elizabeth's poor health, but had his love also been unnatural? That would explain much of Elizabeth's problem. And I sent Alexa to him, he thought, in anguish.

'Where is Alexa now? Bring her home!' he said wildly.

'Never,' Ace said coldly. 'Rose? Are you leaving?'

'I can't believe it's true,' she faltered.

'Can you ignore it?' Ace asked incredulously. 'Think of Kit. And Melissa's baby. Are you going to invite them to stay here when they're older? Are you going to let him read them bedtime stories?' he asked scathingly. 'Dare you risk it, Rose?' he demanded. For a second she hesitated, a hesitation she would remember and regret for the rest of her life. But, if there was just one chance in a million that Ace was speaking the truth, then no, she couldn't put her grandchildren at risk.

'Rose!' Philip pleaded hoarsely. 'It's not true! I . . .' He stopped speaking, his mouth opened but no sound emerged as he slowly slumped to the floor.

'Oh, my God! Philip!' Rose sank to her knees beside him. 'He must be having a heart attack or something. Call an ambulance!' she told Ace frantically. He did as she asked, but with no great enthusiasm. Rose made Philip as comfortable as she could and strained to hear what he was trying to say.

'What was that? Peter? Who's Peter? Is that what it sounds likc to you?' she appealed to Ace, who just shrugged.

'Probably trying to say paedophile,' he suggested. 'A death-bed confession.'

'Shut up!' Rose hissed at him. 'Look what you've done to him – don't you care?'

'Not really, no,' he replied.

'He could die!'

'It's probably best for everyone if he does,' Ace said, and Rose glared at him, then bit her lip. If Philip survived, the repercussions from this evening's events would be horrific; nothing could ever be the same again . . .

'Perhaps you'd better phone Alexa – she has the right to know what's happening,' she said wearily.

Even if she is the cause of it, she added silently to herself.

Alexa slept deeply and dreamlessly for more than twelve hours, and even then only surfaced gradually as the sleeping pills slowly eased their grip.

Finally, she opened her eyes and stretched her limbs. She yawned, and her mouth stayed half open as the memories she had dredged up the day before hit her with almost physical blows. One. Two. Three. Mummy died! The kidnapping . . . oh, God, poor Magda! Grandpa . . . that was the worst and she physically cringed away, as if he were in the room. Calm down, she told herself sternly, and took several deep, steadying breaths.

Maria had again left freshly squeezed orange juice beside the bed, and Alexa drank it thirstily before heading to the bathroom to freshen up. Feeling better, she clambered back into bed and settled herself comfortably against stacked-up pillows, determined to re-examine the memories and come to terms with what had happened so long ago. And that's the key, she thought firmly; to keep remembering that it had all taken place almost eleven years ago.

I can cope with it now. I can and I will. I must, if I want to finally put it all behind me, if I want to grow . . . to become an adult, with adult relationships . . . that made her think of Ace and she flushed, even though she was alone.

He would be at the television studios, she realized, after glancing at her watch. She had plenty of time to herself before facing him. But, he had been so kind and gentle – who would have thought it? Come on, stop daydreaming about Ace! she chided herself, aware that it was a delaying tactic, albeit an exciting one.

Almost as if she were taking tangible objects out of a cupboard, she cautiously began bringing the dreadful childhood memories into the present day. First, Mummy died. She remembered being told that her mother had gone to heaven, and asking; for how long? Elizabeth Kane had been ill for as long as Alexa could remember; she had been quite surprised when she discovered other children's mothers didn't spend most of their time in bed. Until then, she had assumed that all rich women, with nannies and housekeepers, didn't need to get up in the mornings.

Now, she smiled slightly at that notion, and allowed herself to recall the fun times; playing board games, reading, solving jigsaw puzzles; all things that didn't tax Elizabeth's strength. There had been hugs and kisses, too, she thought, with a rush of love for her mother. She did love me, and she didn't leave because she wanted to, Alexa finally realized, and understood that was what had been so hard for her to comprehend at the time – why her mother had gone, deserted her, and not even said goodbye.

I'll take some flowers to her grave as soon as I get home, she decided. She had done that before, of course, dozens of times, but always with a faint sense of resentment that she could only now understand.

Okay – she drew a deep breath as she contemplated tackling the next awful event, only weeks after Elizabeth's death. She didn't want to think about it, but knew she must. It was far worse for Magda than for you, she told herself sternly. That day was a jumble of confusion and noise and fear; of being bundled roughly into a van, of Magda saying it was just a silly game, but in a voice that quavered with fright. There had been a seemingly endless drive, forced to huddle beneath a blanket, a smelly blanket . . . she wrinkled her nose and moved quickly over to the open window, as if the stench were still in her nostrils.

Below her, Raul was working in the garden, and beyond the ocean rolled gently on to the beach. It was a beautiful day, crisp and clear and sunny, and she breathed deeply for several minutes, granting herself a brief respite from the memories, drinking in the view and listening to the comforting sound of the waves.

A gentle tap on the door startled her and she jumped slightly, her heart thumping. She sighed and shook her head at her own overreaction: who was she expecting – kidnappers? Her grandfather?

'Come in,' she called, and Maria popped her head round the door.

'I thought I heard you moving about – how do you feel?' she asked anxiously.

'I'm fine,' Alexa assured her, but she refused Maria's offer of food. 'I'll come down when I feel hungry,' she said, with a finality that stopped Maria's fussing and she left the room.

Alone again, Alexa drank some more of the orange juice and sat by the window, forcing her mind back. They had finally arrived at a terraced house, and been hustled into a cellar . . . no, a basement flat; she remembered the stone steps and iron railings; remembered trying not to cry . . .

There were three men: '. . . the paper says the kid is worth ten million quid! I say we should ask for more . . .' The hate? Yes, hate and envy in his voice had made an impact, then and still did, and she shivered, rubbing at the gooseflesh that sprang up along her arms.

That same man had taken Magda into the bedroom . . . oh, God. Alexa had tears streaming down her face, then and now, only now she understood. At the time, she hadn't, but the noises had terrified her – and the other two men had just laughed! Again, she shuddered with revulsion; the pigs!

She began shaking with the anger and had to force herself to calm down, to remind herself it had happened over a decade ago. The men had been punished, for the kidnap, but not for the rape. She knew Magda had kept quiet about that, insisting she and Alexa had not been harmed. Surely the men had gone to prison, but they would be free men again now. That realization made her feel vulnerable, as if they still plotted against her and posed a threat. She knew that was irrational, but was nevertheless relieved to be away from England.

She had only hazy memories of the aftermath of the kidnapping, the most poignant of which was Magda's departure. But she didn't desert me either, she thought, with a huge sense of relief and gladness. She hoped Magda was happy now, hopefully married with a brood of children, the nightmare, if not forgotten, at least only a wretched memory that didn't intrude in her present life. I must talk to Daddy about her, she thought, as she realized she had no knowledge of Magda's surname, nor where she lived. But it should be fairly easy to trace her whereabouts, and offer her help if she needed it. Of course, Magda might not welcome the contact . . . She frowned. Yes, she would definitely ask her father's advice about that one, she thought.

She paced restlessly around the room, putting off the moment when she had to examine the last, and worst event of those fateful weeks. Finally, she moved back to the bed and drank the last of the orange juice before climbing onto the mattress and cuddling a pillow for warmth and comfort.

She leaned back against the headboard and forced her mind back. Okay, you've recalled two out of three and it wasn't so bad, she told herself, so just get on with the third! Mummy died, Magda left, and Daddy sent me to my grandparents . . .

She frowned, trying remember other, 'normal' visits, but couldn't. She couldn't even visualize their house. Granny had been a bit distant, stern and disapproving; Grandpa had been the nice one. She shook her head at her innocence, but dammit, I was only ten! she defended herself. He had been kind and funny, making her laugh, buying sweets and ice-creams, taking her to the circus and the cinema. And reading stories at bedtime, when she had been frightened, missing her mother and Magda . . .

Oh, this is too difficult! she thought, in anguish. I can't do it alone, maybe Ace is right and I do need a shrink, she decided miserably. So what? There's no shame in that. No shame for you in what happened, either. *He* should be ashamed, but he's dead.

She closed her eyes and, heart thumping with trepidation, forced herself to conjure up an image of her grandfather: tall and thin, with sparse, greying hair and kind eyes . . . yes, kind eyes and a ready smile, except when talking about his only daughter, Elizabeth.

'You have to be grown-up now, Alexa; you have to take your mother's place . . .' Oh, God! Alexa exclaimed out loud and rushed into the bathroom, retching.

Pale and shaken, she returned to the bedroom and tottered out on to the balcony, leaning against the rail and letting the sight and sound of the ocean exert its calming influence. Poor Mummy. I wonder if Daddy ever knew? she wondered, frowning, and decided he had not. She realized he wouldn't have sent her there if he knew; realized also why there had been no previous visits. Elizabeth would have blocked any such suggestion, fearing for her child's safety, but could never have confided the true reason to her husband.

Still fighting nausea, she forced herself to relive the worst of it; the night he had climbed into her bed . . . He had been gentle, she realized; there hadn't been much pain, just horror and disgust and fear. She shuddered anew and wrapped her arms protectively across her chest, hugging herself. He's dead, she reminded herself, and you are not going to allow him to blight your life any longer!

It was little wonder sex had always been a disaster for her, although she had to admit she had probably made matters worse for herself – the one-night stands, the holiday romances; always she had sought sex with strangers, men she need never see again. Only her first lover had been someone in her own social circle, and his scathing comments about her lack of response had made her determined to choose lovers who couldn't tell tales to her friends.

Well, never again, she decided. Next time, when I'm ready, I'll make love, not have sex, make love with a man I care about and who cares about me. Ace? The prospect both excited and terrified her, and she pushed the thought aside. Not yet. But, maybe, one day. As for Grandpa, well, he's dead. But he was rich, and his money can do a lot to help abused kids, she decided, kids far worse off than me. My ordeal was short-lived and a long time ago; for thousands of kids the abuse is happening right now, every day.

Feeling much calmer and cautiously optimistic about the future, she decided to shower and get dressed. She realized she was hungry, which was surely a good sign? she thought happily.

Downstairs, the telephone rang.

## CHAPTER 12

'Miss Kane? Alexa?' Maria knocked on her door. 'Mr Delaney wants to talk to you.'

'Okay, thanks. I'll be right there,' she called out, and padded barefoot downstairs to take the call. 'Hello?'

'Hi, honey, how are you doing?' Ace asked.

'Fine,' she said brightly.

'The truth,' he insisted.

'Well, a little raw, I guess. It all seems as if it happened yesterday, but I can deal with it and put it behind me, I know I can,' she said positively.

'Sure you can, honey,' he said soothingly, then decided he had no choice but to add to her worries; he had no idea how she might react to the news he had to impart. He cleared his throat. 'Honey, I'm sorry to have to break this to you over the phone, but your father is in hospital after suffering a slight stroke.' It was rather more serious than that, but he could see no point in telling the whole truth. 'Rose thinks you ought to come over – do you feel up to it?'

'A stroke? Did Rose call you?' she asked, puzzled, for she was still under the impression he was in LA.

'No, I'm in London, honey. I was there when he collapsed.' He took a deep breath. 'I guess you'll be mad at me and say it was none of my business, but I felt he had to be confronted about the abuse you suffered.'

'Oh, my God.' Alexa sat down abruptly. She had assumed Philip's stroke had been caused by the overwork, booze and cigarettes his doctors had been warning him about for years. But it was the knowledge of what she had suffered that had caused it!

'Alexa?'

'Yes, I'm still here. I . . .' She hesitated. 'I'm not mad at you,' she said honestly. 'I had already decided I would have to talk to him about what happened, and, well . . .'

'If he was going to have a stroke, you'd rather it was on my conscience than yours,' Ace guessed correctly what she was trying to explain. 'And everyone knows I don't have one,' he added drily.

'Mmm, yes. How is he? Will he be okay?' she asked anxiously.

'Sure he will,' said Ace easily, although he hadn't the faintest idea. 'Will you be okay travelling to London alone, or shall I phone Jack? He could be with you in a couple of hours.'

'Oh, no,' Alexa said, although she was sorely tempted to say yes. But that was an echo of the old Alexa, the girl she was leaving behind. The new Alexa was strong, and was perfectly capable of getting herself on a plane to London. Or was she? she panicked, suddenly remembering something. 'Oh, Ace! My passport! I lost it, remember?' she gasped. Ace grimaced; he'd forgotten about that.

'No, you didn't lose it, honey. Go in my bedroom and look in the top drawer directly to your right as you go through the door,' he said crisply.

'You found it?' she asked, too relieved to question its whereabouts.

'Mmm,' he said, non-committally. 'Do you have a pen handy? Take down this number and phone me with your flight details. I'll pick you up at the airport,' he said.

'Okay.' Alexa rummaged for pen and paper, and jotted down the number he gave her.

She was too busy packing and worrying about her father to ponder the mystery of her missing passport until she was actually on her way. She had settled back in her seat and was trying to relax when it occurred to her to wonder when and where he had found it, and why he hadn't simply handed it back to her.

Entering his bedroom had been something of an anti-climax: she had ventured in as cautiously as she would enter Bluebeard's chamber, and found only a large, pleasant room decorated in dark blue and cream, with splashes of red. There were no black satin sheets, handcuffs or blue movies! Still, a man such as Ace would hardly need sex aids, she thought idly. He was so very . . . male. And that no longer frightened her . . .

As he had promised, Ace was waiting for her at Heathrow and, despite her anxiety over her father, Alexa felt a surge of happiness and excitement when she spotted his tall, dark figure. As usual, most of the females between the ages of seven and seventy around him were taking second and third glances at him, but he ignored them all, his smile of welcome was for Alexa alone, she noted joyously.

'How's Daddy?' she asked first.

'Drifting in and out of consciousness,' Ace told her, taking her bag from her hand and leading her towards the car park. 'Rose has been with him for most of the time. She's exhausted, but insisted on staying until you arrived,' he added, rather disapprovingly, although Alexa didn't notice his tone. Ace couldn't understand Rose's attitude – he thought she should pack her bags and move back to her own flat, not tire herself out sitting by his hospital bed. He had warned her that, if she chose to stay with Philip Kane, he would tell both Jack and Melissa what had happened to Alexa.

Rose was, indeed, exhausted, but felt she had to stay. She'd had plenty of time to think, and had decided that Alexa's story was unbelievable. She also felt her own hesitation over trusting Philip with Kit was to blame for his seizure. Ace's accusations had made him angry, yes, but it had been her own reaction that had caused him the greater anguish.

When Ace and Alexa entered the hospital, Rose was in the corridor, arguing quietly with Nick, who, for probably the only time in their lives and for different reasons, agreed with Ace – Rose should get some rest.

'I promised Melissa I'd bring you back to the flat,' he was saying, as Ace and Alexa approached. 'She's worried about you,' he added, as an extra incentive for her to leave.

'Rose!' Alexa rushed towards her. Automatically, Rose held out her arms to the distressed girl, even though she was almost sure she had lied to Ace, although why anyone would make up such a story was beyond belief. Perhaps to elicit Ace's attention, never dreaming he would head straight to London to confront her father? Her thoughts had buzzed round and round her tired brain during the long hours of her bedside vigil as she tried to make some sense of it all. She no longer knew who or what to believe.

'May I see him?' Alexa pulled away to ask.

'Of course,' Rose forced a smile. 'He's resting; he . . . he can't speak very clearly, because of the paralysis, but it's probably only temporary,' she assured her.

'Oh.' Alexa shot a faintly reproachful look at Ace, who had led her to believe he was recovering well, then she followed Rose into the room. Philip looked to be sleeping peacefully, and she relaxed slightly.

'Daddy?' she said softly, as she moved over to the bed and sat down, gently taking his hand.

After an anxious wait, Philip opened his eyes and tried to smile. It was a somewhat lopsided effort, as the right side of his body refused to obey him. He fumbled for the writing pad and pencil by his left side – he could speak, just, but sounded to his own ears like a drunken village idiot, so elected to write instead.

He had been tormented by guilt over what had happened to his daughter; what he had allowed to happen. It had made him re-examine his entire life; he had, until now, been proud of his achievements, counting himself a success. But he had failed at the most important task: that of a parent. He had failed his little girl when she had been at her most vulnerable. With difficulty, using his left hand, he scrawled just one word: 'sorry'.

'Oh, Daddy.' Alexa struggled not to cry. 'It was a long time ago and I'm okay, really I am,' she tried to assure him. 'We'll talk about it when you're better, but you're not to worry about it now.'

Rose had moved aside to let Alexa sit by the bed, and was standing behind her when Philip wrote his message. She stared in shocked disbelief at the apology, listened to Alexa excusing his behaviour and turned and rushed from the room.

'You were right,' she said shakily to Ace, then she looked at Nick, sitting as far away from him as possible. 'Will you take me to Melissa, please?' she asked, in a small voice.

'Of course I will,' he said promptly, and gently led her away.

Alexa felt happier after speaking to the doctor, who assured her Philip would probably make a full recovery, in time. Even more reassuring was the familiar, stern look of authority in her father's eyes which accompanied his written instruction for her to go home and sleep.

'I'll be back in the morning,' she whispered, leaning over and kissing his cheek. She emerged, yawning hugely, into the waiting area, surprised but pleased to find Ace still there.

'You didn't have to wait,' she said.

'I wanted to,' he replied simply, and she grinned. Of course; he always did what he wanted! 'I'll drop you off at your house . . . is that okay?' he asked, belatedly wondering if she would want to return to the 'scene of the crime'. 'Would you prefer a hotel?'

'Suite 212?' she asked solemnly, and he smiled.

'If you like,' he said casually, and her heart began to thump erratically.

'I think I would like, very much,' she whispered, flushing, then she lost her new-found courage. 'But the hospital has the Eaton Square phone number,' she added quickly.

'Fine; I'll take you there,' Ace said equably. Alexa bit her lip and berated herself for her cowardice as he led the way to the car park.

'When did you find my passport?' she asked, as they began the short journey to Belgravia.

'I didn't find it; I stole it,' he replied, matter-of-factly.

'Stole it? But why?' she asked, puzzled. Ace hesitated, then shrugged slightly.

'A few days ago I'd have told you it was to keep you in LA to give Rose a break from your tantrums. But that wouldn't have been true. I guess I just wanted you to stick around for a while,' he said, as if it was no big deal. Alexa digested the extraordinary news in silence for a few moments.

'But you don't even like me,' she said finally.

'Stop fishing!' Ace grinned at her. 'Let's just say you presented a challenge. The very first night we met, you flirted outrageously with Johnny, then turned your attention to Nick Lennox and Jack . . . everyone but me! It bugged the hell out of me,' he confessed.

'You frightened me witless,' she confided.

'Do I still frighten you?'

'No,' she replied honestly. 'You . . . excite me,' she said, with a sideways glance and a provocative smile.

Ace pretended not to realize she was coming on to him, and drove in silence until he drew up outside her front door. He remembered telling Jack she was trouble – how had he described her? The sort of girl you screw once and then can't get rid of? That was still true; his instinct had been correct – Alexa Kane was extremely fragile emotionally.

But . . . and it was a huge but; he did want her, he finally admitted to himself. He wanted to make love to her until her fears and insecurities fled and the shadows lurking in the depths of her lovely golden-green eyes vanished forever. And then what – say goodbye? That would shatter any new-found confidence he managed to instill in her that she was a desirable woman. He frowned as, for the first time in his life, he contemplated how his actions might affect a girl he wanted in his bed.

'Thanks for bringing me home,' Alexa broke the silence that was rapidly becoming strained, but she made no move to get out of the car. Ace turned to look at her – big mistake. Her eyes were large, luminous pools, begging for . . . what? Comfort? Reassurance?

'Don't look at me like that,' he almost groaned, reaching out to cup her chin in his hand. Of their own volition, it seemed, his fingers gently stroked her cheek. Another big mistake. Hastily he removed his hand. 'Alexa, honey, I have to go back to LA tomorrow – the studio will be going nuts. And you have things to sort out here.'

'I know,' she agreed softly. 'But that's tomorrow. Will you stay here with me tonight? Please?'

'I'm no good for you, honey,' Ace said, rather desperately. 'I'm a selfish bastard – you need a nice guy who'll look after you.'

Alexa bit her lip and told herself sternly to gather up what little remained of her pride and get out of the car. But it was as if she were super-glued to the seat.

'I . . . I'll say goodnight, then,' she finally managed to say, fumbling to release the safety belt. Blinded by tears, she couldn't see what she was doing and struggled with the clasp. 'Sod it!' Suddenly, she was frantic to leave before he saw her crying, and tugged hard on the belt, but only succeeded in tightening its grip around her body. 'Damn thing!'

'I bet your nails are too long again,' Ace said teasingly, as he leaned across to help her. She glanced up at him, torn between laughter and tears, then their eyes met and the laughter stilled.

'Aw, to hell with it!' Ace sighed his capitulation and and reached for her, cupping her face in his hands and bending to kiss her.

The first touch of his lips on hers jolted Alexa, and she sighed with pleasure, opening her mouth to him and welcoming the tantalizing, darting caresses of his tongue as he gradually deepened the kiss.

Ace was still well in control, alert for any sign of tension or distress, but she responded so beautifully to his kisses that he almost allowed himself to be swept along on a tide of desire. Almost, but not quite. Although the seat belts and steering wheel had to take some of the credit for his restraint, he acknowledged ruefully, as the latter dug painfully into his ribs and the former anchored him firmly in his seat.

'I haven't necked in a car for about fifteen years,' he said, when they finally paused for breath. 'Can we at least get into the back seat?'

'In Belgravia?' Alexa asked, in mock horror. 'Let's go into the house,' she suggested. This time, he didn't argue, but got out of the car with an alacrity that matched hers. Alexa scrabbled in her bag for her keys; it took an age for her to find them amongst the clutter, and they were both helpless with laughter when she finally managed to open the door.

Hand in hand they walked up the stairs, and exchanged amused looks of mutual understanding as they both recalled the only previous occasion they had climbed these stairs together; the time which had resulted in her being half-drowned. Only then Ace had been furiously angry with her and Alexa too drunk to care.

'It'd better be me that has the cold shower tonight,' Ace said, as they entered her room.

'Why?'

'Because tonight's for you, not me,' he replied simply, and Alexa smiled slightly.

'I thought you said you were selfish?' she reminded him softly.

'I am,' Ace said promptly. 'I want you to enjoy tonight enough to want a repeat performance. It will do my ego, not to mention my reputation, no good at all if you hate what I do to you,' he said lightly. 'I hate to sound like an agony aunt, but have you ever had an orgasm?'

'I don't think so,' she said uncertainly, and it was his turn to smile.

'In that case, you haven't. But you will,' he promised huskily, and Alexa gulped, nerves warring with anticipation. Ace bent his head to kiss her again, resting his hands lightly on her waist and, within seconds, almost unbearable excitement coursed throughout her body, banishing her apprehension.

'Just one more question – what exactly is it that you hate? Penetration?'

'Yes.' She blushed.

'Then I won't. Not until you ask me to,' he declared, sounding so confident she would ask that Alexa began to believe it, too.

'Will you undress for me, honey?' he asked, his dark eyes glittering. He knew it was a gamble, asking her to strip, but she was such an exhibitionist, and he felt that, this way, she would feel she was the one in control of the situation.

Alexa hesitated only briefly, then she nodded. She was justly proud of her body and she wanted to give him pleasure, despite what he had said about tonight being for her. And she felt sure he wouldn't denounce her as a tease, or something far worse, if she balked later, as some other men had done in the past.

Ace kicked off his shoes and shrugged off his jacket, then moved over to the bed and lay sprawled against the headboard, determined to remove no more items of clothing until she either asked him to or did it herself. He hoped for the latter.

Seemingly casual, he watched her slowly undress, standing in front of him with the light from the bedside lamp bathing her body in a soft glow. He had seen her naked before, of course, the night after

Kit's christening, but his behaviour that evening was something he now wished to forget, and hoped she had, too. She'd certainly been drunk enough to have retained no memory of it, he thought wryly, as he feasted his eyes on each bared part of her body.

She was so slender and fine-boned, but beautifully proportioned. What was that phrase? A pocket Venus? It suited her, he thought; her breasts were small, but high and firm, her waist tiny, her buttocks softly rounded, her legs long and shapely. As he gazed at her, her breasts became swollen, the nipples hardening and jutting out, as if seeking attention. A good sign, he noted approvingly.

'Do you know how beautiful you are?' he asked softly.

'No.' She shook her head, but there was an impish smile on her lips.

'Come here and let me show you,' he said, holding out a hand towards her. Alexa hesitated for a split-second, then moved willingly towards him, her hips swaying provocatively – and quite unintentionally, Ace realized.

'Sexy Lexy.' He smiled at her, and she hung her head.

'Don't tease,' she begged. 'I'm not sexy.'

'You will be,' he promised, reaching for her hand and gently tugging it, encouraging her to take the last few steps to the bed. Then he lifted her hand to his mouth and kissed the palm before leisurely taking each finger in turn into the moist heat of his mouth.

'Oh, wow!' Alexa sat down abruptly. Since when had her fingers become erogenous zones? she wondered dazedly, as the sensual sucking and nibbling continued to make her senses reel. She quickly discovered her other hand was just as sensitive, as were her wrists, her arms, the back of her neck . . . oh, yes! Also her ears, the hollow of her collar-bone . . .

'Ohh,' she breathed, as his hands gently but expertly caressed her body while he held her on his lap and bent his head to suckle her breasts.

Her head fell back and she arched her spine to grant him freer access; tiny, incoherent gasps urged him on and she began to squirm against him, plucking impatiently at his shirt, wanting, needing to feel his heated skin against her own.

Ace contained his own impatience and let her fumble with the buttons; finally, she eased the material from his powerfully muscled torso and ran her hands tentatively over his chest, curling her fingers into the mat of dark curls and smiling in delight when his nipples hardened at her touch.

Hc continued his gentle assault on her body and senses, determinedly ignoring the hard evidence of his own arousal, as he sought to banish every one of her fears until she surrendered to him completely. For the first time in his life, his partner's enjoyment was more important to him than his own, but he wasn't accustomed to denying his own needs and, even now, he had only abandoned them temporarily. So far as he was concerned, neither of them was leaving the bed until both were fully satisfied and complete.

She was half-sitting, half-lying across his body, held firmly against his chest while his long fingers expertly toyed with her flesh, searing a path of pleasure wherever they touched her. He lingered briefly, tantalizingly, at the golden curls between her legs before continuing slowly down her thigh and calf until he captured her foot which, to her amazement, had also apparently become an erogenous zone.

Alexa squirmed in delight as his lips began to follow the burning trail begun by his hands, and she bit back a scream of pleasure as his tongue flicked at the hardened nub of her clitoris. Of their own volition, her legs parted for him; physically, she was ready for consummation, Ace knew, but the emotional barrier still remained. Despite his own deprivation, he was deriving immense gratification from the soft moans and incoherent gasps that greeted every new touch, each new sensation.

'Please,' Alexa said breathlessly; the aching need deep within her cried out to be assuaged. 'Please,' she entreated again. Ace purposely made her wait, silencing her with a long, drugging kiss while moulding her body against his, still-clothed, hips. It was Alexa who reached for the belt at his waist and unzipped him.

'Please, come inside me,' she whispered against his mouth. Ace stripped quickly and efficiently, long experience enabling him to do so without ceasing his caresses for one moment.

He thought briefly of his pack of condoms, still in his jacket, yards away from the bed . . . too far away, he decided recklessly.

His entry was so smooth and rapid that Alexa had no time to feel afraid; she had barely begun to tense in anticipation of pain before she relaxed again, realizing, with a sense of wonder, that he was already deep within her.

She was so hot and tight that Ace had to grit his teeth against climaxing too soon. With sure, practised strokes he drove her slowly towards orgasm; the gasps for breath, her fingers clutching at the sheet, the thrashing of her head from side to side on the pillow, all told him of her mounting excitement.

He watched the deep flush of passion staining her cheeks, then her mouth opened in a round O of surprised wonder, and she arched against him, her muscles contracting around him as she shuddered to a climax. The hot sheath holding Ace, seemingly sucking him even deeper inside, gave him the release he craved and he surrendered to it, then let his head fall on her shoulder as he regained his breath. Belatedly remembering how small-boned she was, he removed his weight from her body and lay by her side, grinning triumphantly at the glazed expression of delight on her face.

'Thank you; you really are as clever as everyone says,' she whispered, then blushed and her eyes filled with unexpected tears.

'Don't cry, honey,' Ace kissed away the salty drops. 'There's nothing to cry about, not now.'

'You don't know what this means . . . I'm happy. I'm normal!' she said wonderingly.

'Sure you are,' Ace kissed the tip of her nose. 'You are also tired and jet-lagged. Get some sleep,' he ordered, wrapping the quilt around her nude body. Alexa snuggled close, her eyes already beginning to close.

'You also need to build up your strength for lesson number two,' he added provocatively, and she fell asleep with a smile on her lips and a happy expectation in her heart.

# CHAPTER 13

When Alexa awoke, she discovered lesson number two was already under way. The mists of sleep departed gradually as wonderfully erotic dreams of Ace slowly became reality. She was lying in her side, her back and buttocks pressed against an obviously aroused Ace, and the knowledge brought only a frisson of anticipatory pleasure and not even a hint of apprehension.

He was nibbling at her shoulders and ears, unerringly finding the ultra-sensitive spot above her collarbone, while his hands roamed over her breasts and tummy, seemingly everywhere, then dipping lower to part her thighs and toy with the already sodden cluster of curls.

'Would you like me to prove last night wasn't a fluke?' His voice was soft and seductive, his breath warm in her ear. She turned to face him, a rosy blush colouring her cheeks.

'Yes, please,' she whispered; the ache of longing between her legs was already unbearable, demanding release, and she gave a gasp of delight when he lifted her thigh and hooked it over his hips to align their bodies perfectly. She pressed eagerly against him, but he held back.

'I won't penetrate you until you ask,' he reminded her teasingly, and this time neither doubted she would do so.

'I'm asking,' she said quickly and breathlessly, with a lack of modesty that made Ace give a small smile of triumph. He turned on to his back, effortlessly carrying her with him so she straddled his hips.

'This time, you're in control,' he told her.

'I'm not sure . . .' she faltered, as the old feelings of insecurity came rushing back.

'I am,' Ace said firmly. Expertly, but gently, he manoeuvred her into position; his hands on her hips guided her movements and she quickly matched his rhythm. Her hair fell in a golden-red curtain around them both and Ace wound one hand into the silky tresses and tugged slightly, bringing her face down to meet his in a long, drugging kiss.

'Don't ever cut your hair,' he murmured.

'I won't,' she gasped. Her breathing became ragged and uneven as the pleasure grew and intensified with each powerful thrust. It's going to happen again, she thought wondrously, just moments before the second climax of her life stopped her thinking at all. There was just spasm after spasm of explosive joy that left her feeling drained but utterly happy.

When her rapid heartbeats had stilled a little, she raised her head and laughed out loud in her relief and gladness. Ace grinned at her and tucked her into the crook of his shoulder, their bodies still entwined. He would have to revise his opinion on bedding virgins, he thought idly, for, in many ways, that was what

Alexa had been. Teaching an untried girl how to give and receive pleasure was more rewarding than he had previously thought.

It was still early, around six-thirty, and he drifted off into a half-sleep. Alexa lay motionless beside him, content to watch him as the room gradually lightened into day. A lock of black hair flopped boyishly on to his forehead, the often harsh line of his mouth had softened in repose and thick black lashes that any girl would kill for fanned his stubble-darkened cheeks. She wondered idly if anyone had ever dared tell him how feminine they were – if a man had, he'd likely still be picking himself up off the floor, she thought, with a smile.

If only we could stay together like this forever, she thought wistfully, but knew it was impossible. I mustn't cling, she told herself firmly, sure he would hate that and back off in alarm. Besides, he had to return to LA while she had to remain in London. She hadn't even phoned the hospital, she realized guiltily, but was loath to make a move now and disturb the man sleeping beside her. They would have phoned me if anything was wrong, she assured herself.

She raised herself slightly on one elbow and watched the gentle rise and fall of his chest, admiring the corded muscles of his arms and torso. His body was still that of an athlete, strong and firm with not an ounce of superfluous flesh.

She reached up to lightly smooth back the errant lock of hair from his forehead. By now, Ace was awake, but pretended not to be and concentrated on keeping his breathing deep and even. He could almost feel the curiosity in her eyes and wondered if she would take the initiative if he feigned sleep. To his delight, she did.

Alexa, once her eyes had feasted on the length and breadth of his body, wanted to do more. She had never enjoyed touching her lovers – if they were even worthy of the name, which she now doubted – and especially not . . . there!

She glanced down, and then her fingers followed her gaze and trailed a leisurely path down to his groin. He had given her so much pleasure and she wanted to do something for him without him having to ask her. When other men had requested oral sex, she had recoiled in horror and flatly refused, but now she was amazed to discover she actually wanted to touch and taste him.

Slowly, she inched down the bed: first, her fingers gently stroked the rapid growing length of his shaft. It was so hard, yet soft and warm to the touch, she thought, continuing her delicate massage. Too delicate for Ace, but he wasn't about to start bellowing instructions like a marine recruiting sergeant, and was content to let her continue her exploration at her own pace.

He couldn't hide his increasing arousal, but Alexa seemed to imagine he was still sleeping, so he stayed as motionless as possible. However, he couldn't prevent a tiny moan escaping when her hot, wet mouth finally closed over him. Again, her movements were tentative, untutored, and he guessed, with machismo triumph, that this was a first time for her.

As before, he elected to say nothing that might shatter the fragile burgeoning confidence in her own sexuality. Besides, she's coming along nicely, he thought complacently, as her tongue flicked sensuously over his engorged glands. He closed his eyes and lay back to give himself up to the enjoyment of what she was doing.

They both heard the noise at the same time, but only Alexa recognized it for what it was – the high-pitched whine of the vacuum cleaner outside in the hall, gradually becoming louder as it neared her door. Then, it was louder still, as the door opened and Mary, the Kanes' housekeeper, entered the room.

'Oh, God!' Alexa scrambled away, snatching up a pillow – the first available cover to hand – and placed it in front of her body. Mary remained, motionless, in the doorway, the vacuum cleaner in her hand still whirring away.

Mary had not even realized Alexa was back in England and could not believe the scene of debauchery she had just witnessed. She stared disapprovingly at Alexa, then glared at Ace, still unashamedly erect and making no effort to hide it. Despite the most inopportune interruption, he was struggling not to laugh.

'Er – have you met Mary, our housekeeper?' Alexa enquired politely of Ace, and her attempt at the social niceties made him laugh even harder. 'Mary, this is Ace Delaney – he – er – brought me home last night,' she explained lamely. Mary finally rediscovered her powers of speech.

'Yes, he was here when your father collapsed and was rushed to hospital,' she said disapprovingly. 'How is Mr Kane this morning?' she enquired.

'Oh! I haven't telephoned yet,' Alexa mumbled guiltily.

'Hm!' Mary sniffed. 'I'll clean up in here later, shall I?'

'Yes, please,' Alexa said meekly. Mary exited and the door closed behind her with a resounding slam. 'Oh, don't laugh, this isn't funny,' Alexa begged Ace, who was still creased up with laughter.

'She's only jealous,' he said dismissively, reaching for Alexa. 'Now, where were we?'

'No.' She pulled away, albeit reluctantly. 'I must phone the hospital first,' she said.

'Okay; I'll go and take a shower. And how about some breakfast? I need to keep up my strength!' He winked suggestively as he sauntered, totally nude and magnificently male, into her bathroom.

Alexa wanted to join him, to hang on to the wonder and joy of the past few hours, for never had she felt so happy and complete. It couldn't last, of course, and she sighed heavily as she picked up the phone and began dialling.

Philip Kane had enjoyed a restful night, she was told. She also learned that the hospital intended running further tests that morning, so no visitors would be allowed until the afternoon.

She felt guiltily pleased about that piece of news. Less welcome was the reply to her query concerning the paralysis affecting him and the probable length of recovery time. Her spirits sank as the doctor explained that Philip would need months of daily physiotherapy; that he might never fully regain the use of his right arm and leg.

He will hate that, she thought, as she slowly replaced the receiver. He became dreadfully bored and bad-tempered if a bout of flu dared to strike him, and his frustration after a skiing accident had left his ankle in plaster for a few weeks had been awful to live with – for the rest of the household. I hope Rose can tolerate his moods, she thought.

However, for the present, she determinedly put depressing thoughts to the back of her mind and went to join Ace in the shower, where she underwent a far different experience from the icy-cold near-drowning to which he had subjected her a couple of months before.

He soaped her thoroughly, seeking out every curve and hollow, his slippery fingers dipping tantalizingly between her buttocks and sliding deep inside her.

'Oh! That's nice!' Alexa gasped, and she reached for a bar of soap and moved towards him, intending to soap him just as thoroughly as he had her.

'Later,' Ace said firmly. 'Feed me first, woman!' he growled. Such caveman tactics ought to have made her bristle with indignation, Alexa realized, but she was too happy to care. Besides, his words implied he would be staying a while longer and that alone far outweighed any feminist principles she might have!

'I don't have to be at the hospital until this afternoon,' she said, stepping out of the shower and handing him one towel and taking another for herself. 'Do we have time for any more lessons before you return to the States?' she asked casually, as if it didn't really matter to her, for she was determined not to beg, or to demand more of his time and attention than he was prepared to give.

'I guess they can manage without me for another day or so,' Ace decided, with a silent apology to Ella, waiting impatiently to begin her new life at the tennis academy. He didn't spare a thought for the dozens of people at the TV studio, twiddling their thumbs at great cost to the backers of *Country Club*, while he dallied in England.

'Great,' Alexa said lightly, feeling dizzy with relief and happiness.

They crept downstairs as quietly as possible, avoiding Mary like two kids bunking off school, and dived into the kitchen. It was not a room where Alexa spent a great deal of time, but she managed to produce a hearty English breakfast of bacon, egg, toast and marmalade, with lashings of hot coffee. To her amazement, she discovered she actually enjoyed waiting on a man.

When Ace was finally replete, Alexa stacked the dishwasher, but only after first attempting to load the dirty crockery into the washing machine! Ace grinned at her discomfiture, but was aware that, not so long ago, her ineptitude would have irritated him intensely, and he would have taken it as yet another sign of her uselessness.

She had been a rich Daddy's girl with no financial necessity or desire to change her ways. Already, with her memory regained, she was beginning to make the adjustments to a more normal life. All she needs is a good shrink and a strong man to sort her out, he thought arrogantly, but he shied away from thinking she might expect him to be that man. He wasn't accustomed to introspection, nor to wondering how his often appalling behaviour affected the girls he dated, but even he realized Alexa needed a man who wouldn't mess her around, leaving her more screwed up than she was already.

But, for now, she looked very fetching, clad only in a negligee that parted down the middle to reveal glimpses of smooth thigh and breast, and clung to her buttocks as she bent over the dishwasher. Ace moved behind her and deftly untied the belt, slipping his hands beneath the flimsy material.

'We can't, not here,' Alexa protested, but extremely half-heartedly. 'Mary . . .' she reminded him.

'. . . can't possibly be more shocked than she is already,' Ace drawled, and Alexa giggled.

'I guess not,' she agreed, and lifted her face to meet his kiss. Even her toes curled with excitement as he moulded her body to his, deepening the kiss and sensuously exploring her mouth with his tongue. He is so good at this, she thought dreamily.

This time, it wasn't Mary who interrupted them, but the insistent ringing of the phone. The machine was evidently switched off and Mary too busy or too outraged to answer it, and Alexa reluctantly pulled away from Ace.

'I'd better answer it – it might be someone from the hospital,' she said.

'Okay.' Ace released her and wandered out of the room, picking up the day's newspapers from the hall table and glancing through them while Alexa took the call.

It wasn't the hospital, but Graham Peters, one of Philip's board of directors, wanting the latest news of Philip's progress. Alexa liked Graham – he was the youngest and also the nicest of her father's colleagues, she often thought – but she had no time for him today. She quickly told him what little she had learned and promised to call him as soon as she knew the results from the morning's tests.

'Knowing Philip, he'll be back on his feet sooner than the doctors predict,' Graham said. 'The hardest part will be making him take things easy once he's out of hospital.'

'I know,' Alexa sighed.

'It's lucky he has Rose to keep him entertained. Perhaps she should take him on a long cruise to recuperate?' he suggested.

'That sounds like a good idea,' Alexa approved. 'I'll phone you this evening, Graham,' she added, and hastily ended the call, aware of Ace lounging impatiently in the doorway. But Graham's remarks had brought back her own earlier fears about Rose's desire and capability of coping with a testy invalid – would she even want to try? If I hadn't been so horrible to her when they became engaged, they might be married by now, she thought sadly.

'Something wrong?' Ace enquired, hearing her sigh.

'No. Well . . . I was just wondering about something. Do you think Rose will still be prepared to marry Daddy? she asked.

'I hope not!' Ace said fervently.

'Why?' she asked, puzzled. Surely he doesn't still harbour feelings for Rose? she thought, feeling sick at the very idea.

'Why?' Ace repeated incredulously. 'You know why.'

'No, I don't. He's going to need her . . .'

'I don't give a damn what he needs! A prison cell is too good for him,' he said wrathfully. Alexa stared at him, utterly confused. 'Look, honey,' Ace continued, in a slightly calmer voice, 'if you want to forgive and forget what happened when you were a kid, that's your decision. And I appreciate that you don't want the whole world knowing, but you must understand that, if Rose marries him, or even continues living here, I have to warn Jack and Melissa.'

'What's it to them?' Alexa demanded, rather belligerently. He seemed more concerned about the Farrells than her!

'Don't be stupid,' Ace said impatiently. 'You don't want another child suffering the same fate as you, surely? Jack and Melissa have the right to know what sort of man your father is.'

'What the hell does that mean?' Her voice rose shrilly.

'Aw, Alexa! You're not suppressing it all again, just because he's in hospital, are you?' he sighed. 'He's a rapist and a pervert . . .'

'How dare you?' Alexa screamed, her hand raised to strike. Ace caught her wrist and pulled her arm back down to her side.

'Don't,' he warned, but with compassion, she thought dazedly. 'Ill or not, he's the same man who raped your nursemaid and abused you,' he said quietly. Alexa stared at him for endless moments as her world came crashing down around her, and she realized the nature of the scene which had resulted in her father's stroke. This was unbearable . . . She swallowed painfully.

'You . . . you accused him of that?' she finally managed to croak.

'Yes, of course.'

'That's why he had a stroke – because of you . . .' She closed her eyes against the horror of it all. And I've just been in bed with him, she thought, with the man who almost killed my father. She shuddered, filled with self-loathing and hatred for Ace. She wrenched her arm free, and turned her back, unable to look at him.

'He thought I'd accused him of . . .' she said quietly, half to herself, then she turned on Ace in a rage. 'You idiot! It wasn't Daddy! It was my grandfather!' she screamed at him. 'I poured out my heart to you, and you weren't even listening!' She flew at him then, pounding his chest with her fists. 'You could have killed him! You didn't even listen to me. You didn't listen!' she repeated, and began to cry, huge heart-wrenching sobs torn from her body.

Ace held her wrists, trying, as gently as possible, to subdue the bundle of fury attempting to harm him. He frowned, not at all convinced she was telling the truth, and considered the possibility that she might want to protect the man who had abused her. Or was she scared of him? Afraid of the repercussions?

'Alexa, honey, you told me he came to your bed after your mother died, after he had raped the nursemaid and she left. Are you trying to tell me now that it didn't happen?' he asked carefully.

'I'm never telling you anything ever again!' she said hysterically, then went on to do so. 'Magda . . . oh, that didn't happen here!' she said impatiently. 'After she returned home to Germany, I went to stay with my grandparents. It was my grandfather who came to my bed – I told you that. I told you!' she reiterated, hot tears coursing down her cheeks. 'Poor

Daddy. He thought I'd told you he had done that?' she choked. It was just too appalling to even imagine how he must have felt . . .

She turned and ran from the room; she just had to go to the hospital, now, tests or no tests. Ace ran after her, the increasingly familiar and uncomfortable emotion of guilt squeezing his heart. And maybe he felt something else for the distraught girl, but he refused to consider that.

Alexa reached her room and began feverishly pulling clothes out of the wardrobe.

'I hate you! Get out!' she spat, when Ace appeared in the doorway. 'How dare you mess with my life? You, with your amateur psychology and your sex therapy! Get out of my life,' she said venomously.

'I might have been wrong about the former, but you can't deny the latter was successful,' Ace remarked, somewhat unwisely.

'Oh, sure; thanks for that! I'll be able to make up for lost time now, won't I? In between hospital visits, of course.'

For some reason, the thought of her practising what he had taught her with other men enraged Ace. Also, he hated admitting to making mistakes, even small ones, let alone a huge one such as wrongly accusing a man of incest. He took refuge in his earlier suspicion that she was covering up for her father, out of a loyalty as twisted as Philip's love for her.

'I think you were telling me the truth back in LA,' he said coldly. 'So my earlier warning stands – if Rose stays with him, I'm telling Jack and Melissa to keep their children away from here.'

'Rose! Jack and Melissa!' she mimicked, angrily discarding her robe and pulling on her outdoor clothes as if he weren't in the room. Suddenly, she paused. 'Why did you fly over here? Was it because of me, or to stop Rose marrying him?' she asked, with some difficulty.

'I came to get Rose away from here, of course. Why else? I'm very fond of Rose,' he said coolly.

'Just leave me alone, will you?' Alexa asked quietly, suddenly feeling more sad than angry. 'I never want to see you again.'

'That suits me fine,' Ace said, and turned and stormed out of the house. His hire car had been clamped and, after cursing roundly for several minutes, he left it where it was, merely removing his overnight bag and leaving the keys in the ignition before hailing a cab to take him straight to Heathrow.

When she heard the slamming of the front door, Alexa's face crumpled and she sank to the floor, burying her head in her hands and sobbing as if her heart would break. She cried for her father, lying in hospital, struck down by false accusations of the vilest kind, and cried for the loss of what she might have had with the only man to make her feel happy and fulfilled . . .

Huh! Well, we'll soon see about that! she vowed, fumbling for a handkerchief. She had worked through her problems all by herself; there was no longer a barrier preventing her enjoying a full sexual relationship with someone else. Anyone else. But not Ace Delaney; never again. She must have been mad . . . He had bewitched her . . . I didn't even insist he used condoms, she realized, with horror at her own stupidity. And I performed oral sex . . . I should have bitten it off! she thought wrathfully.

After a while, with no tears left to shed, she calmed down sufficiently to bathe her swollen face and reddened eyes in cold water and finish dressing. She realized the futility of sitting in the hospital waiting room until the tests had been completed, and instead phoned Melissa, to check if Rose was still there, and how she was feeling.

'Can I come over to see her?' Alexa asked hesitantly, when Melissa confirmed Rose's presence.

'Of course,' Melissa said promptly, for she was dying of curiosity. Her mother had been very distressed when Nick had brought her home the night before, yet she had said that Philip's condition was improving. It didn't make any sense. Nor did Ace's involvement. That was a real mystery. Frowning slightly, she went to tell Rose, still abed, that Alexa was on her way over.

'Oh, God. That poor girl . . . I don't know what to say to her,' Rose said, obviously still very upset.

'What's going on?' Melissa asked.

'Oh,' Rose glanced away, 'I can't really tell you, darling,' she said apologetically. 'It's not my secret to divulge and, besides, it's just too awful . . .' She broke off.

'That's okay,' Melissa said easily. And, when Alexa duly arrived, she offered to take herself off shopping and leave them alone.

'Nick and I have bought a house, Nine Elms, just five miles from Bellwood,' she told a pale, but red-eyed Alexa, and pretended not to notice the signs of recent tears. 'We're moving in just as soon as the baby's born, so I'm busy buying furniture and pictures – nesting, Nick calls it,' she added cheerfully.

'Oh, no, please don't go,' Alexa begged; she was not sure how much Melissa already knew, and wanted to put the record straight. 'Rose, you were there when Daddy collapsed, weren't you? Well, you have to know the truth. Ace lied . . . well, he was mistaken,' she amended fairly; even though she hated him for the damage he had caused, she realized he hadn't done it deliberately. 'It is true that I was abused as a child, but not by my father. It was my grandfather. Ace got it wrong. Dreadfully wrong,' she repeated sadly.

'Oh,' Rose digested that in silence for a few moments, not knowing what to believe. It occurred to her, as it had to Ace, that Alexa could be deluding herself; that she wanted to bury the memories again. Had it not been for Philip's note of apology, she might still think Alexa had invented the whole story as a way of gaining Ace's attention. All the possibilities were just too awful to contemplate. She rather wished she had never met Philip Kane or his troubled and troublesome daughter.

Melissa had listened in appalled and shocked silence; it was the first time child abuse had been mentioned to her and instinctively she crossed the room to Alexa and gave her a warm hug. They were hardly friends, barely knew each other, in fact, but Alexa clung to Melissa as if to a lifelong friend.

'Come and sit down,' Melissa urged her, and held her hand as they sat together on the sofa. 'Mum?' Melissa prompted, bemused by her mother's attitude – surely she ought to be overjoyed at this piece of news?

'Yes, well,' Rose fussed with her empty coffee cup, and finally looked up at Alexa. 'Are you quite certain Ace made a mistake?' she asked gently.

'Of course I am!' Alexa insisted hotly. 'Daddy never hurt me. Surely you can't believe he would ever do such a thing!' she exclaimed in horror.

'I don't want to believe it,' Rose agreed. 'But . . . I saw the note he wrote for you last night. He said he was sorry,' she reminded Alexa.

'Oh. I assumed he was apologizing for sending me to stay with my grandfather,' Alexa said slowly.

'But Ace never mentioned your grandparents. He said you had told him your father raped Magda, and then abused you,' Rose said painfully. Alexa shook her head violently in denial.

'I know what Ace said, but I'm sure Daddy must have realized what really happened,' she said firmly.

'How could he?' Rose asked doubtfully. 'If you had no memory of it until a couple of days ago, how could your father have guessed? Just a moment – your grandfather? Is his name Peter?'

'It was. He died six or seven years ago. Why?'

'Your father was trying to speak to me while we were waiting for the ambulance. He kept saying "Peter".'

'So he did guess!' Alexa sagged with relief. 'I've been torturing myself, thinking he might have believed I'd accuse him of such a vile act. But he knew Ace had got it all wrong.' She took a deep, tension-releasing breath, then her expression hardened again. 'But Ace still caused him to have a stroke.'

'Mmm, well, I'm afraid I might have to accept some of the responsibility for that,' Rose confessed miserably. 'Your father was furious with Ace, no doubt about it, but he looked really stricken when Ace asked me if I would risk having my grandchildren near him, and . . . I hesitated,' she whispered. 'If there was one chance in a million that the accusation was valid, then I couldn't, wouldn't risk it. My hesitation hurt your father more than anything Ace said to him. I'm so sorry I wronged him,' she said wretchedly.

'I . . . I think I can understand how you felt,' Alexa acknowledged fairly. 'I'm sure Ace was very persuasive,' she said bitterly. 'He doesn't care about what happened to me – he flew over here to stop you marrying Daddy. But you will still get married, won't you? When he's better?' she asked eagerly.

'I'm not sure he'll still want to marry me,' Rose prevaricated. She had harboured doubts about the marriage even before all this awful business had reared its ugly head. And, of course, it was a hundred times worse because Ace had been Philip's accuser.

She was also aware that, wrongly and irrationally, her feelings for Philip had altered dramatically. If anyone had dared suggest Daniel Farrell had molested a child, she would have defended him with her dying breath, but she had to face the fact that she had wavered in her loyalty to Philip Kane.

And, in his rather obsessive jealousy of Ace Delaney, he would no doubt accuse her – quite justly – of betrayal: she'd had to choose between Ace and Philip and had chosen, however briefly and reluctantly, to believe Ace. Lost in thought, it was quite some time before she realized Alexa was watching her expectantly, and she forced a smile.

'We'll just have to wait and see,' she said gently. 'I expect he'll need a long time to recuperate.'

'I realize that. But Graham Peters phoned this morning and suggested you and Daddy take a long cruise as soon as he feels well enough. Don't you think that's a good idea?' she enthused.

'Well,' Rose glanced at Melissa, 'I'm sorry, Alexa, but I don't want to be away from England when Melissa has her baby,' she said apologetically. It was true, but it was also an excuse and she avoided Melissa's quizzical gaze.

'Oh.' Alexa's face fell. 'Of course you don't,' she agreed flatly. 'I . . . I wish I had been nicer to you when you and Daddy became engaged,' she mumbled. 'I was a bitch, I know, but I'd really love for you to be my mother.'

'Oh, Alexa.' Rose moved over and put her arm around the girl. 'I could never be that, but I'll always be your friend. I'm just relieved you don't blame me for your father's illness.'

'No,' Alexa sniffed. 'Ace Delaney's to blame for that!'

'Why on earth did you confide in Ace, of all people?' Melissa asked, rather tactlessly, but she was dying to know. Ace was hardly the kind of man one turned to with emotional problems.

'I don't know. I didn't intend to. Ella – a kid he's coaching – said something that triggered my memory, and I began talking about it, to myself mostly, I think, just remembering out loud. I remember Ace was there. I was upset and he gave me some sleeping pills. I had no idea he intended coming to England or that he hadn't even been paying attention!' she added bitterly.

'He must be feeling gutted,' Melissa said. 'Where is he now?

'In hell, I hope,' Alexa said viciously. 'No, he's gone back to LA. And I hope he stays there and I never set eyes on him again!'

## CHAPTER 14

Ace arrived back in LA in the early afternoon, local time, more tired and depressed than he could ever remember feeling, and certainly in no mood to deal with the problems awaiting him at home.

Ella had skipped school to hang around his house waiting for him, desperately afraid her dreams were about to vanish as suddenly as he had. Johnny Dancer was there, too, frantic with worry because the studio bosses, finally losing patience with Ace, were threatening to axe *Country Club* and sue Ace for breach of contract. Johnny had been working his way steadily through a bottle of Ace's finest brandy and was, as a consequence, belligerent as well as morose.

'Where the hell have you been?' he demanded, as soon as Ace appeared. Ace, noting the near-empty bottle, merely raised one brow at Johnny's tone and then ignored him. Glancing around, he spotted Ella down on the court, practising with rather less enthusiasm than usual.

'Ella! Get up here!' he bellowed. She was delighted to see him and dashed across the court and up the steps to the terrace.

'Are you taking me to the academy?' she asked breathlessly.

'No, he's not. He's coming to the studio with me!' Johnny put in.

'Shut up, both of you. I'm going nowhere until I've caught up on my sleep,' Ace said irritably; he couldn't remember when he had last slept properly. 'Ella.' He turned to her. 'Tell me exactly what transpired between you and Alexa,' he said, rather sternly. Ella hesitated, choosing her words carefully, not altogether sure she wasn't to blame for Alexa's breakdown.

'Well, I was watching those videos, like you told me to,' she began slowly. 'Alexa said something about not being allowed to watch stuff like that when she was at school . . .'

'Stuff like – what?' Ace interrupted.

'Um, incest,' she mumbled, crimson with embarrassment at discussing such a topic with two men listening avidly. 'There were girls on the tape telling how they had been abused by their fathers,' she told him.

'Just fathers? Or other family members, too? Grandfathers, perhaps?' Ace asked intently.

'The bit I saw was just about fathers and daughters,' Ella said. 'I suppose it could have featured other relatives too, but I didn't notice.'

'Hm. Then what happened?' Ace enquired.

'I told you at the time – she just went nuts,' Ella said simply.

'That I can believe!' Johnny put in caustically. 'Don't try and rationalize her behaviour, Ace. She's psychotic, if you ask me.'

'No one did, Johnny, so just shut up!' Ace snapped. 'In fact, bugger off,' he added irritably.

'What about *Country Club*?'

'Sod it,' Ace said dismissively.

'But . . . when will you be back on the set?' Johnny persisted.

'When I feel like it – okay?' Ace stared him down, and Johnny shrugged, backing off from a confrontation.

'Okay, but don't blame me if they sue you.'

'I don't much care if they do. This is my last series, anyhow,' he said casually. 'It's become rather boring.'

'You can't mean that!' Johnny was appalled. 'They're paying you a fortune!'

'I already have a fortune. Several, in fact,' Ace reminded him smoothly. 'You should be pleased at the opportunity to take on other parts, Johnny; I'm sure your agent doesn't want you to become typecast. After all, you can't make a career out of being my sidekick,' he added mockingly. Johnny's lips tightened in annoyance.

'You can't chuck everyone on the scrap-heap just because you're bored!' he bit out.

'I can't?' Ace enquired blandly. Johnny sighed and ran his fingers through his hair.

'I can see you're knackered,' he said placatingly. 'Give me a call when you're ready to talk, huh?' Ace nodded tersely and Johnny, shoulders hunched, made his way back to his own house, miserably aware that it might not be his for very much longer. If *Country Club* was axed, he would never be able to keep up the repayments, not on the house, not even on the black Porsche, identical to the one Ace drove, that he had recently bought.

'Damn the bastard!' he muttered darkly. 'And damn that English bitch, too!' He and Ace had had a great time, on and off the set, until that trip to London last Christmas when Alexa Kane had fallen, literally, at their feet. I should have left her in the gutter! he now thought wrathfully. All the bad fortune stemmed from that meeting; if she hadn't placed drugs in Ace's luggage, he would never have met Ella, and that had rekindled his passion for tennis. As that had grown, his interest in acting had dwindled.

When Johnny was out of sight, Ace turned his attention to Ella. She was watching him anxiously, her large brown eyes wide with apprehension.

'If I said or did something to upset Alexa, I'm real sorry,' she ventured.

'No, honey,' Ace smiled tiredly. 'I upset her, not you.' He sighed heavily and rubbed his hand over his eyes, stifling a yawn. 'Get Raul to drive you home,' he said, and her face fell. 'You'll have to learn to mask your emotions better than that,' Ace told her sternly. 'On court, you must never let your opponent know if you're injured or depressed,' he warned.

'Okay, I understand that.' She nodded eagerly, all smiles again and encouraged by the piece of advice which implied he hadn't given up on her, after all.

'Pack your things and I'll take you and your mom to the academy tomorrow,' he promised.

'Oh, thank you! I do love you!' Ella reached up impulsively and kissed his cheek. Briefly, he hugged her, then pushed her away.

'Thanks for the sentiment – but don't repeat it to anyone else. It's liable to be misinterpreted,' he warned lightly. There was going to be enough speculation about their relationship without her innocently adding fuel to the fire. 'Go on, get outta here – I'm asleep on my feet,' he told her.

When she had gone, waving happily from Raul's truck, he trudged wearily upstairs on his way to bed, pausing only to glance inside the guest room. Maria had cleaned and tidied it; it was as if Alexa Kane had never stayed there.

The drive to Santa Barbara was an enjoyable one. It was years since Ace had travelled the beautifully scenic route of the Californian coastline by road, and it was the first time for both Ella and Linda. Ace wished he had thought to bring Alexa to see some of the best California had to offer, instead of giving her a tour of the slums of LA.

Ella chattered brightly all day, unbearably excited by the beginning of what she was sure was going to be a wonderful new life. Even Linda lost some of her reserve and began to believe in Ella's change of fortune. Her own life would change, too, for she intended remaining in Santa Barbara to find work near the academy so she would still be close to Ella.

The academy was all Ella had hoped for. She hung back a little shyly while Ace talked to Hal Renwick, her eyes wide with wonder as Hal showed them around: the immaculate courts, the well-equipped gym, the recreation room and the dormitories, functional but comfortable – and single-sex, Linda noted with relief.

Hal assigned a girl of Ella's age to introduce her to the other pupils and she went off happily, with barely a backward glance. Hal noticed Linda's distress at the parting.

'You're welcome to stay for a while, if you'd like,' he suggested kindly. 'We can find you a bed for the night, just to ease your mind about Ella settling in,' he added, making the offer sound like a favour to Ella, not to Linda.

'I'd like that, thank you,' she accepted gratefully. 'And I want to thank you, too.' She turned to Ace, finally convinced that Ella would be happier – and safer – here than in LA. Ace brushed her thanks aside.

'She'll repay me, one day,' he said casually. He had just handed over a sizeable cheque, and wanted to be on his way. The countless hours of practice Ella needed were Hal's responsibility now. Ace fully intended reaping the financial rewards later.

'Are Jack and Lisa still in San Francisco?' he asked Hal.

'They're staying at Rose Arbor, Melissa's place in the Napa valley,' Hal said, rather cautiously.

'Got the number?'

'Yes.' Reluctantly Hal gave him the information, offering up a silent apology to his sister as he did so.

Ace took his leave of Ella, promised to come and see her soon, then climbed back into his car and headed north towards San Francisco, punching out the number for Rose Arbor as he hit the freeway.

'Jack? Are you busy?'

'Oh, it's you,' Jack sighed. 'I was in bed,' he told him.

'In bed? It's only five-thirty . . . oh, second honeymoon going well, is it?' Ace grinned as realization dawned.

'Yes, great. No thanks to Kit, though. Whoever coined the phrase "sleeping like a baby" was obviously a childless cretin. Or deaf,' he added morosely, and Ace laughed.

'Will Lisa allow you out tonight? I'm on my way to San Francisco.'

'Sorry, I'm babysitting. Lisa's going out with some old school friends. Come over here if you want to,' he suggested. Ace grimaced – babysitting?

'Okay.' He decided he would as he was already so near. 'Give me directions to Rose Arbor,' he said. Jack obliged, wondering how Lisa would take the news of the arrival of an unexpected guest. But she merely smiled and shrugged good-naturedly when he told her. She was relaxed and happy these days back in California, and looking forward to meeting up with old friends. And their sex-life was finally back to what it had been before Kit was born.

'Don't drink too much, and don't let Ace anywhere near Kit,' was all she said before she left for her evening out.

Ace, of course, showed no inclination to go near the baby and settled comfortably in Melissa's living room with a glass of scotch in his hand.

'Have you spoken to Melissa or Rose in the past couple of days?' he asked casually.

'Melissa phoned to tell me about Philip Kane's stroke – I gather Alexa was still at your place when it happened?' Jack said, just as casually. He had been wondering how the two of them were getting along, figuring they would either kill each other or fall into bed. The spark between them was such that anyone unwary enough to stand in the crossfire would receive an electric shock.

'Yeah,' Ace said, unhelpfully.

'Did you escort her back to England, or send her on her own?' Jack persisted. Ace looked up sharply.

'Melissa didn't give you any details, did she?' he asked slowly, wondering if the whole matter was to be swept under the carpet, and, if so, was it to protect Alexa? Or Philip? Either way, he decided Jack deserved to know.

He quickly gave Jack a brief explanation, including his own part in events, but omitted to mention sleeping with Alexa. He guessed she would definitely want that to remain a secret, and that was fine with him. So far as he was concerned, it had never happened.

'The poor girl,' Jack said slowly. 'And Philip . . .'

'I'd reserve your sympathy for him,' Ace cut in. 'I'm still not convinced he wasn't responsible.'

'Why? Because it's easier to live with putting a pervert in hospital instead of a decent man?' Jack asked shrewdly. 'Why the hell did you go charging over to England, anyway?' he frowned.

'I was being a responsible godparent, thinking of Kit,' Ace said, rather defensively. Like hell, Jack thought; a brief call to me would have ensured Kit was never placed in danger. He looked at Ace closely, noting the dark circles beneath his eyes, denoting lack of sleep, and the deep grooves running from nose to mouth that he guessed had more to do with depression than jet-lag.

'You and Alexa must have become pretty close for her to confide in you,' he ventured.

'No,' Ace denied quickly. 'She's the only female guest actually to sleep in my guest room!' He forced a grin. Besides, that part was true. 'I told you – she had a bust-up with Johnny Dancer when he tried to get her into bed. She was more upset than you'd expect and I think that half-triggered her memory, and the video Ella was watching finished the job.'

'I see.' Jack regarded him quizzically, but forbore to ask why he had procured the videos in the first place. Ace was obviously resisting the attraction he felt for Alexa and, with Philip Kane lying in a hospital bed for God knew how long, it was probably as well that nothing had happened between the two of them. They would both feel even guiltier than they did already. 'Have another drink,' he said, and changed the subject.

Later, the baby-alarm announced Kit was awake and hungry, and Jack brought her downstairs to give her her bottle. She soon stopped crying and settled happily, gazing wide-eyed at Jack as he fed her, and reaching out a tiny hand to touch his face. Once replete, she seemed to notice Ace for the first time, turning in response to his voice.

'She's smiling at me,' Ace said, pleased. Jack hid a grin.

'She smiles at everybody,' he said drily, holding her securely against his shoulder and gently rubbing her back.

'You seem very expert,' Ace commented.

'I think it's what's called a steep learning curve,' Jack said ruefully. 'I can recommend it, though,' he added lightly.

'What do I know about being a father?' Ace said dismissively.

'About as much as I did before she was born,' Jack retorted. Ace shrugged, and silently disagreed. Jack had excellent role models in his own parents.

'How long will you be staying here?' Ace asked.

'A couple of weeks, maybe more. Dad's holding the fort at Bellwood, and I've no TV commitments until April. I'm covering the tournaments in Berlin, Rome and then Paris. Will you be coming over for the French Open?'

'I doubt it; I'll still be working on *Country Club* – if they don't sack me,' he amended, not too bothered if they did. 'I'll probably be over for Wimbledon, though,' he added casually. That was three months away – surely Philip Kane would have recovered by then? If the man is innocent, I owe him one hell of an apology, he thought. And, as for Alexa . . . he couldn't blame her for hating him, but he would try to make amends. Hopefully, she would have calmed down by then and realize he had meant no harm. Yes, he would definitely go to England for Wimbledon fortnight . . .

As May gave way to June, the professional tennis players left the red clay courts of Europe and headed for Britain, to compete in the warm-up grass court tournaments leading to the biggest and most prestigious of them all – Wimbledon.

For the first time in her life, Melissa was dreading what had always been her favourite tournament. Not only could she not take part, but her reign as the Ladies Singles Champion was drawing to an end. As she confided to Jack, her timing was lousy; if she had conceived just a couple of weeks earlier, she would already have her baby as compensation, but, as things were, she had to endure the last days of her pregnancy watching others compete on the world-famous grass courts.

She was finding the last month arduous, uncomfortable whether she sat, lay down or tried to move about, and the time dragged. She had always been so active and found her condition irksome. In addition, she was carrying alone a secret dread – Gulf War Syndrome. Nick had been a serving officer in the Gulf War and had, along with all the other troops, been given a cocktail of drugs to combat the effects of any biological and chemical warfare waged by the Iraqis. Nick had no symptoms of illness, but she was tormented by the knowledge that thousands of war veterans had since sired deformed babies. She kept her fear to herself, afraid speaking of it out loud would make it more of a reality.

Their new house, Nine Elms, was fully furnished and redecorated, awaiting occupation. They already loved the elegant Georgian country house, set in several acres of paddocks and orchards on the edge of a village only five miles from Bellwood, but within easy commuting reach of London.

It wasn't as large or as impressive as Bellwood, but was a comfortable family home and they were looking forward to moving in. They had decided to remain in the Chelsea flat until after the baby's birth, partly so Melissa would be near the hospital and partly because they wanted to spend their first night in their new home as a family.

To add to Melissa's discomfort, a sudden and intense heatwave hit southern England and, on the first day of the Championships, she elected to stay in the flat and watch the coverage on TV. She didn't much feel like lumbering around the All England Club, nor did she want to mix with her former rivals, still agile and able to run! Skinny bitches! she thought morosely.

Nick was at the office of Lennox and Coupland, Rose was running errands for Melissa, so she was alone and glad of the interruption when Alexa dropped by mid-morning to see how she was feeling.

Philip Kane was out of hospital and back at Eaton Square with a resident nurse. He was receiving daily physiotherapy, but had proved to be as bad a patient as Alexa had feared he would be, and the turnover of staff was awesome.

'I thought Rose might be here,' Alexa said, after she had prepared cold drinks for herself and Melissa, and took a seat in the airy drawing-room, still fairly cool and pleasant at that time of the day.

'She'll be back soon,' Melissa assured her. 'Did you want her for something important?'

'No, not really,' Alexa hedged. 'I just wondered if she'd be coming to see Daddy today.'

'Doesn't she always?' Melissa asked, wondering if that was the real reason for Alexa's visit; she seemed rather nervous and tense.

'Yes, but I thought she might be looking after Kit if both Jack and Lisa wanted to go to Wimbledon,' Alexa explained. Actually she was afraid Rose's visits might cease – it seemed to her that, more and more,

Rose was prompted by compassion and duty, not love.

Alexa had clung rather desperately to the Farrells in the past few months, ironic considering her attitude towards them last Christmas, when Philip and Rose had announced their engagement. Ace had been right: she should have counted herself fortunate to have been accepted into the family. Ace . . . of course, the Farrells were also a link to him . . .

She wished she could stop thinking about him, but it was impossible. Every time she looked at her father, wheelchair-bound, his right arm and leg almost useless, she hated Ace with a passion, but at other times she craved his touch. She dreamed of him constantly, wildly erotic dreams that made her wake feeling frustrated and aching with longing . . .

Soon after he had left London, she had begun dating, with Philip's encouragement, Graham Peters, the youngest member of Philip's board of directors. Philip considered Graham to be his heir apparent and thought it would be ideal if he were also to become his son-in-law.

Alexa had known and liked Graham for years and, high in confidence after sleeping with Ace, had willingly gone to Graham's house after an enjoyable evening out. But, as soon as he had tried to do more than kiss her, she had experienced the old fear and revulsion, and had pleaded tiredness and fled from the house.

She hadn't repeated the exercise, although Graham was a constant visitor to Eaton Square and she had been out to dinner with him on several occasions since. It was a dreadful thought, but she was beginning to conclude that Ace Delaney was the only man who could give her pleasure in bed – he hadn't 'cured' her at all, merely ensured she would respond to him and him alone. Bastard.

'Oh, excuse me,' Melissa said, as the phone beside her rang, and she picked it up. 'Hi, Katy! How are things with you?'

Alexa stood up and wandered over to the window, not wanting to appear to be eavesdropping on a personal conversation, and let her mind wander back in time.

A lot had happened since her father's stroke and her own painful remembrances. She had undergone therapy, with an expert in the field, and had been able to talk it through with someone who understood, someone who urged her to talk about it endlessly until she became almost bored with it and was able to let it go, back into the past where it belonged.

Much of her grandfather's tainted money had been anonymously donated to various children's charities; in addition, she had become a sponsor to a dozen children in the Third World, giving them an education, health facilities and hope for the future. She had a box full of photographs of smiling children of all colours and nationalities and intended one day visiting her 'foster' children. She derived great pleasure from reading of their progress and was touched to receive drawings and paintings they sent her.

As for the kidnapping: of the perpetrators – she didn't want to know their names, as that would give them more validity – one had died in prison, the other two had been released, but had since re-offended and were serving further sentences. Nick had been a godsend; he'd guessed her fears and lack of confidence, expecting to see kidnappers lurking on every corner, and had arranged for two of his 'minders' to accompany her wherever she went until she had relaxed and felt comfortable travelling alone.

She had hired a private detective to check on Magda: he had discovered that she had married a GI stationed in Germany and gone to live with him in New York. Alexa had written to her and suggested a visit, which Magda had vetoed, for now, but the correspondence was continuing and Alexa hoped one day for a reunion. At least Magda was happily married and had two children; her nightmare was no doubt still painful, but buried firmly in the past.

'Sorry about that,' Melissa apologized, as she ended her call. 'It was Katy Oliver, my ex-coach. She's over for Wimbledon with some American juniors,' she explained, before realizing Alexa wasn't even listening.

Melissa frowned slightly as she watched her; there was something about Alexa that was different, and not just the hairstyle, either – in a gesture of defiance, pointless since he wouldn't even know of it, Alexa had disobeyed Ace's command and had her hair cut so it now framed her face in a sleek, shiny bob. It's her clothes, Melissa realized; Alexa had forsaken her short, tight outfits and today she looked very Sloaney in an ankle-length floaty skirt and long, loose sweater.

'Aren't you hot, dressed like that?' Melissa asked idly, for she was sweltering in a sleeveless smock and very little else.

'No.' Alexa, jolted out of her introspection, turned away from the window to face Melissa. As she did so, her body was briefly in silhouette, and her sweater pulled taut across her full breasts and rounded tummy.

'You're pregnant!' Melissa exclaimed unthinkingly. The first outward sign of her own pregnancy had been sprouting boobs to rival Pamela Anderson! Evidently, Alexa was the same.

Alexa opened her mouth to deny it, but realized the futility of doing so. She had hoped to keep it a secret for a little while longer, particularly as she knew Ace was in London for the Wimbledon Championships.

'Yes, I am, but please don't tell anyone,' she begged.

'Okay, but you won't be able to hide it for much longer,' Melissa told her. 'When is it due?'

'Oh, late January or early February,' Alexa lied. She had already thought about dates. She didn't want Ace to guess the child was his, and that meant deceiving the Farrells, too, much as she disliked doing that as they had all been so kind to her. Her baby would be 'premature', of course, but she would worry about that later. Ace would have lost interest in her by then – if he hadn't already, she thought glumly.

'February? It can't be – you must be further along . . .'

'Late January,' Alexa insisted. 'I've seen a doctor and he confirmed it.'

'Oh, well, he should know,' Melissa shrugged. Alexa was very fine-boned, her wrists and ankles as slender as a child's; perhaps that explained the apparently early fullness of her figure. She was dying to ask the name of the father, but didn't quite dare.

'Actually, I . . . I'm not a hundred per cent sure I should go ahead with it,' Alexa burst out.

'Oh.' Melissa shifted uncomfortably, trying to find an easier position, plumping up a cushion behind her aching back. 'Are you asking my advice about abortion?'

'I . . . I suppose I am,' Alexa said, ashamed of herself for making Melissa re-live her own experience, but she felt young and very scared. And Melissa had brought up the subject of her pregnancy, she excused herself. 'I know from what little Rose had said that you regretted having a termination . . .' She halted, and waited for a response.

'It's not the easy option you might think it is,' Melissa said finally. 'The guilt never goes away.'

'Not even now?' Alexa gestured to Melissa's swollen stomach.

'Especially not now,' Melissa shook her head. 'Thanks to the Press, the whole world knows I once aborted a child, so, one day, I'll have to try and explain to this one,' she patted her tummy, 'why he or she doesn't have an older sibling. I'm already dreading it – how would I have felt if Mum had aborted Jack?' she asked, appalled at the very thought.

'God, yes, how awful,' Alexa regarded her sympathetically. 'But at least you had a good reason – I don't have a career to consider, as you did, and I can afford to bring up a child alone. I suppose I'm just afraid of the responsibility.'

'What about the father? Won't he help? Isn't it what's-his-name – Graham?' Melissa asked.

'No,' Alexa shook her head vigorously, perhaps too vigorously she realized at once, and she sighed, for Melissa's inquisitively arched brow signalled that she expected further clarification. Alexa bit her lip and struggled to find the words, desperately afraid she might let slip the truth.

'It was just a one-night stand that should never have happened,' Alexa continued unwillingly. 'I don't intend telling him about the baby. For one thing, he wouldn't be interested and . . . oh, it's all very complicated,' she sighed.

'I see,' Melissa said, although she didn't. She guessed the man must be married, or at least in a settled relationship with someone else. 'What about your father? Won't he help?' Melissa asked next. Alexa shuddered at the very thought of telling him.

'That bad, huh?' Melissa had noticed her reaction. 'Well, he'll have to know some time,' she pointed out. 'Obviously, you know how he'll react better than I do, but have you considered that he might be pleased to have a grandchild?'

Alexa shook her head vigorously.

'Are you sure?' Melissa persisted. 'My father's besotted with Kit; he says being a grandfather is even better than being a parent – all the fun and none of the responsibility!'

'I don't think Daddy will feel that way,' Alexa said doubtfully.

'Because you're unmarried? Will he go ballistic if you refuse to name the father?'

On the contrary, he'll go ballistic if I *do* name him! Alexa thought, and had to bite back a burst of hysterical laughter. 'I just don't feel up to coping with any scenes. It might be better if I go away somewhere for a while,' she said out loud.

'You're welcome to stay at Rose Arbor, my place in California, if you want to,' Melissa offered. 'It's very quiet and off the beaten track, in a beautiful spot in the Napa valley. I used it when I was on the tour and needed a few weeks' respite from the Press. The paparazzi never found me there, so I think you'll be safe enough,' Melissa told her.

'Thanks, it sounds lovely; I'll certainly think about it,' Alexa said gratefully. But Rose Arbor was in California . . . though hundreds of miles from Ace in LA. It was ridiculous to think she might actually bump into him!

Just then the intercom buzzed, announcing the arrival of a visitor.

'Shall I go and see who it is?' Alexa offered, and jumped to her feet to answer the summons. 'Yes?' she enquired.

'Hi, honey,' drawled an achingly familiar voice. 'Is your bastard of a husband out of the way?' God, it's Ace! And he thinks I'm Melissa! Stupidly, she felt hurt that he hadn't instantly recognized her voice, as she had his. Even more stupid was her jealousy that he had come to call on a nine-months pregnant Melissa!

She automatically pressed the button to release the downstairs lock and unlatched the door to the flat.

'It's Ace,' she called back to Melissa, struggling to sound casual. She had to fight an urge to flee, but there was no way out other than to bump into him on the stairs . . . besides, pride dictated she stay, at least for a short time.

'Oh, God! Why him? I look awful!' Melissa wailed, too absorbed in her own dilemma to notice Alexa's discomfiture. Although she was deeply in love with Nick, she still harboured a little of her teenage infatuation with Ace, and didn't want him to see her in the last weeks of her pregnancy.

But it was too late to forestall him; he entered the building and ran up the stairs, tapping lightly on the door before walking in.

'Hi, I . . .' Ace stopped dead when he saw Alexa, still hovering uncertainly in the hallway, but he recovered his composure quicker than she, and his voice and face was expressionless when next he spoke.

'How's your father?' he asked evenly; Jack had assured him weeks before that Philip Kane was innocent of any wrongdoing, an assurance that only served to deepen his feelings of guilt.

'In a wheelchair, thanks to you!' Alexa said bitterly.

'I understood from Jack that he was recovering?'

'He is, but very slowly.'

'I'm sorry,' he said quietly. He studied her for a moment; she was angry, but very jumpy, he noted, with some satisfaction. He noticed the short hair and silently approved, despite remembering vividly the scent and feel of her long mane wrapped around their entwined bodies. He was pleased she had defied him to cut it; it proved he was on her mind, he decided arrogantly. Casually, he picked up her hand and lightly caressed her fingers.

'Long nails again, and short hair,' he murmured. 'You obviously need some more lessons . . . in obedience,' he added, after a pause during which Alexa blushed furiously. How dared he refer to her 'lessons'? she fumed.

She snatched her hand away and hurried back into the drawing room, where Melissa was trying to look as slim as possible and failing miserably. To Melissa's surprise, Ace didn't comment mockingly on her size. Instead, he grinned amiably and handed her a parcel.

'It's a gift from my protégée – Ella Cortez. She's a fan of yours and insisted I bring it to you. Jack says you've been inundated with gifts, but Ella bought this without mentioning it to me first,' he explained.

'Oh, that was sweet of her.' Melissa tore off the wrapping to reveal a teddy bear, one that was similar to dozens she and Nick had already passed on to hospitals and children's homes. 'Is she competing at Wimbledon in the juniors?' she asked.

'No, not this year. She's coming along very well, though. Hal's doing a great job,' he acknowledged. 'Although he is working with the best material – she's a natural,' he enthused.

'I'll write and thank her.' Melissa put the teddy aside. 'What have you been up to recently?' she asked. 'Give me all the gory details – if it's sufficiently shocking I might go into labour!'

'Don't you dare! Not while I'm here,' Ace looked alarmed. 'You're not likely to, are you?' he asked, edging towards the door. Melissa grinned.

'Relax, I was only kidding! Tell me all the gossip,' she commanded.

He sat down, comfortably a-sprawl in an armchair, outwardly at ease as he told her the latest scandals in the tennis world, and about the row over his quitting of *Country Club*. He ignored Alexa, but was acutely aware of her, and of her tension.

'I think I'd better get back home,' Alexa jumped up suddenly. 'The doctor's coming to see Daddy this morning.'

'I thought you were waiting for Mum?' Melissa said in surprise.

'Er – no, I'm sure she'll be along later,' Alexa mumbled.

'Okay, well, I'll tell her you called,' Melissa struggled to rise and followed Alexa out into the hall. 'About the other thing,' she said, in a low voice. 'Just give me a ring if you want to go to Rose Arbor. It's empty at the moment, so all I have to do is call the couple who look after the place for me, and they'll pick you up at the airport and stock up on food and suchlike.'

'Thanks, I'll let you know what I decide to do,' Alexa smiled warmly, then visibly jumped and coloured as Ace loomed over them. How much had he heard?

'Secrets?' he asked mockingly.

'Yes, girlie stuff – you wouldn't be interested,' Melissa said tartly. 'Are you going to Wimbledon?'

'Yeah.'

'You've got a car? Give Alexa a lift home, will you?'

'Sure,' Ace agreed, smiling slightly at Alexa's obvious reluctance. 'My pleasure.'

'No, it's okay; I'll get a cab,' she yelped.

'Don't be silly,' Ace took her wrist in his strong grip, then relaxed his hold and instead caressed her inner wrist with his thumb. Oh, help! Alexa thought weakly.

''Bye, honey,' Ace kissed Melissa's cheek. 'Come along, Alexa, don't just stand there; Melissa probably wants to rest,' he rebuked her, putting her in the wrong and tugging firmly at her hand so she had no choice but to accompany him, unless she wished to engage in an undignified struggle that she would no doubt lose. Inwardly sighing, she forced a smile for Melissa, then followed meekly after Ace.

## CHAPTER 15

'I'll get a cab!' Alexa repeated, rather desperately, as they emerged on to the pavement.

'Don't be childish – you're not afraid of me, are you?' Ace asked mockingly.

'Of course I'm not!' she bristled.

'Good. Anyhow, this is as good a time as any for me to call on your father,' he said casually. Alexa stared at him in horror: he actually sounded as if he meant to do just that!

'Are you insane? You are the last person on earth he wants to see,' she told him.

'Really?' A small smile tugged at the corners of his mouth. Alexa wanted to either slap him or kiss him; maybe both. 'In that case, I won't call – on condition you come out for dinner with me this evening,' he said. 'Is that a deal?'

'No, it is not a deal!' she said furiously.

'Fine. I'll call on your father . . .' He slanted a sideways look, confident of getting what he wanted.

'There's an ugly word for your tactics,' Alexa ground out.

'Effective?' Ace suggested.

'No! Blackmail! You mustn't come to the house,' she pleaded. 'Don't you realize what could happen? Do you want to kill him?'

'No, I'd quite like to apologize,' Ace said sincerely. 'But, if that's out of the question, my second choice is to take you to dinner.' He paused and raised one eyebrow questioningly. Alexa ground her teeth in annoyance.

'Oh, all right, I'll meet you for dinner, if I must,' she accepted grudgingly. 'Are you staying at your usual hotel?'

'No.' He opened the car door for her and walked around to the driver's side. 'I'll pick you up outside your house at seven-thirty – okay?'

'Okay – but you're not to come to the door,' she warned. 'I'll be watching out for you.'

'How sweet; I'm touched,' Ace drawled, deliberately misunderstanding.

'Oh! You're impossible,' she told him.

'I know,' he said, with a sudden bleakness to his voice that startled her. She glanced at him quickly, but there was something about the stern, cold set to his features that stilled her tongue.

They travelled in silence to Eaton Square and he drew up a safe distance from the house without being asked. He didn't shut off the engine, merely leaned across to open the passenger door for her.

His arm brushed lightly against her breasts as he did so, and she caught her breath in a gasp: her glance flew to his; his jet-black eyes bored into hers but she could read nothing of what he was thinking or feeling. However, she was uncomfortably afraid that he could read every conflicting emotion that assailed her.

'Seven-thirty,' was all he said, and she nodded speechlessly, then got out of the car and fled into the house.

It frightened her, just how much she was looking forward to spending the evening with him; she was in a fever of impatience throughout the long afternoon, unable to settle to anything, and glancing at her watch every few minutes.

She was also consumed with guilt as she watched her father struggle with everyday tasks, listened to his stilted, awkward speech. He hated his infirmity, almost as much as he hated the man who had caused it; the man whose child she carried, the man she craved to see . . . oh, God, she thought wretchedly.

Fortunately, Rose arrived in time for tea, and Alexa was able to slip away to shower and change. It was still unbearably hot, and she chose to wear a cool loose-fitting, softly draped dress in cream silk, and examined herself critically in front of a full-length mirror, searching for giveaway signs of her pregnancy.

Melissa's recognition of her condition had been a shock, although perhaps Melissa, absorbed in her own imminent motherhood, was the person most likely to guess, she mused. Apart from an increase in the size of her bust, there were no other visible signs, she decided, pulling in her tummy until it appeared as flat as usual.

However, Melissa was right about one thing – she couldn't ignore it for much longer. If she was going to have the baby, she had to tell Philip, and soon. But the identity of the father must remain a secret! She had no idea how Ace would react to the news, but that was of less importance right now than her father's response.

She was sure the news that Ace Delaney was the father of his grandchild would kill him, or, at best, induce another stroke. She shivered despite the heat and went to sit on a chaise-longue in an upstairs window alcove overlooking the square.

Ace pulled up shortly before seven-thirty – again at a safe distance from the house, she noted, relieved that he was evidently prepared to consider her wishes regarding her father's health.

She picked up her bag and ran downstairs, pausing outside the study which now doubled as a bedroom for Philip, and poked her head around the door.

'I'm going out for dinner, Daddy. Bye. Bye, Rose.' She smiled, and left hurriedly before she could be questioned about where she was going and with whom.

'I ought to be going, too,' Rose said, getting to her feet. 'Melissa's feeling the heat terribly, poor girl, and I said I would go over and prepare a meal for Nick.' It was true, but it was also an excuse not to stay too long, and Philip knew it. But they both kept up the pretence that their relationship hadn't altered, and he nodded, patting her hand understandingly.

'I'll come tomorrow,' Rose promised, as she always did, and bent to kiss his cheek before leaving.

She paused outside the front door, guiltily relieved to be out of the house, and glanced around for a taxi. She caught her breath sharply as she saw the occupants of a black Mercedes leaving the square. Surely that was Alexa! With Ace?

She glanced fearfully over her shoulder, lest Philip should suddenly appear in the doorway, or at a window. That girl's playing with fire, in more ways than one, she thought worriedly as she hailed a cab to take her back to Chelsea. Quite apart from Philip's distress if he ever discovered there was something going on between Ace and Alexa, the girl was too immature and vulnerable to cope with a man like Ace, uncaring of the heartbreak he inflicted on most of the girls foolish enough to fall in love with him . . .

Melissa was watching the Wimbledon coverage on TV with mixed emotions. She loved the sport, this tournament in particular, but today she envied and almost hated those who were taking part.

A Ladies Singles match was in progress, featuring the American Bev Hunter, and Juliet Stanton, Nick's detestable niece, the girl who had betrayed the secret of Melissa's abortion to the Press.

'Come *on*, Bev!' Melissa muttered. 'Don't let the bitch win!'

'Melissa!' Rose admonished, with a laugh. 'Remember your blood pressure!'

'Sod my blood pressure,' Melissa muttered rebelliously, and grimaced as Juliet hit a perfect two-handed backhand down the line to break Bev's serve.

'Oh, I say! Lovely shot!' enthused the commentator. 'Reminiscent of Melissa Farrell.'

'Reminiscent of Melissa Farrell!' she repeated disguistedly. 'I'm pregnant, not dead!' she yelled at the screen, snatching up the remote control handset and hurling it at the set. 'Ouch!'

'What's wrong?' Rose asked sharply.

'Nothing. Just a twinge in my back.' Melissa shifted about, trying in vain to find a comfortable position. 'Oh, I forgot to tell you – Alexa was here earlier; she might be going to hide out at Rose Arbor for a while,' she said, simply to divert Rose's attention from herself.

'Hide out? What's she done – robbed a bank?' Rose asked absently.

'Not unless it's a sperm bank – she's . . . oh, God!' Melissa clapped a hand to her mouth.

'She's pregnant?' Rose was stunned.

'Yes, but it's a secret. She daren't tell her father, or the baby's father for that matter. I promised I wouldn't tell anyone, so please don't say anything to Philip, Mum,' Melissa begged, distressed at having been so indiscreet.

'Of course I won't mention it; don't worry about it,' Rose soothed her, and returned to the kitchen to finish preparing a meal. She pondered Alexa's pregnancy for a while, but an unmistakable cry of pain from Melissa drove all thoughts of Alexa from her mind.

'What is it?' She rushed anxiously to Melissa's side. Really, this is more nerve-racking than having one's own babies, she thought. She rather hoped that Jack and Lisa would provide any future grandchildren . . .

'It's getting worse. I've been uncomfortable all day, but . . .' She stopped speaking and drew in her breath sharply. 'That was a bad one,' she said shakily, and glanced at her watch. 'They're sharper and more regular . . . but it's too early, Mum,' she said, her dark eyes huge with pain and apprehension.

'Both you and Jack were in a hurry to see the world, and you were both fine, healthy babies,' Rose reassured her. 'I think I'd better phone the hospital,' she decided.

'And Nick? Find Nick,' Melissa pleaded.

'Of course I will.'

'I'm so glad you're here; I'm scared,' Melissa admitted.

'Oh, darling, I know,' Rose hugged her. 'If I could do it for you, I would,' she said.

'Now you tell me!' Melissa forced a smile, then she burst into tears of relief as Nick walked through the door.

He was as anxious as Melissa, but didn't show it, and calmly took charge. His military training had prepared him for most of life's emergencies, but childbirth was not one of them; least of all the birth of his own child. He would sooner walk, in uniform, unarmed and with a Union Jack draped around his shoulders, down the Falls Road in Belfast on a Saturday night yelling anti-IRA slogans, than watch Melissa in pain.

While Melissa was definitely not having a good time in hospital, Alexa was enjoying herself immensely.

'Where are we going for dinner?' she'd asked Ace, as she climbed into the Mercedes.

'My place,' he had answered enigmatically, and she had quickly discovered that, instead of booking into a hotel, he had rented a house near the All England Club for the duration of the Championships.

'It's a habit I got into while I was competing,' he explained. 'It was more convenient to stay near the

Club than in central London. It's easier to relax between matches in a home, even a temporary one, than in a hotel. And there was no hassle with traffic and worrying about being late for the start of a match.' His tone was light, conversational, but Alexa knew that, by going alone to his house, she would end up in his bed. If she didn't want that to happen, she had better say so, quickly.

She glanced covertly at him while he drove, admiring his sun-darkened, muscular body, emphasized by the open-necked white shirt he was wearing, the sleeves rolled casually over his elbows in deference to the heat.

His forearms were strong and corded with muscle, covered with a sprinkling of dark hairs, his hands firm and sure on the steering wheel. Wonderful hands, she thought, beginning to shiver with excitement.

His black hair, now longer than hers, hung to his shoulders and, in profile, he did indeed resemble the Apache he claimed as an ancestor, with those proud, aquiline features and black, hypnotic eyes . . . Maybe that's why he's so brilliant in bed, she thought, a little light-headedly: hypnosis. Whatever it was, she knew she wanted a repeat performance . . .

If only . . . She sighed, and tried to banish a mental image of her father, wheelchair-bound and seeming to have aged twenty years in the past few months.

But Daddy need never know, she decided recklessly. Ace would only be in London for the two weeks of the Wimbledon Championships; if she was very careful, her father need never discover the identity of the man she was dating – after all, who's going to tell him? she thought, with a complacency that lasted for all of five minutes.

'Who are all those people? Not the Press?' she yelped, as Ace slowed the car and turned into a driveway.

'Yeah, but don't worry about it. Becker's renting a house across the street – they're waiting for him,' Ace told her casually.

'They mustn't see me with you!' Alexa sank down in her seat until she was almost horizontal, half-strangled by her safety belt and scrabbling at the same time for her dark glasses.

'I love your impatience, honey, but can you possibly wait until we get indoors?' Ace drawled, his lips twitching in amusement at her supine state as he admired the smooth length of thigh which was exposed as her dress rucked up around her hips.

'Oh, please, be serious!' Alexa begged. 'I'm not being melodramatic, really I'm not. If those photographers get a picture of me with you, Daddy will have a fit – literally,' she said earnestly. Ace's amusement vanished.

'He still hates me, huh?'

'Can you blame him?' she shot back.

'No, I guess not,' he said heavily. 'Stay down, and I'll put the car in the garage – there's a door through to the house from there.'

Alexa nodded and relaxed slightly, but, as he got out of the car he waved to the assembled Press.

'Hi, guys!' he called cheerfully, and Alexa ground her teeth in annoyance, half-expecting camera flashes at every window. Why did he have to draw attention to them? she wondered angrily, not realizing, as Ace did, that trying to avoid the Press was a sure fire way of arousing their interest.

Alexa kept her eyes closed, like a child deciding that, if she couldn't see the monster lurking under the bed, then he couldn't see her, either. Only when the car was safely in the garage, with the door closed behind them, did she cautiously open her eyes.

'Okay, you can come out now,' Ace said, opening the passenger door for her. 'This is like having an affair with a married woman!'

'Well, you should know!' Alexa retorted, struggling to sit upright while he unbuckled her seat-belt.

As at lunchtime, the casual touch from his fingers caused her to catch her breath, and she gazed at him helplessly. His hands stilled for a moment, then he lifted her from the car and crushed her to him, one arm holding her firmly around the waist while the other hand gently tipped up her chin. He held her gaze for a moment, then his mouth descended on hers and they clung desperately, each as hungry for the other after more than three months apart.

'I intended feeding you before I pounced,' Ace said shakily, when they finally drew apart, both breathing heavily. Alexa rested her head against his broad chest, feeling the heavy pounding of his heart beneath her cheek.

'I'm not hungry,' she said guilelessly, and heard a rumble of laughter.

'Bed?' he suggested huskily, and she nodded, her mouth dry, her legs weak and trembling as he took her hand in his and led her upstairs.

Ace had closed the bedroom curtains earlier as a precaution against photographers, and the room was cool and dimly lit.

Alexa sat on the edge of the bed, her eyes large and luminous with excitement – and just a hint of apprehension, Ace thought, and cautioned himself to take it slowly. But that was difficult, when he wanted to rip off her clothes and ravish her. It dismayed him to acknowledge just how much he had missed her; how much he wanted her.

He knelt and eased off one high-heeled shoe, then the other, kneading her delicate, slender feet in his hands before slowly sliding his palm up her calves and then her thighs, pushing aside the flimsy material of her dress.

'Magical hands . . .' Alexa said breathlessly, as his thumbs slid inside her briefs, and then moved oh, so slowly around to caress her intimately, rotating ever nearer to the core of her excitement and need. She squirmed against his hands, and reached blindly to try and pull him on to the bed with her.

'Not yet,' Ace resisted her urgent tugging. 'Lie back and enjoy,' he said softly.

She gave a soft whimper of mingled need and acquiescence and did as he instructed, biting her lip as he slowly drew her briefs down her legs and cast them aside, leaving her feeling gloriously free and wanton.

He nudged her thighs apart and buried his face in the soft, damp mound of curls, his tongue teasing and tasting, then searching ever deeper inside her. Alexa clutched the coverlet in her hands, biting back screams of pleasure.

Her head moved restlessly from side to side; the sensations were unbearably exquisite, but still she craved more, needed him inside her, filling her completely. She caught his head in her hands and pulled, then tugged feverishly at his shirt, wanting, needing, his naked flesh against her own.

'If you want me to penetrate you, you have to ask – remember?' he said huskily.

'Every time?' Alexa asked, unthinkingly, and his black eyes gleamed with triumph.

'Every time,' he confirmed, expertly removing her dress in one fluid movement before stripping off his own clothes. He covered her body with his, and a sigh of mutual satisfaction escaped them both as his heated skin touched and inflamed hers even more.

'Now.' Alexa arched insistently against him. He grinned, loving her impatience, and moved to comply.

She was hot and welcoming; her soft moans urged him on, the nails he had once complained of raked his back and he revelled in it. Her hands roamed down his spine and grasped his buttocks, as she strained to have him even closer and deeper.

His thrusts filled her completely, and she began to cry out as the elusive crest came nearer and nearer until she arched upwards, her entire body racked with shuddering spasms of release. She felt the hot gush of his climax and smiled slightly. If I hadn't already had his baby inside me, I would have now, she thought dazedly.

Reality intruded with the thought; she wanted to tell him about the baby, their baby, but she couldn't divulge her secret, not unless she was willing to risk breaking her father's heart. Or worse. She pushed the unpleasant thought aside; she'd have tonight, and maybe the rest of his stay in London. After he had returned to LA would be time enough for her to plan her future.

'Wow. That was incredible' she said, shakily, and he smiled, then began raining kisses on her eyes, the tip of her nose and finally, her mouth.

'Sexy Lexy,' he murmured, and this time she knew he wasn't making fun of her.

'I feel sexy when I'm with you,' she admitted. 'But only you.'

'Good.' He shifted his weight slightly and gazed down at her passion-filled eyes and swollen mouth. Her hair was mussed, lipstick erased, and he thought she had never looked more lovely or desirable. 'You don't still hate me for what happened to your father, do you?'

'No. I hate to see him suffering,' she said slowly. 'But I know you didn't act out of malice. I think he does, too, but . . . it's very hard for him . . .' She shrugged helplessly, then forced a smile. 'Don't let's talk about it,' she begged. 'Not tonight.'

'Okay,' Ace agreed. 'Are you hungry?'

'Yes, but not for food.' She moved suggestively against him, wanting to forget unpleasant reality and lose herself in his lovemaking. He was still deep inside her, and her eyes widened as he hardened, swelling to fill her once more.

'Oh, wow,' she breathed, and arched her head back as his mouth trailed kisses of fire down the column of her throat. Her breasts, already full, became even more swollen as his lips and teeth tugged gently at first one engorged nipple, then the other.

'Your boobs are bigger,' Ace murmured, and she tensed as his hands sought out the curves of her waist and tummy. 'Have you been comfort-eating in my absence?' he teased.

'N-no, but I have gained a little weight,' she stammered. For one wild moment she contemplated telling him the truth, but her courage deserted her. 'I . . . I switched to a different brand of the Pill,' she was inspired to say.

'It suits you,' he commented lightly, and the moment for confession passed.

She gave herself up to his expert touch; this time, they made love slowly and languorously, savouring each delicious sensation until desire for consummation could no longer be held in check and they moved, as one, to a mutual orgasm even more shattering than the last.

Alexa was too sated and exhausted to move, but Ace, declaring he needed sustenance for the night ahead, went to fetch the lobster salad he had ordered earlier, together with champagne and, since it was Wimbledon fortnight, strawberries and cream.

Alexa couldn't eat a thing, but sipped sparingly at the chilled wine.

'Try this.' Ace dipped a ripe strawberry into the champagne and popped it into her mouth.

'Mmm, lovely.' She decided she was hungry, after all, and picked at the food with her fingers. She made him laugh by telling him how Ella's 'lobster' tennis machine had made her think longingly of seafood for supper. 'Does Ella still have that huge crush on you? Or has she lost her illusions?' she teased.

'She still adores me, of course,' Ace replied, rather smugly, but his acceptance of Ella's adoration as his due no longer irritated her.

'How about her stepmother – Linda? Have you won her over yet?'

'She's fine. She's working as a cook at the academy, to keep an eye on Ella.'

'Oh, good.' Alexa was pleased to hear that. 'I'm glad she doesn't live in that slum any more.' She grimaced, forgetting that Ace had once lived in a similar place.

'Don't be such a snob – being born poor isn't a crime,' he rebuked her, quite sharply, and she bit her lip.

'I'm sorry; I didn't mean to imply that it was,' she apologized hastily, looking so distressed that he forgave her instantly. Besides, she looked too cute to stay angry with for very long, clad only in his unfastened shirt, and his plans for the rest of the night didn't include quarrelling . . .

He began demonstrating to her just what those plans *did* include and was delighted with her response. She had lost her fears and inhibitions with a speed that surprised him; she was eager to learn from his years of experience and especially keen to give pleasure as well as receive it.

Finally, if temporarily, exhausted, they lay in companionable silence; Alexa was so comfortable and replete she almost fell asleep, and was instinctively snuggling closer into his arms when she realized how dark it was, and how late it must be.

'I have to go,' she said regretfully, glancing around for her discarded clothes.

'Stay,' Ace said sleepily.

'No, I can't!' Alexa began to panic. If she stayed, and the wretched morning sickness assailed her, he might easily guess her condition.

'Why not?' he asked lazily, and for a moment her mind was a blank.

'Daddy, of course,' she lied. Philip went to bed early these days, and would be fast asleep by now, and would probably never know if she stayed out all night. 'He'll be worried.'

'Phone him . . . oh, all right,' he sighed. 'I'll drive you back.'

'That doesn't matter; I can easily call a cab,' she said quickly.

'I'll drive you,' he insisted, and reached for his own clothes.

'Thank you.' She smiled tremulously, grateful for the solicitude rather than the lift itself.

He drove slowly, one hand on the steering wheel, one arm around her shoulders and his thigh pressed against hers. They spoke little on the journey, and again he pulled up, without being asked, a safe distance from the house.

'Thank you,' she said again, kissing him quickly and reaching for the door handle, nervous of being spotted. 'I'll make it up to you,' she promised.

'When?' Ace held firmly on to her arm.

'Tomorrow? Are you busy?'

'I'm supposed to be taking part in Jack's programme,' he said thoughtfully, 'but he'll understand if I tell him I have other plans!' He grinned. Alexa tried not to think how many other times he had cancelled meetings with friends because of a woman . . .

'You won't tell him you're seeing me, will you?' she asked anxiously. 'He might let it slip to Rose, and she comes to visit Daddy every day.'

'I won't tell him,' he promised. 'I'll pick you up here – seven-thirty again?'

'Wonderful.' They exchanged another long kiss and this time it was Ace who broke away.

'You'd better get out of the car before I take you back to Wimbledon,' he said ruefully.

'Okay.' Alexa climbed out and blew him a kiss, watching until he was out of sight before turning and quietly letting herself into the house.

Alexa slept until mid-morning and lay still for a moment, with a smile of happiness curving her mouth. But as soon as she raised her head from the pillow, a wave of nausea washed over her and she rushed into the bathroom to retch miserably. The only consolation was relief that she had made the right decision by insisting on coming home last night.

When she finally ventured downstairs, she entered her father's room rather apprehensively, afraid he might somehow guess what had transpired. Guilty conscience, she told herself drily, as he turned and smiled at her, the lop-sided smile caused by the paralysis and which always tugged at her heartstrings, but never more so than today.

'Rose phoned a few minutes ago – Melissa had her baby at eight o'clock this morning,' he told her. 'A little girl, seven pounds, two ounces. They're calling her Suzanne, after Nick's mother, Suzy for short.'

'Oh, how wonderful!' Alexa exclaimed. 'Are they both okay?'

'Fine, according to Rose. She didn't say much, she was very tired; she's been at the hospital all night. But Melissa's asleep now, so Rose and Nick have gone home to rest.'

'I'll call Rose this evening, then,' Alexa decided. 'I don't suppose Melissa will want visitors today, will she? I can go out and buy a present for the baby, though,' she said excitedly. 'Oh, and something for Kit, too. I wouldn't want her to feel left out.'

'I think she's a little too young to notice,' Philip commented drily.

'Well, I'll still buy her something,' Alexa said. 'And I'll send flowers to Melissa today.'

'Add my best wishes to the bouquet, will you?' Philip asked.

'Of course. I'll organize it while I'm out shopping.' Alexa consulted her watch. 'Is there anything I can do for you before I go? I thought I might go to Wimbledon this afternoon,' she added casually, 'Jack gave me tickets for the whole fortnight,' she lied. Actually Ace had provided the tickets . . .

'I'd rather you didn't go there.' Philip frowned, and she felt a flush of guilt stain her cheeks.

'Why?' she asked innocently. As if she didn't know!

'I've nothing against Jack Farrell – it's the company he keeps! If you go to Wimbledon, you'll probably run into Delaney!' He spat the name and Alexa bit her lip.

'Daddy, I understand how you feel about Ace, really I do,' she began earnestly. 'I felt the same way, but he never meant to harm you . . .'

'He threatened to kill me! Damn near succeeded, too. And what do you mean – you felt the same way; past tense!' he glared at her accusingly.

'I'm sorry, but I don't, can't, hate him any more. Obviously he misunderstood what I told him about Grandpa, and I have to take some of the blame for that . . .'

'You've changed your tune suddenly,' Philip eyed her suspiciously, then, 'You've seen him, haven't you?' he rapped out.

'Er – yes, he called in to see Melissa while I was there yesterday,' she said, which was true, so far as it went. 'He would like to call on you, Daddy, and try to make amends.'

'Never!' He thumped the arm of his wheelchair in frustration and anger. 'I won't have that bastard in my house!' he roared. 'And I don't want you speaking to him ever again!'

'All right, calm down, please! I won't go to Wimbledon; I can watch it on TV here instead,' she said soothingly, alarmed by the sudden angry rush of colour to his cheeks. To her relief, he relaxed visibly and nodded. So much for trying to build bridges, she thought sadly. He would never accept Ace in her life . . . or Ace's baby? She sighed heavily.

'I'll see you later; I won't be long.' She forced a smile.

'Take your time, but don't forget Graham's coming over later,' he reminded her. She had forgotten, and she bit her lip. Ace was only in

London for two weeks, and she couldn't bear to miss a single moment.

'I've made other plans for this evening,' she said lightly, praying he wouldn't ask for details. 'Besides, Graham calls to see you, not me,' she pointed out, with a slight smile.

'That's not strictly true. His visits are only partly business. You've been out with him quite often recently, and I know he's very fond of you.'

'I like him, too, but there's no romance – you're not trying to marry me off, are you, Daddy?' she asked, forcing a laugh.

'You're twenty-one now; it's time you began thinking of a husband and family,' he said. Yes, but not necessarily in that order, she thought, with an inward sigh.

'Well, I'll just have to wait until someone proposes, won't I?' she asked cheerfully, and slipped quickly from the room.

Philip said nothing, but his shrewd eyes narrowed as he watched her leave. She had been out last night, and again this evening, and not with Graham; nor with one of her girlfriends, or she would have said so. He had never quite understood what had transpired between her and Delaney in LA, and now Delaney was in London. His lips tightened; she wouldn't be so disloyal. She wouldn't dare betray him . . . would she?

# CHAPTER 16

On Wednesday afternoon Alexa went to visit Melissa in London's Portland Hospital, weighed down with gifts for both mother and baby, including a teddy bear that was much larger than the tiny bundle lying asleep in the cot beside Melissa's bed.

'I know you've received lots of these,' Alexa said, brandishing the bear, 'but I couldn't resist it.'

'It's lovely; thank you,' Melissa said warmly.

'Isn't she small?' Alexa was bending over the cot. 'I've always thought Kit was little, but she's enormous by comparison,' she said softly, so as not to disturb the baby. 'Which one of you does she look like?'

'We're not sure yet – she's just a blob,' Melissa said cheerfully, but her eyes were soft with love as she gazed at her daughter.

'Melissa!' Nick chided her, but he was laughing. He had barely left her side; the flat was unbearably empty and lonely without her, and he couldn't wait to take his family to their new home, Nine Elms. His family; what a lovely word, and what a perfect family. He had said nothing to Melissa, but the spectre of

Gulf War Syndrome had haunted him at times over the past months, and he had joyfully counted every single one of his daughter's fingers and toes.

'How are you feeling?' Alexa turned to Melissa.

'Fine, thanks. Although I wish I hadn't laughed at Lisa when she complained she couldn't sit down comfortably for a week after Kit was born!' she grimaced.

'Was it . . . bad?' Alexa asked, rather apprehensively.

'No,' Melissa said quickly, knowing that Alexa would be thinking ahead to when she would give birth. She knew the feeling exactly – she had experienced it while listening to Lisa describing her own ordeal six months earlier. 'No, it wasn't as bad as I thought it would be,' she said encouragingly.

'That's not what you said at the time,' Nick said ruefully, unaware of Alexa's condition. 'At one point you were threatening to have me castrated with a rusty knife and no anaesthetic!'

'Just joking,' she assured him blithely.

Oblivious to Alexa's presence, Nick leaned over and kissed his wife, the love of his life, and now the mother of his child. He had adored Melissa since he had first seen her, seven years earlier at a junior tennis tournament in which his elder niece, Jessica, was taking part, but now his heart swelled with even greater love and gratitude for the happiness she brought him.

Alexa watched enviously; who would look at her in such a way when she had her baby? Not Ace, she was sure of that. She bit her lip and glanced away; Nick and Melissa's absorption in each other and their child was too painful to witness. Perhaps I should tell Ace the truth, she thought, and tried to imagine his reaction; he would probably want her to have an abortion . . .

Well, I won't do that, she resolved, placing gentle fingers against Suzy's soft cheek. Oh, I wish he loved me, she thought longingly, and with the thought came the shock realization that *she* loved *him*! Not just in love, because he made her come gloriously alive as a woman, although that certainly meant a great deal to her. She also loved his humour, his strength, although there was a vulnerability there, too, she thought, which he would deny vigorously!

They were a lot alike – something else he would deny hotly! They had both been damaged in childhood, despite coming from vastly different backgrounds. She had hidden her pain, even from herself, while Ace had turned his back on his roots and moved away from his past, ruthlessly cutting all ties . . . until I was instrumental in sending him back there, courtesy of his community service, she realized guiltily.

'Don't look so worried – it really isn't that bad,' Melissa whispered, mistaking the reason for Alexa's troubled air. Nick had temporarily left her bedside to admit more visitors – Jack and Lisa, together with Kit. Another family group was too much for Alexa and she got hastily to her feet.

'I'd better go,' she said, smiling warmly at Jack and Lisa to prove they weren't the reason for her departure.

'Thanks for the flowers and the pressies,' Melissa said. 'Come and see me when we're settled at Nine

Elms,' she suggested. 'You know how to get there, don't you?'

'Yes, and I have the phone number, so I'll ring you first,' Alexa said. She paused to have a quick cuddle with Kit, glad she had brought an extra gift after all, then took her leave, tears blurring her vision as she stumbled along the corridor. Oh, please, let Ace fall in love with me, she prayed.

While Alexa was visiting Melissa, Rose called at Eaton Square to see Philip. They chatted amiably for a while, then, 'I'm going to stay with Melissa until she's on her feet and confident with the baby,' she said neutrally. Philip nodded, then reached over and, using his left hand since the right still refused to do his bidding, eased off her engagement ring.

'What are you doing?' Rose asked, rather stupidly, she realized at once.

'Making things easier for you,' he replied gruffly, dropping the ring into her palm. 'Keep it, as a memento.' He paused, and tried hard to sound calm and matter-of-fact as he continued. 'You don't want to marry an impotent cripple. And I don't want you to, either,' he said firmly.

'Oh, Philip. You're improving all the time,' she said wretchedly.

'If and when I'm fully recovered I'll come after you,' he said. 'But I won't marry you now. You forget, I was married to an invalid, and it's hell. Love turns to pity, and then you begin to feel trapped . . . I don't want your pity, Rose.'

She regarded him silently, guiltily aware of a burden being lifted from her shoulders. She could never have brought herself to break off the engagement, of course, and probably he guessed that. She slipped the ring on to her right hand and kissed his cheek.

'You're a wonderful man, and I'll look forward to the day when you walk into my flat and propose again,' she told him. 'May I still come and see you? I'd really like to,' she said, earnestly and truthfully.

'Please do. Any time. And bring those grandchildren of yours,' he said.

'I will.' Guilt showed in her dark, expressive eyes; she would never forgive herself for doubting him.

'That wasn't meant to hurt you. I'd love to have babies around the house again.'

'Well, you'll soon have . . .' She stopped and gasped, appalled by her indiscretion. She began floundering for an appropriate ending to the sentence she had so tactlessly begun. 'I mean, Alexa will fall in love and marry one day,' she said, but that only served to remind her of seeing Alexa drive off with Ace two nights earlier, and made her even more flustered. Not that Ace would propose, of course . . .

Philip merely nodded, pretending not to notice her discomfiture, but, alone later, he mulled over her words. He ate a solitary dinner, for Alexa was out yet again, then watched TV before retiring early to bed. But it was a long time before he slept; he was still wakeful at two o' clock and knew Alexa hadn't yet come home . . .

Philip watched Alexa carefully over the days that followed, watched and brooded, and laid his plans. Alexa was too preoccupied with her nights spent with Ace to take much notice. She vaguely realized he was quieter than usual, but put that down to depression over Rose. The news that there was to be no wedding, at least not in the near future, had saddened but not surprised her. But she was confident the Farrells would remain a part of their lives.

She waited until Melissa and Suzy had been installed at Nine Elms for a week before phoning and asking if she might come over the following day.

'What time will you be leaving in the morning?' Philip asked casually, when she told him of her plans.

'About ten,' she replied absently.

Next morning, Philip purposely delayed his breakfast, and, most unusually for him since his stroke, was tucking into a hearty cooked meal when Alexa ventured downstairs.

'Alexa? Can you come in here for a moment, please?' he called, and she got as far as the dining room door before the aroma of bacon almost sent her scurrying away to be violently sick.

'Yes?' she managed to ask, fighting back nausea.

Philip regarded her ashen face for a moment in silence, then, 'I can't manage to cut this sausage – can you do it for me?' he asked politely. Alexa gulped and glanced wildly around, hoping to see Mary or the nurse, or anyone at all to whom she could delegate the task! There was no one.

'Of course.' She forced a smile, took a deep breath, and hurried over to quickly chop up the sausage, and managed not to inhale again until the chore was finished. Even so, the sight of the fried egg and crispy bacon brought bile to her throat and a grey-green tinge to her skin.

'Thank you. Enjoy your day, and do give my best wishes to Melissa,' Philip said pleasantly, and watched as she rushed from the room and into the downstairs cloakroom.

He pushed his unwanted breakfast away and sighed, his suspicions, aroused by Rose's unwitting comment, confirmed. Now, all he had to do was ensure that his plans for her future, and that of his grandchild, proceeded as he wished. Immediately, he phoned Graham Peters and asked him to come to the house as soon as possible.

'Is anything wrong, Philip?' Graham asked.

'Not with the business, no; I'm very pleased with the way you've taken over as acting managing director,' Philip assured him. 'No, this is a personal matter.'

'I'll be right over,' Graham promised.

Graham Peters was, at thirty-eight, the youngest member of Philip's board of directors, and had long been Philip's candidate to take over when he retired – a retirement that had come sooner than he had expected, of course, thanks to Ace Delaney's interference!

Philip forced himself to calm down and turned his thoughts back to Graham. He had a keen brain, a shrewd nature hidden beneath an easygoing, smiling exterior. More importantly to Philip, he was still single and had shown a romantic interest in Alexa, taking her out to dinner on several occasions. Whether he had done rather more than that, Philip now intended to find out!

Philip surveyed the younger man in silence when he was shown into his study. He was pleasant-looking rather than handsome, with sandy hair and neat, even features, and hazel eyes. He was in good shape physically, working out regularly in the gym. He'll do, Philip decided, with some satisfaction.

'What's the problem, Philip?' Graham asked, beginning to find the silence unnerving. If the old man intended stepping down permanently, why didn't he just say so?

'It's Alexa. And it's not a problem, exactly. You've taken her out quite a lot recently . . . did you sleep with my daughter?' he rapped out.

Graham blinked, taken completely by surprise. He wondered uneasily if Alexa had complained to her father that he had tried to seduce her. But why would she? It had happened weeks before, and he had hidden his frustration and annoyance, and continued to invite her out to dinner or the theatre – invitations which she had readily accepted. They had been getting along pretty well, or so he had thought.

'Why do you ask?' he prevaricated.

'It's a simple enough question! I think she's pregnant – is the child yours?' Philip asked bluntly.

'Pregnant!' Graham repeated incredulously. 'I . . .' He started to deny all responsibility, then paused to consider the situation. 'Alexa hasn't mentioned anything to me,' he said finally, and evasively. Philip's eyes narrowed.

'If you're responsible for her condition, I trust you'll do the right thing,' he barked. It was a command, not a question, Graham realized.

'Leave it to me, sir,' Graham said. He was quickly beginning to see the advantages of 'doing the right thing'. Alexa was beautiful, young and extremely wealthy. Okay, she seemed to have a hang-up about sex, but she'd loosen up, in time. If not, well, finding willing bed partners had never been a problem in the past and he could see no reason why it should become one in the future, married or not.

Alexa, with a little coaching, could easily become the ultimate trophy wife. She often acted as hostess for Philip's business dinners, and performed well. The men adored her; the wives were often not quite so enthusiastic, but a wedding ring on her finger and a baby in the nursery would alter the women's attitude soon enough. The baby wasn't his of course, but being the 'father' of Philip Kane's grandchild and custodian of its future vast wealth outweighed any biological drawbacks, he decided.

Philip watched him, cynically aware that Graham was more keen to become his son-in-law and managing director of all of Kane Enterprises than to be Alexa's husband. But he was a kind enough man, from the right sort of family background, and, despite changing public opinion in recent years, Philip was determined his daughter would have a husband before she had a child.

'Don't tell Alexa we've had this little chat.' Philip cautioned, breaking into Graham's almost visible weighing-up of the pros and cons of the situation.

'No, no, of course not. Is she here? I'll invite her out to dinner this evening,' Graham said.

'No, don't do that,' Philip's lips thinned: no doubt his daughter would be busy tonight – yet again! Besides, invitations could be refused. 'Take her to lunch tomorrow,' he suggested instead. 'Pick her up here at noon.'

'Fine; I'll do that,' Graham nodded.

'Good,' Philip said briskly. 'Now, while you're here, I want to go over the details of the Dickinson project . . .'

Alexa, blissfully unaware of how her future was being mapped out, thoroughly enjoyed her day at Nine Elms. The elegant Georgian house, so recently occupied, was already very much a home, a family home, and her admiration of the furnishings and decor was sincere. The nursery was especially pretty, a cheerful, bright and airy room, full to the brim with toys and clothes for Suzy

'We've hardly bought a thing for her,' Melissa told Alexa cheerfully. 'My fans –' this said with a self-mocking grin '– sent most of it. It's just occurred to me – perhaps they sent the stuff out of relief at seeing the back of me!'

'I doubt it – there was practically a national holiday declared when you won Wimbledon,' Alexa said drily. Melissa smiled slightly at the memory of the Press furore; it seemed to her now as if all that had happened much longer ago than a mere twelve months, and to a different person. That's because I *am* a different person now, she realized suddenly.

Lisa drove over from Bellwood with Kit to join them for lunch; Rose, of course, was already there, and intended staying until Melissa felt able to cope alone.

'Which will probably be about the time Suzy starts school!' Melissa said ruefully to Alexa. 'I'd panic every five minutes if Mum weren't here,' she added, before remembering Alexa's motherless state. 'Sorry,' she mumbled, in an aside.

'That's okay; I'll manage,' Alexa said determinedly. 'If my father doesn't want me – us – to stay at home, I'll find a place of my own and hire a nanny, someone with experience of caring for young babies,' she added.

'You've definitely decided to keep it, then?' Melissa asked, relieved.

'Oh, yes.' Alexa glanced at Kit, then Suzy, lying contentedly in Rose's arms, and she nodded. 'Yes, I'm definitely keeping it,' she repeated firmly.

'I'm glad. I gather you still haven't told your father?'

'No.'

'Nor the baby's father?' Melissa persisted.

'No. As I said before, it's all rather complicated. I am seeing him tonight, though,' she confided.

'Why don't you tell him? He might be pleased,' Melissa said optimistically. Alexa smiled, rather sadly.

'I doubt it.'

She stayed longer than she had intended; it was such a friendly, comforting atmosphere and she was loath to leave. Only the prospect of being late for her rendezvous with Ace spurred her into finally saying goodbye.

She arrived back at Eaton Square with only half an hour to shower and change, not that her choice of what to wear was of any importance, since her clothes were usually discarded before many minutes had passed!

They had quickly fallen into a routine: Ace waited in his hired Mercedes a short distance from the house, away from spying eyes, then they went to his rented accommodation in Wimbledon for dinner and . . .

They pretended it was fear of publicity that kept them away from restaurants and hotels; it was a valid point, since Ace was still hot news with the paparazzi, and a photograph of him with Alexa at his side would appear in the gossip columns, but mainly they shunned public places so they could make love whenever and wherever they wanted. Not even Ace Delaney could get away with making love to his companion in the Savoy Grill!

Her 'lessons' continued apace; she delighted in each new technique and position; she had lost her anxieties and revelled not only in the pleasure she received, but in that which she was able to give to the sexiest man in the world.

Tonight would be no exception, she thought happily, totally unaware of the car parked across the square, and of the driver who had watched and waited, and then pulled out to follow behind them as Ace drove away.

The driver's name was Simon Daniels, a private detective hired by Philip Kane to discover exactly where his daughter spent her evenings, and with whom. This same detective had discovered the truth about Dimitri – Philip Kane wished he were again dealing with an impecunious, opportunistic Greek fisherman instead of the man he feared was stealing his daughter's heart.

'I went to visit Melissa today,' Alexa told Ace during a lull in lovemaking, lying sated and drowsy in his arms.

'Yeah?'

'Yes. Suzy's so sweet. And I just adore Kit now she's a little older,' she enthused.

'Mmm,' Ace grunted by way of a response. It was hardly encouraging, but she ploughed on.

'Don't you sometimes envy Jack?'

'No, he was a lot more fun when he was single,' Ace commented, then he eyed her with sudden suspicion. 'Seeing Kit and Melissa's baby hasn't made you feel broody, has it?' he asked.

'A bit.' She shrugged, as if it were no big deal. 'I'd quite like to have children,' she added airily.

'You're too young,' Ace said flatly.

'Melissa's only three years older than I am,' she pointed out.

'Melissa's too young to be a mother,' Ace retorted. 'She could have had another five years as a top player.'

'But I'm not a professional athlete – there's no reason for me to wait,' she said, forcing herself to speak lightly and to smile, when what she really wanted was to rant and rave and hurl the truth at him.

'Look, honey, you've come a long way from the spoilt brat I met last Christmas,' Ace said patronizingly, 'but you've a lot of growing up to do before you should consider having a kid.'

Disheartened, Alexa dropped the subject; she had been a fool to hope there might be a happy ending. Even if – fat chance – Ace had been delighted at the prospect of fatherhood, there was still her own father to consider. He might, just, accept an illegitimate grandchild – but not one sired by the man he held responsible for his stroke and subsequent disability.

She pushed the problems that awaited her in the near future to the back of her mind; there were only three days remaining of Ace's stay in London, and she wanted to gather as many happy memories as possible, memories she could bring out and savour in the months ahead. She would say nothing more to antagonize him, and possibly spoil what little time she did have with him.

But then he climbed off the bed and sauntered into the bathroom, returning with a packet of condoms, for the first time ever. Tears and temper warred for supremacy. The pig!

'It's too late for those!' she snapped.

'What do you mean?' Ace looked horrified – and angry – and Alexa back-pedalled hastily.

'I mean, if either of us has a nasty disease, the other has probably already caught it,' she said acidly.

'Oh.' He looked so relieved she wanted to hit him, and her fingers curved into claws, ready to strike at his face. 'I'm clean,' he informed her.

'So am I. But that's hardly the point – you should have been using those all along,' she said loftily. Ace arched one dark brow sardonically.

'I don't recall your mentioning it before now,' he drawled. 'It's all my responsibility, is it? Honey, I'm thirty-two – when I started screwing, "safe sex" meant not telling the girl where I lived!'

'Very funny,' she scowled. 'Admit it – you're terrified I'll "forget" to take my Pill, in an attempt to trap you into marriage. You are so arrogant,' she said wildly. 'Any woman who would marry you would need her head examined! Hell, what am I talking about – I'm the one who needs her head examining! I must be mad!' She scrambled off the bed and began searching for her clothes. 'I want to go home!'

'No, you don't.' Ace caught her arm and pulled her back against him; his mouth unerringly found the ultra-sensitive spot above her collarbone while one hand fondled her breast, teasing the nipple until it hardened, betraying her desire.

Alexa put up a half-hearted token resistance for a moment more, then gave up the unequal struggle – she couldn't fight him as well as her own needs.

'You don't play fair,' she said weakly.

'I know,' he murmured, with the slow, heart-stopping smile that melted her resolve, and she forgot all about wanting to go home . . .

Simon Daniels, the private detective, called on Philip early the following morning, while Alexa was still sleeping off the excesses of the night before.

Simon had spent a boring evening, following Ace to Wimbledon, watching and waiting outside the house, guessing correctly what was happening behind the closed curtains, and then tailing the Mercedes back to Eaton Square. He quickly briefed Philip on what he had seen.

'And the man she was with – do you know his identity?' Philip asked tersely, although, deep down, he was sure he already knew.

'I recognized him at once – it was the American tennis player, Ace Delaney,' Simon informed him. Philip nodded, and forced himself to remain calm.

'You said they remained at this private house all evening. Were they guests of the owners?' Philip demanded, clutching at straws.

'No; I talked to some of the paparazzi hanging around – Delaney has rented the house for the duration of the Wimbledon Championships.'

'I see.' Philip nodded curtly, and turned away, indicating the meeting was at an end.

Alexa returned from shopping – after buying, yet again, more, looser clothing – shortly before noon, just in time for the start of the Wimbledon coverage on TV.

She dashed into the drawing room and switched on the set; it was the men's semi-finals day, and Ace was being interviewed for his opinion on the likely outcome of the matches.

Alexa gazed at his darkly handsome features and listened to the American drawl she had come to love: the adoration she was careful to mask whenever she was with him was apparent in her face for all to see. It was certainly obvious to Philip Kane as he silently manoeuvred his wheelchair into the room, with Graham Peters following behind. If Philip had not already learned of her liaison with Delaney, her rapt expression now would certainly have given him the answer he'd sought.

'Good morning, Alexa,' Graham said, rather formally.

'Oh, hi.' She reluctantly tore her gaze away from the screen, but only for the second it took to smile briefly at Graham.

'Graham's here to take you to lunch,' Philip told her.

'Huh?'

'Graham's here. It's time for lunch. He's booked a table at San Lorenzo,' Philip said loudly.

'Oh, great. Have a nice time,' she said vaguely. 'I'll see you when you get back.' Philip, yet again, had to force himself to calm down, and made a concentrated effort to control his breathing – and his temper.

'I had rather hoped to take *you* to lunch,' Graham said, with a forced joviality. 'I hadn't realized you were such an ardent tennis fan,' he added, rather edgily, as she continued to ignore him. 'Who got through to the semis?'

'Um . . .' Alexa hadn't the slightest idea, and finally lost interest in the TV when the interview finished and the cameras switched to a Doubles match already in progress on an outside court. She gazed blankly at Graham for a moment, then, 'Lunch, you said?'

'Yes. We have something to discuss,' he gritted out.

'We do? Oh, the dinner party you mentioned for the Dickinsons?' She looked to Philip for confirmation.

'Yes,' he agreed hastily, with a warning glance at Graham. 'Graham will be holding it at his house, but we'd like you to organize it and act as his hostess.'

'When?' she asked anxiously.

'Next Friday, probably,' Graham put in, and she relaxed: Ace would have returned to LA by then, and she would be glad of something to occupy her mind.

'That's fine. I'll see to it. But you don't have to take me to lunch, Graham,' she told him.

'I want to,' he insisted, so she went to quickly change into one of her new dresses. For the first time in her life she was unable to squeeze into a size eight, and she wondered gloomily just how big she would become in the months ahead.

'Don't have a pudding,' Philip couldn't resist advising her, with some malice. 'I'm sure you're gaining weight.' Alexa flushed, but made no comment, and merely mumbled a goodbye.

Philip watched her go, with a dark scowl and even darker thoughts. I hope to hell Graham's the father of that baby, he thought, and prayed for a fair-haired child, preferably a replica of Alexa. If it was black-haired and dark-eyed . . . he shook his head at that prospect, and tried to console himself with the thought that it would still be his grandchild; that it would be brought up decently – an interesting experiment in nature versus nurture, he decided, with black humour.

Strangely, he felt he could love a girl, whoever her sire, but not a son of Delaney's. He shuddered at the very idea of a small version of Ace Delaney living in his house. Still, it will be my job to ensure that environment triumphs over heredity, he thought, envisaging a future with himself, Graham, Alexa and the child forming a family group; maybe, in time, there would be other children. For the first time since the stroke, he saw a glimmer of light at the end of a very long, dark tunnel.

## CHAPTER 17

Alexa was quite relaxed and at ease with Graham over lunch; the awkwardness she had initially felt after the night she had repudiated his lovemaking had long vanished. She quite enjoyed holding dinner parties for her father's business colleagues, and was especially pleased to have something to fill the empty days and nights following Ace's departure after the weekend.

'I didn't really bring you here to discuss the dinner party,' Graham finally broke in, bored by talk of menus and seating arrangements, and anxious to get the other matter settled as quickly as possible. He reached into his pocket and brought out a small, heart-shaped box that could only contain a ring. Alexa stared at it in perplexity.

'You're getting married?' she ventured. He smiled faintly.

'I hope so.' He opened the box and took out a large, square-cut emerald, then leaned across the table to take her hand.

'Me?' Alexa said, with less than flattering astonishment tinged with dismay. 'You must be joking,' she said flatly, snatching her hand back and hiding it under the table. 'You don't love me.'

'I'm very fond of you, and you're a beautiful girl. I think we could make a success of it,' he said.

'Maybe,' Alexa said doubtfully. 'But this isn't necessary; I'm sure Daddy already intends appointing you managing director,' she told him, and he raised one eyebrow in mock dismay.

'Such cynicism in one so young,' he remarked. 'I'm sure you're right – I will be the next MD,' he said confidently, 'but that isn't why I'm asking you to marry me.'

'Then why are you?' she asked bluntly. 'I don't understand.' Graham lifted his hands in a gesture of helplessness.

'Don't you? I've been watching you, wanting you, ever since that night at my house,' he said, lowering his voice. 'I'm sorry I tried to rush you into something you're not ready for,' he said earnestly. 'We could have a good marriage, Alexa. Wouldn't you like to be married? To start a family?' he added. Alexa drew in her breath sharply at that, and glanced away. 'Alexa?' Graham prompted. 'What's wrong?'

'I . . . I'm pregnant,' she blurted out. 'So you see why I can't marry you. But I haven't told Daddy, so please don't mention it to him,' she begged. Graham raised one eyebrow at that, but decided there was no point in telling her Philip had already guessed, so merely nodded his agreement. 'Graham, I appreciate your offer, but obviously it's out of the question now. I suggest we both forget we ever had this conversation,' she added.

'Who is the father?' Graham asked, after a pause.

'I'd rather not say.' She lowered her gaze.

'Will he marry you?'

'No, he's not the marrying kind,' she said bitterly, and Graham relaxed.

'Then my offer still stands,' he said quietly. Alexa's head jerked up in amazement, then she frowned slightly and bit her lower lip worriedly. Ace didn't want her, not permanently, anyway, and he had made it perfectly clear he didn't want a child . . . She sighed and looked at Graham.

'Marry me,' he urged. 'It would please your father,' he added.

'I'm sure it would.' She hesitated, then, 'May I think it over? Just for a few days?' she asked. That would give Ace the opportunity to say something, anything, to give her hope for a future with him. She wasn't being fair to Graham, of course, but then he wasn't being entirely truthful with her – if she weren't Philip Kane's daughter he wouldn't be offering marriage, baby or no baby.

'Very well,' Graham agreed. 'But just a few days, no longer. We don't have much time to waste.'

'I suppose not.' Alexa glanced down at her fuller figure; there was a definite roundness to her stomach now. 'I'll let you know as soon as possible,' she promised.

'All right.' Graham pocketed the ring, and turned the conversation to neutral topics, discussing mutual friends and business acquaintances, letting her know, whether by accident or design she wasn't sure, that they had matching lifestyles, came from similar backgrounds, and could live together in comfortable compatability.

After lunch, Graham dropped her off at Eaton Square and she went straight to her room, where she remained throughout the afternoon, worrying over her future and that of her baby, not sure what she ought to do for the best. The sensible solution was to marry Graham, but she couldn't quite rid herself of the fantasy that Ace might fall in love with her and decide he wouldn't return to LA on Monday, after all. She knew he had filmed his last episode of *Country Club*, so there was no urgent reason for him to rush back.

As usual, she slipped out of the house at seven-thirty, and hurried over to where Ace had parked the Mercedes.

'Hi, honey.' He leaned over to open the door and kissed her as she climbed in, not a light kiss of greeting, but a deeply passionate embrace that made her temporarily forget her dilemma. 'Wimbledon?' he suggested huskily. She nodded her acquiescence, then abruptly changed her mind. The suspense was driving her insane; she simply had to know how he really felt about her, if there was any hope or if her fantasy was just that – a dream that could never come true.

'No – can we go somewhere to talk?' she asked. If they went to his house, they would go straight to bed.

'Talk?' Ace queried. 'We can talk at the house.'

'Oh, sure,' she said tartly. 'I need to talk to you – before we go to bed,' she emphasized.

'Okay.' Ace shrugged, and started up the car. 'Where do you suggest we go? Presumably public places are still off limits?'

'Oh.' Alexa had forgotten the need for secrecy. 'Why do you have to be so damn famous?' she groused. 'Turn left here, and again,' she directed him. 'There's a place to park just ahead,' she said.

'So. What's on your mind?' Ace asked idly, turning to face her. Alexa gazed down at her hands, clasped loosely in her lap. This was so difficult – why couldn't she have left it alone?

'I've been doing some thinking,' she began slowly.

Oh, hell! Ace grimaced: when a woman started thinking, it usually spelled trouble!

'Yes?' he asked idly.

'I've been really happy these past couple of weeks, but, well, what's going to happen in the future?' she asked tentatively, praying for a miracle, for him to declare he loved her and would stay in London to be with her.

'Who knows? Come back to LA with me on Monday and we'll find out,' he said; which was a perfectly reasonable suggestion, he thought.

'Oh, right! I just pack my bags and step over my father's corpse on my way out of the door, I suppose,' she said, disappointment making her voice hard and cold. Ace frowned.

'You said he was much better.'

'He is, but I can't risk causing him to have another stroke!' she glared at him. 'Surely you can understand that?'

'Does he suspect you've been seeing me?'

'No, I don't think so. But I can't just go to LA without any explanation, can I?' She looked at him beseechingly, waiting and hoping for him to contradict her. He didn't. His expression, or lack of one, told her nothing of what he might be feeling.

Ace realized he did want her to return to the States with him, but he shied away from the commitment she seemed to hanker after. And, if Philip Kane were to have another seizure, and possibly die . . . It was too big a risk; besides, Alexa was too emotionally insecure for him. He knew himself too well; sooner or later he would cheat on her, and he didn't think she could handle that.

'I guess you can't,' he finally replied lightly. Alexa bit her lip and blinked back tears. She had been a fool to hope she had meant more to him than just another temporary fling. She had only herself to blame; he'd never promised anything more.

'I had lunch with someone today. His name's Graham Peters – he's on Daddy's board of directors. He asked me to marry him,' she said, in a rush.

'Does he know you've been in bed with me every night for the past couple of weeks?' Ace asked, after a long pause.

'No, of course not. It's none of his business,' she said quickly, lest he think she had been two-timing him. 'But I have known Graham for years; he'll take over as MD when Daddy officially steps down. And he's keen for us to have a family,' she added softly.

'It all sounds very neat,' Ace commented acidly. 'No doubt your father approves?'

'Yes, he does.'

'What answer did you give him?' he asked idly, sounding totally unconcerned, Alexa thought wretchedly.

'I . . . I asked for time to think about it,' she stammered.

'What's to think about? You've obviously made your decision,' he said carelessly. 'I think you're making a mistake, but that's your problem.'

'What do you mean?' she asked, hope flaring.

'I think you ought to stand on your own two feet for a while. You've been a Daddy's girl all your life, and now you want this other guy to take over the task of looking after you. I realize this is a revolutionary idea,' his voice dripped sarcasm, 'but why don't you get a job? Find a place of your own to live and be independent for the first time in your life. Do you know something?' he asked, but didn't wait for a reply. 'All this bleating about how much your father needs you is rubbish! You need him far more than he needs you.'

'That's not true.' Alexa was once again near to tears. He sounded so cold and distant, clinically dissecting her life and emotions.

'Isn't it?' His eyes bored into hers and she looked away. 'Do you love him – this Graham?'

'I . . . I like him a lot. He'll be a good husband and father . . . what are you doing?' she asked, as he started up the car.

'Taking you home – you can phone Graham and give him the good news,' he said coolly.

The short journey passed in silence; Alexa was too near to breaking down to try and speak, and Ace was too angry. He wanted to throttle her, drive her to the airport and drag her on to a plane, go and confront Philip Kane and/or Graham Peters . . . He wanted to take any or all of the courses of action that occurred to him in rapid succession, but something held him back. He refused to take control of her life

– something he felt sure she would gladly allow him to do. She had to make her own decisions, right or wrong, he thought grimly. But he was uneasily aware of just how tempted he was to keep her with him.

He pulled up outside the house and stared stonily ahead; only his knuckles, gleaming whitely as he gripped the steering wheel, betrayed any emotion. Alexa didn't notice that sign of tension; she glanced only at his stony visage as she fumbled for the door handle. As she climbed out on to the pavement, Ace turned his head slightly towards her.

'Coward.'

That one word – coward – rang in her ears throughout the sleepless, tearful night. Saturday was a wretched day; at seven-thirty, the customary time for Ace to arrive, she sat by an upstairs window and waited. Only when darkness fell did she stretch her cramped limbs and go to bed, to spend another night sobbing into her pillow.

On Sunday, while flicking listlessly through the stack of newspapers, she came across a photograph of Ace, taken at a nightclub. He was locked in an embrace with Lucia Conti, the very pretty Italian-born American professional player with whom Ace was rumoured to have had several affairs in the past. The accompanying paragraph quoted a happily smiling Ace as saying he was consoling Lucia for her semi-final defeat at Wimbledon earlier in the week.

It hasn't taken him long to find a replacement! Alexa thought savagely, screwing up the offending paper and tossing it aside, again blinking back tears. I will *not* cry for him any more! she vowed furiously, and before she could change her mind she phoned Graham to tell him she would be happy to accept his proposal.

Melissa also noticed the item of gossip concerning Ace and Lucia, her one-time rival, on court and off it, both for sponsorship deals and for Ace's attention! The rivalry had been intense, but it all seemed so long ago now, and irrelevant to her life, and Melissa was genuinely sorry that Lucia, in her last year on the tour, had again failed in her bid to win a coveted Grand Slam.

She quickly forgot about the article, and certainly made no connection between it and Alexa's phone call to tell her she was marrying Graham Peters, and that her father now knew about the baby, and seemed to be not displeased by the news.

'It will be a very small register office "do",' Alexa explained. 'We're getting a special licence. As you know, we don't have much time to waste! As it is, everyone will be counting the months once the baby's born,' she said ruefully. Except Ace, she thought silently.

'Who cares? So long as you're happy,' Melissa said, with a faintly questioning tone to her voice.

'I'm doing the right thing,' Alexa said, after a pause. 'For everyone concerned,' she added, which sounded a little strange to Melissa. But she was distracted from asking further questions by an urgent cry for attention from her daughter. 'Here's Mum – tell her your news,' she said hastily, and handed the phone over to Rose.

Rose listened to Alexa with a huge sense of relief. She had been so anxious since seeing her drive off with Ace! Perhaps he had been simply giving her a lift somewhere, she thought again. She had tried, rather unsuccessfully, to convince herself there was nothing going on between the two of them, but now Alexa's engagement to Graham reinforced her view. But still she refrained from asking Alexa just why she had been in Ace's car. It's none of my business, she told herself firmly, but knew, deep down, that she didn't really want to know the answer.

However, Alexa wouldn't be the first girl to indulge in a final fling before settling down to matrimony. Graham was a pleasant young man, as well as being clever and shrewd enough to take over the running of Philip Kane's empire. Everything was working out perfectly, she decided happily.

'Will you come to the wedding?' Alexa asked, rather tentatively. 'I know it's a bit mother-of-the-bride, but I'd really like you to be there,' she said earnestly.

'Of course I will; I'd love to come,' Rose said promptly. She ended the call soon after, for Suzy's wails weren't lessening but seemed to be getting louder. Melissa was almost as distressed as her baby when Rose arrived in the nursery and took over; within minutes, Suzy was sleeping contentedly.

'You're so good with her,' Melissa sighed enviously.

'I've just had a lot of practice,' Rose said calmly, settling Suzy back into her cot. Melissa switched on the baby-alarm and they returned downstairs.

'I'm so relieved to hear Alexa's marrying Graham,' Rose said. 'Philip will be pleased, too; I know it's what he hoped would happen.'

'I'm not so sure – talk about a marriage of inconvenience!' Melissa retorted.

'It's a very suitable match,' Rose said firmly.

'Maybe, but she didn't sound too thrilled about it, did she?' Melissa asked thoughtfully, remembering how excited she had been when Nick had proposed. 'And I'm sure she told me Graham isn't the baby's father – although I was in the early stages of labour at the time, so I could be wrong!'

'I expect she hadn't made up her mind about marriage at that stage. I'm sure they'll be very happy,' Rose insisted, refusing to acknowledge any doubts. Melissa grimaced slightly, but let the matter drop.

On Monday, Ace, hungover and unusually depressed, arrived at Nine Elms. He had been to Bellwood to say goodbye and decided to call in on Melissa on his way to the airport.

'Hi, honey; you're looking good,' he approved, noting that she had already regained her slim figure.

'That's more than I can say for you,' Melissa eyed him sourly. 'Lucia, I suppose?'

'That's right,' he lied smoothly: he'd seen the Press reports and guessed, hoped, Alexa had too. If he told Melissa the truth, she might well tell Alexa – why the hell should he be the only one to be miserable? he thought dourly, as he followed Melissa into the drawing room. Suzy was there, in her pram, and he glanced uninterestedly at the small bundle.

'This is what has made Alexa so broody, is it?' he asked idly. Melissa nodded proudly as she took Suzy out of the pram for a cuddle. She was too absorbed in her baby to register the import of his words; to realize he must have seen Alexa more recently than on his visit to the Chelsea flat on the day before Suzy's birth.

'Will you be seeing Ella when you get back to the States?' she asked him next.

'Sure. I go and check on my investment most weekends. It drives Hal Renwick nuts!'

'I bet it does. He's a good coach; why don't you just let him get on with it?' she asked absently, searching for a photograph she wanted Ella to have. It was one Nick had taken, of her and Suzy with the teddy bear Ella had sent. On the reverse, Melissa had written, 'Good luck with your career', and signed it 'Melissa Farrell'.

'Thanks, honey; she'll treasure this,' Ace said, pocketing it.

'Melissa, do you . . . oh!' Rose halted in the doorway, startled to see Ace. 'Hello,' she greeted him, rather stiffly, then ignored him and held up the burgundy suit she was carrying. 'Do you think this will do for the wedding?' she asked Melissa. 'I've a rather nice hat that matches it; I'm never sure what to wear for a register office.'

'That's lovely; you always look good in it,' Melissa assured her. She turned to Ace as Rose exited hurriedly. 'Alexa's getting married next week,' she told him casually. The information hit him harder than he had expected it would, despite knowing of the marriage proposal; it certainly hurt more than he wanted to admit, even to himself. He reached for his cigarettes, then, at Melissa's look of horror, put them away again.

'That's a bit sudden, isn't it?' he asked lightly. 'And a register office? I'd have thought she would want to hire Westminster Abbey or something. What's the rush?'

'Oh, the usual,' Melissa said blithely.

That hit him even harder; that was why she was so interested in babies? Was she trying to tell me she's having my child? he wondered suddenly.

'She's pregnant?' he asked hoarsely.

'Yes.'

'Not another baby! It must be contagious,' he tried to joke. He looked awful, grey and shaking, but Melissa put that down to his obvious hangover. His eyes were bloodshot, his hands trembling, and he looked as if he hadn't slept for a week. He took a deep breath.

'When's the happy event?'

'The wedding? Next week,' Melissa said. He almost shook her.

'You already told me that!' he ground out. 'The baby!'

'Oh, not for ages. January, or early February,' Melissa unwittingly passed on the misinformation, having forgotten she had originally thought Alexa had got her dates wrong.

Ace counted back. It's not mine, he thought, and wondered why he felt angry instead of relieved. In fact, he was so furious he wanted to break something or someone, and he quickly took his leave of Melissa, claiming he would miss his flight if he didn't hurry.

But, once out of sight of the house, he stopped the car and lit the cigarette he craved. The little two-timing bitch! He recalled her saying, that awful morning when she had discovered he had accused her father of abuse, that she intended making up for lost time in her sex-life, but he hadn't believed she would. Obviously, he had been wrong.

'My father mustn't know I'm seeing you!' he mimicked out loud. It wasn't her father's finding out that bothered her, but this other guy! He must have been out of town for the past couple of weeks, Ace decided grimly, and she had taken the opportunity to have a little fun during his absence.

Briefly, he considered going to confront her. Two things stopped him: her comment about stepping over her father's corpse might have some validity, and there was the knowledge that the baby wasn't his.

He re-started the car and drove to the airport, pleased to find Lucia also waiting for a flight. He purposely let the Press believe they were leaving together, and another photograph and article appeared in the British tabloids the following day.

For a couple of days after Ace had so publicly taken up with Lucia Conti, Alexa clung to Graham. She was under no illusions that he bore any great love for her, but he was comfortable and familiar; he would look after her and her baby, and competently take over all the Kane business interests. Married to Graham, she would be safe.

Philip had suggested Graham move into Eaton Square after the wedding, and Graham was amenable to the idea. Once the baby is born, the house will be a happy, family home, Alexa concluded, but with rather more determination than confidence.

Graham organized everything for the wedding, to take place the following Friday: he arranged the special licence, booked the register office and a small reception afterwards, he even ordered flowers and cars. All Alexa had to do was buy her dress, and even that failed to rouse any enthusiasm in her.

'What colour did you have in mind?' enquired the saleslady brightly.

'Black,' Alexa said dolefully.

'Excuse me?'

'Nothing. Sorry.' She tried to shake off her lethargy, and glanced at the racks of frothy creations such as she had always dreamed of wearing for her wedding. But they weren't suitable, not for her mood, nor for a simple civil ceremony.

'That suit is pretty,' she admired a cream two-piece on a model, then realized it was very similar to the one she had worn for Clarissa's wedding; the one Ace had splashed with mud . . . after he had slept with Clarissa! I hate him, she thought, I truly hate him. And Lucia Conti. I'm glad she didn't win Wimbledon, she thought childishly, and was instantly ashamed of herself. She left the boutique without buying anything.

On Thursday, she awoke with a sense of dread. Today is my wedding day, she thought, then realized, with a surge of relief, that she still had another day. Another day – for what? For Ace to come charging in to the house and insist she marry him instead? Yeah, sure, with Lucia Conti offering to be bridesmaid. And Daddy having apoplexy, at the very least. She sighed heavily and climbed out of bed. At least the nausea had stopped.

She wasn't really aware when she made the decision not to go ahead with the wedding, but the final straw was Graham's arrival on Thursday evening, with some of his personal belongings, which he proceeded to put in her bedroom!

'You can't leave those there!' she snapped.

'Why not? Are we moving to a different room?' he enquired.

'No, it's not that.' She glanced down at the ring she had worn for less than a week and slowly slipped it off her finger. 'I'm sorry, Graham,' she said, as she held it out to him.

His face darkened with anger. 'You're being silly; it's all arranged,' he said tightly. 'You're just suffering from last-minute jitters.'

'No, it's more than that,' she said quietly. 'I'm sorry, but I just don't want to marry you.'

'You cannot do this to me! I will not be made a fool of! Have you forgotten you're pregnant? You should be grateful I'm willing to take on another man's . . .' he stopped abruptly.

'Another man's bastard? You said that didn't matter to you,' Alexa pointed out slowly.

'I lied,' he snarled. 'Your father guessed you were pregnant and hinted that I would have to marry you if I wanted to be made MD,' he told her callously.

'Daddy had guessed, before you proposed to me?' Alexa frowned, wondering what else her father had guessed. Had Mary told him about Ace being in the house? Surely not; she would be too concerned for his health to do that.

'Yes. And now you can come downstairs with me and explain to him what's going on here.' Graham grabbed her arm. 'I'm not losing my chance at MD because of your waywardness,' he said grimly.

Still stunned by the news that her father had known about her condition, Alexa allowed him to pull her down the stairs and into Philip's study.

'Alexa has something to tell you, sir,' said Graham, tightening his grip on her wrist.

'Yes.' She took a deep breath. 'I'm sorry, Daddy, but I don't want to marry Graham. I won't be part of a business deal. He doesn't love me and I don't love him.'

'Aren't you forgetting something?' Philip asked, after a long pause, gesturing to her stomach. She flushed and placed a protective hand over the slight bulge.

'No, I'm not forgetting anything. I can look after my baby.'

'I'll have no bastards in my house!' Philip roared. 'You'll marry Graham tomorrow, or you'll get rid of it!'

'You don't mean that,' Alexa said, aghast.

'I damn well do mean it! Do you think I'm stupid, girl? I know why you want to cancel this wedding, and I know . . .' He stopped, belatedly remembering Graham's presence. This was better settled without him. 'Leave her to me, Graham. She'll be at the register office on time tomorrow; I'll see to that,' he said briskly. Graham hesitated briefly, glancing from father to daughter.

'Very well,' he capitulated, and took his leave, after another stern glance directed at Alexa.

Philip waited until he heard the front door close before turning to his daughter. But Alexa spoke first.

'I'm truly sorry to upset you, Daddy, but I won't marry him,' she said quietly. She could tell he was agitated, his colour worryingly high, but she wouldn't back down merely to avoid – no, postpone a scene. 'And I won't have an abortion,' she said firmly.

'Graham's not the father, is he?' Philip said heavily; it was a statement, not a question.

'No,' she admitted, bracing herself for the next, inevitable question. She mustn't divulge Ace's name, not ever . . .

'It's Delaney, isn't it?' Philip spat, his features contorting with rage. Alexa stared at him, too shocked to confirm or deny it. 'Well? I'm right, aren't I?'

'Yes,' she whispered finally.

'He damn near kills me, takes Rose away, and you . . . you let him . . .' He struggled for control. 'When did it happen? While you were staying with him in LA, I suppose? Before he came over here to ruin my life!' Alexa couldn't meet his gaze, but fortunately he didn't press for a reply.

'Does he know you're pregnant?'

'No.' She shook her head. Philip grunted his satisfaction at hearing that small piece of good news.

'At least you have the sense to realize he'll never marry you.' He paused and looked at her, her pale face and worried eyes, and his voice gentled somewhat. 'Marry Graham, Alexa.' He tried coaxing where bullying had failed. 'He's willing to give the child his name . . . oh, I know,' he put up a hand to forestall her argument. 'He's not doing so out of the goodness of his heart; he'll be well rewarded, but he'll be a good enough husband and father.'

'I know all that, but I can't, won't, settle for second-best,' Alexa said wretchedly. 'I thought I could, but I can't. I'd prefer to bring up my child alone.'

'Then do that! Alone!' Philip shouted. Alexa blinked and swallowed painfully.

'You want me to leave this house?' she whispered.

'Yes!'

'I . . . I understand. I'll go, first thing tomorrow morning,' she said quietly. 'I do love you, Daddy . . .'

'Go away,' he said, but with more sadness than anger. He was sure she would be back; she had never coped alone and certainly wouldn't now.

Alexa hurried away, relieved to have finished with Graham, but filled with sadness at leaving her father. She felt the least she could do was to go right away, somewhere abroad, far enough away to avoid meeting any of his friends or business colleagues.

It was Melissa who provided her with a solution, promptly renewing her offer to let Alexa stay at Rose Arbor, in California, for as long as she wished. And it was Melissa who made all the travel arrangements; she also contacted the couple who acted as caretakers in her absence and asked them to keep an eye on Alexa and call her if there were any problems.

Alexa didn't tell her father her destination, nor did he ask, and his study door was closed to her when she slipped quietly out of the house; the house which had been her home for her entire life. As she closed the door behind her she wondered if she would ever be welcome there again.

## CHAPTER 18

Nick had been in favour of purchasing Nine Elms for many reasons, not least of which was its lack of a tennis court! However, as July gave way to August, he began to change his mind for, more and more, he arrived home to an empty house. Melissa was usually to be found five miles away at Bellwood, out on the tennis court with either Jack or Lisa, while Rose tended to the two babies.

It became such a regular occurrence that he began driving directly to Bellwood, instead of his own home! He understood Melissa's desire to regain her figure and her fitness, but he secretly worried that she was intending making a comeback on the professional tour.

The quarrel, when it came, was unwittingly triggered by Jack's innocently telling Melissa of his TV work for the US Open which was due to begin at the end of August.

'I wish I could be there,' Melissa said wistfully. 'Why don't we ask the tournament director to grant us a wild card entry into the Mixed Doubles?' she suggested idly.

'You can forget that idea! You're not going to New York!' Nick snapped. Melissa stared at him for a moment, then her chin jutted stubbornly. Uh-oh, trouble, Jack thought, recognizing the signs. He was surprised at Nick – surely he knew Melissa wasn't serious? He should also have learned by now that telling her she couldn't do something only made her more determined to have her own way. Nick was usually more subtle in his dealings with her.

'I've decided I am going to New York with Jack and Lisa,' Melissa informed Nick coolly.

'Leave me out of this – it wasn't my idea,' Jack said hastily, when Nick glared at him, as if it was his fault for mentioning it. He quickly left the room and resisted the temptation to eavesdrop.

'I said no,' Nick told his wife, his grey eyes steely as he regarded her. 'What about Suzy? Or had you forgotten you have other responsibilities now?'

'Of course not! She'll be fine in New York – they do have babies there, you know. There's even a crèche at Flushing Meadow,' she informed him. 'Or I can get a babysitter at the hotel . . .'

'Why don't you try looking after her yourself?' Nick asked sharply. 'She spends more time with your mother than with you.'

'And she spends even less time with you,' Melissa pointed out sweetly.

'I have a business to run,' Nick snapped.

'Oh, sure,' Melissa sneered. 'You were only a sleeping partner for eighteen months while you travelled with me on the circuit, and they managed to survive without you. You work because you want to – we hardly need the extra money!'

'Are you telling me you want to re-start your career?' asked Nick slowly. It was what he had dreaded, and he would fight her all the way, for his daughter's sake as well as his own.

'Of course not!' Melissa said impatiently, annoyed that he didn't realize the impossibility of such a move. 'I could never get back into the top ten. I don't even want to try,' she added quickly. 'It would take me away from you and Suzy too much, but I still want to be part of the sport; part of the major championships. Is that really too much to ask? Just two weeks in New York? You could come too,' she added.

'Thanks for that afterthought,' Nick said bitterly.

'You know I didn't mean it like that,' she sighed. Nick watched her, noting the sad droop to her mouth, and felt ashamed of himself.

'I'm sorry, sweetheart.' He moved swiftly to her and pulled her gently into his arms. She didn't resist, but nor did she respond, remaining stiff in his embrace. 'I overreacted, but you've been working so hard at your tennis recently, and I've been afraid you might be preparing for a comeback,' he explained.

'Oh, Nick.' Melissa relaxed and melted against him, her anger and resentment vanishing in an instant. 'Why didn't you tell me? I promise you it's never even occurred to me to rejoin the tour. Even if I could become strong enough physically, I couldn't summon up the necessary mental and emotional commitment to the game. I love you and Suzy too much for that. I knew, when I decided to start a family, that my career as a top professional would end, and I have no regrets, none at all,' she assured him earnestly.

'That's good to hear.' Nick rested his chin on her hair, and hugged her close. 'I was beginning to think Suzy and I aren't enough to make you happy.'

'That's not true,' she denied quickly. 'I'm very happy with my life, but I'm not the baking-cakes-and-knitting type of wife and mother,' she told him – as if he didn't already know! 'I still love the sport, and I really would like to remain a part of it,' she added, watching anxiously for his reaction.

'Doing what, exactly?' Nick asked warily.

'Nothing that would take me away from you and Suzy,' she said promptly. 'I'm talking about exhibition matches, pro-am tournaments, endorsing my line of sportswear – it's still selling well despite my retirement, but it won't for much longer if I don't soon do some promotion work.'

'Okay,' Nick capitulated. 'New York, here we come!'

'You'll come with me?' Melissa beamed.

'I certainly wouldn't let you go alone,' Nick said firmly. 'No doubt that reprobate Delaney will be there, hanging around you as usual?' he growled.

'He only does that to wind you up,' Melissa grinned. 'He practically ignores me when you're not around!'

'Hm!' Nick wasn't entirely convinced of that, but he let it drop, relieved that she wasn't contemplating a return to the gruelling schedule of constant travel, practice and competition.

They arrived in New York at the end of August; Nick, Melissa and Suzy, together with Lisa and Kit.

Jack had gone on ahead a few days earlier to prepare for his TV coverage. He was in the studio for much of the day and late into the night, so Lisa joined Nick and Melissa in sightseeing until the championships got under way.

It felt good to be back – all the fun and excitement, but none of the hard work! Melissa joked to Lisa. Melissa, as a Brit, would always consider Wimbledon to be the most prestigious of the four Grand Slams, but the US Open was the biggest in terms of prize money and numbers of spectators who flocked to Flushing Meadow.

There was always an incredible buzz around the vast concourse – Stadium Court alone had seating for twenty thousand, and the noise was indescribable – the vociferous New Yorkers had none of the polite restraint generally exercised by the crowds at Wimbledon.

The two babies received a great deal of attention from the players; Kit, at nine months, especially enjoyed the fuss while Suzy slept through most of it, despite being handed around the locker room as if taking part in a game of Pass of Parcel!

'You are lucky,' sighed Bev Hunter, one of Melissa's friends from her playing days, as she cuddled Suzy.

'I know,' Melissa agreed, rather smugly. She felt fitter, healthier and happier than she had in years; the niggling injuries that were an accepted part of a professional player's daily life had healed. No longer did she need regular physiotherapy – the only massage she required was that provided by Nick!

'I have to go practise for my match,' Bev said, reluctantly handing Suzy back. 'See you later?'

'Sure, but I'm meeting up with Katy for lunch,' Melissa told her.

Katy Oliver, Melissa's ex-coach and great friend, hadn't changed at all over the years; her hair was still the same riot of red curls, her tongue as sharp and caustic as when she had bullied and cajoled Melissa into producing the best tennis she was capable of. Katy still felt Melissa had blown a brilliant career by deciding to have a baby at such a relatively young age, but grudgingly conceded that Suzy was, perhaps, worth the sacrifice.

Since leaving Melissa's employ, Katy had also taken a break from the constant travelling entailed by being part of the pro circuit, and had taken a post coaching young kids in her home city of New York. Several of her charges were taking part in the junior event, as were half a dozen of the teenagers from Hal Renwick's tennis academy in California, including Ella Cortez.

'Do you know much about this girl Ella?' Katy asked Melissa, when they had caught up on gossip and the subject had turned to tennis. 'She's playing against one of my kids in the first round of the juniors,' she explained.

'I know Hal's fed up with Ace's constant interference,' Melissa told her. 'Apparently he's down there most weekends, checking on her progress.'

'I suppose he feels entitled, since he's picking up her bills,' Katy mused, eyeing Melissa curiously. 'Just *why* is he sponsoring her?' she asked. 'Everyone's speculating about it.'

'I know; poor kid,' Melissa grimaced in sympathy. 'He's convinced she's a good investment – I really think it's as simple as that. I haven't seen her play, but Ace told Jack she has loads of talent but has a lot of catching up to do, which is why she's at the academy. She's a hard worker, and also desperate to please Ace!'

'Oh, no, not another besotted teenager!' Katy groaned, with a sideways glance to remind Melissa she had been similarly infatuated when she was Ella's age.

Ella was bursting with excitement, tinged with apprehension. This was her first trip to New York and, instead of staying with the other juniors, Ace had arranged for her and Linda to have a suite in an hotel on Fifth Avenue!

She longed to explore the city, but was even keener to play well and justify all the money Ace was investing in her. She was out on the practice courts as much as possible, and eagerly awaiting her first match in a Grand Slam – the US Open! She couldn't believe she was actually taking part in an event she had only previously watched on TV. Okay, so the junior events took place on the outside courts, with no TV coverage, but it was still the US Open, the biggest and best of them all!

Her opponent was Shanna Douglas, a native New Yorker, so the rather meagre crowd was rooting for her. But Ella, far from being downcast, was delighted to see, not only Ace and Hal, but Melissa Farrell in the stands, waiting for the match to begin. Ella grinned broadly at them all, but Ace scowled in return.

'Concentrate on what you're doing,' he growled, but not loud enough for her to hear.

'You're tetchy,' Melissa commented. He looked hungover and rather gaunt, and thoroughly disreputable. Still sexy, though, she had to admit, and sternly reminded herself she was a respectable wife and mother! 'Lucia keeping you on your toes?' she teased.

'My elbows, you mean,' Ace grunted, reluctant to admit there was no affair with Lucia; his sleepless nights had nothing to do with the sultry Italian.

He hated to admit it, even to himself, but a green-eyed, tawny-haired, toffee-nosed Daddy's girl was keeping him awake – which would be okay if she were in the room, in his bed, but she wasn't. The two-timing witch was also married and pregnant and had caused him nothing but trouble. He should be glad she was some other guy's problem, but he wasn't.

In an effort to distract his thoughts from Alexa Kane, he had finally got around to listening to the tapes his mother had provided for Flanagan's biography. Ironically, Loretta's 'revelations' – which could be true, or just as easily be the product of a drugged-up, drunken imagination – were also making restful sleep an impossibility. He had tried to dismiss her tales as being mere fantasy, but it wasn't that simple. And he shied away from the next, logical step of investigating her claims; that could too easily add to his problems instead of lessening them.

'Sorry, Hal, what was that?' He forced himself to stop thinking about either Alexa or Loretta and concentrate on what Hal was saying about Ella.

She had played a couple of junior tournaments in California, but this was in another league. In the big time, nerves or a poor mental attitude could quickly negate talent and endless hours of practice.

'I said, I think she'll be okay,' Hal repeated. 'She seemed quite relaxed when I hit with her earlier, and she was timing her shots well. Oh, hi, Katy.' He turned to greet her as she took a seat beside Melissa. Ace glanced enquiringly at her, wondering at her presence.

'You're not trying to persuade Melissa back on to the tour, are you? You'll have to step over Nick's dead body first,' he drawled, but his words only served to remind him of Alexa's excuse for keeping their relationship a secret. His lips tightened in anger; damn the lying bitch! He should have known there was another man involved – and not her father. After all, Philip Kane was already in a wheelchair, and presumably taking medication to prevent another stroke – how much more damage could I have done? he brooded bitterly.

'No.' Katy shook her head, and pointed to the tall, blonde girl facing Ella across the net as they warmed up for the match. 'That's Shanna Douglas – she's in my squad,' she explained.

'Any good?' Ace asked casually.

'Wait and see. I'm not telling you anything about her game – you'd probably signal instructions to Ella,' Katy said shrewdly.

'That would be against the rules.' Ace tried, and failed, to sound affronted. 'Are you happy with the job you're doing here?' he asked Katy a little later. She shrugged.

'Yeah, it's okay. Not as interesting – or as demanding – as looking after a superstar, though,' she added loudly, for Melissa's benefit.

'You know you enjoyed it,' Melissa retorted. 'You never stopped giving me earache when I decided to quit!'

'Seriously, Katy, would you consider travelling the circuit again?' Ace persisted. He'd never liked Katy overmuch, but he had seen how she had propelled Melissa to the top, and had a healthy respect for her ability as a coach.

'With Ella, you mean?' she guessed.

'Mm. Not yet, of course. But Hal's already said he wants to stay where he is, so I'll soon be looking to hire a travelling coach. If she's good enough,' he added, frowning as Ella dropped her first service game. 'If she does well here and at the Orange Bowl in December, I'll be aiming to get her on to the tour next year,' he continued. The Orange Bowl in Florida was the unofficial junior world championships and winners there were generally tipped for the top.

'I might be interested,' Katy said thoughtfully, mentally weighing up the pros and cons. Immediately after Melissa's retirement, she had enjoyed not having to pack her bags and get on a plane almost every week, but now, more than a year later, the idea held some appeal. She had certainly missed the excitement of the tour. As Melissa Farrell's ex-coach, she could easily get a job with an established player, but she would prefer to take on a newcomer, as she had with Melissa, and hopefully guide her to a successful career. Some of the players and coaches swapped places regularly, as if playing musical chairs, but Katy wanted none of that.

'I'll keep an eye on Ella's progress over the next few months,' she said now. 'And get to know her a little,' she added, for she would find it impossible to work and travel with someone she disliked. 'And there's one other thing.'

'What?' Ace asked warily.

'You,' she said bluntly. 'I couldn't coach her if you're going to pop up every few weeks and undermine my authority. I would have to have the final say on coaching – and which tournaments she should enter,' she added as an afterthought, afraid Ace would be more interested in financial gain than computer points.

'Agreed. I wouldn't set up any exhibition matches without consulting you, but I'd deal with the sponsors and the business side,' Ace said. 'I want her to succeed, but I also intend making money. I'm not picking up her bills now out of the goodness of my heart.'

'Tell me something I don't know!' Katy retorted.

'What heart?' Melissa put in, and he scowled at her before turning back to Katy.

'So? If she makes the grade in the juniors, you'll take her on full time?'

'If I think I can work with her, and get the best out of her, then yes,' Katy agreed cautiously.

'Great,' Ace said casually, then fell silent for a while as he watched Ella play. She was improving daily, but was struggling against her opponent, still distracted by the crowd as well as the excellent standard of play from the other side of the net.

'That blonde's pretty good,' Ace commented grudgingly. 'What did you say her name is?'

'Shanna Douglas,' Katy supplied, with a sigh. 'You're not thinking of collecting a harem of young players, are you?'

'I thought he already had!' Melissa interrupted.

'Will you shut up?' Ace demanded irritably. 'Haven't you got a baby to feed or something?'

'She's with Nick,' Melissa told him, poking out her tongue – boy, was he in a filthy mood! Then she too lapsed into silence and they all concentrated on the match. Ella finally made the scoreboard and perceptibly relaxed, breaking Shanna's serve with some beautiful shots – a difficult top-spin lob, then a delicate drop-shot. Ace grunted his approval at the improvement.

'There's certainly a lot of talent there,' Katy acknowledged, and Melissa nodded her agreement. She glanced up as a petite blonde woman arrived and was promptly taken under Hal's protective wing.

'This is Linda Cortez – Ella's stepmother,' he introduced her casually. Melissa smiled broadly; the proud look of happiness Hal was bestowing on Linda was one she recognized and she was extremely pleased that he had evidently found someone he could love. Her own happiness with Nick had hurt Hal tremendously and she felt suddenly as if a weight had been lifted from her shoulders.

'Hello, Linda, I'm pleased to meet you. You must be very proud of Ella,' Melissa said warmly.

'Oh, yes! I hope she didn't notice I wasn't here for the start of her match. I'm afraid I got lost,' she confessed, blushing. 'It's such a huge place, isn't it?'

'Yes, I was just the same on my first trip here,' Melissa confided, and Linda smiled gratefully.

'How is she doing?' she asked Hal, holding on to his arm.

'She started badly but she's got herself together now,' Hal replied. 'There! That's 3–3,' he said, relieved.

Ace had ignored Linda's arrival, but he wasn't, for once, being intentionally rude – he was watching a group of youths who seemed to be hassling Ella, calling out ribald comments.

They were sitting behind her but, when she moved to change ends at 3–4, they also stood up and walked to the other end of the court. He frowned, then nudged Hal to appraise him of the situation and both men continued to watch.

Ella spun around to confront her tormentors, obviously upset by what was being said, then she hunched her shoulders against them, trying to ignore them. But, as she turned her back, one produced a camera and crouched low, aiming for a shot of her thighs and bottom as she bent to receive serve.

'That's enough,' Hal muttered angrily, and got to his feet intending to intervene, but Ace grabbed his arm to stop him.

'No, leave it!' he snapped. 'She has to learn to ignore idiots like those. Besides, if she were concentrating properly she wouldn't even be aware of them,' he added.

'God, you're a hard bastard!' Hal said disgustedly, but he sat down again. He knew Ace was right, dammit!

By this time, Ella was scarlet from the rude comments as well as her physical exertions, and lost the first set 6–3. She sat miserably in her chair at the changeover and gave herself a stern talking-to. Hal was watching her, as was Ace, and Melissa Farrell! I will not lose in the first round of the juniors in front of my heroes! she decided firmly, and there was a new determination in her step as she walked back on to court that was evident to the ex-pros in the stands.

Hal relaxed a little and even Katy smiled in satisfaction, despite Ella's opponent's being one of her charges. Ella ignored the disruptive behaviour of the louts and won the second set easily. She faltered slightly when serving for the match at 5–2 in the third, but then played brilliantly to break Shanna to win it 6–3.

She beamed her delight at the spectators but they all noted, with varying degrees of unease, that she singled Ace out for special attention. He either didn't notice, or chose to ignore it, offering only a brief 'Well done, honey,' by way of congratulations before leaving the stand.

Ella watched him go wistfully, her adoration plain to see, then she began talking shyly to Melissa, who knew exactly how the youngster was feeling. At Ella's age Melissa had been just as infatuated – and similarly ignored, she remembered ruefully.

She made an effort to draw Ella out, chatting about tennis and Suzy, and had tea with her later. Katy joined them, anxious to get to know the girl before committing herself to coaching her. To help Katy make her decision, Melissa offered to help Ella prepare for her next match and they arranged a time when Katy could be present, to further her assessment of Ella's capabilities.

'She's a nice kid, isn't she?' Melissa remarked, when Ella left to return to her hotel.

'Mmm, she reminds me a bit of you – although she's from the wrong side of the tracks and you're a snooty upper-class Brit.' Katy grinned at Melissa, who merely grimaced by way of reply. The difference in their backgrounds – for Katy, like Ella, came from a poor family – had caused dissension at the start of their coach-pupil partnership, until Katy realized that Melissa was prepared to work hard to achieve her ambitions and not merely bask in Jack's reflected glory.

'Seriously, she does remind me of you,' Katy continued. 'She's a natural serve-volleyer, she has lots of talent, oodles of enthusiasm – and she's nuts about Ace! If I agree to take her on, I'll need to be her chaperone as well as her coach, just as I was with you!'

'Do you think you will take her on?' Melissa asked.

'What do you think I'll do?' Katy countered.

'You'll do it,' Melissa said, without hesitation.

'You're right. I will. And I'll turn her into a champion,' Katy said positively.

Later that evening, Ace joined Jack in his hotel suite for a drink before the evening matches began, when Jack would again return to the TV studio to present the late-night coverage for British viewers.

'It's quiet in here,' Ace commented. 'And tidy,' he added; on his one earlier visit, to say hi, Kit had been screaming the place down and baby paraphernalia had littered the suite. His visit had been a brief one.

'Mmm, too quiet,' Jack sighed. 'Lisa's taken Kit to visit her parents. I'm joining them after the tournament,' he explained, with a notable lack of enthusiasm.

'In-laws still giving you grief? Can't you go and stay at Melissa's place?' Ace asked idly.

'Not really. Alexa Kane's staying at Rose Arbor,' Jack informed him.

'Oh?' Ace stood up to refill his glass, keeping his back turned. 'A strange choice for a honeymoon,' he commented lightly.

'Oh, no, she's not on her honeymoon – she's there alone,' Jack told him. 'She dumped her fiancé at the altar!'

'Really?' Ace was both surprised and annoyed by the surge of relief he experienced at the news.

'Well, it wasn't quite that dramatic. She called it off the day before. There was quite a fuss, apparently. Philip Kane did his nut; told her not to darken his door again, or words to that effect, and Melissa suggested she go to Rose Arbor for some peace and quiet.'

'I'm glad she's shown some guts at last. The guy she was to marry sounded like a clone of her father,' Ace said, unthinkingly.

'You knew about him?' Jack asked, startled. He looked at Ace curiously, remembering how, months earlier, he had thought there was something going on between Ace and Alexa. He had dismissed the notion after her engagement to Graham Peters, but now he wondered if he had been right all along.

'Oh, Melissa mentioned it,' Ace said vaguely. 'I called in to see her the day I left England and Rose was wittering on about what she should wear for the wedding,' he explained. Despite his telling Alexa to stand on her own two feet, he found he didn't like to think of her all alone and pregnant at Rose Arbor.

'I see,' Jack said neutrally, but he continued to watch Ace closely. Ace was aware of the scrutiny and forced himself to stop thinking about Alexa, and to keep his face expressionless.

'Do you remember I told you about some tapes I got from Flanagan? The interviews he did with Loretta?' he abruptly changed the subject.

'Yeah, sure. Have you checked them out?' Jack asked interestedly, diverted from thinking about a possible liaison between Ace and Alexa Kane.

'Mmm, well, I've listened to them. It's hard to work out when she was telling the truth and when she was simply angling for more money . . .' He laughed suddenly and shook his head slightly in genuine amusement. 'She really gave him the run-around; didn't tell him much at all, just hinted that she could tell him a lot if she chose to! The tapes that are really interesting are the two she used when she was alone . . .' He sighed. 'But she was obviously either drunk or high on drugs and I have no idea how much of it is true.' He stopped speaking and gazed moodily down at his glass, as if the answers he sought lay in its depths.

'So?' Jack prompted. 'What exactly did she say?'

'Well . . . if you laugh, I'll kill you,' Ace threatened, but he had to tell someone. 'I think I may have a brother, possibly even a twin,' he said slowly. Jack choked on his drink. Another Ace Delaney? If that piece of news became public knowledge, men the world over would lock up their wives and daughters! The manufacturers of chastity belts would be pleased, though, he thought, but wisely refrained from saying so. Ace was obviously deadly serious.

'Did she come right out and say that?' he asked instead.

'No, that's the problem,' Ace frowned. 'She was slagging off the Press – it sounded to me as if she and Flanagan had just had a row. She said all journalists were assholes, and he was the worst of the lot. She said it amused her whenever they described me as a one-off, an original character, because, and I quote: "they were like two peas in a pod", unquote. And, at another point in the tape, she begins talking about me when I was a baby, but several times gets confused and says "they", not "he".' He paused and looked at Jack. 'What do you make of it? What else could she have meant?' he asked. Jack considered his words carefully before answering; there was an intensity about Ace that surprised him – he'd have expected him to simply shrug it off. 'Family' was a dirty word to Ace.

'Could she have been referring to your father?' he ventured finally.

'No,' Ace said positively. 'The one thing I have to thank Loretta for is the way I look.'

'Did you inherit her modesty, too?' Jack couldn't resist asking. Ace scowled.

'Get serious!'

'Okay, sorry.' Jack stood up and refilled both their glasses. 'I don't see how you could have a twin, not an identical one, anyhow,' he said slowly. 'Your face is too well known throughout the world for him to be unaware of the resemblance, and it wouldn't take much effort on his part to discover you share a birthday.'

'Mmm, I take your point,' Ace said thoughtfully. 'Not a twin, then, but I could still have a brother somewhere,' he said moodily, sounding neither pleased nor horrified at the prospect. Yet it had obviously been on his mind.

'Do you want to find him?' asked Jack.

'I'm curious,' Ace admitted.

'I suppose you've considered hiring a private detective?'

'Sure, but what if I don't like what he finds? Once the truth has been uncovered, I might find it impossible to re-bury it.' He paused, thinking of Alexa and Philip Kane – the last time he had opened Pandora's Box, the results had been horrific. 'Once questions have been asked, people will start to remember . . .' He shrugged. 'A wealthy man once said, "I find that the richer I become, the more relatives I have." If word got out that I was searching for a family, there would be a queue of people stretching around Central Park, all holding out begging bowls,' he said cynically.

'Yes, I see that. But it's a risk you'll have to take. Either that, or stay curious,' Jack told him.

'Thanks, you're a great help.' Ace sighed, no nearer to a decision.

# CHAPTER 19

Ella's second-round opponent was a young French girl, Yvette Dubois. Yvette had defeated one of Katy's pupils the day before, so Katy had learned something of her style of play and passed on the information to Melissa, thereby enabling her to imitate the shots Ella could expect to face later that afternoon.

Melissa was enjoying herself immensely; it felt great to be back on a court at Flushing Meadow, even if it was only on a practice court, helping out a junior player. She thought briefly of her glory days here; of the matches on the Stadium Court in front of twenty thousand noisy and exuberant New Yorkers. She hadn't won a title here, but had come close to the Mixed Doubles with Jack, and reached the semis in Singles. Great matches. Great days.

She sighed a little wistfully, then glanced over to the stands where Nick was sitting with Suzy. He was so good with her, so gentle; it always brought a lump to Melissa's throat when she watched them together – her tough, strong soldier tending his baby so carefully and lovingly.

Nick sensed her gaze and looked up to smile at her. She grinned back; she had no regrets, none at all. She loved her sport, but she loved Nick and Suzy far more.

'Come on, Melissa. Let's get to work,' Katy ordered; it was as if the years had rolled back and they were once again coach and pupil. 'I shouldn't really be here,' Katy added. 'Three of my kids are playing today as well, but I wanted to watch Ella.'

'Okay.' Melissa signalled to Ella, and they moved out on to court, trading shots to warm up before getting down to work.

Melissa had to abandon her own natural serve-and-volley game and take on Yvette's baseline play, heavy with top-spin. Yvette's serve was a 'dolly-drop', according to a contemptuous Katy, so Melissa accordingly took most of the pace off her own serve. She also allowed Ella to win most of the points to boost her confidence.

Ella had initially been terrified at the prospect of practising with Melissa, afraid she would humiliate herself by dumping every shot into the bottom of the net. However, she gradually lost her nerves, and began to play well, delighted and amazed to discover she was actually outplaying Melissa Farrell by getting shots past her!

Hal appeared briefly to check on Ella, but vanished just as quickly, partly because he, like Katy, had other juniors preparing for matches later that day and he could see Ella was in competent hands. Also the sight of Nick Lennox holding his and Melissa's child caused him a stab of pain. Despite his growing closeness to Linda Cortez, part of him would always mourn the loss of Melissa. But at least he had lost her to a decent guy and not to Ace Delaney, he consoled himself as he left the court.

Finally, Katy called time on the practice session and Melissa went over to talk to Ella, offering encouragement and good wishes for her match.

'Why don't you and I play for real?' Ella asked eagerly. Melissa's brows rose in astonishment and she glanced at Katy, who was suppressing a grin.

'At least she's not daunted by a challenge,' Katy murmured to Melissa, then she raised her voice. 'Okay, Ella, but just a tie-break, then you should go and eat and take a rest before your match.'

Melissa moved back out on to the court, a little aggrieved that Ella's hero-worship had vanished so quickly, and that the kid now considered herself on equal terms with a former Wimbledon Champion!

Ella served first, just the one point to begin the tie-break. The speed of Melissa's return took her by surprise and she lunged for, but completely missed the shot. 1–0.

Melissa served the following two points. Her serve had always been one of her strongest weapons, fast and deep, hard for even an experienced player to read and return. The first point was a clean ace; the second, Ella did manage to return, just, but Melissa almost sauntered to the net to put away an easy volley. 3–0. Not so cocky now, huh? Melissa thought, as she went back to the baseline to receive serve.

The first was a fault; so was the second, but Melissa hit it back anyway, and then proceeded to keep Ella pinned to the baseline, effortlessly swinging her from side to side and then blasting a trademark Melissa Farrell double-fisted backhand down the line for a winner. 4–0. Melissa felt great! She grinned across at Katy and Nick as she moved back again to receive.

Once more, she deliberately kept the ball in play longer than she needed to, forcing Ella to rush to the net to scoop up a drop-shot and then to scurry back to the baseline in a vain attempt at retrieving a lob. 5–0.

'What the hell do you think you're doing?' Ace's furious voice caused Melissa to spin around to face him. He had just arrived and watched the display in growing disbelief and anger. His eyes glinted with fury as he marched on to court to confront Melissa.

'I've been helping her prepare for her match!' Melissa snapped, annoyed by his tone.

'Helping her? You're undermining her confidence!' Ace raged.

'Oh, come on! We're only playing a tie-break, not a three-set match,' Melissa said scornfully. Nick was watching the exchange; although he was too far away to actually hear what was going on, it was obviously nothing pleasant. He stood up, intending to intervene, and belatedly realized he was hampered by Suzy.

'Here.' He thrust the baby at Katy, who stared down at her in bewilderment.

'Don't you dare cry!' she hissed, then her sharp features softened and she smiled, cuddling Suzy close.

'How the hell do you think Ella feels, losing every point to someone who hasn't played a competitive match in over a year, someone who's just had a kid, for God's sake? You had to prove you're still a champion, didn't you?' Ace was snarling at Melissa, oblivious to Nick's rapid approach. 'Well, I've news for you, honey, you're not a champion, you're a has-been,' he said cruelly.

Nick had heard more than enough; Melissa's shocked, pale face showed plainly her hurt at the words flung at her. Years of dislike erupted and Nick grabbed Ace by the shoulder, spun him around and drove his fist into his midriff. Ace, caught by surprise, went down on one knee beneath the blow, expelling his breath in a grunt of pain.

'Come on, sweetheart,' Nick said calmly, placing a protective arm around Melissa's shoulder. She gazed up at him, then glanced at Ace and hesitated, then walked away without a word. Her body was stiff with tension but, as she took Suzy from Katy, she began to relax.

'He was right,' she said quietly to Nick. 'I was trying to put her in her place, and I shouldn't have done, not before a match.'

'I hope you don't expect me to apologize to him?' Nick asked, somewhat taken aback.

'No.' She smiled impishly. 'He deserved it!' She reached up and kissed Nick. 'My hero,' she said mockingly, but he read the message of love in her eyes and held her close.

Ace watched them leave, his jet-black eyes narrowed and glittering with fury. He was humiliated, rather than hurt, by Nick's blow and angrily shrugged off Ella's anxious enquiry before stalking off to drown his sorrows.

'That damned soldier of Melissa's has probably ruptured my spleen,' he groused to Jack later. 'It's a pity he never volunteered for the Bomb Squad!' he added viciously. But Jack was unsympathetic and sided with Melissa, and proceeded to deal Ace a severe dose of earache.

'It sounds to me as if you were asking for it!' Just what's got into you? You're unbearable these days,' Jack told him coldly. 'If it's this business with Loretta, then either hire a private detective and check it out, or forget it,' he advised tersely. 'Your mother's dead and buried, and her secrets are probably buried with her. It's a little late to be interested in her now, isn't it? If you were that concerned, you should have talked to her occasionally while she was still alive!'

'Have you quite finished?' Ace snapped.

'Yes. No,' Jack quickly changed his mind. 'Apologize to my sister!' he instructed, before turning on his heel and walking away.

Ace scowled and ordered another scotch, rubbing his sore midriff and trying not to wince. Jack's words had struck a chord; he knew he was being irritable and unreasonable. But not because of Loretta's secrets, as Jack called them. It was Alexa Kane, unmarried and therefore available – not that Ace considered a wedding ring to be an insurmountable obstacle if he really wanted a woman – but still pregnant with another man's child. Now *that* was an obstacle . . .

He stayed in the bar, brooding, and forgot all about Ella's match. She, upset by what had happened earlier, kept looking anxiously out for him, infuriating Hal and Katy by her lack of concentration. She played badly and was quickly a set down.

When Ace finally put in an appearance, his mood darkened as he watched her poor performance. He had persuaded several sponsors to come and watch her, with an eye towards future endorsements, but this display would impress no one, he thought furiously. He glared at Hal Renwick, and vented some of his pent-up anger and frustration on him.

'I'm not paying you a blasted fortune to teach her how to lose!' he snapped, most unfairly. Until this moment, he had been more than satisfied with her progress under Hal's tutelage.

'Coach her yourself, then,' Hal retorted. 'I'm sick of your constant interference! You . . .' He broke off as he became aware of Linda Cortez tugging at his arm, her eyes wide with apprehension and silently pleading with him. She and Ella were so happy at the academy and would hate to leave. Hal hesitated, prepared to back down for her sake, but it wasn't necessary, for Ace knew he hadn't the patience to be a full-time coach, nor did he want to remove Ella from the academy. He back-pedalled hastily.

'Sorry, Hal; you're doing a great job – it's that business with Melissa showing off earlier that's undermined her confidence,' he said sourly.

'That's not true – they only played a few points!' Katy contradicted hotly. 'Ella's the show-off – she's got too much confidence, if you ask me . . .'

'No one did,' Ace said curtly.

'You asked me to coach her when she leaves the academy,' Katy reminded him sweetly. 'But, for now, she's just a junior. She should be staying and practising with the other kids, not be in a luxury suite in a five-star hotel and working out with players of Melissa's calibre. You've led her to believe she's special, but she's not. Not yet. Right now she's a kid with a lot of talent and even more to learn. She's totally . . .' Katy paused as Ella loudly queried a line-call, too loudly and for too long, appealing to the umpire to overrule, which he refused to do '. . . totally undisciplined,' Katy finished smugly.

Ella was desperate now, trailing a set and 2–5, and one look at Ace told her plainly how angry he was. She had to serve to stay in the match; the first point was a double-fault, the next, a good first serve but an even better return from Yvette clipped the side-line for a clean winner.

'That was out!' Ella screamed, storming over to the umpire's chair again.

'Oh, God,' Katy grimaced. 'She seems to have picked up your bad habits,' she said innocently to Ace. In his days as a pro, Ace could out-shout and out-tantrum anyone, and had been defaulted and thrown out of more than one tournament for his bad language and abusive behaviour.

'You'd better sort her out, Hal. Fast!' Ace said grimly.

'I'll be able to, if you keep out of it,' Hal retorted. 'She's always unsettled and over-excited after a visit from you. Katy's right – you've made her think she's better than the rest.'

'Well, she's learning now that she isn't,' Katy said, with grim satisfaction, as Ella dropped her serve and advanced to the net to exchange a surly greeting and brief handshake. 'She deserved to lose that match.'

Ella collected up her rackets and towels, her eyes welling with tears that spilled over despite her best efforts to hide them.

'Good. It's hurting her,' Katy murmured to Hal, earning herself a look of outrage from Linda.

'Katy means Ella will learn from this, and not just shrug it off,' Hal explained quickly. 'If a loss doesn't hurt, she's in the wrong game.' Linda nodded her understanding, but rather doubtfully. Ace meanwhile had moved over to intercept Ella on her way to the locker room.

'That was the most abysmal performance I have ever seen,' he raged at her. 'One more match like that and you'll be back in the gutter! And don't you ever again yell at the linesmen or umpire,' he added.

'My God. What's that phrase about poacher turned gamekeeper?' Katy muttered, hardly able to believe her ears.

Hal, flanked by a frightened but angry Linda, hurried over to stop Ace. Linda glared at him and put her arm around Ella's shoulders to give her a comforting hug. Ella's tears had dried, mostly from the shock of witnessing at first-hand the notorious Ace Delaney temper.

'That's enough!' Hal called sharply. 'I'll do the post-mortem on the match when she's calmed down a little.'

'Oh, okay; she's all yours,' Ace said wearily. He glanced across at the stands, but the sponsors' reps had long gone.

He turned on his heel and walked away. What a day! Even Jack wasn't talking to him. He sighed and left Flushing Meadow, heading back to his hotel but stopping off first at Cartier to buy a peace-offering for Melissa; a gift that would both placate Jack and enrage Nick. Two birds with one stone, he thought, with grim satisfaction.

Later, his good humour somewhat restored after a workout in the gym followed by a relaxing massage and several glasses of scotch, he wandered the two blocks to Jack and Melissa's hotel. He mended fences with Jack first, then went and knocked on the door of the adjoining suite. Nick opened the door, his eyes chips of ice as he surveyed his unwelcome guest.

'I haven't come to fight,' Ace said hastily.

'Pity,' Nick replied grimly.

'I just want to apologize to Melissa . . .'

'She's having a bath.'

'That's okay, I've seen . . .' Ace began. Nick's eyes became positively glacial, and even Ace recognized the folly of reminding Nick he had seen Melissa naked. '. . . plenty of women taking a bath,' he amended, holding out the gift-wrapped box containing a diamond and sapphire bracelet. 'I bought this for her, to say sorry for yelling at her this morning.' Wordlessly, Nick took the package and slammed the door shut. He dropped the gift into the waste-paper basket, then retrieved it, deciding to give it to the chambermaid as a tip when they left. One thing was for sure, he was never going to let Melissa wear it!

Ella was desperate to make amends with Ace, both upset and frightened by his outburst. Hal had taken Linda to dinner, and Ella had excused herself from joining them, claiming to need time alone.

Without her even realizing it, the sly digs about being Ace Delaney's pet, the murmured comments about his cradle-snatching, had filtered into her subconscious and now she felt there was only one way to regain his favour, and that was to offer herself to him. It was what she had fantasized about, what she wanted, but not like this. She had dreamed of the day when he would propose and she would waft down the aisle in virginal white . . .

Instead, she now stripped naked, brushed out her glossy dark brown hair, applied make-up, then, wrapped only in a bath towel, opened the door and peeked nervously into the corridor. No one was about, so she sped along the hall and banged on Ace's door before she could lose her nerve.

'Ace! Quickly!' she called, and had no need to pretend to be terrified. She was, but was even more afraid of his coldness; that he might wash his hands of her. 'Ace!'

'What is it?' He opened the door and stared at her in perplexity. 'What's wrong? Are you ill?'

'No, I'm fine. But come quickly! There's a man in my room!' she said desperately.

'What?' Ace pushed past her and dashed to her room. He glanced around quickly, then checked the bathroom. 'There's no one here now. I'll call security.' He moved to pick up the phone and Ella panicked; this wasn't what she had planned at all – he hadn't even appeared to notice her state of undress!

'No, don't do that!'

'Why not?' Ace paused. 'Did you recognize him?'

'No. I lied.' She hung her head. 'I'm all alone,' she mumbled, trying to summon up the courage to drop the towel and stand naked before him. He'd take her in his arms, declare he had only been waiting for her to grow up a little before making a move, he'd say he had known all along they were meant for each other; he'd say he loved her . . .

'What stupid game are you playing?' he demanded harshly. 'Haven't you caused me enough trouble today? Not to mention costing me a fortune,' he added disgustedly. Ella burst into tears.

'I'm sorry,' she sobbed. 'I just wanted to apologize. I promise I'll work hard at my tennis, I know I've got a lot to learn. Please, don't be angry with me, I love you so much . . .' Ace stared at her, belatedly realizing why she had come to him dressed, or rather not dressed, in a towel. He had been blind – how had a silly teenage crush developed into this attempt at seduction? he wondered. Then he understood why she had chosen this moment – she was offering him her body in an attempt to win back his favour. A wave of fury swept over him. The little slut!

'You are a sick little girl! Don't you ever pull a stunt like this again, not with me, not with anyone! I am not interested in your girlish charms – just your ability to play tennis. Is that quite clear?' he asked coldly.

'Yes,' Ella sniffed, experiencing a strange mixture of relief and disappointment at his words.

'You and I need to do some serious talking . . . for God's sake, stop crying and put some clothes on!' he snapped irritably, and turned his back on her as she reached for the clothes she had discarded earlier.

It was then he noticed for the first time the array of photographs she had placed by her bed. There was one of him, he noticed with a grimace, one of Melissa and Suzy, another of Linda with a man he assumed was Marcelo Cortez, Ella's father, and one other . . . He stared at it in disbelief, then reached out and picked it up to study it more closely, noting the colour of hair and eyes, the bone structure . . . A picture of a young Loretta?

'Where did you get this?' He rounded on Ella.

'I've always had it,' she stammered. 'That's my mother.'

'Your mother?' he echoed incredulously.

'Yes. You knew Linda is my stepmother,' she said, perplexed. 'My real mom died when I was three. I don't really remember her, and that's my only picture of her,' she said pleadingly, stretching out her hand for it as if afraid he intended destroying it.

'Your mother,' Ace mused, studying the likeness once more, and hearing again Loretta's slurred voice on the tape: '. . . they were like two peas in a pod . . .'

'What was her name?' he asked, more quietly, and Ella relaxed slightly.

'Teresa,' she told him.

'And her surname – before she married?'

'Mmm, the same as my grandparents, I guess – Chapman.'

'Your grandparents!' Ace exclaimed. Of course! They would have the answers, he thought. 'Are they still alive?' he asked urgently.

'Yes. Well, I think so. They quarrelled with my dad when he married Linda, and I haven't seen them since I was a little girl,' she said.

'Do you have a photograph of them?'

'Not here, but I have some in my album at the academy.'

'And their address?' Ace asked.

'I can't remember.' She was becoming flustered by his intensity. 'They still live in Florida, so far as I know.'

'Don't you have the exact address?' he persisted, trying to curb his impatience.

'Yes, but that's at the academy as well,' she said miserably; she was trying to be helpful, but knew it was a poor effort. And she couldn't understand why he was asking so many questions, unless . . . 'They don't have much money,' she told him.

'Money? What the hell's that to do with anything?' Ace frowned.

'I thought, maybe you're expecting them to repay you what you've spent on me,' she stammered, her lower lip trembling.

'Don't be stupid,' he said, but not unkindly. 'Phone the academy and get that address for me. Oh, and ask them to fax a photo of your grandparents,' he added, heading for the door. 'Bring it to my room as soon as you have it – I'm going to pack.'

While he waited for a flight, he quizzed Ella and, later, Linda about Teresa Chapman, but neither knew very much about her. To Ella she was a distant memory, an image conjured up only with the help of the one, treasured photograph; to Linda, she was merely Marcelo's former wife.

The answers had to lie with Teresa's parents, John and Sheila Chapman; the photograph showed a nondescript couple, ordinary, both grey-haired, she a little plump in middle age, he, tall and slim. There had to be a connection between Teresa Chapman and Loretta, and her parents must know what it was. He didn't know why it suddenly mattered, why he felt this need to know about his roots. For years he had shrugged aside his illegitimacy, contemptuous of the father who had abandoned him and mentally sticking up two fingers at the unknown man, hoping he was aware his unwanted son was now a success, a millionaire.

At Fort Lauderdale he hired a car and took the highway north to Pompano Beach. When he located the small bungalow, he remained in the car for a time, uncertain how to proceed. He might be on a wild-goose chase, or these two people might know Loretta's secrets. He sighed and got out of the car, striding up the short path and stabbing at the door-bell.

It seemed an age before the door opened and Ace found himself face to face with the man in the photograph, slightly older now. Ace had been wondering how to begin the conversation, but he needn't have worried. John Chapman took one look at him, nodded slightly, and held the door open in invitation to enter.

'We wondered if you'd ever show up here,' he said mildly.

'Here I am – is that good or bad?' Ace asked, unable to discern either pleasure or annoyance in the older man's expression or voice.

'Neither.' John Chapman smiled slightly. 'Come in; I'll make some coffee. My wife's away, I'm afraid; she's staying with her sister for a few days.' Ace followed him into a neat kitchen and accepted a cup of strong black coffee.

'Why did you think I might turn up? Because of Ella?' he asked curiously.

'Ella?' John sounded surprised. 'You've met Ella?'

'Met her? She's costing me a fortune!' Ace said ruefully. 'I'm paying for her tennis tuition.'

'Ah, I hadn't heard about that. So you already know?'

'I don't know a damned thing!' Ace said, exasperated. 'I saw a photograph of your daughter, Ella's mother. She bears a remarkable resemblance to my own mother, Loretta Delaney.'

'Yes, well, she would.' John said slowly. 'Teresa was Loretta's daughter,' he continued. It was what Ace had half expected to hear, but it was still a shock. He had a sister, but she was dead . . . He drew a deep breath and took another scalding gulp of the strong coffee.

'You and your wife adopted Teresa?' he asked.

'In a way.' John hesitated. 'It wasn't strictly legal . . . I think I'd better start at the beginning. Did Loretta ever tell you about the time she lived in New York?'

'No, she was very secretive about her past,' Ace said, although he had to admit he had never been sufficiently interested to actually ask.

'Well, back then I owned a coffee shop in Brooklyn. One day, I put a card in the window advertising for a waitress and in walked Loretta.'

'You knew her?'

'Oh, yes.' John smiled fondly. 'She told me she was eighteen, but I think she was younger. She was a runaway, so don't ask me where she was from originally, because I don't know. I gave her the job; she was pretty, bright and cheerful – the customers loved her. And so did I,' he admitted quietly.

'You!' Ace exclaimed.

'Yes,' he sighed. 'My wife and I . . . we couldn't have children, which was no excuse for me to have an affair, but Loretta . . . she was hard to resist.'

'You're Teresa's natural father?' Ace guessed.

'Yes. Loretta discovered she was pregnant with my child. She didn't want to keep it . . .'

'That I can believe!' Ace said caustically, his lip curling with disdain.

'Don't talk about your mother in that tone!' John Chapman rebuked him sharply. 'She was young and frightened; it wasn't easy for girls to be unmarried mothers thirty-five years ago. I wanted the child, and eventually talked to my wife – she suggested we raise the child as our own.' He sighed heavily, and Ace could only guess at the tears and recriminations he'd endured before the decision had been made! 'I paid all Loretta's medical bills, of course. And she used my wife's name, so Teresa's birth certificate names my wife and me as the natural parents,' he explained. 'After the birth, we moved here to Florida, where my wife's family lived. Loretta stayed on in New York.'

'Did you ever see Loretta again?' Ace asked, the words 'Are you my father?' hovering on his lips.

'Not for several years. I sent her money, and photos of Teresa from time to time, without my wife knowing – she hadn't wanted any further contact, but I felt Loretta deserved to know how her daughter was faring. One day, Loretta turned up at my place of work, quite unexpectedly. You were about a year old, the image of your sister at that age; half-sister, I should say,' he amended. Like two peas in a pod, Ace thought.

'My father?' he asked tentatively. John Chapman shook his head regretfully.

'I'm sorry, I don't know. I did ask Loretta, but she just laughed it off and said she'd been up to her old tricks . . .'

'Now that does sound like her! She became expert at turning tricks!' Ace said bitterly.

'Will you stop bad-mouthing your mother!' John glared at him.

'Sorry,' Ace said quickly. 'Please, go on.'

'Hmm. As I was saying, she'd had an affair with a married man – she never mentioned his name, so I can't help you there. I don't think he knew about you; she simply disappeared without a word.'

'His wife obviously wasn't as forgiving as yours, or Loretta would have dumped me on them!' Ace said scornfully.

'I warned you!' John said sharply. 'And you're wrong. Loretta said she knew she ought to give you up for adoption, for your sake not hers, but she couldn't bear to give away another child.'

'Huh!'

'Loretta was a very warm, loving person. Too loving, perhaps.'

'Promiscuous, you mean?' Ace sneered.

'And you're not?' John shot back. 'If half of what I've read about you is true, you've no grounds to criticize!' Ace shrugged: maybe he was guilty of double standards, but at least he hadn't produced unwanted children. 'Is it true Loretta became addicted to heroin?' John continued.

'Yes.'

'Why didn't you help her?'

'Give me a break – I was only about eight years old at the time!' Ace said. John made a dismissive gesture with his hand.

'Not then. But later, you could have, should have helped her. You could have afforded to put her into a rehab clinic,' he said accusingly.

Ace fell silent; it had never occurred to him. By the time he'd reached his mid-teens all he had wanted was to turn his back on his background and get out, never to return.

'Will you tell me more about Teresa?' he asked finally. 'Did I ever meet her?'

'Yes, twice, in a park not far from here. I wouldn't be surprised if you still bear the scars! You took one of Teresa's toys; a clockwork musical clown, which was made of metal and was quite heavy. Teresa snatched it back and hit you over the head with it! There was blood all over – you screamed blue murder, and Teresa started crying, too,' John remembered with a slight smile.

'I had a clown like that . . .' Ace frowned.

'Yes. Teresa gave you hers when you left, to make amends,' John told him. Ace swallowed painfully.

'I wish I could remember her,' he muttered, then drew a shaky breath. 'How did she come to be living in LA? Did she go looking for Loretta?'

'No, that was a coincidence. Marcelo Cortez was from LA. She met him on holiday, dropped out of school and went back to California with him. We disapproved strongly – he was much older than her, and had already been married and divorced, with a young child.'

'A child?' Ace's head jerked up. 'Ella's never mentioned that.'

'I don't suppose she's had much contact with him. He must be ten or twelve years older than her, and lived with his mother, Marcelo's first wife,' John explained.

'How did Teresa die?' Ace asked.

'It was one of those senseless, stupid killings,' John's voice was raw with pain. 'She was just in the wrong place at the wrong time. She had gone to buy groceries, in broad daylight. There was a hold-up at a nearby liquor store, someone got trigger-happy and Teresa was caught in the cross-fire.' He paused and took several deep breaths before continuing. 'My wife and I offered to take Ella, but Marcelo refused and made access difficult. We were too old, too tired to fight him . . .' He looked at Ace. 'I'm glad you're looking after her now,' he added quietly. Ace nodded; strangely, the responsibility didn't weigh heavily on his shoulders.

He stayed overnight, hearing more about Teresa and a young, happy Loretta who, according to John, brightened up the lives of those around her with her laughter and gaiety, a Loretta who loved her children, both the one she had given up to its natural father, and the one she had kept with her.

It was difficult for him to equate the two Lorettas – the drug-addict he remembered was vastly different from the woman John had known. He regretted never having known Teresa, but there was Ella, Teresa's daughter, in his life, needing him. Ella would be delighted to discover the link between them, he thought, and looked forward to breaking the good news.

# CHAPTER 20

'You're my uncle? That's awful!' Ella shouted. 'I don't believe it. Don't you dare tell anyone!' With that, she burst into tears and ran off. Bewildered, and not a little affronted, Ace turned to Linda, who had been listening in silence.

'I thought she'd be pleased,' he said, rather helplessly. 'What's wrong with her?' Linda knew exactly what the problem was, but refused to tell him, to spare Ella's feelings. The poor girl had convinced herself – and hinted to her friends – that, one day, she would marry Ace.

'She'll come around, in time,' she said calmly. 'You haven't told anyone else, have you?'

'No, not yet, I wanted to tell her first. But going public would put a stop to all the stupid speculation about my interest in her,' Ace pointed out.

'Hmm.' Linda refrained from mentioning that Ella actually enjoyed the speculation!

Ace decided to keep the news a secret; it was true that, as his niece, Ella would have to cope with added pressure to succeed, to match his victories on court.

Over the following weeks, Ella gradually adjusted to their changed relationship, aided enormously by the arrival at the academy of a new coach. Juan Garcia was twenty-one, drop-dead gorgeous with coal-black hair and piercing sapphire eyes. All the girls, Ella included, fell madly in love with him and ran themselves ragged on the court to gain his attention and praise.

The Orange Bowl junior championships took place in early December, and Ella acquitted herself well, reaching the semi-finals in both Singles and Doubles. Ace, pleased with her results, phoned John Chapman and suggested taking her to visit her grandparents while they were in Florida.

Ella was delighted at the prospect, and this time Sheila Chapman was present. She made both Ace and Ella feel welcome, and it became obvious she had deeply loved Teresa, despite her resemblance to Loretta, her natural mother. They stayed for two days before heading back to California.

During the flight home, Ella began asking questions about Loretta, her real grandmother; questions Ace found hard to answer – truthfully, at least. But Ella had grown up in the same kind of neighbourhood and understood, with a wisdom beyond her sixteen years, how easily young women, especially those with young children and no husband, could be drawn into a world of drugs and prostitution.

She discomfited him by asking to visit Loretta's grave, and he was ashamed to admit he didn't know where she was buried. He had to ask his lawyer, Larry Knight, for he had arranged the funeral, and one Sunday afternoon he and Ella took flowers to the cemetery.

'Do you really have Apache blood?' she asked unexpectedly. 'Do I?'

'Nope. Years ago a kid called me a Spic, and I beat him up and cut off his hair. I told him I was descended from an Apache chief and promised to scalp him if he ever called me Spic again!' Ace grinned at her. 'When I turned pro, I grew my hair and repeated it so often I almost believed it myself. The fans and sponsors loved it, so I stuck with it over the years. It was worth a lot of money to me, so keep the truth to yourself!' he warned.

'I will.' She smiled, then, 'Did Loretta play tennis?' she asked.

'I don't think so – why?'

'I was just wondering if sporting ability is hereditary. Do you think it is?'

'I doubt it; maybe good co-ordination and quick reflexes can be handed down,' he shrugged.

'You and my mom had different fathers, so our talent, our love for the sport has to come from Loretta, don't you think?' she asked eagerly.

'It's a nice theory,' Ace acknowledged. 'We also inherited her good looks!'

'Did we? Thanks, Grandma,' Ella said softly, arranging the last of the flowers, then getting to her feet.

'Yeah. Thanks, Mom,' Ace echoed. He stayed by the grave for a moment longer, then stood up and followed his niece back to the car.

At Bellwood, preparations were under way for Christmas but, before that, there was Kit's first birthday to celebrate. She was an adorable child, with a mop of dark hair and large navy blue eyes that lit up whenever she caught sight of her father. Invariably sunny-tempered, she toddled happily and inquisitively around the house, running Lisa ragged.

However, at this particular moment she was curled on Jack's lap, pretending to read a book, but spoiling the effect somewhat by not realizing it was upside down.

'This birthday party is going to be bedlam,' Lisa sighed, consulting the ever-growing list of names. 'Oh, damn! I . . .' She clapped a hand to her mouth and glanced guiltily at Kit, who thankfully appeared not to have heard. She was already proving to have ears on elastic when unsuitable words were uttered by adults.

'I forgot about her godparents,' Lisa continued. 'I don't suppose Alexa will feel like travelling back from California, but what about Ace? Do you think we ought to invite him?' she asked, with a noticeable lack of enthusiasm.

'Yes, but don't worry, he won't come, not when I tell him how many kids will be here,' Jack said confidently. He checked his watch to calculate the time in LA, then reached for the phone. He was right; Ace sounded appalled at the very idea of attending a toddlers' tea-party.

'I hadn't forgotten her birthday – there's a present on its way,' he said quickly. 'Alexa can represent me on the day.'

'She won't be here, either,' Jack told him. 'She's at Rose Arbor.'

'Still? Hasn't Philip Kane mellowed yet?'

'I don't know about that; she seems to like it there. She even asked Melissa if she would consider selling the place,' Jack told him.

'But surely she'll be returning to England for Christmas?' Ace asked.

'Doubt it,' Jack said casually.

'Is what's-his-name – Graham with her?'

'No, she's alone,' Jack said, even more casually; there was a slight smile tugging at the corners of his mouth and Lisa glanced up and regarded him quizzically.

'Alone? For Christmas?' Ace persisted.

'Mmm.' Jack sounded bored.

'Is she okay?'

'So far as I know,' Jack replied vaguely, wondering if a yawn would be a bit over the top. 'Mum isn't marrying Philip, so Alexa isn't our problem.'

'That's a callous attitude,' Ace said stiffly.

'Yeah, well, you live nearer to her than we do.' Jack's grin broadened as the silence lengthened. 'Give me a call if you decide to come over for the holidays,' he said, and ended the call. He looked across at Lisa. 'I bet he's at Rose Arbor within twenty-four hours,' he said, rather smugly.

'To see Alexa?'

'Mmm. I thought there was something going on between them months ago, but when she got engaged to Graham Peters I assumed I'd got it wrong. But now I think I was right the first time,' he said thoughtfully. 'Melissa mentioned the other day that Alexa told her Graham wasn't the father, which rather begs the question of who is . . .' He arched one brow.

'Ace and Alexa? They don't even like each other. I think you're nuts,' Lisa told him.

'Do you want to bet?' Jack challenged her.

'No,' she said, after a moment. 'You know him better than anyone.' She paused again. 'You didn't tell him that Alexa . . .'

'No, I didn't, did I?' Jack smiled broadly.

Jack was a little optimistic in his calculations: it was actually three days later when Ace flew north by helicopter to visit Ella. An earth tremor had hit LA early that morning and a stronger one shook the ground at Santa Barbara while he was there.

'It was real scary earlier,' Ella told him. 'Did you hear on the news? There was a big 'quake north of San Francisco; it caused a lot of damage, but no one was killed.'

'North? Napa valley?' Ace asked sharply.

'Somewhere up there.' Ella shrugged.

'Frank!' Ace yelled to his pilot. 'Have you got enough fuel to get us to the Napa valley?'

'Yeah.'

'Come on, then, let's get moving!' He said a hasty goodbye to Ella and scrambled back into the helicopter, gripped by a sudden urgency to reach Rose Arbor.

'Give me your map,' he said, cursing as he tried to recall the exact location of Rose Arbor. He had to trace the route he had taken by car on his one earlier visit. 'There!' He stabbed his finger on the map and Frank glanced down, then nodded. 'You'll be able to land on the tennis court . . . can't this thing go any faster?' Ace grumbled, looking down at the land rushing by below.

From the air there was evidence of structural damage, to both roads and buildings, and there were a lot of police and ambulance crews in evidence. Oh, God, Ace found himself praying. The poor kid must have been terrified, all alone and heavily pregnant. It was probably the first time she had experienced an earthquake, and no one seemed to give a damn about her, not her own father, not the Farrells.

'Down there!' Ace shouted, recognizing the white-washed, red-tiled building, with its adjacent tennis court. Frank nodded and gradually lost height, hovering above the court before dropping down. Ace was out of the door before he had landed, ducking low to avoid the blades as he began to run towards the house.

Alexa had heard the noise of the approaching helicopter and glanced out of the window in some alarm as it landed. She couldn't believe her eyes when she saw the tall, lithe figure of her dreams, his dark hair whipping around his face as he ran towards her.

'Ace!' She hurried from the house and laughed with delight when he lifted her off her feet. 'What are you doing here?' she asked joyously.

'I came to check if there was any damage to Melissa's property,' he began, his instinct to betray no emotion kicking in before he could stop it. But the crestfallen look on Alexa's face, the brightness dimming from her green-gold eyes, made him pause. 'No, that's not true, I don't give a damn about Melissa's house – I came because I was worried you might be hurt, or frightened,' he said honestly, pulling her tight against him and wrapping his arms around her. 'I know I told you to stand on your own two feet, but I was an asshole. I've missed you like crazy and I want to look after you, and the baby. I don't care who its father is, I know who its mother is, and that's enough . . . you're not pregnant,' he suddenly realized, and pulled away slightly. 'Why not? You didn't . . .'

'No,' she said quickly.

'Was it a false alarm? Is that why you didn't marry Graham?' he asked, feeling a guilty surge of relief. Sheila Chapman had shown him it was possible to bring up a child not one's own, but he would prefer Alexa to have *his* children.

'Come inside,' Alexa pulled at his hand; she had debated for weeks, months, when and if she should tell him. But he's come to me, she thought wondrously, and was glad she had kept her secret. This way, she was sure he wasn't here out of a reluctant sense of responsibility.

'You're impatient,' Ace drawled, assuming he was about to be dragged off to bed. 'Have you missed me, honey?'

'Yes, but this is better than sex!' she laughed at him over her shoulder. 'Oh, this is Magda,' she said, as they passed a woman emerging from the kitchen. 'She and her children are staying for a while.'

'Jack said you were alone,' Ace said, smiling vaguely at Magda.

'You must have misunderstood,' Alexa said. 'He knows Magda's here. All the Farrells have been wonderful – Rose has offered to come out here when Magda returns to New York,' she told him.

'I see,' Ace said, rather grimly. Jack Farrell, you lying, manipulative, conniving bastard! he thought, but he was smiling.

He followed Alexa upstairs and she paused outside a door, then took a deep breath and tiptoed into the room. Ace was a step behind her and stood stock-still in shock when he caught sight of the crib. 'Like two peas in a pod . . .' He could hear Loretta's voice clearly, and he swallowed, his gaze moving from one black-haired, creamy-skinned baby to the other.

There was a strange, almost painful emotion tugging at his heart: he couldn't put a name to it and he certainly couldn't deal with it. He turned on his heel and walked out. Alexa, after one stunned moment of immobility, raced after him, her hopes, so recently and amazingly raised, now cruelly dashed.

'Ace!' The anguish in her voice stopped him, or maybe it was the cry from one of the babies; whichever, he paused and turned back to Alexa.

'They're mine,' he said flatly; a statement, not a question.

'Yes.' Alexa nodded and licked her lips nervously.

'You weren't going to tell me, were you?' he went on, in an almost conversational tone of voice.

'I tried to, back in England, but you said you didn't want a family,' she reminded him miserably.

'How was I supposed to know you were talking about a baby that had already been conceived?' he demanded grimly. 'I thought you just wanted the latest designer accessory, to keep up with Lisa and Melissa,' he said scathingly. Alexa flinched; this was all going horribly wrong . . .

'Did you know they were mine?' he asked next.

'Yes.'

'But you were willing to marry someone else!'

'No, I called it off; I couldn't go through with it,' she protested, but it was as if he didn't hear her.

'I know why you didn't tell me – you think I'm a bastard from the slums, not good enough for you,' he said bitterly, 'certainly not good enough to be a father to your child . . . children.'

'You're insane if you think that,' Alexa told him flatly. 'Have you forgotten my grandfather was a molester of little girls? Do you honestly think there can be anything as bad as that in your bloodline?' she asked incredulously. Ace stared at her, then raked his fingers through his hair.

'I guess not,' he muttered finally. 'So why didn't you tell me? Dammit, I had the right to know!' he raged at her. 'I grew up without a father, and those two in there . . .' He broke off.

'Come back inside,' Alexa pleaded softly, certain of the babies' powers of persuasion, if not her own. She reached hesitantly for his hand, and he let her lead him back into the nursery. Alexa went and carefully picked up the crying baby.

'Shush, darling, you'll wake your brother,' she crooned. Ace tried to protest when she handed the squirming baby to him, but instead found himself awkwardly cradling the soft bundle.

'Meet Pippa Kane,' Alexa said softly. 'Pippa, here's your daddy.'

'I'm scared I'll drop her.' Ace finally managed to speak. 'I should have practised on Kit Farrell . . .' He gazed down at his daughter, a maelstrom of emotions assailing him: love and a powerful surge of protectiveness, terror because she was so little, fragile and vulnerable. He swallowed convulsively several times as he looked at her, marvelling at her perfectly arched brows, thick black lashes surrounding inky blue-black eyes, button nose and a slightly pursed rosebud mouth.

'She's so tiny,' he muttered.

'They're both gaining weight now. You should have seen them when they were born,' Alexa said, unthinkingly. Ace looked up and stared at her.

'Yes,' he said quietly. 'I should have.' They locked glances for a moment, then Alexa turned away to pick up Pippa's twin brother.

Ace returned to his inspection of Pippa. Her hands were loosely curled into fists and, when he carefully stretched out a finger to touch her, she grabbed it and held on with a surprising strength.

'She's obviously your daughter – she's growing her nails already,' he tried to joke. Alexa smiled but said nothing, content to watch the transformation taking place before her eyes, and once again daring to hope for a happy ending, or, rather, a happy beginning to a new life.

'Don't you want to say hello to your son?' she finally asked. 'I thought I'd call him Andrew.' Ace nodded and she carefully placed Andrew in the crook of his other arm, enabling him to hold both babies.

'A year ago I had no family; now it's like *The Waltons*!' Ace said. 'I'll have to sell the Porsche, and the Harley Davidson; trade them in for a station wagon. Or a Greyhound bus,' he amended, looking around rather helplessly at the mass of baby paraphernalia in the room. He looked directly at Alexa; he could understand why she had not told him, not trusted him, but that had to change. He was not going to be a part-time father, a visitor in their lives.

'Pippa and Andrew Kane . . . Delaney sounds better,' he said quietly.

'Oh, Ace, you don't have to marry me,' Alexa demurred, fearing he was feeling trapped. If so, she would never hold on to him; of that she was sure. 'It's enough that you'll be a part of our lives.'

'I know I don't have to. I never do anything I don't want to,' he said simply, and she made a sound of agreement that was a half-laugh, half-sob. 'Will you marry me?' he asked. 'Will you trust me? I've always been a sod to women . . .'

'I know; I think I understand why,' she broke in.

'You do? You're wiser than me,' he said lightly.

'I've had a lot of time to think about it recently,' Alexa paused. 'In a different way, you were as damaged in childhood as I was. Those women who paid for your tennis tuition when you were young in return for sex – that was a form of abuse.'

'No boy of thirteen turns down the opportunity to have sex!' Ace told her.

'Maybe not,' Alexa conceded. 'But those women had the upper hand, didn't they? As soon as you were old enough, and rich enough, to do as you pleased, you started exacting revenge by treating women badly. You were determined never to let another woman be in control.'

'You could be right.' Ace shrugged. 'But it doesn't matter now.' As he spoke the words, he knew it was true. Loretta . . . well, she had probably done her best as a mother until drugs had ruined her life; the bored and restless fun-seeking women at the tennis clubs . . . they were in the past. He had serviced them, true, but in return he had become rich and successful beyond his wildest dreams. There were worse ways of climbing out of the ghetto.

'You didn't answer my question – will you marry me?' he asked gruffly. Alexa nodded joyously, her eyes swimming with tears.

'No more tears,' he ordered, reaching over to kiss her gently, careful not to crush the precious children he was holding. Suddenly, the words he had always shied away from, the words he'd hated even hearing, came easily to him. 'I love you. I love you all.'

A few days later they flew to England, booking the flights separately and pretending to be strangers throughout the journey to fend off any Press speculation before Alexa had the opportunity to see her father. The cabin crew made a huge fuss of the twins and Alexa was able to relax; it was enough, for now, that Ace was there, silently watching over them.

In London they booked into the same hotel, but separate suites, again out of a discretion Ace was beginning to find irksome. But he understood Alexa's need to attempt a reconciliation with Philip, and that was more likely to happen if he hadn't already had journalists camped on his doorstep!

Ace waited outside the house in Eaton Square while Alexa went inside, taking the twins with her. She felt, as she had with Ace, that they could melt Philip's heart easier than she. But first she left them in the lobby with Mary and, straightening her shoulders, walked into the drawing room.

Philip hadn't heard her arrival and was absorbed in the evening paper, squinting slightly as he had once again mislaid his spectacles.

'Where are your glasses, Daddy?' Alexa asked softly. He looked up and felt only a surge of pleasure at the sight of her. With the help of a walking stick, he got to his feet and moved towards her.

'Oh, Daddy! You're walking!' she exclaimed.

'Just about,' he confirmed. He stopped a few feet away from her and just looked at her, then held out his arms. She went into his embrace gladly, and smelled the familiar scent of him, the soap he used, the tweed of his jacket, the aroma of cigars . . .

'Daddy! You're still smoking!' she chastized him.

'Not often,' he said shiftily. 'And you. Are you home for good?'

'No.' She shook her head. 'I'm getting married. To Ace.'

'I see.' He drew a deep breath. 'You can come home, to me. You and your baby. Where is it?' he asked eagerly.

'In the lobby. And there are two of them, a boy and a girl,' she said proudly, going to retrieve the double-sized carry-cot from Mary. 'Would you like to hold them?'

'I'm rather shaky on my legs, and my right arm still isn't strong . . .' he demurred.

'Come and sit down with them; you'll be fine,' she said confidently. He lumbered back to his chair and Alexa carefully placed first Pippa and then Andrew in his arms.

'She's a beauty; his colouring but your features,' Philip decided, then, rather reluctantly, looked at

Ace Delaney's son. But all he saw was another beautiful baby, his grandson, and he smiled. 'When are you getting married?'

'As soon as possible. We were going to get married in the States, but I rather hoped you'd give me away . . .' she ventured.

To him? Philip thought, but bit back the words. He had missed her, and he would miss these little ones' lives if he refused her now. 'Of course I'll walk you down the aisle,' he said firmly.

'Thank you, Daddy.' Alexa kissed him.

'Are you sure that's what you want?' he couldn't resist asking. 'You can come and live here, you and your babies.'

'No, Daddy, I'm marrying him. I love him,' she said simply. 'He's waiting outside now . . . can he come in?' she asked, rather anxiously, for Ace had threatened to kick down the door if she was gone too long. Philip stifled a sigh and nodded his agreement.

The wedding took place four weeks later. It was snowing and bitterly cold, but the sun shone brightly on the Christmas card scene and the church was frosted with a fresh new covering of brilliantly white snow.

Despite their caution, the Press had discovered the time and place of the ceremony and were out in force, stamping their feet and blowing on their hands in an effort to keep warm while they waited for the bride to appear. A large crowd of onlookers had also gathered, and were being kept at bay behind crash barriers by a police presence.

'She's late – do you think she'll show up?' asked one cynical journalist.

'More to the point – will he?' responded one even more jaded by the human foibles he'd witnessed over the years.

'He's already here. He and Jack Farrell slipped in through the vestry an hour ago,' replied the first.

Ace felt as if he had been waiting for far more than an hour; he was perspiring despite the chill, constantly checking his watch, miserably convinced Philip would even now be doing his utmost to persuade her to change her mind. Jack was watching his agitation with barely concealed amusement.

'Why is she late? Have you got the ring? Show me,' Ace demanded of Jack for the umpteenth time. Jack sighed heavily and produced the gold band from his pocket.

'I can't believe this is the same man who tried to talk me out of getting married!'

'I did not,' Ace denied.

'You did. You even had a getaway car waiting outside the church!' Jack reminded him.

'So I did. Sorry.' Ace turned and grinned briefly, then resumed his anxious watching for Alexa's arrival. Finally, she was there, ethereally beautiful in ivory lace, and Ace didn't even hear Jack's final comment.

'I've been thinking of the thousands of women who've tried to find the key to your heart,' he mused out loud. 'Not one of them ever thought of having you arrested for drug-smuggling!'

# QUESTIONNAIRE

Please tick the appropriate boxes to indicate your answers

1 Where did you get this Scarlet title?

Bought in supermarket ☐

Bought at my local bookstore ☐ Bought at chain bookstore ☐

Bought at book exchange or used bookstore ☐

Borrowed from a friend ☐

Other (please indicate) ____________________

2 Did you enjoy reading it?

A lot ☐ A little ☐ Not at all ☐

3 What did you particularly like about this book?

Believable characters ☐ Easy to read ☐

Good value for money ☐ Enjoyable locations ☐

Interesting story ☐ Modern setting ☐

Other ____________________

4 What did you particularly dislike about this book?

____________________

5 Would you buy another Scarlet book?

Yes ☐ No ☐

6 What other kinds of book do you enjoy reading?

Horror ☐ Puzzle books ☐ Historical fiction ☐

General fiction ☐ Crime/Detective ☐ Cookery ☐

Other (please indicate) ____________________

7 Which magazines do you enjoy reading?

1. ____________________

2. ____________________

3. ____________________

And now a little about you –

8 How old are you?

Under 25 ☐ 25–34 ☐ 35–44 ☐

45–54 ☐ 55–64 ☐ over 65 ☐

*cont.*

9 What is your marital status?
Single ☐ Married/living with partner ☐
Widowed ☐ Separated/divorced ☐

10 What is your current occupation?
Employed full-time ☐ Employed part-time ☐
Student ☐ Housewife full-time ☐
Unemployed ☐ Retired ☐

11 Do you have children? If so, how many and how old are they?

______________________________

______________________________

12 What is your annual household income?

| | | | | |
|---|---|---|---|---|
| under $15,000 | ☐ | or | £10,000 | ☐ |
| $15–25,000 | ☐ | or | £10–20,000 | ☐ |
| $25–35,000 | ☐ | or | £20–30,000 | ☐ |
| $35–50,000 | ☐ | or | £30–40,000 | ☐ |
| over $50,000 | ☐ | or | £40,000 | ☐ |

Miss/Mrs/Ms ______________________________
Address ______________________________
______________________________
______________________________

Thank you for completing this questionnaire. Now tear it out – put it in an envelope and send it, before 31 January 1998, to:

Sally Cooper, Editor-in-Chief

*USA/Can. address*
SCARLET c/o London Bridge
85 River Rock Drive
Suite 202
Buffalo
NY 14207
USA

*UK address/No stamp required*
SCARLET
FREEPOST LON 3335
LONDON W8 4BR
*Please use block capitals for address*

MIDOU/11/97

***Scarlet*** **titles coming next month:**

**HARTE'S GOLD** Jane Toombs
No-nonsense rancher Carole Harte can't believe that she, of all people, would fall for a film star. But that's exactly what she's done! Trouble is, she's never heard of 'the star', Jerrold Telford, and fears he's out to con her grandmother!

**THE SECOND WIFE** Angela Arney
When Felicity decides to marry Tony she thinks the decision is theirs alone, and that love will conquer all. What she's forgotten is that other people have a stake in their future too, and then Felicity realizes just how difficult it is to be *the second wife* . . .

**WILDE AFFAIR** Margaret Callaghan
Rich, powerful, ruthless – the Jared Wildes of this world don't make commitments. Oh yes, Stevie has come across men like Jared before. Her daughter Rosa's father for one!

**A BITTER INHERITANCE** Clare Benedict
'A scheming little gold digger. Her husband not cold in his grave and she's involved with another man!' That's how Sam Redmond thinks of Gina. How can she change his mind, when he clearly can't forget or forgive how badly she treated *him* in the past?